POWER OF KIDS

SUNSHINE AND SOUL OF KIDS

THIERRY KOUAM

ISBN 978-1-957943-53-4 (paperback)
ISBN 978-1-957943-54-1 (digital)

Rushmore Press LLC
1 800 460 9188
www.rushmorepress.com

Printed in the United States of America

INTRODUCTION

This story is happening in the kingdom called Manitoba. Manitoba is located in North America between Canada and the United States. Manitoba is ruled by a bloodthirsty king named Kalus. Kalus, also called the King, had inherited his late father's throne.

Because according to the tradition and the constitution of Manitoba, the first child of the king or queen is the heir or the heiress to the crown and throne of Manitoba. And in the future, the king or queen was born with natural powers, and these natural powers were used by the future king or queen to rule the kingdom.

The King had all the powers, and he had duties to create his government and change the laws as he wanted, and the members of the government were the king's advisors. The King had the duty to watch over the traditions of Manitoba and make sure that its inhabitants respected and practiced the tradition.

And God was included in the tradition of Manitoba. And the only thing that the King could not change was tradition because even the King had the duty to respect and practice tradition. Tradition and religion were untouchable.

God had a great importance on the lives of the inhabitants of Manitoba, and their daily life was dictated by God's word, which was taught in the churches by priests. Children were educated with the word of God. A ll families of Manitoba paid taxes to the king on their activities. And the inhabitants of Manitoba lived in peace and in joy.

But everything changed in the kingdom of Manitoba when the king Kalus sat on the throne, and the kingdom became a hell for its inhabitants. Kalus was thirsty for power, and the natural powers with which he was born were not enough for him, and Kalus wanted to become immortal. To realize this dream of becoming immortal, Kalus made a pact with the devil called "god of land," also known as Lord.

Kalus had received the satanic powers from the god of land, and these satanic powers were going to allow Kalus to stay immortal, but in exchange, Kalus was going to fill some devilish conditions.

And to stay immortal, Kalus was going to use these satanic powers to mystically kill and torture children of the kingdom. Kalus must also mystically drink the blood of children, thanks to his satanic powers. And even worse, Kalus was also going to make some changes in the kingdom of Manitoba.

Lord and Kalus had a plan for the kingdom, and their plan was to turn the kingdom of Manitoba into the kingdom of vampires. Lord and Kalus were going to mystically turn the population into vampires, and the future generations would be born vampires. And to turn the kingdom of Manitoba into a Vampire the kingdom, everything must change in the kingdom; the kingdom of Manitoba was going to stop with its traditions, cultures, and values.

Lord and Kalus must mystically own the souls of the future generations to be able to turn the future generations into vampires. Lord and Kalus had the plan to establish the laws of the world of the vampires in the kingdom of Manitoba. And to ban the traditions, cultures, and values of the kingdom, Kalus had established the laws called the laws of Kalus.

And during the war of Kalus and Lord to turn the kingdom of Manitoba into the kingdom of vampires, they felt that a powerful enemy was about to be born. Then Kalus and Lord established the new laws of Kalus that banned births in the kingdom and forced all pregnant women to have abortions to prevent this powerful enemy from being born.

Even worse, Lord and Kalus used their satanic powers to make the monsters appear in the kingdom, and the monsters had the mission to kill all pregnant women who had not aborted, as well as to kill all newborns.

The whole kingdom was surprised to hear the king Kalus announce that tradition and religion were prohibited. And even worse, the king Kalus had banned education for children, and Kalus had ordered the inhabitants of the kingdom to pray on his behalf and to believe in him because he was the god of the kingdom.

And these changes made by Kalus were like a miracle for the inhabitants of the kingdom, and no one was understanding what was going on with the king Kalus. And for the population of the kingdom, their king was crazy.

Kalus made something unreal by prohibiting the tradition and education in the kingdom, no one could understand or explain why the king prohibited the tradition and education, and Kalus was the first king to do that. And since the existence of the kingdom, the kings and queens had always promoted tradition and education. And many natural disasters have begun to strike the kingdom.

Suddenly, the kingdom became a cemetery, and the dead bodies of children were found every day in the houses and in the streets. The children were mysteriously killed and children were dying in the same way, and there was a small wound that looked like a hole in the neck of children who were found dead.

And the corpses of children were taken to the hospital to find the cause of death, but the doctors were unable to find the cause of the death. And the doctors were surprised to notice that all the corpses of children were empty of blood, as if something or someone had drunk their blood.

And children were tortured day and night while sleeping, and no one could understand what was going on, and no one could imagine that children were mystically tortured and killed by the king

Kalus. And Kalus was torturing and killing these children because he mystically controlled children's souls, and even worse the king Kalus mystically prevented pregnant women from giving birth.

Suddenly, one night a miracle happened and this miracle was going to change the destiny of the kingdom, a woman gave birth to a girl named Sunshine. Sunshine was born with the powers, and she suddenly became the enemy of the king Kalus and god of land. Sunshine started to fight the king Kalus and Lord to save the kingdom and to free the souls of children that were controlled by Lord and the king Kalus.

And during the fight Sunshine was joined by Luna to fight Lord and Kalus. Luna was the first child of the king Kalus and the heiress to the throne and crown of the kingdom of Manitoba. And Luna was born with the powers as all the heirs and heiresses of the kingdom were born with the powers that would help them to rule the kingdom when they would become the kings or queens.

But Kalus had hidden from Luna how to use her powers and magic as the traditions of Manitoba required that the king must show to the heiress how to manage the powers. And Kalus had hidden from Luna that she was born with the powers and magic. And even worse Kalus had tried to steal the powers of Luna, but it was impossible to steal these powers.

Then Kalus tried to destroy Luna's powers, but he failed because Luna's powers were natural and it's impossible to destroy the natural powers. Then Kalus mystically tried to kill Luna, but he failed because Luna was protected by her powers. And Kalus wanted to kill Luna because he knew that Luna could be a danger for his plan to turn the kingdom of Manitoba into a Vampire kingdom.

And although the fact that Kalus had hidden from Luna her powers, Luna had found out that she was born with the powers and she also found how to use these powers. And Luna understood that she was born with the powers because she was the heiress to the crown and throne of the kingdom of Manitoba.

Luna was shocked and angry to find out that Kalus had made a pact with the devil named Lord to turn the kingdom of Manitoba into the kingdom of Vampires. And Luna was more shocked to find out that Kalus and Lord had the plan to own the souls of the future generations and to turn the future generations of the kingdom into vampires.

And Luna understood that Kalus had destroyed the traditions, cultures, and values of the kingdom because Kalus wanted to install the traditions, the cultures, and the values of the world of the vampires in the kingdom of Manitoba.

Then Luna understood that it was her responsibility as the heiress to the throne and crown of the kingdom to save the kingdom by fighting Kalus and Lord to prevent Lord and Kalus from turning the kingdom of Manitoba into the kingdom of the vampires.

Then Luna found out that there was a young girl of her age named Sunshine who was born with the powers and who was fighting Lord and Kalus to save the kingdom. And Luna joined Sunshine in the fight to save the kingdom of Manitoba. Then Sunshine, Luna, and their friends started fighting against the laws of Kalus.

Sunshine and Luna would succeed in saving the kingdom of Manitoba by preventing Lord and Kalus to turn the kingdom of Manitoba into the kingdom of Vampire? Sunshine and Luna would succeed in freeing the souls of the children that were owned by the Lord?

Sunshine and Luna would succeed in saving the future generations of the kingdom by preventing Lord and Kalus from turning the future generations into vampires? Sunshine and Luna would succeed in ending the laws of Kalus so that the kingdom regains its traditions, cultures and values?

Sunshine and Luna would succeed in killing Lord and Kalus who were immortals? Or the kingdom of Manitoba would become the kingdom of Vampire with the traditions, cultures, values and laws of the world of the vampires and with a population who would be the vampires?

CHAPTER I

THE BIRTH OF SUNSHINE

It had been more than ten years since a great drought had hit the kingdom, and this drought had been triggered by the king Kalus thanks to his satanic powers. And all the rivers of the kingdom had dried up and there were no crops in the fields because all the crops had been killed by the drought.

The animals and livestock had died due to the drought. And even worse there was a hot dry sun hitting the kingdom, and the markets and offices had been closed, and the inhabitants of the kingdom were at home and they were dying of starvation. No one was understanding what was going on and it was the first time in the history of the kingdom that a drought hit the kingdom.

And the worst were children who were mystically tortured and killed. The children were seeing the monsters during the day and night even while sleeping. And children sometimes woke up during the night and cried because they had been woken up by the monsters they had seen while sleeping in their dream.

And sometime during the day, children ran away from the house and cried that they were seeing the monsters, and once children got out of the house by running away from the monsters, these children were found dead in mysterious conditions. The children were found dead everyday in the streets, in the houses and on their beds.

And the parents were all surprised to notice that all the children's corpses had a wound that looked like a hole in the neck. And children's corpses were taken to the hospital to find the cause of death, but unfortunately, the doctors were unable to find the cause of death, but the doctors were astonished to notice that all children's corpses were empty of blood as if their blood had been drunk by someone or something.

And the doctors were completely lost by seeing children's corpses who were empty of blood. And the doctors could not only explain the cause of death of these children and they could not also explain why children's corpses were empty of blood.

The parents were very worried about their children, and they did not know how to protect their children, and no one was understanding what was going on. The inhabitants of the kingdom were very afraid about what was going on, they were all very worried about their kingdom and some were even saying that what was going on was the wrath of their ancestors and God because Kalus had prohibited the tradition and religion in the kingdom. Mostly, that it was the first time in the history of the kingdom that the kingdom lived this kind of drama.

The parents were trying to save their children without success, children were tortured day and night. Children were feeling thirsty, tired, hungry, dizzy and violent headaches, and they were also always sad. Although the children felt hungry, they did not have the appetite to eat, and they always vomited when they put something in their mouth.

And they did not even want to smell the food, and despite the fact that they were thirsty, they did not want to drink water. Children spent the months without eating and drinking water. The parents and adults did not feel these tortures that children felt.

Children were acting as if their bodies were controlled by someone else, and children were saying strange words that even themselves could not explain or understand the meaning of their words. And the children were doing things that themselves did not know what they were doing, and they were walking in the house without knowing where they were going or what they were looking for. And children were always crying and running away from the monsters, and only children were able to see these monsters because the parents were not seeing them.

And sometimes, children sat in the chairs and suddenly they got up, crying and pointing their hands, saying that they were seeing the monsters. And that these monsters were coming towards them and they started running away from the monsters that they were seeing. And the parents started to run after their children to save their children from the monsters.

But unfortunately, the parents were unable to protect their children not only because the parents were unable to see these monsters. But because once children started running away from the monsters, children had only a few seconds to die. And most of the time when children wanted to die, they screamed while holding their necks. The parents did not know how to help their children because the doctors could not diagnose what their children were suffering from.

And there was no solution to help children, and the two solutions that could be used by the parents to save their children were prohibited by the king. And these two solutions were the traditional remedies and the prayers. In the kingdom, tradition and prayer had an important place in the lives of the inhabitants, and most inhabitants were cured by the traditional remedies when they were sick, and almost all diseases were cured using traditional remedies.

And certain serious illnesses were cured by the practice of certain traditional rites, and there were also some traditional remedies that were taken by the inhabitants even when they were not sick. And the inhabitants were given these traditional remedies when they were not sick because these traditional remedies were like the vaccine.

And these traditional remedies kept people from getting sick. And the prayers were used by the people to keep their faith, and the events for the sick were organized in the churches by the priests to pray for the sick.

But unfortunately, the inhabitants of the kingdom could no longer use the traditional remedies to cure their illness or even to cure these children who were sick. Because the king had banned the inhabitants from using the traditional remedies to cure the illness, and he had also forbidden people to go to the sacred forest.

And people could no longer make the traditional remedies because they had been forbidden by the king to go to the sacred forest because the ingredients to make the traditional remedies were in the sacred forest.

And people could not go to church to pray for children, and they could not go see the priests with children for the priests to pray for their children because the churches had been closed, and the priests had been sent to prison by the king. And the king Kalus had even killed some priests who had tried to protest when he had banned the religion in the kingdom.

And the kingdom had another problem, and this problem was pregnant women. Despite the fact that pregnant women were doing well and they were not feeling any illness, they were unable to give birth. And there were women who had been pregnant for many years, but they were unable to give birth.

And the doctors had even examined these pregnant women, but doctors were surprised to notice that these pregnant women were doing well. But when the doctors made the ultrasounds to these pregnant women, the doctors were very astonished to notice that the bellies of these pregnant women were empty, that there were no babies in their bellies.

And the doctors were completely lost to see that the ultrasounds showed that there were no babies in the bellies in any of these pregnant women. And the doctors could not explain why there were not the babies in the bellies of these pregnant women. And despite the fact that these pregnant women had large bellies, they did not feel the symptoms of pregnancy.

And between these pregnant women, there were some who had been pregnant before the king Kalus was crowned the king of the kingdom. And these women who had been pregnant before the king Kalus sat on the throne of the kingdom were followed by the doctors.

And everything was going well for these women, they had the symptoms of pregnancy, and the ultrasounds had shown the babies in their bellies, and they had even felt their babies moving in their womb.

But after that Kalus had been crowned the king and that he had changed everything, the babies had mysteriously disappeared in their bellies of these pregnant women, and even the symptoms of the pregnancy had disappeared.

And even women who had gotten pregnant after Kalus had been crowned the king were in the same situation as women who had gotten pregnant before he had been crowned the king. But with the difference that women who had got pregnant before Kalus had been crowned the king had had the symptoms of pregnancy and they had even seen their babies in their womb through the ultrasounds, and they had felt their babies moving in their womb.

While women who had been pregnant after Kalus had been crowned the king had never had the symptoms of pregnancy, they had never felt their babies moving in their wombs, and they had never seen their babies through the ultrasounds.

And even the doctors did not understand why these pregnant women did not have the babies in their bellies. And the doctors could not practice the surgery on these pregnant women to find out why there were not the babies in their wombs because the operation on pregnant women had been banned by the king. Some people said that the reason why pregnant women could not give birth was because God and ancestors were angry against the inhabitants of the kingdom, like the king had banned tradition and religion.

But people had noticed that all these dramas started in the kingdom when the king had prohibited the tradition and religion in the kingdom. And when the king had planted the satanic trees in all the streets of the kingdom, and the satanic trees were also planted in the yard of all the houses of the kingdom.

And the king had ordered the inhabitants of the kingdom to never touch or cut these satanic trees. And people were very surprised to notice that these satanic trees were more important to the king than the drama that was happening in the kingdom because since this drama had started Kalus had not said a word about it. And Kalus was acting as if everything was going well in the kingdom.

It was an evening at eleven o'clock, the whole kingdom was asleep, and suddenly in the house of David, a pregnant woman named Estelle also called Sarah who was David's wife started to cry in pain while holding her belly, and she was crying the contraction pains. And Sarah, also called Estelle, was taken to the hospital by her husband. In the hospital, the doctors were very astonished to notice that Sarah was crying the contraction pains, and she was taken to the delivery room.

It was midnight, Estelle gave birth to a baby girl, and the nurse carried the baby in her hands and the nurse tried to make the baby cry without success. And the nurse even shook the baby to make the baby cry without success. Then Estelle carried her baby and lifted looking at the baby, then Estelle smiled at her baby and said, "Sunshine."

Suddenly, baby Sunshine started crying, and people who were in the room turned their heads through the windows when they heard the noises that hit the window's glass like the water. And the surprise appeared on their faces, and they had their eyes wide open like they were staring at the rain that was hitting the window's glass. They were all surprised and they were wondering if it was really raining.

Then one of the doctors who were in the room asked if it was really the rain? And a nurse answered that it was the same question that she was wondering herself. Then they all turned their heads through the bed when they heard Sunshine who was crying louder, and it was raining more and more harder.

And no one could imagine that it was raining harder and harder because Sunshine was crying more and more loudly. Then they turned their head through the window and they looked through the window's glass that it was raining more and more, and a nurse walked near the window and this nurse opened the window.

And suddenly, the smile appeared on the face of everyone in the room, and they were watching the rain that was raining outside through the window. And the thunder that was rumbling in the sky and the wind blowing.

The eyes of everyone in the room were focused on the rain that was outside, and they had even forgotten that a woman had just given birth. And it's been years now that they had not seen the rain, and they were watching the rain outside through the window with a violent wind that was blowing as if they were seeing the rain for the first time.

Suddenly, other doctors got in the room, and they said that they needed more staff because the hospital was full of pregnant women who wanted to give birth. Then the doctors and nurses left the room by running and they were going to help other pregnant women to give birth.

Although the heavy rain was falling with the wind that was blowing and the thunder that rumbled in the sky, the streets of the kingdom were full with the cars and ambulances that had transported pregnant women and went to the hospitals.

All the hospitals in the kingdom were full of pregnant women, and the hospitals lacked the staff that doctors and nurses who were at home to rest were called to the hospitals for help, and even the doctors and nurses who were retired were called to the hospitals for help.

Except the king Kalus who was in his bed deeply asleep, the rest of the inhabitants of the kingdom had woken up and they were watching through their windows the rain that was falling outside and the cars and ambulances that had transported pregnant women and going to the hospitals.

And they all had a smile on their faces by watching the rain outside, and it was like a miracle for them, and they did not believe that it was really raining. And there were even the cries of joy coming over the kingdom, and these screams were coming from the houses and hospitals, and it were people who were screaming because their relatives or a member of their families had given birth.

And all the children of the kingdom were deeply asleep in their beds, and the parents were very surprised to notice that since the rain had started children had not woken up. And that was the first time that children were asleep without any problem, and without waking up crying because they had seen the monsters while sleeping.

Except the king Kalus and children who were deeply asleep in their beds, the rest of inhabitants of the kingdom had spent their whole night at the windows of their houses watching the rain outside through the window's glass. Other people like the doctors, nurses, hospital's staff, pregnant women, some relatives, and newborns had spent their whole night in the hospitals.

It was six in the morning, the rain was over, and a miracle had happened in the kingdom. All the pregnant women had given birth, even those who had been pregnant before Kalus was crowned the king, and even those who had been pregnant for less than nine months had given birth.

And all the babies who were born were doing well. And even the king's wife named princess Diana had given birth to a baby girl named Luna, and Luna was the last baby to be born, and Sunshine was the first baby to be born.

And for the first time in years, children woke up with a smile on their faces, and they were running around the house with joy on their faces, and they were jumping and playing. The parents were very amazed by the attitude of their children, they did not understand what was going on with their children, and it's been years that they had not seen their children happy like that.

And it was also the first time in years that children had slept all night without being woken up crying because they had seen the monsters while sleeping. And it was also the first time in years that a child was not dead during the night or while sleeping, and that a family was not mourning the death of their child.

The whole kingdom was very happy, and everyone was hoping that the curse and drama that had plagued the kingdom during the years were over. And that the population of the kingdom was going to live in peace forever, mostly that children would not be tortured and killed by the mysterious monsters. The rain that had fallen during the whole night was a great miracle because since the drought had started in the kingdom it had not rained, and they were all hoping that the drought was over.

Then some people started to get out of their houses and their eyes widened once they put their feet in the yard. And they were staring at the satanic trees that had been turned into the magic trees also called the peace trees.

And people were getting out of their houses more and more to see the magic trees that were outside. And no one was understanding what was going on, and no one was understanding how it was possible that the satanic trees that were outside had become the magic trees.

And they were wondering how it was possible that the satanic trees had turned into the magic trees, but none of them could explain this miracle, and some of them were afraid. And those who were afraid said that the rain that had fallen during the night was a curse, that things would be worse with this rain that had fallen.

Because the satanic trees of the king Kalus had turned into the magic trees. While others said that the rain that had fallen was a good sign of the peace in the kingdom not only because all pregnant women had given birth, but mostly because children were doing very well.

All the inhabitants of the kingdom were outside and they were staring at the magic trees that were in the yard of their house. And even the satanic trees that were in the streets had turned into magic trees. But they were all afraid about the reaction of the king.

And they knew that the king Kalus would not be happy to see that his satanic trees had turned into the magic trees, not only because these satanic trees were very important to Kalus. But mostly because the king had banned the magic trees in the kingdom.

At the palace, except the king who was still asleep in his bed, the rest of the inhabitants of the palace were in the yard of the palace and they were staring at the magic trees with astonished faces. Then Albert, who was one of the king's security guards, said that he was going to wake up the king, then Albert turned and left.

Kalus was in his bed deeply asleep, then he opened his eyes when he heard the noises coming from the door. And he got out of the bed and walked till the door, then he opened the door and he saw Albert who was staring at him.

Kalus was a tall man with long black hair, with green eyes and with a short line in the middle of his forehead that looked like a scar. Kalus and Albert were looking at each other with silence, and the king was looking tired, and Albert was very surprised to see that the king looked tired.

Then Albert broke the silence and asked Kalus if Kalus was doing well? Kalus answered Albert that he was doing well, but that he was feeling very tired. Albert told Kalus that a miracle had happened during the night. Kalus asked Albert what was this miracle? Albert answered Kalus that the satanic trees that were outside had turned into the magic trees. And suddenly, the expression on the face of Kalus changed and he was looking at Albert with an amazed face, then he cried out, "What?"

Albert answered that the satanic trees that were outside had turned into the magic trees. Kalus asked Albert how the satanic trees had turned into the magic trees? Albert answered that he had no idea. Kalus said that he had banned the magic trees in the kingdom, so that it was impossible that the satanic trees had turned into the magic trees.

Then Kalus pushed Albert who was at the door, and he got out of the room and ran towards the front door. Suddenly, the facial expression of Kalus changed when he put his feet on the veranda. And he had a face full of fear by staring at the magic trees that were in the yard, and he was turning his head around looking at the magic trees as if he was watching the miracle.

And looking at the expression on the king's face, he was completely lost, he did not believe what was going on, and he did not understand how it was possible that the satanic trees had turned into the magic trees. Then the king turned and ran inside the palace without saying a word.

Kalus got into his secret room also called the magic room. The secret room was the room where the king communicated with the Lord, also called god of land. And the king communicated with the Lord through the voice of his Lord because the king had never seenLord. And nobody in the palace knew the existence of this secret room.

Then Kalus knelt in the secret room and called, "Lord, Lord, Lord." No one answered. Then Kalus took a deep breath and asked, ""Lord, are you here?""

A voice answered, ""Everything is over."" And this voice was Lord.

""What does this mean, my Lord?"" Kalus said.

""You lost everything,"" Lord answered.

Kalus said, ""My Lord, I do not understand.""

"You failed your mission,"" Lord said.

"Still, I do not understand,"" Kalus said.

Lord said, "She is born at midnight.""

""Who is born?"" Kalus asked.

"Sunshine,"" Lord answered.

"Who is Sunshine?"" Kalus asked.

""Sunshine is your enemy,"" Lord retorted.

"My enemy?" Kalus cried out.

Lord said, "Sunshine is the baby girl who is born tonight at midnight, and she is born with natural powers, and she used her powers to put an end to the curse and drama that were happening in the kingdom."

"My Lord, can you tell me exactly who Sunshine is?" Kalus asked.

Lord answered, "Sunshine is a very powerful girl, she succeeded through her powers to trigger the rain, to free children's souls and to turn the satanic trees into the magic trees."

Kalus cried out, "What?" And Kalus added, "Sunshine is the one who dared to turn my satanic trees into magic trees?"

"Yes," Lord answered.

"I am going to kill this cursed girl named Sunshine," Kalus said with a voice full of anger.

"Do not dare to approach Sunshine!" Lord snarled.

Kalus asked, "Why not Lord?"

"Do you want to die?" Lord asked.

Kalus said, "I do not understand."

"You can not kill Sunshine!" Lord snarled.

Kalus asked, "Why can I not kill Sunshine?"

"Sunshine is more powerful and stronger than you," Lord said.

"Sunshine is just a baby who was born a few hours ago," Kalus snarled.

"Yes, Sunshine is just a baby who was born a few hours ago, but she is born with the powers and she can kill you by using her powers," Lord retorted.

"Kill me?" Kalus asked.

"Sunshine is more powerful than you!" Lord snarled.

Kalus asked, "How is it possible that Sunshine is more powerful than me?"

"The fact that you were unable to prevent what happened in this kingdom during the night means that Sunshine is more powerful than you because you were not even aware of what was going on in your kingdom," Lord said.

"I lost control of the kingdom tonight because I was feeling very tired," Kalus said.

Lord said, "You were very tired because you were less powerful than Sunshine, and Sunshine's powers had mystically controlled your powers. And it's the reason why you were so tired and it's also the reason why your powers did not succeed to prevent Sunshine's powers to trigger the rain and to turn the satanic trees into the magic trees."

Kalus said, "I was so tired that I even forgot to kill children and to drink children's blood during the night."

Lord said, "You did not forget, it's Sunshine who mystically prevented you from killing children and drinking children's blood."

"I would kill children today and drink their blood," Kalus said.

"You lost the control on children's souls," Lord said.

"How I lost control of the children's souls?" Kalus asked.

Lord answered, "It was the satanic trees that allowed you to control children's souls, and you were able to mystically kill children and drink children's blood because there were satanic trees outside. But now that Sunshine mystically turned these satanic trees into the magic trees, you could no longer kill children and drink children's blood."

Kalus said, "My Lord, even without the satanic trees I can still mystically kill children and drink their blood. Because I mystically kill children and drink their blood through the satanic powers I had received from you, and I still have these satanic powers in me."

Lord said, "It's true that you still have the satanic powers in you, and it's also true that you kill children and drink their blood through your satanic powers. But what you forgot is that you can not kill children and drink their blood without controlling children's souls, even with your satanic powers, it would be impossible for you to mystically kill children and drink their blood if children's souls are not controlled. And you already lost the control of children's souls because the satanic trees that controlled children's souls to allow you to kill children and drink their blood had been turned into the magic trees by Sunshine."

Lord went on and said, "You can no longer use your satanic powers to turn into monsters and go outside to kill children and drink their blood because the magic trees that are outside would mystically destroy your satanic powers, and these magic trees could even kill you. Because these magic trees could not match or function with the satanic powers that are in you. And it's also the reason you would stay in the palace till I destroy the magic trees that are outside." Lord added, "It was the reason why I had asked you to always control the satanic trees that were outside."

Kalus said, "It means that I would stay inside this palace till you destroy the magic trees that are outside."

"Exactly," Lord retorted.

"Like I can not kill Sunshine, I would kick her and her family out of this kingdom," Kalus said.

"Do not even dare to touch Sunshine's family because she will not hesitate to kill you if you approach her family," Lord retorted.

Kalus said, "I would ask Sunshine's parents to change her name because you had ordered me to make sure that a child would never be named Sunshine in this kingdom."

Lord said, "It's too late, you already lost the control of the kingdom. You can not ask Sunshine's parents to change her Sunshine's name because Sunshine will kill you if you send your men to her house to talk to her parents."

Kalus said, "My Lord, please, kill this cursed girl of Sunshine as soon as possible."

"Congratulations!" Lord said.

"Congratulations?" Kalus asked.

"You are the papa of a little girl named Luna," Lord retorted.

"Me?" Kalus asked.

"Your wife gave birth to a little girl this morning that she named Luna," Lord said.

"My wife?" Kalus asked.

"All the pregnant women of this kingdom gave birth this morning, Sunshine was the first baby to be born and Luna was the last baby to be born," Lord said.

Kalus said, "You know that I am not supposed to have a child because I must stay immortal."

"You know well that your wife was pregnant," Lord retorted.

"I thought that she should never give birth," Kalus said.

"Sunshine used her powers to allow all pregnant women to give birth," Lord said.

Kalus said, "This cursed girl of Sunshine is destroying all my dreams."

"Do not make a mistake to teach the secrets of powers to Luna because Luna is your heiress and she is the future queen of this kingdom according to tradition. And that means that she is born with the powers so make sure that Luna would not get in contact with her powers and she would not know how to use these powers she is born with," Lord said.

"My Lord do not worry for Luna because I would kill her," Kalus retorted.

"Make sure that Luna would not be a danger for us because we can not have Sunshine and Luna against us. And it's the reason why you must watch Luna to prevent to get in contact with her powers because it would be dangerous if Sunshine and Luna mystically communicated through their powers," Lord said.

"Do not worry my Lord because these two cursed girls who are Sunshine and Luna would never communicate together through their powers," Kalus said.

Lord said, "Do not forget that you would not get out of this place till I give you order." And the Lord added, "Have a great day." Then Kalus called the Lord three times and the Lord did not answer, and Kalus understood that the Lord had left, then Kalus got up and left the room.

The inhabitants of the kingdom spent a great day, and they were all happy with the only hope that the curse and the drama were over. And all the babies who were born had come home with their parents, and all these babies were well.

And for the first time since Kalus had been crowned the king, the kingdom had spent a day without a dead body, without a child being tortured by the monsters, without a drought, and without a sadness and tears on the faces of people. And for the first time, children had spent the day running outside and playing with the smiles on their faces.

The years were passing, and everything was going well in the kingdom, and the inhabitants had never seen the drought again, and the weather was beautiful every day. And children were doing well, children were happy and they were no longer tortured by the monsters, and there were no more children's corpses. And the weather was beautiful, the activities had resumed, and the market had reopened, and especially that the crops and cattle were going well.

And the children who were born a few years ago were all doing well, and they were growing up very well, except Sunshine who was always sick. And Sunshine was always sick because she was mystically tortured by god of land, and god of land was trying to kill Sunshine. Sunshine's parents were living with fear everyday because most of the time, Sunshine's body was full of scars, wounds and bites of animals.

Sunshine was always sick and tired, and she was always in the hospital but unfortunately the doctors were unable to diagnose what Sunshine was suffering from. Even all the results of the blood tests that the doctors had done on Sunshine were negative, and the doctors were not understanding what was going on with Sunshine.

And no one could explain what caused the wounds, scars and bites that were on Sunshine. And sometime when Sunshine was asleep, she suddenly woke up trembling, and most of the time Sunshine was shaking in her cradle. And Sunshine was shaking because she was mystically fighting with the god of land, and all these wounds, scars and bites on Sunshine's body were made by the god of land during their fight.

After the years, the kingdom was at peace, the population was doing well and all babies who were born were going to be twelve years old, and they became almost teenagers. And people had almost forgotten the trauma and drama that they had experienced over twelve years ago.

And many women had continued to give birth again without any problem and Sunshine had succeeded to survive against the Lord so far. And the parents were worried about the education of their children because the school was still banned in the kingdom by the king. But there was a question that all the inhabitants of the kingdom were wondering, and this question was where the king was.

Because it's been almost twelve years now, most of the inhabitants of the kingdom had not seen their king, and the king had not left the palace. And some people were even saying that Kalus was very sick, and Kalus had not even made a speech on television for twelve years now. And even in the palace, people were wondering where the king was because although the king was in the palace, it's not everyone in the palace who could see the king.

Only a few people in the palace were in touch with the king, and these few people who were in touch with the king were his family and people who worked directly for him like people who served his food. Even people who were in touch with the king were wondering why he was not going outside, but they had noticed that the king was always sad and nervous, as if there was something going wrong.

It was midnight, Sunshine was lying in her bed on her back and she had her eyes open and she was staring at the ceiling with her blue eyes and long blond hair. And Sunshine was thinking about what she was going to do during the day. And suddenly, the expression on Sunshine's face changed and she started to breathe deeply as if she was feeling something strange.

Then Sunshine turned her head and looked at the table that was near to her bed like she had heard the noises coming from this table. And she was staring at the table that was shaking with a worried face.

Then Sunshine turned her head around and she noticed that the whole bedroom was shaking, and she was shaking in bed. Then she tried to focus on herself and her eyes started to turn, then the light shone into her eyes and she disappeared.

There was the moon that was shining in the sky, and the weather was beautiful with the wind that was blowing. And suddenly Sunshine appeared in the yard of her house in front of a tall man, and she was staring at this tall man with his red eyes, big ears, long chin and with long gray hair. And this tall man was also looking at Sunshine with her blue eyes, her little pointy nose and long blond hair. And they were staring at each other with silence, but we could see the anger in their eyes.

Then Sunshine broke the silence and said, "Lord?"

This man answered, "Yes, I am Lord, also called god of land."

"What do you want?" Sunshine asked.

"Leave this kingdom," Lord answered.

"Leave this kingdom?" Sunshine cried out with a surprised face.

"Yes," Lord retorted.

"To go where?" Sunshine asked.

"Go anywhere, but leave this kingdom," Lord answered.

"This kingdom is my land!" Sunshine snarled.

Lord walked a step towards Sunshine and he looked into Sunshine's eyes and said, "I am the owner of this kingdom, and I order you to leave my kingdom."

"This kingdom does not belong to you, you are not even a child of this kingdom," Sunshine retorted.

"This kingdom and the inhabitants of this kingdom have belonged to me since the day I made the pact with the king Kalus," Lord said.

"The pact of blood to kill children, right?" Sunshine asked.

"Yes, the pact of blood of blood to kill children and to torture them," Lord answered.

Sunshine looked into Lord's eyes, and said, "You and Kalus would regret it, I swear I would make Kalus and you pay for all the harm you did in this kingdom."

Lord lifted his head and looked at the sky with his face full of anger, then he looked into Sunshine's eyes and said, "I am the one who would make you pay to be born in my kingdom and to stop all my plans."

"I am not afraid of you," Sunshine retorted.

"You should be afraid," Lord replied.

"It's been twelve years now that you are trying to kill me without success, so you are just a poor weak devil who was unable to kill me in my cradle when I was baby," Sunshine said.

Lord said, "You got a chance when you were a baby, but do not forget that the chance can not be with you forever."

"It was not a chance, you were just too weak," Sunshine replied.

Suddenly, the terror appeared on Lord's face, and he was staring at Sunshine with the eyes that were spinning. And suddenly, Sunshine pushed aloud and yelled while holding her shoulders like she was feeling pains coming from her shoulders. Then Sunshine started moving her hands all over her body still screaming in pain, and these pains that she was feeling were caused by the Lord.

Then Sunshine understood that she must fight back to stop these pains, and she looked at Lord and her eyes started to turn, and Sunshine's eyes were spinning very slowly because it was hard for her to focus because she was still feeling pain all over her body.

And the fact that Sunshine's eyes were spinning slowly had no effect on the Lord. And Sunshine was feeling pains and the torture coming from Lord because Lord was still staring at Sunshine with the eyes that were spinning. Sunshine was trying to concentrate more and more on herself to make her eyes turn faster.

After a few seconds, Sunshine started to sweat and her eyes were spinning faster and faster, then Sunshine's eyes turned yellow. And suddenly, Lord pushed a loud yell when he felt his body that was burning as if he was in the fire, and he started to lose concentration.

Because it was impossible to focus on himself with his body that was burning, and Lord's eyes started spinning slowly.

And Sunshine's eyes were spinning faster and faster like Lord's eyes were spinning slowly, and Sunshine had taken advantage in the fight. And Lord was feeling his body that was burning more and more that he could not bear pains.

Sunshine and Lord were still looking at each other in the eyes, and their eyes were still spinning, with the difference that Sunshine's eyes were spinning faster than Lord's eyes. And another difference was the fact that Lord was feeling more pains in his body because his body was still burning as if he was in the fire, while Sunshine was feeling less pains in her body.

Suddenly, there was the sweat that was running down Lord as if it were the water, and looking at Lord, it was as if the water had been sprayed on him. Then Lord started to breathe deeply and he gave up the fight, while Sunshine was still staring at Lord with her eyes that were spinning. And Sunshine had more concentration because she was no longer feeling any pain in her body like Lord had given up the fight.

And Lord was feeling his body that was burning more and more because he was no longer fighting Sunshine to prevent her from using her magic to burn his body. Then Lord lifted his head through the sky and he started staring at the moon that was in the cloud by breathing slowly, and he was trying to focus on getting his energy.

After a few seconds, there was a strange light that was shining on Lord's face coming from the sky, then Lord started to breathe faster, and Lord's eyes turned into blue and his eyes started spinning. Then Lord turned his head and he looked into Sunshine's eyes, and suddenly Sunshine's eyes stopped spinning.

Sunshine's eyes had stopped spinning because Lord was more powerful than her, and it was Lord's magic who had mystically blocked Sunshine's magic, and Lord's magic had also prevented Sunshine from using her magic to fight. Sunshine was trying to focus on herself to make her eyes turn, but she was too weak to do so and she started to become weak.

Then a light got out from Lord's eyes and went through Sunshine, and suddenly Sunshine flew in space once this light coming from Lord's eyes had shone on her. Sunshine was spinning in the space, and she had lost all her strength, and Lord had lifted his head through the space with his eyes focused on Sunshine, and Lord's eyes were still spinning.

And Sunshine was spinning in space because Lord's eyes were in contact with her body, and it was Lord who was controlling Sunshine through his magic, so she was spinning because Lord's eyes who were in contact with her body were spinning too.

Then Lord started walking with his eyes still focused on Sunshine, and Sunshine started flying in the direction that Lord was walking through. And Lord was walking through the wall of Sunshine's house, and Sunshine was moving through the direction of the house wall too.

Suddenly, Sunshine started screaming in pain while she was hitting her body against the wall, and Lord's eyes were still focused on Sunshine. And Lord was moving his eyes between Sunshine and the wall, so Lord was using his eyes to hit Sunshine against the wall.

After more than an hour, Lord started walking through the middle of the yard still with his eyes focused on Sunshine, and Sunshine was flying in the direction of the yard. Then Lord stopped in the middle of the yard and Sunshine had stopped flying in space, but Lord's eyes were still focused on Sunshine, but Lord's eyes had stopped spinning.

And Sunshine's face was full of blood, and she got hurt by hitting her face and her body against the wall, and Sunshine was looking very tired and she was bleeding. Then Lord's eyes started spinning, and Sunshine started turning in the space, and Lord's eyes were focused on Sunshine, and Lord's face was full of smiles as he was watching Sunshine who was spinning in the space.

After a few minutes, Lord's eyes were still focused on Sunshine, he had started to feel tired because Sunshine's body was absorbing the energies of his magic, and he could no longer control Sunshine through his magic. Sunshine was still flying in space and she was flying very slowly because Lord's eyes were spinning very slowly, and Sunshine was retaking control of her body because Lord's magic did not really have an effect on her anymore.

Then Sunshine started to fly away by controlling her movement, and it was no longer Lord who was controlling Sunshine's movement in space. Lord was turning his head looking at Sunshine who was flying in space with an astonished face, and looking at Lord expression's face, he was completely lost and he was not understanding how he had lost control of Sunshine.

Then Lord tried to regain control on Sunshine in space without success, and Lord's magic had no longer effect on Sunshine's body despite the fact that Lord's eyes were turning very slowly. Then Lord understood what was going on and why he had lost control of Sunshine.

Then Lord lifted his head through the sky and he was staring at the moon that was in the cloud, and he was trying to focus on getting the energy. Then Sunshine saw Lord who was staring at the moon, and she understood that he was trying to get the energies to fight her, and he understood that she must do something to prevent him from getting the energies.

Then Sunshine flew till where Lord was, and she stopped through the Lord and the cloud, so Sunshine's body was between Lord and the sky. And Lord's eyes were not anymore in contact with the sky, but his eyes were in contact with Sunshine's body.

And Lord's magic had no effect on Sunshine although the fact that his eyes were spinning, his magic had no effect on Sunshine because the energies of his magic were very weak. And Sunshine was using her magic to mystically absorb the energies of Lord's magic through her body.

Then Lord started walking in the yard to try to be in contact with the sky, but Sunshine was flying in the direction of Lord, to prevent him from being in contact with the sky. And each time when Lord tried to be in contact with the sky to get the energies of his magic, he was prevented by Sunshine because she was always between him and the sky.

After more than an hour, Lord had still not succeeded to get the energies of his magic from the sky to fight Sunshine, and he did not have the energies of his magic to fight Sunshine. Then the light shone in Lord's eyes and she disappeared. And Sunshine noticed that Lord had left, and her eyes started turning, then the light shone in her eyes and she disappeared.

After a few minutes, Sunshine was in the washroom of her house, and she was in front of the mirror and she was cleaning the blood that was on her face. Sunshine was feeling very tired and she was feeling pain all over her body.

Then Sunshine made the bandages on her wounds and she went into the bedroom. Sunshine laid in her bed, and she started thinking of the god of land, and she was not only thinking about the fight that happened a few minutes ago between him and her. But she was mostly thinking of the words of the Lord, like he ordered her to leave the kingdom.

And even if Sunshine was not surprised that Lord had ordered her to leave the kingdom, not only because it's been twelve years now that Lord was trying to kill her without success. But mostly because since she was born, she had destroyed all the projects of Lord and Kalus.

And Sunshine was wondering why the king had mystically killed children and drunk their blood, but unfortunately, she could not answer these questions. Then Sunshine turned her head and looked at the light bulb on the ceiling, and her eyes started spinning and the light went off. Then Sunshine closed her eyes and she fell asleep.

It was six in the morning, Sunshine's parents named David and Sarah walked till in front of Sunshine's bedroom, and they opened the door and they got in the room by singing, "Happy birthday, happy birthday Sunshine." By clapping their hands, they were staring at Sunshine who was in her bed and who had covered her face with the blanket.

Then David and Sarah walked till near to bed still by signing, and they got on the bed and they removed the blanket on Sunshine. And suddenly, the expression on their faces changed, and they were staring at Sunshine with their eyes full of fear, as they were seeing the bandages on Sunshine's forehead.

Then David asked Sunshine what happened? And Sunshine lied to David that she fell in the stairs when she was going to the kitchen during the night. David asked Sunshine if she had not turned on the light? Sunshine answered that she had forgotten to turn on the light. David asked Sunshine who made the bandages on her forehead? Sunshine answered that she made these bandages herself.

Then David told Sunshine that they must go see the doctor with her wounds, but Sunshine refused and said that she was doing well. Then Sunshine got out of the bed, and her parents saw the injury marks on her hands, and her parents tried to convince her to see a doctor with her wounds, but she refused.

Sunshine's parents asked her why she did not want to go see the doctor? Sunshine answered her parents that she did not have time to go to the hospital because her day was going to be busy. And David asked Sunshine what she was going to do? Sunshine looked at her dad and answered that she was going to celebrate her birthday.

And suddenly, David and Sarah looked at each other with surprised faces and they were very surprised to hear Sunshine say that she was going to celebrate her birthday because since Sunshine was born, she had always refused to celebrate her birthday.

Sarah asked Sunshine why she wanted to celebrate her birthday now if she always refused to celebrate it? Sunshine told her mom that she was going to celebrate her birthday today because today was going to be a great day. Sarah asked Sunshine what she meant by today was a great day?

Sunshine looked into her mom's eyes and answered that today was a great day because everything was going to chance. Sarah asked Sunshine what was going to change? Sunshine smiled at her mom and answered that it was a surprise, and that they would discover the surprise at one in the afternoon, and she added that she was going to invite her friends for her birthday party.

David asked Sunshine if she wanted a birthday party? Sunshine smiled at her dad and answered that she wanted a big party because she was going to invite not only children of her age, but she was also going to invite the parents.

Sunshine added that it was not only her birthday, but it was also the birthday of her friends and many children of this kingdom because twelve years ago many children were born in this kingdom. Suddenly, the expressions on the faces of David and Sarah changed, and they looked at each other in surprise without saying a word.

Then David looked at Sunshine and asked her who told her that twelve years ago many children were born in the kingdom? Sunshine looked into her father's eyes and answered that she knew a lot of things. David asked Sunshine what she knew?

Sunshine took a deep breath and answered that she knew that the drought had hit the kingdom for many years before her birth. And that the night she was born it was a memorable night because a few seconds after her birth it had rain, and all pregnant women gave birth that night. David asked Sunshine who told her that? Sunshine answered her father that no one told her.

And David told Sunshine that if nobody told her about what had happened in the kingdom before she was born, it meant that she had heard a conversation between him and her mom talking about. Sunshine replied to David that she had never heard a conversation between him and her mom about the drama that had occurred in the kingdom before her birth.

David looked into Sunshine's eyes and said he hated the lies, and that he wanted the truth about how she knew what had happened in the kingdom before she was born. Sunshine looked at her father with the mouth open, but no word was coming out from her mouth, and she was thinking what to say. But she could not tell her dad that she was born with magic and powers, and that she was the one who had put an end to the drama in the kingdom. And there was silence in the room.

After a few minutes, David broke the silence and said to Sunshine that he was still waiting for her to tell him how she knew the drama that had occurred in the kingdom before she was born. And Sunshine replied to her father that she was not going to tell him how she knew about the drama that had happened in the kingdom before her birth.

And suddenly the expression on David's face changed, and he looked at Sunshine with a face full of anger. Then David shouted at Sunshine that he wanted to know how she knew about the drama that had happened in the kingdom before she was born.

Then Sarah looked at her husband and noticed that he was very angry, and she told him that Sunshine probably heard about the drama that had happened in the kingdom before she was born when she was with her friends. And that her friends had probably heard of this drama from their parents. Sunshine looked at her mother and said that no, that she had not heard about this drama from her friends.

Sarah asked Sunshine how it was possible that she knew about something that had happened before she was born if she did not hear it from someone? Sunshine told her mother that she could not answer this question.

Sarah asked Sunshine if she did not want to answer or if she could not answer? Sunshine answered her mother that she wanted to answer but that she could not answer. Sarah asked Sunshine why she could not answer? Sunshine looked at her mom without saying a word. Then there was silence in the room.

After a few minutes, David broke the silence and he told Sunshine that as she refused to tell them how she knew about the drama that had happened in the kingdom before she was born, she was not going to celebrate her birthday. And Sunshine replied to her father that he could not punish her just because she had refused to answer a question that she could not answer.

David told Sunshine that she could answer the question because she knew the answer to the question, but just that she refused to answer the question. Sunshine replied to her father that it was his right to punish her, and that she deserved to be punished.

But he could not prevent her from celebrating her birthday, not only because it was the first time that she was going to celebrate her birthday, but mostly because this birthday was important and this birthday was going to change everything.

David told Sunshine that it was true that it was the first time that she was going to celebrate her birthday. But that it was also the first time that she refused to answer a question and it was also the first time that she was going to be punished.

Sunshine told her dad that it was not fair to prevent her from celebrating her birthday, and that she always refused to celebrate her birthday, and that for the first time that she decided to celebrate her birthday, he could not refuse.

David replied to Sunshine if she wanted to celebrate her birthday, she would answer the question that he wanted her to answer. Sunshine told her dad that she would respect his decision and she would not celebrate her birthday, but that she would hold her meeting with her friends and with her parent's friends.

David asked Sunshine what the meeting that she was going to hold was about? Sunshine answered her father that it was a surprise that he was going to find out the content of the meeting at one in the afternoon, and that this meeting was going to change the destiny of the children of the kingdom forever. Sarah and David looked at each other with astonished faces without knowing what to say, but looking at the expression on their faces, they were very surprised by the attitude of Sunshine.

Then David looked at Sunshine and said that it was important that he knows the reasons why she wanted to hold a meeting, and what this meeting was about. Sunshine replied to her father that she was sorry, but that she could not tell him the reasons why she was going to hold a meeting. And that it was a surprise, and if she told him the reasons why she wanted to organize a meeting it would no longer be a surprise.

David looked into Sunshine's eyes and he told her that she was not going to organize a meeting in the house if he did not know what the meeting was about. Sunshine replied to her father that if she could not call the meeting in the house, she was going to organize this meeting in the street.

David looked at Sunshine without uttering a word, and he took a deep breath, then he told her that she was punished and that she was not going to celebrate her birthday and that she was not going to organize a meeting. Then David and Sarah left the room.

Then Sunshine started walking in her room thinking what to do, and she did not expect her father to prevent her from celebrating her birthday and to call a meeting. And Sunshine was thinking how to organize this meeting even against the wishes of her father because this meeting was very important for her.

And mostly that this meeting was going to change everything in the kingdom, and this meeting was not only for the children, but it was also the meeting that would save the kingdom. Then Sunshine got an idea, and she concentrated on herself, and her eyes started spinning, then the light shone in her eyes and she disappeared.

After a few seconds, Sunshine appeared on the road that was in front of her house with her pajamas on her. Sunshine spent the hours inviting her neighbours to her house at one in the afternoon, but Sunshine did not tell them that she invited them for the meeting.

She just told them that she was sad and that it was her birthday and her parents had refused to celebrate her birthday. And that she wanted to spend just an hour with people she loved. And all people that Sunshine had met, had accepted the invitation of Sunshine.

It was one in the afternoon, David and Sarah were sitting in the living room, and they were talking about Sunshine. And Sarah was asking her husband to forgive Sunshine and to let Sunshine celebrate her birthday, and that if Sunshine wanted to organize her birthday, they must let her do it.

Because it was the first time that Sunshine really wanted to celebrate her birthday, and they could not punish her by preventing her from celebrating her birthday. David replied to his wife that Sunshine just needed to tell him how she was aware of the drama that had occurred in the kingdom before her birth.

And Sarah told David that he could find another way to punish Sunshine, but that he could not stop her from celebrating her birthday. David replied to Sarah that he would not change his decision, and that Sunshine was going to celebrate her birthday only in one condition.

And this condition was that Sunshine told him how she was aware of the drama that had occurred in the kingdom before her birth. Sarah told David that he must allow Sunshine to celebrate her birthday, and after her birthday party, they would talk with Sunshine, and they would try to find out how she was aware of the drama that had happened in the kingdom before her birth.

And David replied to Sarah to forget the idea of the birthday party because Sunshine would not organize the birthday party this year because if Sunshine told them how she was aware of the drama that had happened in the kingdom now, she was no longer going to celebrate her birthday. Because they could not allow Sunshine to choose her time to talk or to answer a question because it was not a good way to educate a child.

And David went on and said that Sunshine must learn to obey and to follow the rules, and she must mostly understand that the kingdom was not a land where everyone could express his thoughts without being killed on the orders of the king. Because if Kalus's men were in their house when Sunshine talked about the drama that had happened in the kingdom before her birth, she would be in her grave now.

Because it was forbidden by the king to talk about the drama that had hit the kingdom more than twelve years ago. And David added that it was important that Sunshine be aware of the rules of the kingdom, and that the kingdom was not a safe land where people were safe to do whatever they wanted. Because everyone in the kingdom must live according to the rules of Kalus also called the laws of Kalus.

Sarah replied to David that he was right, and that they must try to find a way to explain to Sunshine the rules of the kingdom, also called the rules of Kalus or the laws of Kalus. But they must not forget that Sunshine was just a child of twelve years old, and that they must be a little patient with her.

And that they must celebrate their daughter's birthday with her, and after her birthday party, they would try to explain to their daughter the laws of Kalus. David looked at Sarah and said that Sunshine would celebrate her birthday next year when she would be thirteen years old, and that Sunshine must learn a lesson this year, and next time she would learn that she must obey her parents.

Sarah replied to her husband that their daughter could be traumatized if she did not celebrate her birthday, mostly that their daughter was the one who asked to celebrate her birthday for the first time. And that their daughter had always refused to celebrate her birthday, and they did not know if she would accept to celebrate her birthday the next year.

And Sarah added that she had been in the kitchen since the morning when they left their daughter's room to bake cakes and food to celebrate her birthday. Suddenly, David and Sarah turned their heads and they looked at the front door as they had heard the bell ring.

Then Sarah got up from her chair and she walked till the door, then she opened the door and suddenly the expression of her face changed, and she was seeing her neighbours and their children at the door.

And some of their neighbours had carried the cakes, drinks and other stuff in their hands. And Sarah asked them what was going on? And one of the neighbours answered Sarah that they had been invited by Sunshine to come celebrate their children's birthday with her because she had been forbidden by her parents to celebrate her birthday.

And Sarah welcomed her neighbours in her house with a smile of joy on her face, then they all walked till the living room. David was astonished to hear from his neighbours that they had been invited by Sunshine to come spend her birthday's day with her. And some of David's neighbours told him that it was also the birthday of their children, and their children had decided to celebrate their birthday with Sunshine.

Then Sarah went to Sunshine's bedroom, and she saw Sunshine who had worn a nice outfit, and who was sitting on the bed. Sarah was not really surprised to see Sunshine who had worn a beautiful outfit, but she was surprised to see that Sunshine had almost removed her bandages, and that there was only a small bandage on Sunshine's forehead and on Sunshine's hand.

Then Sarah looked at Sunshine's hands and she was more astonished to notice that there were no more marks of injuries on Sunshine's body, and Sarah did not understand what was going on. Then Sarah asked Sunshine if Sunshine was doing well? Sunshine answered that she was doing fine.

Sarah asked Sunshine how it was possible that almost all her wounds had been healed. Sunshine answered her mom that she had taken the medicines. Sarah replied to her daughter that it's been less than nine hours that she saw Sunshine's body full of wounds, and she was very amazed to see that almost all these wounds had been healed in less than nine hours.

Sunshine asked her mother why she was surprised? Sarah answered that because it was her first time to see the wounds that had been healed in less than nine hours because the wounds usually take days, weeks, and even months to heal. Sunshine looked at her mom without saying a word, and she could understand that Sarah was surprised, but she could not tell Sarah that almost all her wounds had healed in less than nine hours.

Because she was born with the magic and powers, and that she had used her magic and powers to heal her wounds. Then Sarah told Sunshine that her friends were waiting in the living room. Sunshine smiled at her mom and said that she was eager to spend time with her friends. Then Sunshine and her mom left the room.

Then Sunshine and her mother reached the living room, and suddenly the smile appeared on Sunshine's face when she saw her friends, and she was even more surprised to notice that there were some children of her age in the room that she did not know.

Then everyone in the room started singing happy birthday when they saw Sunshine. Then Sunshine greeted everyone and she thanked them for coming, and mostly to those who came to celebrate their birthday with her. Then Sunshine was introduced to some people that she did not know, and who had come to celebrate their birthday with Sunshine. Those people were the relatives of Sunshine's friends.

There were three people between those people that Sunshine made their acquaintance who had caught the attention of Sunshine. Between these three people, there was a boy named Aaron with short gray hair, blue eyes, and a small chin; a girl named Mia with long black hair, a sharp nose, and green eyes; and a boy named Asher with long black hair, green eyes, and a small nose. But there was also a young girl, who was twelve years old like them, named Nany with long black hair and blue eyes; she caught the attention of Sunshine. And Sunshine sensed a lot of courage coming from Asher but fear emanating from Nany.

Then the cakes, drinks and food were served at the table, and the names of all children who were celebrating their birthday were written on the cakes, and there were also the burning candles on the cakes. Sunshine was very surprised to see that her mom had made the cake and food for her birthday because her parents had told in the morning that she should not celebrate her birthday. They all stood up around the table and they sang happy birthday, then children hugged each other and they wished each other a happy birthday.

The parents clapped their hands and children blew on the candles which were on the cakes, then children cut the cakes. Then they all started to eat, drink and talk. After more than an hour, they had all finished eating and drinking.

Sunshine made a speech and she thanked everyone for coming, and especially children, and she also thanked all parents who had taken their time to make the delicious cakes for them. And Sunshine thanked her parents for the surprise because she did not expect to have a cake in her name because she had been punished by them.

And David looked at Sunshine and said that she had not respected her punishment because she organized her meeting, despite the fact that she was forbidden to do that. Sunshine replied to her father that she had respected her punishment, that she was not forbidden to get out of the house, and she was not also forbidden to spend time with her friends.

But she was instead forbidden to organize her meeting and to celebrate her birthday. And Sunshine went on and said what she did was go out and invite her friends to come celebrate their birthday with her because she could not celebrate her own birthday.

Suddenly, Asher started to clap his hands and he looked at Sunshine and said, "I am amazed by your thinking skills, you are very smart because you succeeded in organizing a wonderful birthday party by respecting your punishment."

Mia looked at Asher and said that she was impressed by Sunshine, that Sunshine had not broken the rules that were imposed on her by her father, but she had succeeded to do what she wanted to do. Then the parents started to laugh, and David said that he admitted that Sunshine was very smart, and that she always succeeded in finding a way to do whatever he wanted to do.

Then Sunshine said that she would like to talk about something that concerned children of the kingdom and the future of the kingdom. Then Sunshine posed, and the eyes of everyone were focused on her, and Sunshine's mom had the feeling that Sunshine would say something that would be against the laws of Kalus.

The expression on Sunshine's face changed, and she was looking nervous and she opened her mouth and said that she would like to talk about the education of children, the destiny of children and the rights of children in the kingdom.

Suddenly, the eyes of all the parents in the room opened wide, and they were looking at Sunshine with surprised faces, then the parents turned their heads and looked at each other still with the same expression on their faces, and some even had their mouths opened.

While children were looking at the parents wondering what was going on, they were also wondering what Sunshine had said so the parents suddenly reacted like this. But Sunshine was not surprised by the attitude of the parents and looking at the expression on the face of Sunshine, it was obvious that she was expecting this reaction from the parents.

Then Asher looked at Sunshine and asked her what was going on? And why the parents were reacting as if they had heard that the devil was coming. Sunshine answered Asher that exactly, that the parents were reacting like this because she had broken the laws of the devil.

Asher asked Sunshine who was the devil? Sunshine answered Asher that the devil was the king Kalus. Mia cried out, "the king Kalus is the devil?" Mia was looking at Sunshine with an astonished face. Sunshine looked at Mia and replied that the king Kalus was a real devil.

Nany looked at Sunshine and said that the king Kalus was instead the god of the kingdom, and that it was the reason why they prayed in the name of the king Kalus. Sunshine looked into Nany's eyes and said that the king Kalus was not a god, but instead a devil, and that they must stop praying in the name of Kalus.

Suddenly, Sunshine was interrupted by David who asked her to stop talking about the king of the kingdom like this. And David also told Sunshine that he did not want to hear something again coming out from her mouth about the kingdom and children.

Sunshine looked at her father and replied that she would not stop talking, and that it was unfair what the king was doing to children because Kalus was stealing the life, the destiny, the dream, the future and the happiness of children.

David looked at Sunshine angrily and he ordered her to leave the room and to go to her bedroom. Sunshine replied to her father that she was sorry to not obey because she would not go to her bedroom, and that she was tired of staying at home and that she was going to fight for her destiny, even if she was going to die while doing it.

Everyone in the room was looking at Sunshine in the room with astonished faces, wondering what was going on with her. And the parents were very afraid because they knew exactly what Sunshine was talking about, even if they did not understand why Sunshine was calling the king Kalus a devil. While children in the room were completely lost because they did not know what was going on and what Sunshine was talking about.

Then Asher looked at Sunshine and he asked her to explain what she was talking about because he was completely lost. Sunshine looked into Asher's eyes and said that she was talking about children's lives, the future of children, the dream of children, the rights of children and the destiny of children.

Asher asked Sunshine who the children were? Sunshine answered Asher that they were children, their little brothers and sisters were children, the future babies who would be born were the future children, their babies would be children, their grandbabies would be children and all babies who were not yet born and who would be born would be children.

Asher asked Sunshine what harm was with the children's lives, and Sunshine replied by asking if he had a dream. Asher smiled at Sunshine and asked what was the dream? Sunshine asked Asher what he wanted to become in his life? Asher answered Sunshine that he wanted to become a doctor. Sunshine asked Asher what he would do to become a doctor? Asher answered Sunshine that he had nothing to do to become a doctor. Sunshine replied to Asher that he could not become a doctor by a miracle. Asher asked Sunshine what she meant by he could not miraculously become a doctor?

Sunshine looked into Asher's eyes and said, "There's only one way to become a doctor—education. Nobody could stay at home and miraculously one day become a doctor."

Asher asked, "What's education?"

Sunshine answered, "Education is the path that everyone uses to achieve their dream, and that only education would allow them to become what they wanted to be. Only with education would their dreams come true; doctors, lawyers, nurses, chefs, instructors, and others were trained through education."

Suddenly, Sunshine was interrupted by Sarah. "Enough. You've said a lot and went too far."

Sunshine looked at her mother and asked her, "Why should I stop if I'm telling the truth? This is a reality. I know the risks that I'm taking by breaking the laws of Kalus, by talking about education, but that I can no longer close my mouth and pretend to be blind so as not to see things. I'm tired of pretending to be happy, tired of pretending that everything was going well, tired of lying to everyone, saying that I'm doing fine. I'm tired of lying to myself every day."

Sunshine, getting more emotional, added, "I was born from lies, and I grew up among lies, but today is my twelfth birthday, and the gifts I'm giving to myself is to fight for my dream, for the dream of all children of the kingdom, for the dream of the future generations of the kingdom. For the future of the kingdom! And the fight for my right, for the rights of all children of the kingdom. And for that, nobody should stop me because I am ready to get into my coffin and grave, if that's what it takes."

Suddenly, everyone in the room was looking at Sunshine with fear on their face, including children who were not really understanding what was going on. On the other hand, Sunshine's friends were very surprised by the attitude of Sunshine because it was their first time to see her like this.

The parents were very afraid, and they knew that they were in danger because they knew that Kalus would not hesitate to kill them if Kalus knew that they were talking about education. But at the same time, the parents were very surprised by Sunshine's courage. And the parents were understanding the reasons why Sunshine had invited her friends and her parent's friends to come spend their day with her.

David and Sarah were understanding why Sunshine wanted to organize a meeting, and why she had refused to talk about the content of her meeting and why she had said that the content of her meeting was a surprise. But David and Sarah were wondering how Sunshine was aware of the problem of education in the kingdom, and other problems in the kingdom.

Because Sunshine's parents could see that Sunshine had not heard the problems of the kingdom through her friends because all her friends who were in the room were completely lost, and her friends were not even aware of the problems that Sunshine was talking about. Sunshine's parents were thinking how to stop Sunshine because they knew that Sunshine was in danger, that Kalus would not hesitate to kill all of them if Kalus knew that they were breaking his laws.

Asher asked Sunshine what exactly education was and how education would help them to realize their dream? Sunshine looked at Asher and said that the education was school. And Sunshine went on and said that all the doctors, the engineers, the lawyers, the chefs, the instructors and others went to school. And that all those who wanted to become doctors, the nurses, the lawyers, the receptionist and others must spend the years in school to study.

Asher asked Sunshine if the doctors, the nurses and the lawyers who were in the kingdom went to school? Sunshine answered Asher that yes, and that not only the doctors, the nurses, the lawyers, the journalists and the technicians of the kingdom had been in school, but that ninety-eight percent of workers in the kingdom had been to school.

And even the king Kalus had been to school because the king Kalus was a former lawyer. And Sunshine added that even their parents who were in the room listening to her had been to school, and they had studied to practice the job that they were doing now.

Asher asked Sunshine why his parents told him that when he would grow up, he would become a doctor and he would go to work at the hospital? Sunshine looked at Asher and said that she hated what she was going to say, but she must say it because she was going to say that their parents had lied to them by saying that they could become doctors, lawyers, engineers, technicians without an education. And Sunshine added that her own parents had lied to her that she could become a lawyer without an education.

Suddenly, Sunshine was interrupted by a tall man with short hair and yellow eyes named Moise, and Moise said that the meeting was over, and that they had to return home. Asher turned and looked at Moise and said that the meeting was not over yet, and he was interested in what Sunshine was saying.

Moise replied to Asher that children would talk about what Sunshine was talking about with their parents at home. Asher replied to Moise that he was no longer interested in what his parents would say to him because his parents had already lied to him. Moise told Asher that the parents had not lied. Asher asked Moise if everything that was said by Sunshine was a lie? Moise answered Asher that everything that was said by Sunshine was the truth.

Then Mia looked at Moise and said that if everything that was said by Sunshine was the truth, it meant that the parents had lied to them. Moise told Mia that the parents would find time at home and explain everything to the children. Mia asked Moise why not continue to listen to Sunshine because Sunshine was already telling the truth.

Moise answered Mia that it was true that Sunshine was telling the truth, but that the parents would explain to them exactly what was going on in the kingdom. Mia told Moise she was not going home to listen to the lies of her parents, and that she was going to listen to Sunshine because she had lost the confidence in her parents.

David said that it was already late, and that they must find another day to talk about the problem of education. Asher looked at David and said that it was just 3: 00 p.m., and that it was not late yet. David replied to Asher that the parents were very tired because last night the parents were busy with the preparations for the birthdays, so that the parents wanted to rest.

Asher told David that the parents were not tired, but the parents did not want Sunshine to talk. David told Sunshine that he wanted to clean his house and get rest. Asher replied to David that he, Sunshine and other children were going to the street to continue their meeting.

And suddenly, Mia joined the idea of Asher and said that they were going to the street to continue their meeting. And Aaron said that if he could not listen to Sunshine in the house, he was going outside to listen to her.

Then the rest of the children in the room said that they were going outside to listen to Sunshine, and that they were ready to continue their meeting outside. And the parents were very surprised by the attitude of the children and looking at the expression on the faces of the parents, it was obvious that they did not expect this situation to happen.

And the parents did not know what to do because they had lost control of their children, and they knew well that they could not send children in the street to continue their meeting. Because children could be caught on the street by Kalus's men, and if their children were caught by Kalus's men, their children would be killed on the orders of Kalus. Then a woman with short black hair and green eyes named Victoria looked at Sunshine and asked Sunshine to continue. Then all the eyes were focused on Sunshine.

Sunshine thanked all the children in the room for their support, and she said that she understood their parent's concerns because it was prohibited by Kalus to talk about education in the kingdom. Because when the devil named Kalus had been crowned the king of the kingdom after the death of his father, Kalus changed everything, he banned the tradition and religion in the kingdom.

And Kalus even went far and he decided to steal the dream of children, children's lives, the destiny of children, the happiness of children, the future of children and the future of the kingdom. And even worse Kalus stole the lives of many children in the kingdom and he established the laws called the laws of Kalus, also called the laws or rules of the kingdom.

And the laws of Kalus forced all the inhabitants to shut their mouth on everything that was going on in the kingdom. And these laws of Kalus obliged the parents to not talk about the education to their children, to not teach to children how to read and write, to not talk to children about the history of the kingdom, to not talk to children about the tradition and culture of the kingdom, to not talk to children about the religion and God.

And even worse the laws of Kalus obliged the parents to lie to their children, and these laws of Kalus forced the inhabitants of the kingdom to believe in Kalus as god, to pray in Kalus's name. And of course, all those who would dare to break only one of the laws of Kalus would be killed on the orders of Kalus.

And the laws of Kalus were created only by Kalus to kill people and to make the inhabitants of the kingdom poor. Because Kalus was using his laws to steal the money of the inhabitants of the kingdom by forcing the inhabitants of the kingdom to pay more taxes.

Sunshine went on and said that what she did not understand it's why Kalus prohibited education in the kingdom knowing well that a nation could not survive without an education because education was the heart of a nation. Some people were trained through education, like doctors, engineers, lawyers, pilots, technicians, and others. Education is the air of a nation, and if this air died, it would mean that the nation would die too.

Sunshine continued and said that the kingdom was in a coma because Kalus had killed the air of the kingdom, which was education, and that the kingdom was on breathing assistance and the kingdom was breathing on oxygen.

And that this oxygen that was helping the kingdom to breathe and to stay alive was going to finish very soon, and once this oxygen would finish, the kingdom would be buried. Because they would have nothing possible to do to save the kingdom or to prevent the kingdom to be buried once this respiratory assistance that allowed the kingdom to stay alive would stop.

And that the kingdom was in grave danger now. And that also meant that the population of the kingdom was in grave danger because the fact that the kingdom was on respiratory assistance and breathing on oxygen that also meant that it was all the inhabitants of the kingdom who were on respiratory assistance and breathing on oxygen.

And that when the oxygen would finish and the respiratory assistance would stop, the lives of all the inhabitants of the kingdom would also stop. And the kingdom would be buried with all its inhabitants.

Sunshine continued and said that the respiratory assistance of the kingdom were all the parents of the kingdom who were working now to allow the kingdom to stay alive, and the oxygens of the kingdom were the energy and strength that these parents had now.

And that it was these oxygens that were the energy and strength that allowed the parents who were respiratory assistance to maintain the kingdom alive by working. But that the energy and strength that were the oxygen would run out soon, and once it's depleted, the respiratory assistance who were the parents would stop working to maintain the kingdom alive.

And it meant that when the parents who were working now to maintain the kingdom alive would be tired because they would have no choice but to retire because they would no longer have the strength and energy to wake up each morning and go to work. And once the parents would have retired, the kingdom would die because there would no longer be the doctors, the nurses, the engineers, the technicians, the researchers, the lawyers, the judges, the chefs, the pilots and others in the kingdom to replace the parents who retired.

Because the parents who were working now had just replaced the great parents when the great parents had retired, and the great parents had replaced the great great-parents when the great great-parents had retired.

And that is how the things worked since the existence of the kingdom and it's how the kingdom succeeded to stay alive till when Kalus had been crowned the king of the kingdom. And once Kalus sat on the kingdom throne, Kalus decided to kill the kingdom with its inhabitants by putting the kingdom on respiratory assistance for the reason that only himself knew.

Then Sunshine posed, and there was silence in the room and everyone was looking at Sunshine with amazed faces. And children were completely lost about what Sunshine was saying, and they were still not realizing what they were hearing from Sunshine.

And they were mostly surprised to hear that the king Kalus that they had grown up watching on television and who was introduced on television like god, was just a real devil who had stolen their dreams, their lives, their happiness and their destiny. And children did not understand why their parents did not prevent them from believing in Kalus like their god, and why their parents did not throw away the status of Kalus that they had received from Kalus's men like the status of the god of the kingdom.

And most of the children were very angry, and they were realizing that since they were born, their lives were based on lies. And the parents in the room were very surprised to notice that Sunshine was aware of what was going on in the kingdom, and they were wondering how Sunshine could be aware of the situation of the kingdom, even to be aware of all the details.

Mostly that Sunshine was not yet born when Kalus had been crowned the king of the kingdom, and the parents were wondering who had told Sunshine about the situation of the kingdom, mostly that the laws of Kalus forbade everyone to talk about the situation of the kingdom.

Then Sunshine broke the silence and said that she was going to fight for her dream, but she was also going to fight for the dream of children of this kingdom, and she was going to fight for the destiny of the future generation, and she would mostly fight to prevent this kingdom from dying.

Sunshine went on and said that it was useless to try to convince her to not fight for her dream because she had already made her decision and she was determined to fight. And that she was not afraid of Kalus, and that she was going to break all the laws of Kalus, and she was not also afraid to die or to be killed by Kalus's men on the orders of Kalus.

Suddenly, Sunshine was interrupted by Asher and he looked at Sunshine and said that he was going to fight with Sunshine for their dream and the dream of children of the kingdom. And Asher went on and said that he just changed his dream, he was no longer interested in becoming a doctor.

But he was going to become a soldier to protect the kingdom and the rights of the population of the kingdom from the devil people like the king Kalus. And Asher added that the only thing he needed right now was a gun and with bullets to shoot on this devil named Kalus. Sunshine smiled at Asher and she thanked him for his support.

Then Aaron started walking towards Sunshine, and everyone in the room had their eyes focused on Aaron, and they were all wondering why Aaron was walking towards Sunshine, and even Sunshine's eyes were focused on Aaron. Then Aaron stopped near to Sunshine and he looked at everyone in the room and said that this day was not only a great day, but it was a memorable day because this day would be in the history of the kingdom forever.

Because this day was going to change the history of the kingdom, and this day would write a new page in the history of the kingdom, and this day would be remembered like Sunshine's day. Because it was Sunshine who had made history this day.

Aaron went on and said that the kingdom was lucky to have a child like Sunshine, that Sunshine was sent by God to save the kingdom to prevent the kingdom to be buried because the kingdom was already almost dead because they were all living in the kingdom that was in a coma.

And if they were all living in the kingdom that was in a coma, that meant they were all also in the coma, and that they must fight to survive because if the kingdom was going to be buried, it meant that they were going to be buried too.

And that the kingdom did not belong to Kalus, but the kingdom belonged to all the inhabitants of the kingdom, and it was the responsibility and duty of all the inhabitants of the kingdom to take care of the kingdom, to make the kingdom a better place for everyone and a safe place for the future generation.

And Aaron added that he was going to take his own responsibilities like a child of this kingdom. And he was going to fight near Sunshine not only for his dream, but for the love of the kingdom, and mostly for the destiny and the dream of the future generation.

Because, if they failed to save the kingdom, their little brothers and sisters, their children and the future generation would have no place to live because the kingdom would be buried. And that it was not only the fight of Sunshine, but it was the fight of everyone, mostly the fight of children.

Suddenly, Aaron was interrupted by Sunshine who was clapping her hands, and Asher followed Sunshine by clapping his hands, then the rest of the children started clapping their hands. Mia said that she was going to fight near Sunshine, Asher and Aaron to save the kingdom and to make the kingdom a better place.

And immediately, the rest of the children in the room said that they were going to fight to save the kingdom. And the parents were very amazed by what was going on, and they were realizing that children had taken control of their destiny.

But the parents were very afraid of Kalus because they knew well that Kalus would not hesitate to kill their children when Kalus would hear that their children wanted to fight for their right of education.

And the parents knew well that they must prevent children from fighting Kalus or to break the laws of Kalus. And the parents knew well that it was not going to be easy to convince children to forget about their dream, and they were thinking about how to talk to children.

Then the parents started trying to talk to children, and saying that it was dangerous to fight Kalus because Kalus would not hesitate to kill them. And Asher replied to the parents that the children were already dead, that Kalus had already killed them by stealing their dream, their lives, their destiny and their happiness.

And Asher went on and said that children were not afraid of Kalus, and that it was this devil named Kalus who should be afraid of children because children had nothing to lose but every to gain. And Asher added that the fight was not the fight of the parents, but it was the fight of children. And that he was going to kill this devil named Kalus by himself because this devil named Kalus had no place in the kingdom.

A parent with short gray hair and green eyes a little tall named Jacob told children that he understood their anger and their desire to go school to realize their dream. But that it was more important to stay alive because life did not have a price, and no one could realize a dream in a grave because they would not realize their dream of going to school when Kalus would kill them.

Asher looked at Jacob and said that he was not ready to live at any cost, and for that he was not going to accept the laws of Kalus just because he wanted to stay alive. And that he was already dead because he had been killed since before his birth by this devil named Kalus.

Victoria looked at Asher and said that she understood his desire to fight for his dream, but that he would also understand that it was not without a risk to fight the king Kalus because Kalus was not a nice person. And that was the reason why they would all calm and find a time to think very well about how to approach Kalus to talk to Kalus about the situation of the kingdom.

Asher replied to Victoria that the worst thing that Kalus could do to him was to kill him, but that he was not afraid to die because he was not really different from a corpse. And Asher added that he was not going to talk to Kalus because the devil Kalus was not his king, but Kalus was his enemy, and that he was not going to beg his enemy for his rights, and for that he was going to fight.

Aaron said that he was against the violence, and that he did not want people to die, and for that he would join Victoria's idea to find a time and to think how to approach the king Kalus with this problem of education. And Asher looked at Aaron and said that he was not going to join Victoria's idea to beg the devil Kalus for his rights, and that he was ready to burn this kingdom just to kill Kalus, even if by burning the kingdom, many people would die.

Aaron replied to Asher that they must talk to the king Kalus, even if they did not like Kalus because Kalus was the king of the kingdom, and Kalus was the one who had the powers in the kingdom to decide if children would go to school or not.

Asher told Aaron that the devil Kalus was not his king, and this same devil named Kalus had not the powers in his life, so it was not Kalus who would decide if he would go to school or not, and that he was not going to beg Kalus.

Because he was going to put the fire on all the status of Kalus that was in the kingdom, to send a message to this devil named Kalus even if it would be the last thing he would do. Nany looked at Asher and said that Aaron's idea was perfect, that it was important and necessary to go talk to Kalus because Kalus was not only the king of the kingdom, but he was also the father of the kingdom, and Kalus was mostly the father of children who love children.

Asher replied to Nany that Kalus was not his father, and that Kalus was just a monster for the kingdom who destroyed the lives of children, and who did not care about the kingdom and the inhabitants of the kingdom.

Because if Kalus loved the kingdom, Kalus should never ban education in the kingdom knowing that education was the engine of the kingdom, and that Kalus was just a monster who wanted to kill the kingdom with its inhabitants.

Mia said that she joined Asher's idea because Kalus had no right to ban the education to children because this monster named Kalus knew well the importance of the education in a nation, and although the fact that this devil of Kalus had been in school, he did not hesitate to ban the education to children.

Mia added that if Kalus had banned education in the kingdom, that meant that they could not talk with this monster of Kalus about education because Kalus would not give them their right to education, and that's why it was important to use the violence to get their right to education.

A young boy named Isac said that the ideas of Aaron and Nany were the best because it would be useless to use violence against their king because he had no doubt that there was a reason why Kalus had banned education in the kingdom, and they must listen to their king why the education was banned by him in the kingdom.

And that they must stop calling their king a devil or a monster because they loved their king and their king loved them, and it was the reason why it was important to have a conversation with their king.

Sunshine said that she joined the ideas of Asher and Mia because they would not negotiate with the devil Kalus, and that Kalus had no reason to ban them education because all the schools that were in the kingdom were built by their ancestors. And the instructors of the school were paid by the money of their parent's taxes, so that Kalus had no right to steal their dream.

And that Kalus was just a monster who hated children, and who did not love the kingdom because if Kalus loved the kingdom, he should never ban education, knowing very well the importance of education.

Then Sunshine went on and said that Kalus was not her king, and he was just a devil for her who hated children. And that she did not understand how people could love this devil named Kalus and even pray in his name, and that since she was born, she had never seen this devil walk in the streets of the kingdom to talk with his people, he had never even visited hospitals or the orphans.

And even worse he had never made a speech to his people even on television. Because it was always Kalus's men who made the speech on television on behalf of Kalus. And that the king who loved his people and his kingdom did not behave like this devil named Kalus.

Then the parents tried to convince Sunshine that the idea of Aaron, Nany and Isac was good, and they would think how to approach Kalus because the violence would not solve the problem, but the violence would make the situation worse.

And that Kalus would probably understand if they approached Kalus in peace and tried to talk to him by begging him to allow children to go to school. Sunshine replied to the parents that she was not going to beg for her rights, and that it was a waste of time to try to have a conversation with Kalus because Kalus would never accept to give education to children.

Sunshine went on and said that there was no time to waste because the kingdom was already in a coma, and it was time now to save the kingdom. And that the parents who were working now would be retired in a few years, and there were not yet people who would replace the parents. Because children who were supposed to replace the parents were not going to school to study to be ready to replace the parents who would be retired in a few years.

And that meant that in a few years, there would be no doctor, no engineer, no technician, no lawyer, no nurse, no pilot, no judge and there would be nobody in other areas. And that she was wondering how people would live in a kingdom that did not have doctors, lawyers, engineers, judges and chefs? And how people would heal when they would be sick? Who would help women to give birth? Who would create and make things?

Then Sunshine posed and all the eyes were focused on her, and there was silence in the room. And after a minute, Sunshine broke the silence and said that no one could answer these questions because she had spent time trying to answer these questions without success.

And she would be very happy if someone could answer these questions for her, if someone in the room could tell her how people were going to live in the kingdom without doctors, lawyers, nurses, engineers, researchers, judges, prosecutors, and with the offices empty.

Suddenly, there was silence in the room, and the parents were really realizing the problem that there was in the kingdom, and they were understanding that Sunshine was right to say that the kingdom was in a coma. Then Sunshine broke the silence and said that no one answered her question, and that if no one answered her question, that meant that the kingdom was really in danger, and the kingdom was very sick in a coma with no future.

That children were those who were going to give a future to the kingdom because children were the future. And that Kalus could not cure the kingdom that was sick in a coma because Kalus was not a medicine for the kingdom, but Kalus was instead a cancer for the kingdom, and that meant that if they wanted to cure the kingdom, they would not work with Kalus.

Sunshine added that only children could cure the kingdom from its coma because they were the future of the kingdom, and for that, children would do everything, even the impossible things, to heal the kingdom that was sick. Because children would not let the kingdom in a coma because children would not let the kingdom die, and children would never allow someone or even the king Kalus to kill the kingdom.

Suddenly, Sunshine was interrupted by Asher who was clapping his hands, and Asher was followed by the rest of people who were clapping their hands too. And Asher said that he was going to throw Kalus's status that was in his bedroom in the garbage, and that from today he would stop praying in the name of this devil named Kalus.

And Sunshine said she had never prayed in the name of Kalus because she always knew that he was not a god, but instead a devil. Sunshine added that she invited all children in the room to stop praying in the name of Kalus, and to destroy Kalus's status that was given to them as the status of god.

Then the parents asked the children that they had heard them, and they supported them in their fight for their right of education. And the parents asked the children what was their plan? Sunshine answered the parents that she had a plan, but she would talk about her plan only with children, and she would decide with her friends.

Then the parents insisted on knowing Sunshine's plan, but Sunshine refused, and the parents told the children that Kalus had killed the students, the priests and other people who had tried to protest when he banned the religion, the tradition and the education in the kingdom. And the parents asked the children to be careful because Kalus would not hesitate to kill them if they were a danger for Kalus.

Sunshine told the parents not to worry, that they would be fine. Then Sunshine took the children to the basement of the house. Sunshine and friends, also called fellows, spent three hours in the basement to plan a plan for the next day.

It was midnight, Kalus had knelt in his magic room and he was talking with Lord. And Kalus asked Lord if Sunshine was already dead? Lord answered Kalus that Sunshine was still alive. Kalus replied to Lord that Sunshine was already twelve years old, and that it's been twelve years today that he had not put his feet outside of the palace.

Lord told Kalus to be patient, that he had failed to kill Sunshine mystically during twelve years, but that he was not going to fail to kill her physically by fighting her. And Lord added that he had his first fight with Sunshine yesterday during the night, and she was lucky during this fight.

Kalus said that he hated this cursed girl of Sunshine, and that he wanted to kill her by himself with his hands. Lord told Kalus to be patient because Sunshine was very strong and powerful. And Sunshine was also dangerous, and he had noticed that she was very smart too.

Kalus replied to Lord that Sunshine had kept him prisoner in his own kingdom, that since Sunshine was born, he had not put feet outside, that Sunshine had even stopped his projects. Lord told Kalus to be patient and that Sunshine would soon die. And Lord asked Kalus to be ready because he would receive a visit in a few hours.

Kalus asked Lord who was coming? Lord answered Kalus that it was a surprise, just that Kalus must be ready to receive his guests. And Kalus asked Lord how many guests were coming? Lord answered that he did not know exactly the number, but that it was more than one person. Kalus asked Lord for which reasons these guests were to the palace? Lord answered Kalus that these guests were coming with the news. Kalus asked if these guests were coming with the good news?

Lord replied to Kalus that it would depend how Kalus was going to take the news. Kalus asked Lord if he knew people who were coming. Lord asked Kalus to stop asking the questions and get ready to welcome his guests. Then Lord told Kalus to go sleep and Lord wished good luck to Kalus with his guests, and that they would talk the next day. Then Lord left. Then Kalus got up and left the room.

CHAPTER II

THE FIGHT OF THE CHILDREN FOR THEIR RIGHT TO EDUCATION

It was nine in the morning, Sunshine and her fellows were in the basement of her house, and they had made the protest signs and Sunshine was writing on these protest signs with the chalk. And Sunshine's fellows were watching at Sunshine who was writing on the chalk with astonished faces.

And if Sunshine's friends were surprised, it was because they were noticing that Sunshine knew how to write, and they were wondering what Sunshine was writing on these protest signs. But they noticed that Sunshine had written different words on the protest signs even if they could not read these words.

After a few minutes, Sunshine had finished writing on the protest signs, and there was silence in the room, and they were all looking at Sunshine. Then Asher broke the silence and asked Sunshine how it was possible that she knew how to write? Sunshine looked at Asher with a surprised face, and she did not understand the meaning of his question.

Then Sunshine opened her mouth and asked Asher what meant by how it was possible that she knew how to write? Asher answered

Sunshine that the children of the kingdom had never been in school, so they did not know how to write.

Then Sunshine understood why this question was asked to her by Asher, and she was thinking how to answer, but she knew well that she could not tell her fellows that she was born with the powers and magic, and that she could do everything through her powers and magic. Sunshine opened her mouth and lied to her friends that it was her parents who had taught her how to write.

Asher told Sunshine that her parents had broken the laws of Kalus because these laws of Kalus banned the parents from teaching children how to read and write. Sunshine replied to Asher that her parents had broken the laws of Kalus to teach her how to write and read because she had insisted.

Mia looked at Sunshine and said that Sunshine was lucky that her parents had taught her how to read and write. Mia asked Sunshine how Sunshine knew about the existence of education. Sunshine lied to Mia and said that she knew the existence of the education through a conversation with her parents.

Aaron told Sunshine that she was very lucky to have the nice parents who talked about important things with her. Aaron added that his parents had never told him about the existence of the education, and that he found out about the existence of the education last night during their meeting.

And other children replied that they did not know about the existence of education, and that it was last night during their birthday party, that they found out the existence of education and how it was important. Sunshine said that if they did not know about the existence of education it was because the laws of Kalus had forced the parents to never talk about the education to children.

And Sunshine added that it was not really the fault of the parents to not talk about the education to children because Kalus was a real monster who killed all those who broke his laws. And the parents were afraid to be killed with their children by Kalus if they broke the laws of Kalus.

Asher told Sunshine that it was a big mistake on the part of their parents to remain silent face to Kalus because the parents should never accept these laws of Kalus. And Asher added that the parents had just unconsciously helped Kalus to destroy the kingdom by accepting these laws of Kalus.

Sunshine replied to Asher that she agreed with him that the parents had helped and even encouraged Kalus by accepting the laws of Kalus. But just that the parents thought to protect their children by accepting the laws of Kalus, mostly that Kalus had killed many people who had tried to protest against his laws.

Then Sunshine added that it was time to leave and to go to war against the laws of Kalus. Asher asked Sunshine what was written on the protest signs? Sunshine answered Asher that she had written many slogans on the protest signs like:

"Children need education."

"Education is the right of children."

"Children have a dream."

"Ban the laws of Kalus and open schools for children."

"Children are the future."

"Save the kingdom."

"Save the future of the kingdom."

"Children are powers."

Then Sunshine said that it was time to carry the protest signs and leave. Then each of them carried a protest sign and they left.

After a few minutes, children were walking in the streets and they had lifted the protest signs, and they were walking in the direction of the palace. And people were very surprised to see children who were walking in the streets and holding protest signs with the slogans that were written on these protest signs.

And people were more astonished to read the slogans that were written on these protest signs because all the words that were written on these protest signs were the words that were forbidden to be used in the kingdom by the king Kalus.

And people were wondering who had sent these children in the streets to protest for their right to education. And they were wondering if the parents of these children knew that their children were in the streets with the protest signs to protest against the laws of Kalus. And some people tried to convince children to return at home, that they would be killed by Kalus's men, but children refused to return at home and they said that they were ready to die.

After an hour, children were downtown, and they were suddenly surrounded by a huge crowd, and they were all amazed to see children in the streets with the protest signs asking for their right to education. And the opinion of people was divided about children, and there were people who wanted to prevent children from walking till the palace, while there were other people who encouraged children to walk till the palace and to fight for their right to education.

And those who were against the protest of children said that children would be killed by Kalus's men on the orders of Kalus, and that Kalus would not hesitate to kill these children. Those who encouraged children to protest said that children were right, and that it was time to put an end to the laws of Kalus and save the kingdom.

Because Kalus was not only killing the future of children but he was also killing the kingdom. Both sides started to argue, and those who were against the protest were determined to prevent children from walking till the palace, while those who supported children said that they could not keep supporting the laws of Kalus. And that children had the right to education.

Then the police arrived, and the police wanted to arrest children but the population opposed the police, and even people who were against the protest of children opposed the police. And despite the fact that the police threatened to use their guns and to shoot, people were determined to protect these children against the police and people were also ready to die to protect these children. Then the police lost control of the situation when other people arrived to support the protest of these children, and even worse, children who were downtown joined other children in the protest.

Then the police wanted to call their colleagues for reinforcements but the phones and guns of the police were taken to them by the population. And the population had taken the phones and guns of the police to prevent the police from calling for reinforcement.

And it was the first time that people were breaking the laws of Kalus in the kingdom because laws of Kalus prohibited people from attacking the police because the police worked for Kalus, and the police obeyed the laws of Kalus.

Then even people who were opposed to the protest of children changed their ideas, and they joined the ideas of those who supported the protest of children. Then people wanted to join children in the protest, but Sunshine refused and she said that it was the fight of children. Then children continued to walk towards the palace.

After three hours of walking, children arrived in front of the palace. And the security men who were in front of the palace were very astonished to see children in front of the palace with the protest signs. And these security men were staring at children with surprised faces without saying a word and wondering who had sent these children.

And security men were more amazed when they read the slogans that were written on the protest signs that children had held in their hands. And looking at the expression on the face of security men, they did not believe what they were reading on these protest signs.

Then a tall security man with short black hair and red eyes named Jadis asked the children who had sent them. Sunshine told Jadis that nobody had sent them, and that they had come by themselves.

Jadis asked, "Who had written the slogans that were on the protest signs?"

Sunshine answered, "We had written these slogans on the protest signs."

Jadis replied, "T that could not be true because children could not write."

"Not all children are incapable of writing," Sunshine stressed.

Jadis just looked at her with a frown. "Children of your age have never been to school. There's no way children like you know how to write."

With a determined gaze, Sunshine looked into his eyes and said, "My fellows and I are not here to give you an explanation; we are here in the place to ask Kalus to give us our right to education."

And suddenly, security men started laughing, and the children just stared at them. There was anger on the faces of Sunshine, Asher, Mia, and Aaron.

After a few seconds, security men had finished laughing. Then Sunshine looked at Jadis and said that they wanted to see Kalus. Jadis told Sunshine to take her fellows and go home because Kalus would not hesitate to kill them if Kalus knew that they were outside of the palace with the protest signs asking for their right to education. And Sunshine replied that they were not afraid to die because they were ready to die for their rights. Full of anger, she added that she would prove to him that she and her fellows were not afraid of the devil named Kalus.

She raised her protest sign and yelled, "Children need education; education is children's right!" And Asher raised his protest sign and screamed, "Children need education; education is children's right!" The rest of the children raised their protest signs and yelled, "Children need education; education is children's right!" They were screaming louder and louder.

Security men were staring at children with astonished faces, wondering what was going on with them. Security men were amazed by the courage of the children, and they were wondering if these children were drunk because they did not understand where these children were taking their courage to confront the King Kalus. Then a short, bald man with green eyes named Albert got out of the gate. And Albert was astonished to see children yelling with the protest signs in their hands.

Albert asked Jadis, "What's going on?"

"Jadis answered, "Children are demanding to see the king for their right to education."

Albert looked at children who were still screaming with surprised faces, and he was very amazed to read the slogans that were written on the protest signs.

And Albert tried to talk to children, but unfortunately children did not pay attention to him, and they were still screaming. Then Sunshine looked at her friends and made a sign with her left hand, and she asked her friends to calm down.

That made the children shift their focus toward Albert. And Albert asked them what they wanted. Sunshine responded, "We want to see Kalus."

"You're not allowed to see Kalus."

"Why not?"

"The King Kalus is busy."

"We'd keep screaming in front of the palace till Kalus received them."

"You'd better leave."

"We won't leave! We're ready to spend weeks, months, and even years in front of the palace till Kalus receives us!"

Albert sighed. "What exactly do you want?"

Sunshine said with pride, "We want to go to school."

Albert almost scoffed. "The word school does not exist."

"We're not stupid. We know that education is one of children's rights, and all children on the planet had access to education, except in this kingdom."

Sunshine went on and said that in the past, children of the kingdom had access to education, but when Kalus became the king, he decided to prohibit education for the reasons that only himself knew. Sunshine added that children of the kingdom had decided to fight for their rights, and children needed to go school.

Then Sunshine raised her protest sign and screamed, "Children need education!" And children followed Sunshine by yelling,

"Children need education!" Then Albert turned and left. And the children continued to yell by asking for their right to education.

After a few minutes, Albert got out and looked at children who were still screaming, and he tried to talk to children without success because children were still yelling. Then Sunshine noticed that Albert wanted to talk to them, and she asked her fellows to calm down.

Then there was silence and all the eyes were focused on Albert. Albert told the children that the king Kalus asked them to leave and if they did not leave, they would be sent to jail. Sunshine replied to Albert that they would not leave, and that they were ready to go to jail. Then Sunshine shouted, "Education or death." And the rest of the children followed Sunshine and yelled, "Education or death."

Albert and security men were surprised to see the rage and determination on children's faces as the children were screaming the words education and death. Then Albert told Jadis that they were going to use the violence to kick children out of the palace because Kalus did not want to hear the screams of these children, and that Kalus had also said that if children refused to leave, they must lock up children in prison.

Then Jadis told his colleagues that they would use the violence to kick children out of the palace. And security men took their big sticks that they worked with, and they started to walk towards children. And children were staring at security men who were walking towards them with the sticks in their hands, and the faces of some children were full of fear, while other children were still screaming, "Education or death."

The security men stopped to face the children, and Jadis tried to talk to the children, but unfortunately the children did not pay attention to him, and children continued to scream. Then security started to push children, and children were trying to resist. And Sunshine told her fellows to not run away and to resist even if they were going to be hurt.

Then the worst happened, and most of the children were on the ground bleeding because they were beaten and kicked by security men. While other children were still trying to resist the security men.

And security men were beating children by using their sticks, and they were asking children to leave. And despite the fact that children were bleeding at their knees, foreheads, elbows and other parts of their bodies, children were determined not to leave. And most of the children were screaming in pain, and they were feeling very weak, and they were unable to defend themselves from security men.

After half an hour, all the children were on the ground bleeding, and feeling pains on their whole bodies, but they were still determined not to leave. Then Albert told security men to lock up children in the prison of the palace.

And this prison of the palace had been built by Kalus to torture his enemies before killing them. Then children were taken to a prison in the palace. Children were locked up in a dark cold prison, and some of them were sitting on the floor, while others were lying on the floor, and the floor was wet.

Children were feeling pains, and they were trembling with cold. And they were talking about Kalus. And Nany said that their king was really mean because he ordered his security men to beat them and to lock them up in a dark cold prison.

Mia replied to Nany that she was not surprised at all that Kalus locked them up in this cold prison because since she was born, she had never heard anything good about Kalus. Mia added that Kalus was seen by the inhabitants of the kingdom as the worst king in the history of the kingdom, even if people were afraid to speak out loud about Kalus.

Asher said that the death of Kalus was the only solution to save the kingdom because when Kalus would be alive the kingdom would never be in peace. Aaron replied to Asher to forget about that idea to kill Kalus, not only because they were not the murderers but because even if they did not like Kalus, Kalus was the king of the kingdom.

Asher told Aaron that Kalus was not his king but his enemy, and that he was going to be a murderer only to kill Kalus. Aaron said that the death of Kalus would not be a solution to their problem. Asher replied that the death of Kalus would be the solution because their problem was Kalus.

Mia said that Asher was right that their problem was Kalus, but that she was afraid that they could not kill Kalus and that Kalus was going to kill them all. Because she had heard from people that Kalus had killed many people in the kingdom. Nany said that she was afraid and that she did not want to die. Asher replied to Nany that not to worry because everything would be fine.

Then Asher asked Sunshine if everything was fine? And Sunshine replied to Asher that everything was all right. Asher asked Sunshine why she was quiet like this? Sunshine answered Asher that she was thinking. Asher asked Sunshine if she was afraid? Sunshine replied to Asher that no, that she was not at all afraid.

Then Nany interrupted the conversation between Sunshine and Asher, and Nany said that she was feeling pain in her whole body. And Asher replied to Nany that everyone was feeling pain. And Asher added that they were all injured. And Nany said that she was trying to sleep but just that her pain coming from her injuries were preventing her from sleeping. Then Sunshine asked everyone to be quiet because there were some people who were trying to sleep.

Then Sunshine's eyes started to spin, and a light got out from Sunshine's eyes and shone in the room, and no one saw this light coming from Sunshine's eyes and shining in the room. And suddenly, except Sunshine, the rest of the children in the room felt a strange reaction in their bodies, and they were feeling very tired, then they fell asleep. Sunshine turned her head and she noticed that everyone was deeply asleep. Then Sunshine knelt and she started praying with her eyes open. Then the light shone into Sunshine's eyes and she disappeared.

the king Kalus was sitting in his living room, and he was watching television. Then Kalus turned his head to his left when he heard a voice coming from this side. And suddenly, the fear appeared on Kalus's face and he was staring at Sunshine with his eyes widely open. And looking at the expression of Kalus's face, it was as if he was staring at a monster, and Kalus tried to talk but his mouth was shaking that a word could not get out from his mouth.

Sunshine was looking at the fear on Kalus's face, and she said, "I thought that you were a man, but I just notice that you are just a coward."

"Who are you?" Kalus asked.

"I am the one, you are looking for," Sunshine said.

"I am not looking for you," Kalus retorted.

"I am the one you dream of seeing dead," Sunshine said.

"Sunshine?" Kalus cried out.

"Yes, I am Sunshine," Sunshine answered.

Kalus was looking at Sunshine with a face extremely full of terror, and with his mouth open but he did not know what to say, and Sunshine was staring at Kalus with a face empty of expression. Then Kalus got up from his chair without saying a word, and he started running towards the corridor of his magic room. Then Sunshine turned her head and looked at Kalus who was running away, then Sunshine's eyes started spinning.

And suddenly, Kalus stopped running, and he was trying to run without success and the feet of Kalus were not moving, and it was as if a strong glue had stuck on the feet Kalus's floor. Kalus bent his head and he was looking at his feet with his face full of fear, and he was surprised to see that there was nothing that tied his feet, and he tried to move his feet but unfortunately his feet were not moving.

And immediately, Kalus's body started trembling with fear, and he did not understand what was going on. And he was turning his head around to look at what was going on, and what was preventing him from running away.

Then Kalus's eyes met with Sunshine's eyes, and suddenly Kalus started breathing deeply and the sweat started to flow on Kalus's body. And Kalus's eyes were still focused on Sunshine's eyes, and Kalus was seeing that Sunshine's eyes were spinning. And Kalus was understanding that it was Sunshine who was using her magic to prevent him from running away.

Then Kalus opened his mouth to scream, but unfortunately for him, his throat was blocked and he was unable to scream to call for help. And he understood that it was Sunshine who was using her magic to prevent him from calling for help.

And Sunshine had her eyes still focused on Kalus and Sunshine's eyes were still turning, then a blue light got out from Sunshine's eyes and this blue light went towards Kalus and this light started shining on Kalus. And suddenly, Kalus started feeling a strange reaction in his body, and this light coming from Sunshine's eyes was still shining on Kalus.

Then Kalus felt his body moving towards Sunshine as if someone or something was pushing him, and Kalus had completely lost control of his body. Then Kalus stopped near Sunshine and Sunshine's eyes stopped turning and the light stopped getting out from Sunshine's eyes to shine on Kalus.

And there was the sweat that was running down on Kalus's body as if the water had been spilled on him and Kalus was looking very tired. Then Kalus walked till the sofa that was near to him and he sat on this sofa, and he turned his head looking at Sunshine and they were looking at each other in the eyes with silence.

"Are you okay?" Sunshine asked.

"Leave this kingdom," Kalus replied.

"To go where?" Sunshine asked.

"Where you come from," Kalus replied.

"I am from this kingdom," Sunshine retorted.

"I do not want you in this kingdom," Kalus said.

"It's also my kingdom, and it's also the kingdom of all people living on this land," Sunshine said.

"I am the king of this kingdom, and I am the one who decided on this kingdom," Kalus said.

"But you can not decide who would be born in this kingdom or not." Kalus said.

"I can decide who would stay in this kingdom or not," Kalus retorted.

"According to the laws and traditions of this kingdom, all people who are born in this kingdom belong to this kingdom," Sunshine said.

"I am the law and the tradition," Kalus replied.

"Why do you mean?" Sunshine asked.

"I mean, I am the one who makes the law and the tradition," Kalus answered.

"I have noticed it, and you had even prohibited the education, the tradition, the religion and you had even created the laws of Kalus," Sunshine retorted.

Kalus got up from the chair and he walked a step toward Sunshine and looked into her eyes with a face full of anger and said, "But you changed everything."

"I changed nothing because people are still living according to the laws of Kalus," Sunshine said.

"You stopped my projects," Kalus retorted.

"Which projects?" Sunshine asked.

"The projects you destroyed twelve years ago," Kalus answered.

"The night I was born?" Sunshine asked.

"Yes, the cursed night you were born," Kalus answered.

"Why did you not want women to give birth?" Sunshine asked.

Kalus smiled at Sunshine and said, "I thought you knew the reasons."

"I do not know," Sunshine said.

"That's the good news I got since you were born in my kingdom," Kalus replied.

"Why is it good?" Sunshine asked.

"It's good because you do not know my projects," Kalus answered.

"Are you not going to tell me why you spent the time to mystically kill children and torture them?" Sunshine asked.

Kalus looked into Sunshine's eyes and answered, "I am not stupid to tell to my enemy my projects."

"Why can't you tell me?" Sunshine asked.

"Because you are my enemy and if you know my projects, you will prevent me from realizing them," Kalus answered.

Sunshine took a deep breath, and said, "It's cold in the prison where you locked us up."

Kalus looked at Sunshine and replied, "Use your magic to warm the prison."

"My Magic can not warm this prison," Sunshine said.

Kalus smiled at Sunshine and said, "I hope you will all die of cold in this prison."

"We came here for a problem and you did not even listen to us, but you locked us up in a dark cold room," Sunshine said.

Kalus looked at Sunshine and replied, "I hate all children of this kingdom, and especially you." And Kalus added, "I wish you and your friends would die in this cold prison."

"I wish I could kill you," Sunshine said.

Kalus smiled at Sunshine and said, "I know well that you are powerful and stronger, and even more powerful than me, but unfortunately for you, you do not have the special powers to kill me."

"You are just lucky for the moment," Sunshine said.

"You would never succeed to kill me," Kalus retorted.

"We never know," Sunshine said.

Kalus smiled at Sunshine and said, "Stopped dreaming because you would never succeed to kill me because you had mystically failed to kill during twelve years, and it's not today that you would succeed."

"Things might change one day," Sunshine replied.

Kalus looked at Sunshine and said, "I advise you to forget about this idea to kill me one day because I would live forever."

"No one is immortal," Sunshine said.

"I am immortal," Kalus retorted.

"Sunshine said, "We are all human beings who will die one day."

"But I am not a human being like everyone," Kalus replied.

"What do you mean?" Sunshine asked.

Kalus looked into Sunshine's eyes and said, "Return to your prison now, I want to keep watching television."

"My friends and I are here for education," Sunshine said.

Kalus smiled at Sunshine and said, "Children of this kingdom would never go to school."

"Why have you banned education for children?" Sunshine asked.

Kalus looked at Sunshine and answered, "one part of my project does not want children to go to children."

Sunshine looked into Kalus's eyes and said, "Think very well."

"I do not have to think," Kalus retorted.

Sunshine said, "We will see later." And she added, "I advise you to think very well because with your authorization or without your authorization children of this kingdom would go to school."

Then Sunshine turned and she watched the television and her eyes started spinning, then the television went off, then the light shone into her eyes and she disappeared. And Kalus was surprised to notice that Sunshine had turned off the television through her magic.

Then Kalus took the remote control and he tried to turn on the television without success, and he understood that Sunshine had spoiled the television through her magic. Then Kalus turned and he walked towards the corridor of his magic room.

It was eleven o'clock, and the parents of children who were prisoners at the palace were at Sunshine's home, their faces full of fear, and others had even tears in their eyes. And they were all worried about their children who were prisoners at the palace, and they did not know if their children were doing well or not.

And mostly they did not know what Kalus was going to do to their children and they were very afraid that Kalus would kill their children, mostly that Kalus had killed children who had tried to protest in the past. And the parents had spent their whole afternoon and evening in front of the palace to beg the king Kalus to release their children or even to let them see their children without success.

And Kalus had refused to receive the parents but he had also ordered his security to beat the parents before kicking them out of the palace. And despite the fact that the parents had begged security men to let them see their children just for a minute, security men had refused. And even worse, security men had injured some of the parents.

The parents were feeling guilty about the fact that their children were prisoners at the palace because they had done nothing to protect their children, and they had let their children hold their meeting in secret.

And the parents had been surprised when they had heard that their children had gone to the palace because they did not know that their children should go to the palace to protest. And if the parents knew that their children should go to the palace, they should prevent their children from going to the palace. And the parents did not know what to do, and they were thinking how to save their children.

It was midnight, and children were lying on the wet floor in their prison and they were all shaking with cold, and they were feeling very hungry and some were feeling thirsty. And they were feeling pain in their bodies, and this kind of pain was not only coming from their injuries that had been caused by security men, but these pain were also due to the fact that it's been hours that they were lying on the floor. Even worse, some were feeling sick, and some were even coughing, and most of them were feeling headaches.

Sunshine got up from the floor and she walked till the door, and she stared at the door and her eyes started spinning. After a few seconds, Sunshine's eyes were still focused on the door and her eyes were still spinning, then the door started to open, while Sunshine's eyes were still spinning. After a few seconds, the door was completely opened.

Then Sunshine turned and she walked till her friends, and she knelt near to Nany and she started shaking Nany who was deeply asleep. Nany opened her eyes and she asked what was going on? Sunshine replied to Nany that the door was opened, and that they should get out. Nany asked Sunshine how the door was opened? Sunshine lied to Nany that she just found out that the door of their jail was opened. Nany asked Sunshine who opened the door? Sunshine lied to Nany that she had no idea.

And Asher told Nany to stop asking questions, and that they should get out. Nany replied to Asher that she was afraid, mostly that they did not know who had opened the door. Asher said that he did not care about who had opened the door, and that he was going out. Nany told Asher that they should stay in their prison because it could be a trap.

Asher asked Nany which trap it could be? Nany answered Asher that it could be a trap to kill them. Asher answered Nany that the devil named Kalus did not need to trap them to kill them because this devil named Kalus had the powers on the lives of the inhabitants of the kingdom. And Asher added that he did not care to die, but that he was not going to die in this darkness cold prison where they were.

Aaron said that Nany was right that they must know who opened the prison's door and why that one had opened the door. Mia told Aaron that it could be someone who worked at the palace who had opened the door for them, to allow them to escape from Kalus.

Asher replied to Mia that he was not going to run away, that he was to the palace to fight for his dream and he was going to fight for this dream. Aaron told Asher that the violence was not the solution. Asher replied to Aaron that the one who was using the violence was the devil Kalus and not him, and that it was Kalus who ordered his security to beat them and to keep them prisoners.

Then they started to argue if they would get out of their prison or not, and there were some people like Sunshine, Asher and Mia who wanted all of them to get out of the prison, but there were some like Aaron, Nany and Isac who were completely opposed to getting out of the prison. Sunshine tried to convince Aaron, Nany, Isac and other people that they must get out of the prison without success.

Then Asher got out from the floor and said that he was not going to die in this dark cold prison and that he was going outside, then he started to walk towards the door. And Nany said that she wanted to pee. And other people said that they wanted to pee too. Sunshine told them that they must get out of the prison to go to the toilet. But Nany replied to Sunshine that she was afraid to get out.

Then Mia got up and said that she was going outside too, and she started to walk towards the door. Then Sunshine told them that they must follow Asher and Mia. And Sunshine got up and asked the rest of the people to get up and follow her. Then they all got up from the floor and they walked till outside and they joined Asher and Mia who were talking by staring at the moon and the stars that were shining in the cloud. Then Nany said that she wanted to pee. Sunshine asked her fellows to follow her.

Then Sunshine started to walk towards the yard of the palace, and she was followed by her friends. Then the expression on the faces of some of Sunshine's fellows changed and when they noticed that Sunshine was walking towards the entry door of the palace, they were looking with worried faces. And some of Sunshine's fellows were wondering if Sunshine was taking them to see Kalus.

Then Sunshine stopped in front of the door and she was staring at the door, then her eyes started to spin, and the door started to open. And some of Sunshine's fellows were staring at the door that was opening with amazed faces, while others were staring at the door with fear on their faces. And they were all wondering who was opening the door.

Then the door was completely opened, and except Sunshine, the eyes of the rest of them were largely opened, and they were staring at the living room of the palace from where they were. And they were amazed to see how beautiful the living room of the palace was.

Then Sunshine started walking towards the door, and most of them were completely lost to see Sunshine who was getting in the living room. And Aaron asked Sunshine where she was going? Sunshine looked at Aaron and answered that they must look for washrooms. Aaron told Sunshine that it was dangerous.

Sunshine replied to Aaron to stop being afraid, that they were at the palace to show their courage and not to show their fear because they would never get their right to education if they showed to Kalus that they were afraid.

And Asher said that Sunshine was right, that they should not be afraid to walk inside the palace because the palace was not the house of the devil named Kalus, but it was the house of all inhabitants of the kingdom. Then Asher started walking towards the living room. And Mia followed Asher, then other people started walking towards the living room. Then all the rest followed by walking towards the living room.

They walked in the living room and they were staring at the living room with surprised faces, and they were very amazed to notice that the living room was huge. And except Sunshine who was not amazed, the rest of them were astonished to notice that the living room was a luxury place.

And most of them had stopped in the middle of the living room and they were turning their heads staring at the living room, and they were staring at the pictures and the maps that were in the living room. But their eyes were more focused on the skin of the animals that were on the walls, and they noticed that there were the skins of different animals like lions, panthers, snakes and others on the walls.

While other people were walking in the living room, they were staring at the chairs and other things that were in the living room. And they noticed that most of the things in the living room were made with gold. But their eyes were more focused on the different totems that were in the living room, and some of these totems were scary. And they were all wondering why there were the skin of animals and the totems in the living room, and some of them were even frightened by these totems and the skins of animals.

And except Asher who was touching things, the rest of the people were very afraid to touch things, and they started to talk about the living room, and almost all of them said that the living room of the palace was larger than their houses. Then Nany said that she wanted to go to the washroom. And Sunshine's eyes started spinning and a light shone in the left eye of Sunshine. Then Sunshine asked Nany and all those who wanted to use the washrooms to follow her.

Then Sunshine started walking towards the left side of the living room, and she was followed by those who wanted to use the toilets, then they saw a corridor and they walked towards this corridor, and they saw the doors that were on this corridor.

And Sunshine stopped in front of the first door and she stared at the door and her eyes started spinning, then the door opened. Then Sunshine continued to use her magic to open the doors of the bathrooms. And none of Sunshine's friends knew that it was Sunshine who was opening the doors through her magic.

Sunshine was in the corridor waiting for friends, and her eyes were spinning, and if Sunshine's eyes were spinning, it was because Sunshine was visiting all the rooms of the palace through her magic. And she was also seeing the position of all the people who were inside the palace. Then Sunshine's friends got out of the bathrooms, and they walked till the living room and they joined those who were in the living room.

And Asher said that he was hungry, and they had to look for something to eat. Sunshine smiled at Asher and she asked everyone to follow her. Then Sunshine started walking through the right side of the living room, and she was followed by her friends, and they saw a corridor and they started to walk in this corridor.

Then Sunshine stopped in front of the door, and she stared at the door and her eyes started spinning, and the door started to open. And Sunshine's fellows were staring at the door that was opening with amazed faces, and they were wondering who was opening the door, and some of them were a little scared.

Then the door was completely opened, and they all walked in the kitchen. And except Sunshine, the rest of them were staring at the kitchen with astonished faces, and they were surprised to see how large the kitchen was.

And they were more amazed by the stuff that was in the kitchen, and they noticed that the kitchen had three fridges, three freezers, two large cookers and a huge table in the middle of the kitchen. And some of them even said that the kitchen of the palace was larger than most of the houses in the kingdom.

Then they started to walk in the kitchen, and their eyes opened wide when they opened the fridges, and they were surprised to see all the foods that were in the fridges. They opened the freezers and they also were astonished to see that all the freezers were full of food, but they were more amazed when they opened the garbage and they saw all the food that was thrown in the garbage. And some of them like Asher and Mia said that the king Kalus was so mean because he threw the food in the garbage while there were people in the kingdom dying of starvation.

Asher said that Kalus was a real devil because he locked them up in a dark cold prison without giving them food and water, while there was the food full in the garbage of the kitchen of the palace.

And there was also the light on throughout the palace, and even in the kitchen the light was on. Mia said that it seemed that people did not turn off the light in the palace because even in the washrooms the lights were turned on.

Asher said that it was time to eat, and that today was a great day because for the first time in his life, he was going to eat expensive food, and that even if he did not like Kalus, he was going to eat the same food like Kalus. And people started laughing. Then they removed the food from the fridges and they warmed the food in the microwaves. Then they served the food, the drink and the fruits on the table that was in the kitchen.

Then they all sat around the table, and they started to eat by talking, and they were enjoying their food. And Asher said that he was going to live in the palace to enjoy the delicious food. And most of them were eating the food that they had never eaten before, and they were enjoying the new dishes.

Then Aaron looked at Sunshine and he asked her who opened the doors each time that they were near the doors? Sunshine lied to Aaron that the doors of the palace were automatic, and that the doors of the palace opened when people approached the doors.

Aaron asked Sunshine how she knew where the washrooms and the kitchen of the palace were located? Sunshine lied to Aaron that it was not her first time to come to the palace, and that she had come to the palace a few days ago to talk to Kalus about the education of children, and Kalus had refused to listen to her and he had abandoned her in the living room of the palace. And she was alone in the living room, then she walked in the palace and she visited inside the palace that day.

Nany looked at Sunshine and she told Sunshine that her fear was gone, that she was afraid that there was an invisible monster hidden in the palace who opened the door for them, and who was waiting for the right time to kill them. Asher looked at Nany and said that the only monster who was in the kingdom was Kalus.

Mia looked at Sunshine and asked what was the plan? Sunshine answered Mia that they would wait for Kalus in the living room of the palace. Nany told Sunshine that it was dangerous and risky. Sunshine replied to Nany that to not worry because everything would be fine.

After a few minutes, they had finished eating, and they decided to go to the living room. And some of them took the ice creams, the fruits and the drink with them. They sat on the sofa in the living room, and they started talking.

Then Mia said that she wanted to watch television. Aaron replied to Mia that they could not watch television because there were people who were asleep in the palace, and the noises of the television would wake them up. Nany said that she wanted to watch television too but she could not because she must respect the fact that people were sleeping in the palace.

Asher told Nany that he did not care if people were asleep in the palace or not, that he was going to watch television. Sunshine told Asher that they could not watch television because there were children in the palace who were sleeping, and the noises of the television would wake them up.

Asher replied to Sunshine that they were also children, and that if Kalus had not prohibited the education in the kingdom, they should not be at the palace at this time, but they should be in their house asleep in their beds too. And Asher went on and said it was unfair that they were not sleeping because they were fighting for their right to education, while others were sleeping, and that the devil Kalus should be asleep in his bed.

Mia said that she agreed with Asher because this monster called Kalus should not sleep, and he should be in the living room with them to give them an explanation why he had banned education in the kingdom. Nany said that they have to calm down and wait when people would wake up and they would talk with the king.

Sunshine said that she agreed with Nany, and that they could not wake up people with the noises of the television. Asher replied to Sunshine that he was going to watch television, and that if he did not watch television, he was going to make noises to wake up all the people who were asleep in the palace.

Sunshine told Asher that it was not polite to disturb people who were asleep, and that even if they were mad at Kalus, they should respect those who were sleeping. Sunshine added that they were at the palace to fight for their right to education, and not to prevent people from sleeping.

Asher replied to Sunshine that he wanted her to show him the bedroom of the monster named Kalus because he was going to wake up Kalus, and he would ask Kalus why Kalus had stolen the dream of children by banning education in the kingdom.

Sunshine replied to Asher that she did not know where the bedroom of Kalus was. But Sunshine had lied to Asher that she did not know where the bedroom of Kalus was because she had located the bedroom of Kalus through her magic a few hours ago.

Asher got up from his chair and he walked near the television, and he tried to turn on television without success. Then Asher looked at his friends and said that someone had to help him to turn on the television. And that if there was no one to help to turn on television, he would wake up all the people who were asleep in the palace by making the noises.

Sunshine smiled at Asher without saying a word, and she got up from her chair and she walked till near the television, and she took the remote control and she looked at the screen of the television and eyes started spinning.

Then the light shone in Sunshine's eyes and the television turned on. And Sunshine asked her fellows what they wanted to watch. And almost all of them answered that they wanted to watch the movie called Superhuman 2: The Magician Boy and the Magic School of Wizards by Thierry Kouam. Then Sunshine put on the movie Superhuman 2 that was asked by her friends. And almost all of them got up from their chairs and laid on the carpet, and they started watching movies and some were eating their ice cream and fruits.

After three hours, almost all of them were asleep on the carpet and on the floor and only Sunshine who was not asleep. Then Sunshine got up from the chair and she walked to the right side of the living room. And after a few minutes walking, she turned to the left and she saw the stairs and she started to climb the stairs, and she stopped in the middle of the stairs, and she concentrated on herself by staring in front of her, then her eyes started spinning.

After a few seconds, the light got out from Sunshine's eyes and went through the ceiling, and Sunshine turned and she started to climb down the stairs. After a few seconds, Sunshine reached the last stair, and the expression of her face changed, and she was staring at Aaron with a surprised face who was staring at her too.

And Sunshine understood that Aaron wanted to climb the stairs to go upstairs, and she asked Aaron where he was going. Aaron answered Sunshine that he was looking for her. Sunshine asked Aaron why he was looking for her? Aaron answered Sunshine that he did not see her in the living room and he was worried about her. Sunshine smiled at Aaron and said that everything was fine, just that she heard the noises coming from upstairs and she went to check, but that everything was fine.

Aaron smiled at Sunshine and he handed his right hand to her, and Sunshine looked at Aaron's hand that was handed to her, then she looked into his eyes without saying a word, and understood what Aaron wanted. And Aaron asked Sunshine to grab his hand. Sunshine replied to Aaron that she did not need to grab his hand.

And Aaron told Sunshine that he wanted to grab her hand to walk with her till the living room. Sunshine replied to Aaron that it was not necessary, that they could walk till the living room like this. Then Aaron smiled at Sunshine without saying a word, and he moved from behind, and Sunshine climbed down the last stair and they walked till the living room.

And they sat on the long sofa and they were looking at each other in the eyes, and Sunshine was more focused on looking into Aaron's eyes, and she was reading the thoughts of Aaron. Then Aaron broke the silence and said, "You changed our lives."

"Changed your lives?" Sunshine cried out.

"Yes, you changed our lives," Aaron replied.

"I do not understand," Sunshine said.

Aaron smiled at Sunshine and said, "We are here in this palace fighting for our right to education because of you." Aaron added, "the kingdom is happy to have someone like you because if you were not born in this kingdom, children of this kingdom should never know the existence of education."

"We are all fighting for our dream," Sunshine said.

"I hope Kalus would understand that children of the kingdom need education," Aaron replied.

"I am sure Kalus would realize that the kingdom would not survive without education," Sunshine said.

"Your parents would be proud of you," Aaron said.

Sunshine smiled and said, "Your parents would be proud of you too."

"I am not a brave child," Aaron replied.

"You are!" Sunshine retorted.

"I do not think," Aaron said.

Sunshine smiled at Aaron and said, "You are here."

"I do not understand," Aaron said.

"We all here in this living room are brave because we are all fighting for our dreams," Sunshine replied.

Aaron smiled at Sunshine and said, "You are not only beautiful, but you are also very smart."

Sunshine smiled and said, "Thank you." And she asked, "Why are you not sleeping?"

Aaron smiled and answered, "Because I am talking with you." And he added, "I have been looking for this opportunity since I first met you."

"Which opportunity?" Sunshine asked.

"The opportunity to talk to you," Aaron answered.

Sunshine smiled and asked, "What are you going to study?"

"My dream is to become a lawyer," Aaron answered.

"Why a lawyer?" Sunshine asked.

Aaron answered, "To protect this kingdom, to protect people, to protect the future generations and to prevent the future generations from living this situation that are living now, and to protect the right of all inhabitants of the kingdom." Then Aaron looked into Sunshine's eyes with a face full of smiles and he said, "Mostly to protect you."

Sunshine smiled and said, "the kingdom has his hero."

"I am not the hero of the kingdom," Aaron replied.

"Of course, you are," Sunshine said.

Aaron smiled and said, "The only hero of this kingdom is you."

Sunshine smiled and said, "You are the one who is going to protect this kingdom and not me, so you are the hero of this kingdom."

Aaron looked at Sunshine with a face full of smiles and said, "I do not want to be the hero of this kingdom, but I just want to become your hero."

Sunshine looked at Aaron with a face full of smiles and asked, "My hero?"

"Yes, your hero," Answered Aaron.

"Why hero?" Sunshine asked.

"Because I want to look after you, to protect you, to save you and mostly to make sure that you are all right," Aaron answered.

Then Sunshine opened her mouth but no word was coming out, and she was just staring at Aaron with a face full of smiles, and Aaron was staring at her too with a face of smile, and there was silence between them. And Suddenly, the expression on their faces changed, and the smiles that were on their faces turned into fear, then they turned their heads towards the front door as they had heard the cries coming from the voice of their parents.

And those who were sleeping on the carpet woke up when they heard the noises, and they were astonished to notice that these noises were coming from their parents because they had recognized the voice of their parents. And Nany said that it was their parents who were outside. Mia said that they should go open the door to their parents.

Sunshine replied to Mia that they could not open the door to their parents. Mia told Sunshine that she was worried about their parents because security men of Kalus could hurt their parents. Sunshine replied to Mia not to worry that their parents would not be hurt by security men.

Then the expression of their faces changed and except Sunshine, the rest of them had worried faces as they were hearing their parents screaming more and more by making noises, and by shaking the gate. And the parents were yelling by begging Kalus to release their children.

Asher asked if people who were in the palace were dead because he did not understand how people could sleep with these noises coming from their parents. Mia replied to Asher that she was wondering the same question. Nany said that she hoped that all people in the palace were still alive. Asher replied to Nany that he hoped that the devil named Kalus was dead.

And suddenly, they turned their heads to the right when they heard the noises of the footsteps. And suddenly, the expression on their faces changed and some were looking with fear on their faces, while others were looking with worried faces. And except Sunshine who was looking with a face empty of expression.

And all their eyes were focused on Kalus who had worn a pajamas on him, and Kalus was also looking at them with a surprised face, and there was silence between them. And looking at the expression on the face of Kalus, he was completely lost and he did not understand what these children were doing in his living room. And looking at Kalus, it was obvious that he had just got out of his bed.

And except Sunshine in the room, it was the first time for the rest of the children to see Kalus in front of them with their eyes because they had grown up seeing Kalus only on the photos and Kalus's portrait on television.

Then Kalus opened his mouth and he tried to talk but his mouth was shaking that a word could not get out of his mouth. And Asher smiled and said that the devil had lost his word. Kalus looked at Asher and asked, "Who is the devil?" Asher looked into Kalus's eyes and answered, "You are the devil."

And immediately the expression of Kalus's face changed and he was looking with a face full of anger, and Kalus screamed at Asher asking Asher who was the devil? Asher replied to Kalus that Kalus was a real devil. Kalus told Asher that he was the king of the kingdom. Mia looked at Kalus and said that he was a bad king because the king loved his kingdom, cared about his kingdom and mostly the good the king allowed children to go to school.

Kalus looked at the children and he asked them to get up and return to their prison. Asher burst into laughter and said that they were going to luck up Kalus in this prison, and they would make sure that Kalus would spend the rest of his life in this prison.

Kalus looked at Asher and he asked Asher to get up and leave his house. And Asher stared at Kalus and burst into laughter without saying a word. Mia looked at Kalus and said that the palace was not his house. Kalus looked at Mia and said that the palace was his house, and he wanted all of them to get out of his house.

Mia replied to Kalus that the palace was the house of all the inhabitants of the kingdom. Kalus told Mia that the palace was his house, and not the house of all inhabitants of the kingdom. Mia replied to Kalus that the palace was the house of all the inhabitants of the kingdom, and that they were going to stay in the palace.

Then Kalus asked who was making the noises outside? Asher answered to Kalus that it was their parents who were making the noises. Kalus looked at Sunshine and he asked Sunshine to take her fellows and to get out of his palace with them. Sunshine replied to Kalus that they needed education.

Kalus told Sunshine that education was banned in the kingdom, and that children of the kingdom would never go to school. Sunshine told Kalus that if they did not go to school, they would stay in the palace with him. Kalus replied to Sunshine he was going to take his gun and he would come and kill them. Sunshine looked into Kalus's eyes and she wished him good luck. Then Kalus turned and left without uttering a word.

Nany looked at Sunshine and said that they must leave. Sunshine replied to Nany that they would not leave without having obtained their right to education. Nany told Sunshine that they would be killed by Kalus.

Sunshine looked into Nany's eyes and she asked Nany if she was afraid to die? Nany answered Sunshine that she was a little afraid of death. Sunshine replied to Nany that they were in the palace to fight for their right to education, and they would not leave the palace without having obtained their right to education. Asher told Nany to stop being afraid.

Mia said that there was something strange that was happening in the palace. Asher asked Mia what this strange thing was? Mia answered Asher that she was not understanding how people could be asleep with the noises coming outside from their parents. Asher laughed and said that probably people living in the palace were dead.

Sunshine smiled at Asher and she asked him if he wanted to kill people who were in the palace. Asher replied to Sunshine that the only person he wanted to kill was the devil named Kalus. And Asher added that he did not care about people living in the palace because they had done nothing to stop the devil Kalus from banning education in the kingdom. Sunshine smiled at Asher without saying a word.

Kalus was in his bedroom and he was trying to open the drawer to take his gun without success, and Kalus was not understanding why he was not able to open the drawer. Then Kalus tried to break the drawer without success.

Then Kalus left his bedroom, and he went to the bedrooms of his staff and he tried to wake up his staff without success. And he went to the bedroom of his wife and children and he tried to wake them up without success. And Kalus was completely lost, and he did not understand how it was possible that people were asleep in the palace like the corpses.

Then Kalus ran till the house of the security men who were in the yard of the palace, and he got in the house and saw security men who were deeply asleep. And he tried to wake them up without success. And he even poured water on them, but security men did not wake up even with the water that was poured on them.

Then Kalus left the security's house, and he walked till near to the gate and he saw the three security men who had a duty to guard the gate during the night who were deeply asleep in their chairs.

Kalus tried to wake up security men without success, and he even took the sticks that were near to these security men and beat these security men with.

But unfortunately for Kalus, even by beating security men, he did not succeed in waking them up. Kalus tried to open the gate without success, and there were still the parents outside the gate who were making noises. And Kalus did not understand how it was possible that people in the palace were still asleep with all these noises that were being made by the parents.

And Kalus was wondering if people in the palace were all dead because he had poured the water on security men and even beat them to wake them up without success. And Kalus went to the parking lot and he tried to open the doors of the cars that were in the parking lot without success. And Kalus was thinking how to get out of the palace.

Then Kalus went and tried to open other doors to get out of the palace without success, and he even returned to the bedrooms of his employees and family and he shook them on the bed to wake them up without success. But Kalus had noticed that his employees and family were still alive because he had noticed that their hearts were beating and they were also breathing very well.

And Kalus tried to call for help, but unfortunately for him, his phone was not working. And Kalus spent hours walking in the palace trying to find the solution without success, and he even tried to get out of the palace through the windows, but unfortunately, he did not succeed to open the windows.

Kalus was completely lost, and he started to be afraid because it was the first time that he was living in this situation. He was still not understanding why he was unable to wake up people who were sleeping. And why he was unable to open the doors and windows of the palace, mostly why he was the only one who was not asleep in the palace. And Kalus started to run inside the palace like a crazy man without even knowing where he was going and what he was doing.

Children were still in the living room and they were talking about Kalus, and some of them were a little afraid that Kalus would come with his gun to kill them. And except Sunshine, the rest of them were very astonished to see that people in the palace were still sleeping at nine in the morning, mostly with the noises that were coming outside from their parents. Then they turned their heads to the right when they heard the footsteps.

And suddenly, the expression on their faces changed and they were looking at Kalus with surprised faces, and they were all astonished to see Kalus who was sweating and who was breathing deeply and who was looking very tired. And looking at Kalus, it was obvious that he had spent hours running in the palace.

Then Asher smiled at Kalus and he asked Kalus where the gun was? Kalus looked at Asher without saying a word. Mia asked Kalus if people in the palace were dead. Kalus looked at Mia and he opened his mouth to answer but his mouth started shaking that a word was not coming out. And some of them started to laugh at Kalus. And Asher asked Kalus if Kalus swallowed his tongue.

Then Kalus walked till the cupboard that was in the living room, and he took the phone that was on the cupboard and he tried to dial the police number, unfortunately for Kalus, the phone was not working. And Kalus was still not understanding what was going on, mostly that he had used this phone yesterday to make a call.

And he did not understand why all the phones were not working. Then Kalus noticed that children were watching television, and he remembered that yesterday this television was not working. Because Sunshine had used her magic to spoil this television, and that he had even tried to turn on the television after Sunshine had spoiled it without success.

And Kalus was very surprised to see that the television was working and he did not understand by which miracle these children had succeeded in turning on television. Then Kalus asked the children who had turned on the television? Asher answered that it was them who had turned on the television. Kalus asked who between them?

Asher answered that it was not important. Kalus replied to Asher that he wanted to know who had turned on the television.

Sunshine answered that she was the one who had turned on the television. Kalus looked at Sunshine and cried out, "You?" looking at her with a surprised face. Sunshine replied, "Yes, me." Then Kalus and Sunshine were looking at each other in the eyes with silence.

Then Kalus started to understand that it was Sunshine who had used her magic to prevent people from waking up and to spoil all the phones in the palace to prevent him from making a phone call to call for help.

Kalus and Sunshine were still looking at each other with silence. And Sunshine had understood that Kalus knew that she was the one who was preventing people in the palace from waking up. It was the light that had got out from Sunshine's eyes in the stairs and went into the palace that was preventing people from waking up.

And it was still this light that had spoiled the phones and locked the doors and windows. And this light had had an impact only on people and things that Sunshine wanted. Sunshine wanted this light to have an impact on those people and things because she did not want people to prevent her from talking with Kalus, and she did not want Kalus to call for help or to get out of the palace.

Sunshine's friends were very surprised by the way that she and Kalus were looking at each other. And Asher asked Sunshine what was going on? Sunshine answered Asher that everything was fine. Asher asked Sunshine why Kalus was staring at her like this. Sunshine answered Asher that she had no idea why Kalus was staring at her.

Then Kalus asked Sunshine to leave his palace. Sunshine answered Kalus that she wanted to talk about education first. Kalus smiled and said that he was not going to talk with useless people, and that he could not sit and talk with useless children like them. Also, that education was banned in the kingdom forever. Sunshine replied to Kalus that it was his choice.

Kalus told Sunshine to take her friends and leave his house with them because he was leaving and when he would be back, he would not hesitate to kill them if they were still in his living room. Sunshine told Kalus that she wished him good luck. Then Kalus looked into Sunshine's eyes and walked away without saying a word.

Children watched Kalus, walked away, and they turned their heads and looked at each other without uttering a word. Then Mia broke the silence and said that Kalus was acting as if he was crazy. Asher replied to Mia that Kalus was crazy. Mia said that Kalus decided not to open the school in the kingdom.

Asher replied to Mia that Kalus was nobody to make a decision in the kingdom, and that Kalus was not a student to decide if he was going to school or not. And that all the decisions about education in the kingdom concerned only children, and children had decided to go to school, so school would be opened with or without the agreement of Kalus.

Nany said that they would need the agreement of Kalus to go to school, and for that they should beg Kalus to open the school for them. Sunshine said that she agreed with Asher and that only children could decide if they were going to school or not, and for that children had decided to go to school, and with or without the authorization of Kalus, children would go to school.

Mia said that she was tired of talking about this monster of Kalus, and that she was hungry. And other people said that they were also hungry. Asher got up from the floor and said that it was time for breakfast. And except Sunshine, the rest of them went to the kitchen for their breakfast.

Kalus was in his magic room and he had knelt and he was calling the name of Lord, and he was trying to talk to his Lord, but unfortunately his Lord was not answering. Kalus was trying to explain to Lord that Sunshine was in his palace, and that she had taken his palace hostage and he did not know how to get rid of her because she was more powerful than him. And Kalus was sweating and his face was full of fear, and as he was trying to communicate with Lord without success.

After a few minutes, Lord had still not replied to Kalus. And Kalus was wondering where Lord was because it was the first time that he tried to communicate with his Lord without success.

And Kalus was very afraid, and he started wondering if Sunshine had killed Lord because he did not understand why Lord was not answering. Mostly that Kalus had never called Lord more than three times and he was thinking what to do. And Kalus knew well that he could not allow children to go to school because the pact treaty that he had with Lord prohibited the education of children in the kingdom.

And at the same time, Kalus knew well that he could not kick out Sunshine and her fellows outside of the palace. Because he was less powerful than Sunshine, also that Sunshine and her fellows would not leave the palace without getting their right to education. Then Kalus got up and left the room.

Children were still in the living room, and some were lying on the carpet, while others were sitting in the chairs and they had their eyes focused on television and they were watching a movie called Supernatural Beings 1 by Thierry Kouam. And except Sunshine, the rest of them were eating their breakfast by watching the movie. Then they turned their heads to the right when they heard the footsteps and the smiles appeared on the faces of some of them like Asher and Mia, and they were all staring at Kalus who was looking very tired and who was sweating.

Then Mia asked Kalus who he was fighting with? Kalus looked at Mia without saying a word. And Asher told Mia to not forget that the monster Kalus was crazy, so that Kalus was fighting with himself. Kalus said that he needed breakfast? Mia answered Kalus to go to the kitchen and make his own breakfast.

Kalus replied to Mia angrily that he was the king of the kingdom and the one who gave the orders in the kingdom and that he ordered them to go to the kitchen and make him breakfast. Mia replied to Kalus that they were not his employees, so that if he needed breakfast, he should go ask his employees to make him breakfast or he would go to the kitchen himself to make his breakfast.

Kalus told Mia that he was hungry, and he needed his breakfast. Mia replied to Kalus that she did not care if he was hungry or not, but she would be happy if he could die of starvation because at least his death would be useful for the kingdom.

Kalus asked Mia how his death would be useful for the kingdom. Mia answered Kalus that his death would be the end of the laws of Kalus that banned children from going to school. Kalus replied to Mia that he would never die, and he would live forever, mostly children of the kingdom would never have access to education.

Sunshine looked at Kalus and said that they would leave the palace only when they would have the agreement to go to school, and that if children of the kingdom would never go to school. It meant that they would stay in the palace in this situation forever. Kalus replied to Sunshine that the palace was not a house for children of the kingdom, but that the palace was his house. Sunshine told Kalus that the palace was the house of all inhabitants of the kingdom and not his house.

Kalus told Sunshine that he was tired of talking to them and that he wanted his breakfast. Sunshine replied to Kalus to go to the kitchen. Kalus replied to Sunshine that he was the king, and the king did not go to the kitchen for his food. Sunshine told Kalus that if he did not want to go to the kitchen, he must stop complaining that he was hungry because there was nobody to go to the kitchen to make him breakfast.

Kalus told Sunshine that if she wanted to discuss with him about the education of children in the kingdom, he needed breakfast first. Sunshine looked into Kalus's eyes and said that no one was going to give him his breakfast, even if he agreed to allow children of the kingdom to go to school because all children of the kingdom would go to school without any conditions.

Nany looked at Sunshine and said that she could go into the kitchen and cook the breakfast for Kalus, if Kalus was ready to allow them to go to school. Sunshine replied to Nany that no one would make breakfast for Kalus.

Nany said that Kalus was hungry and they could just make him breakfast. Sunshine looked into Nany's eyes and said no one would make breakfast for Kalus, and that Kalus knew the way to the kitchen if he wanted to eat. Asher said that he agreed with Sunshine that no one would make breakfast for Kalus because Kalus was so mean not only because Kalus banned them from education, but because Kalus locked them up yesterday in a dark cold prison.

Mia got up from the chair and she said that she was going to the kitchen to cook the breakfast for the king Kalus, and she asked Kalus what he wanted to eat. Kalus replied to Mia that he wanted to eat salad, carrots and avocados. Mia smiled at Kalus and said that she was coming with his food, and she walked towards the kitchen.

Kalus looked at Sunshine and said that her friend went to make him breakfast. Sunshine replied to Kalus to stop dreaming because Mia would not make him breakfast. Then Sunshine and Kalus continued to talk about education, and Kalus was determined to not allow children to go to school.

After a few minutes, Mia walked into the living room holding a plate in her hand that contained the salad, carrot and avocados that were cut into small slices and with a fork inside the plate. Mia walked till the empty chair that was near to Kalus, and sat in the chair and she put the plate that she had on her hands on her knees, and she glanced at Kalus, then she started to eat.

And Kalus looked at Mia who was eating with an amazed face, and he asked her who ordered her to eat his food. Mia answered Kalus that it was her food and not his food. Kalus told Mia that only he had the right to eat the salad, carrots and avocados in the palace because even his own family did not eat the same food as him. Mia smiled at Kalus and said she was glad to know that she was eating the food of the king, even if this king was a monster. Then People started laughing.

Kalus turned and walked towards the kitchen without saying a word. After a few minutes, Kalus reached the door of the kitchen and he looked inside the kitchen and his eyes opened wide when he saw the mess in the kitchen. Then he turned and he walked till the living room angrily, and he started to shout at children about the mess in the kitchen, but no one was paying attention to him, and they were all focused on watching a movie.

Then Kalus turned and walked till the kitchen and he got inside the kitchen and he walked till near to the fridge and he put his hand on the fridge to open the fridge, but a blue light shone in the kitchen and suddenly the expression of his face changed when he saw a blue light shone in the room. And Kalus was looking with an astonished face as he had understood that this blue light was coming from Sunshine's magic.

Then Kalus tried to open the fridge without success because the fridge's door was locked, and he tried to open other fridges and microwaves without success. And he tried to pick up the fruits on the counter but unfortunately, he did not succeed to take the fruits because it was as if the fruits were stuck on the counter.

And Kalus tried to turn on the water tap without success, and everything that he tried to do he failed, and he also tried basic things like turning off the light without success. Then Kalus understood that Sunshine had used her magic to prevent him from making his breakfast. Then Kalus turned and left.

After a few minutes, Kalus walked in the living room and he started to stare at Sunshine with a face full of anger, but Sunshine's eyes were focused on television. Then Kalus broke the silence and he asked Sunshine to wake up his family. Sunshine looked at Kalus without saying a word. Mia looked at Kalus and said that he could go wake up his family by himself.

Sunshine told Mia that they must stop paying attention to Kalus and they would focus on watching their movie. Then they all turned their heads through the television and they continued to watch their movie. And Kalus continued to talk but no one was paying attention to him, and he even asked them to turn off the television but no one paid attention to him.

Then Kalus started walking in the living room by thinking what to do, and he was trying to find a solution to get rid of these children in his living room without success. And after a few minutes, Kalus got an idea and he looked at Sunshine and said that he was ready to talk with her. Sunshine asked Kalus if he was ready to give them their right to education. Kalus answered that yes, that he was ready to give them their right to education.

Sunshine told Kalus that he must apologize first before they started talking. Kalus cried out, "What?" By looking at Sunshine with an amazed face and he asked her why he should apologize? Sunshine answered Kalus that he must apologize because he insulted them by calling them useless children.

Kalus smiled at Sunshine and said that he could not apologize because he was the king, and the king did not ask for forgiveness, but it was the king who gave forgiveness to people. Sunshine replied to Kalus that they were not going to talk with them if he did not apologize.

Kalus told Sunshine that he agreed to give them their right to education, and that they leave his palace. Sunshine looked into Kalus's eyes and said that they would talk about education only when he would apologise for calling them useless children, and they would leave the palace only after getting an agreement about their education. Then Sunshine turned her head and she continued to watch television. Kalus started thinking without knowing what to do.

After an hour, Kalus was still thinking and he had not yet succeeded to find a solution on how to get rid of the children who were in his palace. And he was very hungry and tired, and he mostly knew that he had not the control of the situation, and that it was Sunshine who had the control of the situation.

Then Kalus understood that he did not have the choice, and that if he wanted these children to leave his palace, he should obey and do everything that they wanted. Then Kalus opened his mouth and said, "I apologize."

Sunshine turned her head and looked at Kalus and she said, "We did not hear you."

Kalus said, "I apologize."

Sunshine asked, "Apologize for what?"

Kalus replied, "I apologize for calling you useless children."

Sunshine said, "You must lift your head and look at us and say it louder."

Kalus lifted his head and looked at the children and said louder, "I apologize for calling you useless children."

Sunshine said, "Sit down and we would talk."

Kalus walked two steps towards the empty chair that was near to Sunshine and he sat, then he looked at Sunshine and said, "I listen."

Sunshine asked, "When are we going to school?"

"I would think about it and I would let you know," Kalus answered.

"We need a day now," Sunshine retorted.

"In five years," Kalus said.

Sunshine cried out, "What?" And she asked, "Five years?" looking at Kalus with an amazed face.

"It's too much?" Kalus asked.

"We would not start when we would be old," Sunshine answered.

"Three years," Kalus said.

"I think you want us to live in this palace with you in this situation where we are now," Sunshine said.

"What do you want?" Kalus asked.

"We are going to school this year," Sunshine answered.

Kalus cried out, "What?" Looking at Sunshine with an amazed face.

"We are going to school this year," Sunshine repeated.

"That's impossible," Kalus said.

"We are the ones who would go to school, so we were the ones who decided when to start school, and we decided to start school this year." Sunshine said.

"You would start school next year," Kalus said.

"We decided to start school this year," Sunshine said.

"At the beginning of this next year," Kalus replied.

"I said this year," Sunshine retorted.

Kalus took a deep breath and said, "Fine." And he added, "You would start school at the end of this year."

"In three weeks," Sunshine said.

Kalus cried out, "What?" Looking at Sunshine with a surprised face.

"Three weeks," Sunshine replied.

"That's impossible," Kalus said.

"Children decided to go to school in three weeks," Sunshine said.

Kalus looked into Sunshine's eyes and said, "Everything could not be ready in three weeks."

"What could not be ready in three weeks?" Sunshine asked.

"The schools could not be built in three weeks," Kalus answered.

"Why do you need to build the schools?" Sunshine asked.

"You would study in the classrooms, and these classrooms need to be built," Kalus answered.

"We would study in the schools where our parents, grandparents and great grand-parents studied," Sunshine said.

"These schools are old, and I would build the new ones for you," Kalus said.

"We do not want to study in the new schools, so we are going to study in the classrooms where our parents and grand-parents studied," Sunshine said.

Kalus took a deep breath and he looked into Sunshine's eyes and said, "I had transformed these schools into factories, that's the reason I need to build the new schools."

Sunshine looked at Kalus with a face full of anger and said, "You are not the one who had built these schools that you transformed into factories because these schools were built by the former kings, our grand-parents and our great grand-parents. And these schools had been built for children of this kingdom, these schools were built for children get access to education, not for the factories." Then Sunshine looked into Kalus's eyes and said, "You have less than three weeks to make our schools suitable and ready for us to start the school in three weeks."

"I would need more than three weeks to make school frequentable," Kalus said.

"Less than three weeks, and we must start school in three weeks from today," Sunshine said.

"It would be impossible for you to start school in three weeks because the kingdom does not have the instructors to teach you, so I need more than three weeks to look for the people who can teach you," Kalus said.

"Where are the instructors who were in the kingdom?" Sunshine asked.

"The instructors are in prison," Kalus said.

"For what?" Sunshine asked.

"The instructors had broken the law," Kalus answered.

"I imagine the instructors had broken the laws of Kalus by protesting against the ban on education in the kingdom, right?" Sunshine asked.

"Yes, the instructors were sent to prison because they had protested when I had decided to ban education in the kingdom," Kalus answered.

"You must release all these instructors, and you would give them back their jobs, so these instructors would teach us lessons in three weeks," Sunshine said.

"I would not release the instructors from the prison," Kalus said.

"Children want their instructors to be released from prison," Sunshine retorted.

"You are not here to talk about the prisoners, but you are here to talk about your education," Kalus said.

"Our instructors are those who would teach us lessons, so we want them to be released from the jail," Sunshine replied.

"I would hire the new instructors to teach the lessons," Kalus said.

"No, we want the instructors who are in prison to teach us lessons," Sunshine said.

"You would have new instructors in three weeks," Kalus said.

"We do not want new instructors, but we want the instructors who are in prisons," Sunshine retorted.

"You are not the one who decides about the instructors who would teach you lessons," Kalus said.

"We are ones who are going to study, so we are those who would choose our instructors," Sunshine said.

"The instructors you have chosen are the prisoners," Kalus retorted.

"Release them, "Sunshine replied.

"I would not release them because they had broken the law," Kalus said.

Sunshine looked into Kalus's eyes and said, "The only prisoner in this kingdom it's you, not only for the education you banned from children, but mostly for all children who had been killed by you." Then Sunshine posed and she was staring at Kalus with a face full of anger and she broke the silence and said, "I promise you that I would make you pay for it."

Kalus smiled at Sunshine and said, "I wish you good luck." And Kalus added, "I hope that you will live long to make your dreams come true."

"Do not worry, I will," Sunshine replied.

"You would have the instructors you want," Kalus said.

"Great!" Sunshine retorted.

"Leave my palace now," Kalus said.

"Not yet," Sunshine said.

"What else do you want?" Kalus asked.

Sunshine said "You would make a speech on the national television at eight o'clock, and in your speech you would announce the back of school in the kingdom in three weeks, and you would ask all parents and children of the kingdom to be ready for the back of school. And you would ask everyone who owns the libraries, the bookstores, and other shops to open their doors for the parents to buy stuff for their children for their back to school."

Then Sunshine went on and said, "You would announce the release of all the instructors who are in prison, and you would also build the new tables in the classrooms. And you have less than three weeks to arrange our school to make it clean and suitable and we want to watch on television the works that would be doing at school, so the national television would make the reportage on school by filming people who are working at school and of course we want the new paint on the school walls."

And Sunshine added, "You would also announce during your speech that a school director would be named before the end of the next week, and this school director would make a speech on television to talk about the school program and to talk about the books that would be used by children at school. Then you would ask the national television, the national radio and newspapers to announce to the whole kingdom that you would make an important speech in news of eight o'clock,"

"Something else?" Kalus asked.

Sunshine looked into Kalus's eyes and said, "Do not even try to play with us because we would be back if you tried to play with us, and if we come back because you lied to us, you would spend a bad moment, and this moment would not be a peaceful moment like this moment"

"Leave my palace now," Kalus said.

Sunshine stared at Kalus with a face empty of expression without saying a word, and after a few minutes, she broke the silence and said,

"Do not dare to send your army or your men to threaten or arrest our families." And Sunshine added, "Have a great day."

Then Sunshine got up from her chair and she told her fellows that they must leave. Then Sunshine's friends got up and they stared at Kalus, and some of them like Asher and Mia were laughing at Kalus. And Asher told Kalus that Kalus was lucky because Sunshine gave Kalus till three weeks to open the school because if it was him, he should give only twenty-four hours to Kalus to open school.

Mia told Kalus that if she did not start school in three weeks, she would come live in the palace and she would enjoy the luxury and eat the good food. Then Kalus watched Sunshine and her fellows leave the living room without saying a word.

Children were walking towards the gate. And except Sunshine, the rest of them were wondering if people who lived in the palace were dead, not only because people were still asleep at noon, but because there were their parents outside who were still making the noises.

They were approaching the gate and Mia started to laugh when she saw the security men who were deeply sleeping in their chairs, and Mia asked her friends to look at security men who were asleep like the dead bodies. Asher looked at security men and he told Mia that they were security men who beat them yesterday, so that it was time to take revenge.

And Nany asked Asher what he meant by that it was time to take revenge? Asher answered Nany that they would beat the security men too. And Aaron tried to oppose Asher's idea to beat security men without success. And Mia supported Asher's idea to beat security men. Then Asher and Mia walked till near security men who were deeply asleep in their chairs, and they took the sticks that were near to these security men and they started to beat security men.

Sunshine, Aaron, Nany and others were watching Asher and Mia who were beating at security men. And Aaron asked Sunshine to stop Asher and Mia, that Asher and Mia would kill security men. And Sunshine replied to Aaron that Asher and Mia were doing a great job and to enjoy it because these security men had hurt them yesterday.

And except Sunshine, the rest of them were afraid that security men were dead. Because they did not understand how security men did not open their eyes, despite the fact that Asher and Mia were beating at them.

Then the fear appeared on the faces of most of them when they noticed that security men were bleeding, and they asked Sunshine to stop Asher and Mia. Then Sunshine told Asher and Mia to stop hitting the security guards, that it was enough.

Then Asher and Mia stopped beating security men and they all continued to walk towards the gate. Then Sunshine had her eyes focused on the gate and her eyes were spinning, and the gate opened and they all walked out of the gate.

And they saw their parents who were waiting for them, and they all ran in the arms of their parents. And their parents were very happy to see that their children were doing well, and they were happier to hear from their children that Kalus would open the school in three weeks.

And even if the parents were very happy to hear that their children were going to start school in weeks, they were concerned for the safety of their children because they knew that they could not trust Kalus. And the parents were very astonished to see that Kalus had not killed their children, and mostly that he had not locked up their children in jail.

And even if the parents did not understand the reasons why Kalus had promised to their children that children were going to start school in three weeks, they could not tell their children to not trust Kalus. Because they did not want to make their children look sad, mostly that children were very happy to know that they were going to start school in three weeks.

Then Aaron's mother invited all the children to her home to celebrate their victory, and she also told them that she had good news to announce to them. Then Sunshine turned her head and looked at the palace and her eyes started spinning, then a light got out from her eyes and went towards the palace. Then the parents and children left.

After two hours, children were at Aaron's home and they were sitting in the living room, and they were eating and drinking juice while talking about their success against Kalus. And some of them were even laughing about the attitude that Kalus had in his palace.

And they were all talking about the school that they were going to start in three weeks and they were very eager to go to school for the first time in their history. And even if they did not know what exactly the school was, they could not wait to start.

Aaron was sitting near Sunshine and they were talking in low voices because they were the noises in the room, and these noises were made by Asher who was screaming their victory against the devil Kalus. Then Asher said that they needed music to celebrate their victory, and he walked till the radio that was in the living room and he turned on the radio. And some people got up from their chairs and they started dancing.

And Asher started dancing in the middle of those who were dancing, and he saw sunshine who was talking with Aaron, and he walked till near to Sunshine. Then Asher grabbed Sunshine's hand and told her that it was time to celebrate their victory by dancing. And Asher invited Sunshine to the dance floor, and she got up from her chair and went on the dance floor with Asher.

Sunshine and Asher started to dance with their faces full of smiles. Aaron's eyes were focused on Sunshine who was dancing with Asher. And looking at the expression on the face of Aaron, we could see that he was jealous by seeing Asher and Sunshine who were dancing together. Then Nany came and she invited Aaron on the dance floor, but he refused and he told Nany that he was tired.

After an hour of dancing, Sunshine told Asher that she was tired, and that she was going to sit. And Sunshine turned and she left the dance floor and she went and sat in her chair near to Aaron. Sunshine and Aaron were watching their fellows who were dancing on the dance floor. Aaron invited Sunshine to dance with him, but Sunshine refused and she told him that she was tired.

Then Aaron's parents walked in the room. And Aaron's mother said that she had good news to announce to them. And Asher went and he turned off the radio, and all the eyes were focused on Aaron's mom. Then, Aaron's mother touched her belly with her right palm's hand and said that the kingdom was going to have a new baby, and they were all going to have a little sister or a little brother. And suddenly, there were the screams of joy in the room, and all those who were sitting got up from their chairs, and they all went and congratulated Aaron's parents.

And Aaron was congratulated by his friends for the little brother or little sister that he was going to have. Then Sunshine was near to Aaron and she was watching her friends who were teasing Aaron if Aaron was ready to be a big brother. And Sunshine was the only one who had not yet congratulated Aaron. After a few minutes, there was nobody in front of Aaron. Then Sunshine turned towards Aaron, and she looked into his eyes and she smiled at him and said, "Congratulations."

Aaron replied, "Thank you."

Sunshine said, "I am sure you would be a good elder brother for your little sister."

Aaron cried out, "Little sister?" Looking at Sunshine with a surprised face.

"Yes, little sister," Sunshine answered.

"What makes you think that I would have a little sister?" Aaron asked.

"Because your mom is expecting a girl," Sunshine said.

Aaron looked into Sunshine's eyes and said, "My mom did not say that she was expecting a baby girl."

Sunshine looked at Aaron and she understood that she had made a mistake by saying that Aaron's mom was expecting a girl, and she did not even know why she said that Aaron's mom was expecting a girl, and she had just guessed it. Then Sunshine opened her mouth and said that she was sorry, that she had just guessed it. Aaron smiled at Sunshine and said that it was okay.

Then Sunshine and Aaron continued talking. And Asher went and turned on the radio, and he asked everyone to walk on the dance floor and to celebrate the good news of the unborn baby that the kingdom was expecting. Then most of the people in the room went to the dance floor and they started dancing.

Sunshine and Aaron were still talking together. Then Sunshine felt that her left hand was grabbed by someone, and she turned her head to her left and she noticed that it was Asher who had grabbed her hand.

And Asher smiled at Sunshine and said that it was not the time for conversation, but that it was time to dance and celebrate the future baby who would be born in a few months. Then Asher pulled Sunshine onto the dance floor before Sunshine opened her mouth to say a word. And Sunshine was walking towards the dance floor with her head turned from behind by staring at Aaron. And Sunshine was seeing the anger on Aaron's face.

Then Aaron turned and went and sat and he was looking at Sunshine who was dancing with Asher. Then Nany came and she invited Aaron to dance, but again Aaron refused, and he told Nany that he did not want to dance. Then Nany sat in the empty chair that was near to Aaron, and she started having a conversation with Aaron about the kingdom. And Aaron was talking to Nany without even looking at her, and Aaron's eyes were focused on Sunshine who was dancing with Asher.

Sunshine was not really focused on dancing with Asher because her eyes were sometimes turned on Aaron while she was dancing. Sunshine had noticed that Aaron's eyes were always focused on her, and she had also noticed the rage on his face, and she knew that Aaron was angry because she was dancing with Asher. Then Sunshine saw Aaron get up from his chair and left the room.

After an hour, the party was over and all children returned to their home, and they were all surprised to see that they had left

Aaron's home without seeing Aaron, and without Aaron wishing them a goodbye. And most of them were wondering what had happened to Aaron for that he behaved like this, mostly that Aaron was in his bedroom, and his parents called him to come say goodbye to his friends but he refused to get out of the bedroom.

Sunshine was very surprised by the attitude of Aaron, and although the fact that she knew that Aaron was angry because she had spent her time during the party to dance with Asher, she did not expect Aaron to behave like this.

In the palace, everyone had woken up, and they were all surprised to see that they had woken up at three in the afternoon, and they were more amazed to notice the mess that there was in the kitchen and in the living room. Diana, who was Kalus's wife, asked Kalus who were the people who were in the palace during the night? Kalus lied to his wife that he had no idea, that he woke up and he was surprised to see the mess in the living room and in the kitchen.

Some security men woke up and were surprised to see that they were wet with water, and other security men woke up feeling pains in their bodies. And they were even astonished to see that they were bleeding. And they were all wondering what had happened and they had also noticed that children were not in their prison. And security men had asked Kalus who had released children? Kalus had just insulted them by calling them useless people who were unable to keep him and his family.

Then National television, the national radio and newspapers had announced the speech of Kalus in news at eight o'clock, and except children who were at the palace and their parents, the rest of inhabitants of the kingdom were wondering what news would be announced by their king.

And most inhabitants of the kingdom were very worried about the speech which would be delivered by their king at eight o'clock because since Kalus had been crowned the king, he had never announced good news in his speeches. And all the speeches that had been made by Kalus were just to destroy the kingdom, and all the decisions that had been taken by their king were against the values of their kingdom.

And people were very afraid, and they were afraid of the news that would be announced by Kalus because for them, they had no doubt that the news that would be announced by Kalus would not be good news. And some people were even hesitating to watch television at eight o'clock because they did not want to listen to their king.

But at the same time, people were very surprised to hear from the television and radio that their king was going to make a speech at eight o'clock because it's been more than a decade that their king had not made a speech.

And it's also been more than a decade that they had not seen their king with their eyes, and that they had not even listened to their king's voice on the radio. And they were wondering if it was really their king who was going to make a speech, and if their king was still alive. Because some had even said that Kalus was dead.

And they knew that if it was really their king who was going to make a speech at eight o'clock, it was not to give them an explanation for the reasons that he had spent more than a decade without talking to them. Because their king did not care about them, and their king did not care about the kingdom, but their king instead hated them and hated the kingdom.

And they knew well that if it was really their king who was going to make this speech at eight o'clock, this speech would be only a disaster for them and for the kingdom. Because they knew their king as someone who made changes only to make things worse. And they were not really interested in the speech of their king because they knew that their king could not announce good news.

But at the same time, although the fact that they were not really interested in the speech of their king, they were curious to see if it was their king who was going to speak to them at eight o'clock, and they were more curious to know about what their king look like after that they had not seen their king in over a decade.

It was 7:45 p.m., all the inhabitants of the kingdom were sitting in their living room in front of their television and they were all watching the national television and they were waiting for the speech of their king. And except for the children who had spent the night in the palace, the rest of the inhabitants were very worried, and they had their hearts beating with fear. And they were wondering what exactly their king was going to announce, but they were sure that it would not be good news.

And even the parents that their children were in the palace were very afraid about the news that would be announced by Kalus. And although the fact that their children had told them that Kalus was going to make a speech in the news at eight o'clock, to announce to them the back of the school in the kingdom in three weeks, the parents did not really believe in the words of their king. And for the parents, Kalus had just lied to their children that he was going to give them their right to education.

It was eight o'clock, and the hearts of people who were in front of their television were beating faster than normal, and they were all waiting for their king to appear on the screen of their television.

And there was silence in the houses of the kingdom, and for the first-time people were watching television without talking. After ten minutes, Kalus had not yet appeared on the screens of their televisions, and most of them started to say that Kalus had just lied to them.

And they were not even surprised to notice that Kalus had lied to them, but at the same time most of them were very happy that Kalus had lied to them. Because if Kalus had lied to them that meant that Kalus had nothing to say.

And like Kalus had nothing to say, it meant that there would not be bad news that would be announced by their king. Because they were sure that if their king had something to announce, it would be just bad news because their king had a reputation to announce only the bad news.

And even if most people were happy to see that bad news would not be announced, there were a few of them who were a little disappointed to not see their king. Because they were curious to see Kalus after more than ten years that they had not seen him. And for some people the fact that Kalus had not made his speech was evidence that he was very sick or even dead. And most people wished that Kalus was really dead.

It was 8:35 p.m., and Kalus had still not yet appeared on the television screen. And Children who had spent their night at the palace were angry in front of their televisions, and the faces of some of them like Sunshine, Asher and Mia were full of rage. And for them, Kalus had lied to them. And although the fact that Sunshine was very angry to see that Kalus had lied to them, she was trying to keep her calm, she had already planned in her head to return to the palace the next day and to face Kalus.

Most of the Children to whom Kalus had promised the back of school in three weeks were very sad, and their parents were trying to calm them. And their parents were not surprised at all that Kalus had lied to their children, and for these parents if Kalus had kept his promise it would be a great miracle. It was very hard for these parents to see the sadness on the faces of their children, mostly that their children were very happy to start school in three weeks.

And their children had even celebrated their victory at Aaron's home for having succeeded in obtaining their right to education. But what was most important for the parents, was the fact that their children were alive and safe, and they were grateful to Kalus for that because Kalus had not killed their children.

It's been almost three hours since Kalus was knelt in his magic room, and he was trying to talk to Lord without success, and he had screamed the name of Lord that he had lost his voice. And Kalus was looking very tired and he was even sweating, and he was very afraid to not hear the voice of Lord, mostly that the kingdom was in a crisis with Sunshine who had taken the palace hostage last night. And Kalus was trying to talk with Lord because he wanted Lord to tell him what to do if he was going to make this speech on the news or not.

And at the same time, Kalus knew well that if he did not make this speech, Sunshine would come back, and the worst could happen if Sunshine came back in the palace because he did not announce the back of school in three weeks on television. And the real problem was the fact that Kalus could not take this decision to announce the back of the school in the kingdom in three weeks without the authorization of Lord.

Because the kingdom was not ruled by Kalus but the kingdom was instead ruled by Lord, and mostly because education was banned in the kingdom by Lord. And Lord had told Kalus that it was important and necessary that the children of the kingdom never had access to education.

And Kalus was just like the spokesperson of the kingdom because the decisions were made by Lord, and Kalus just implemented and announced the decisions that were made by Lord. And Kalus had lost control of the kingdom since the day that he made a pact with Lord. Kalus was completely lost, and he did not know what to do, and he was wondering if Sunshine had killed Lord.

And if Sunshine had killed Lord, it meant that the kingdom would be ruled by Sunshine now. And Kalus did not know if he would continue to obey Lord and not allow children to go to school, or if he was going to obey Sunshine and allow children to go to school.

And Kalus was realizing that he was in trouble because he did not know what decision to make, and if he obeyed Sunshine, he would be killed by Lord, and if he continued to obey to Lord, he would be killed by Sunshine.

Then Kalus took a deep breath and he yelled the name of Lord with a desperate voice. And suddenly the expression of Kalus's face changed and his face was full of surprise and his eyes were widely opened as he had heard the voice of Lord.

Then Kalus asked Lord if he was really in the room. And the smile appeared on Kalus's face when he heard Lord answer him. Then Kalus told Lord that the palace had been taken hostage last night by Sunshine because she wanted their right to education. And Lord told Kalus that he was aware of everything that had happened, and that it was the reason why he had warned him [Kalus] about the visitors that should come in the palace because these visitors were Sunshine and her fellows.

But that was not time to talk about it. Then Lord asked Kalus to get up and go keep his promise by making the speech on television and mostly to mention everything that he had agreed with Sunshine during his speech.

Kalus asked Lord if it meant that they were going to give education to children. Lord answered Kalus that for the moment they did not have a choice, and he hated the fact that children of the kingdom could have access to knowledge but that they did not have another solution.

And that they would make Sunshine more mad if they did not give children their right to education. And Lord added that things could be worse if Sunshine returned to the palace because children were not going to school.

Kalus told Lord that Sunshine was dangerous, and that she had tortured him at his palace this morning. Lord replied to Kalus that he knew everything that had happened in the palace this morning, but that it was not time to talk about it.

And Lord said that he was looking for a way to kill Sunshine, and that children of the kingdom would never have access to education because Sunshine would die in less than three weeks. And they would cancel this decision to give access to education to children that would be made today once Sunshine would be in her grave.

Kalus asked Lord if it meant that his speech would be just the words to calm Sunshine and to show to Sunshine that he had kept his promise? Lord replied to Kalus that exactly that the speech would be just a way to calm Sunshine and to gain on time and to let Sunshine focus on the back of school in the kingdom, while he would be looking for a way to kill Sunshine in less than three weeks.

Because it was necessary that children of the kingdom must never have access to knowledge and for that they must get rid of Sunshine. And it was important to get rid of Sunshine in less than three weeks, before the day of the back of school.

Kalus told Lord that he was very happy to know that children would never have access to education, and he was happier to hear that Sunshine would die in less than three weeks. Lord asked Kalus to leave the room now and go and make his speech because the inhabitants of the kingdom had already lost the hope to see him. And Lord also told Kalus that it was important to apologize for being late, before starting his speech. Then Kalus got up and left the magic room.

It was nine o'clock, people were still sitting in their living room with their eyes focused on the screen of their television, but they were no longer waiting for their king to deliver the speech. Because they thought that their king had lied to them. And some people had already even left the living room.

Suddenly, the expression of the faces of people who were watching television changed, and they were all looking at the screen of the television with surprised faces. And some had even their eyes widely opened. They were all watching someone on television who looked like their king.

And some were wondering if it was really their king that they were watching on television, while others were saying that it was not their king. And there were a few people who were saying that it was their king just that their king looked older and tired.

Then they suddenly recognised the voice of their king, when their king opened his mouth to talk, and they were all very surprised to see that their king looked older with the long beard. And it was their first time to see their king with the long bear. And they also noticed that their king had difficulties speaking, and that the voice of their king was very low.

Then some of them got up from their chairs and went and knelt near the television to listen very well to the speech of their king, while others pushed their chairs in front of the television. Suddenly, the expression on their faces changed and some were watching television with their faces full of surprise, while others had turned their heads and looked at each other with their mouths open. But no word was coming out from their mouths. And they were all surprised to hear their king who was apologizing for being late.

And looking at their expression on their faces, they did not believe that it was really their king who was apologizing to them. And if they were surprised, it was because it was their first time to hear their king apologize, and they had never imagined that their king could apologize one day. And some of them were trying to talk, but their mouths were shaking so that they could not pronounce a word.

And suddenly, there were the louder screams coming from the houses of the kingdom when they heard their king announce that the back of school in the kingdom was in three weeks. And that children were going to start school in three weeks. And that all the instructors who were in jail would be released by tomorrow, and the owners of the libraries and bookstores must open from tomorrow.

And that the parents had the right to talk about the education to their children, and the parents would start to buy the school's books for their children when the libraries would be opened. Also, a school director would be named before the end of the next week, and this school director would make a speech on television to talk about the school program and the books that would be used by children.

Then people continued to yell of joy, and those who had left the living room before Kalus started his speech were running towards the living room to be aware of what was going on, and to know the reasons why people were screaming. And there were the screams in the houses of the kingdom and people were screaming the word, "Education."

Children who had spent their night in the palace were very happy to see that Kalus had kept his promise, and they were very glad to know that they were really going to school in three weeks.

But Sunshine was not particularly happy because she knew that there was a reason why Kalus had started his speech at nine o'clock, and she knew that there was something going wrong, mostly that Kalus had apologized for being late. And Sunshine knew well that Kalus was not the kind of person who could apologize, mostly apologized on television knowing that the whole kingdom was watching him.

Sunshine knew well that Kalus had apologized for calling them useless children in the palace because he did not have the choice because he was a prisoner in his own palace and he apologized to get rid of them. And Sunshine did not understand why Kalus apologized, mostly that he was not under pressure, and he could just make his speech without apologizing.

Sunshine started to think about what was hidden behind the fact that Kalus had not started his speech at eight o'clock, like they had agreed in the palace. And Sunshine knew well that there was nothing that could prevent Kalus from making his speech at eight o'clock, then, Sunshine started thinking.

It was ten minutes before midnight; there was the moon that was shining in the sky and there were the stars that were shining in the clouds, and the wind was blowing. And people were getting outside of their houses screaming of joy, and some were even crying.

Kalus had just finished his speech and the whole kingdom was in joy, and seeing how people were happy, it was as if a miracle had happened in the kingdom. People were hugging each other, and there were the tears that were flowing down from their cheeks.

And people were happy because their king had given the right of education to their children, and they did not expect this to happen, mostly that their king had sworn to them that education was banned in the kingdom forever. And they were very surprised that their king had changed the idea, and he had not only promised to open the schools, but he had also promised to release all the instructors who were in prison.

And they were not expecting it from their king, and they were still not believing what they were living, and some people were even drinking the wine and beers that they had at home to celebrate the return of education in the kingdom, and there were even the fireworks that exploded almost everywhere in the kingdom.

The parents that their children had spent the night in the palace were also very surprised that Kalus had kept his promise because they did not expect Kalus to keep the promise that he had made to their children.

And for the first time, they could trust their king now, and they were wondering what their children had said to the king for that the king changed his idea by giving the right to education to children. And they were very proud of their children, and Sunshine was the heroine of the kingdom for them.

In the palace, it was a big surprise, all the people who lived in the palace were very surprised by the announcement of the king to reopen the schools and to release the instructors who had protested against the laws of Klaus when Kalus had banned the education in the kingdom.

And they were wondering what or who had made their king change the idea about education in the kingdom. And security men who had seen children in the kingdom last night were wondering if it was these children who had made their king change the idea. And they were also wondering if it was the king who had released these children from jail, but unfortunately, they could not answer these questions.

Princess Diana, who was Kalus's wife, was very surprised about the decision of her husband to reopen the schools and give the education to the children. And she was wondering what had happened to her husband because her husband changed his idea about the education of children in the kingdom, and she was not really understanding what was going on with Kalus, mostly that Kalus had sworn the end of the education in the kingdom forever.

And although Princess Diana was very happy that her husband finally authorized the education in the kingdom, she was still not understanding the reasons which had pushed Kalus to allow children to go to school.

Even if Princess Diana had spent time fighting for the right of education of children in the kingdom against her husband, she was a little suspicious. Because she knew well that her husband was not someone to trust. And Diana was also surprised by the fact that her husband had apologized, and it was her time to hear her husband apologize.

Except for the children who had spent the night in the kingdom to negotiate with Kalus about their right to education, the rest of the children did not really understand what was going on. And why people around them were yelling of joy by screaming, "Education is back in the kingdom."

If these children did not know what the meaning of education was, it was because the laws of Kalus prohibited the parents from talking about education to children.

And the parents were just celebrating the victory of the return of education in the kingdom without even trying to know the reasons why their king had changed the idea about the right of education in the kingdom. Or who had forced their king to allow the return of education to the kingdom. And most of them had even said that their king had changed.

And the fact that they had lost the hope to one day see their children go to school, that they had decided to celebrate all night the return of education in the kingdom. And fortunately for them, the next day was a weekend which was Saturday.

It was nine in the morning, and the sun was shining outside, and the streets of the kingdom were almost empty, and most people were still sleeping in their beds. And those who had woken up to clean the houses and to make breakfast and to go to the market looked very tired. And people were still sleeping because they had spent all their night celebrating the return of education in the kingdom.

Downtown was not as crowded as usual, and some stores were still closed. And almost all people who were downtown were in front of the kiosks of newspapers, and they were fighting to get a newspaper.

Newspapers were talking about the return of education in the kingdom, but people were not really interested in the fact that the king had announced plans to reopen the schools in the kingdom. But people were instead interested in the reasons why the king had changed his idea about the education in the kingdom and what had prompted their king to reopen the school in the kingdom.

But there was a newspaper called Kongreshow by J Point Remy Ngono also called Remy who was telling about Sunshine and her fellows who had marched from Sunshine's home to the palace with the protest signs asking for their right to education. And there was Sunshine's photo in front of all newspapers of Kongreshow, and with the highlights like, "Who is Sunshine?"

"How did Sunshine succeed in convincing the king to reopen the schools in the kingdom?"

"How did Sunshine know the importance of education?"

"Sunshine the savior of the kingdom."

And the journalist called Remy had investigated near to children who had protested for their right to education to know exactly what had happened in the palace. And only two children, Asher and Mia had agreed to talk to Remy about what had happened in the palace. And Asher had told Remy about the meeting that was organized by Sunshine to celebrate her twelfth birthday, and Asher had also told Remy everything that had happened to Sunshine's home this day of her birthday.

And how they had planned to go to the palace, and even how they were beaten by security guards of Kalus and locked up in a dark cold prison. And mostly the morning that Sunshine had forced the king to give them their right to education, and to open the school in three weeks.

And Remy had written in his newspapers all the stories that were told by Asher and Mia about the protest that was organized by Sunshine to get the right to education of children in the kingdom.

Also, how Sunshine had forced their king to open the schools in three weeks and to release all the instructors who were in the prisons. And people were fighting in front of the kiosk of Kongreshow to get a newspaper, and they were reading the newspapers with surprised faces.

People did not believe what they read in newspapers, and it was unreal for them to read in the newspapers that children had forced the king to open the schools in three weeks. And each person who read the newspaper of Kongreshow was wondering who Sunshine was. And at the same time, they were amazed by the courage of Sunshine and Sunshine's fellows who had protested to the palace for their right to education.

It was one in the afternoon, and it was very hot, and those who were sleeping had already woken up, and they were reading the newspaper called Kongreshow. And even in the palace people were reading this newspaper. And those who did not have the newspapers went on the website of Kongreshow to read the content of newspapers.

And everyone was astonished about the content of the newspaper, and they were all wondering who children who had gone to the palace to protest were, and mostly whoSunshine was. And it was very hard for them to believe the content of the newspaper, and it was even impossible for them to believe that children had forced the king to reopen the schools in the kingdom.

And all people knew well that the content of the newspaper was true not only because some people had seen children protest with the protest signs by walking towards the palace asking for their right to education.

But they knew that Remy was a fantastic journalist who could not write the lies in his newspaper, and they also knew that Remy was a journalist who fought for equal justice for everyone. And who was opposed to the laws of Kalus in the kingdom, and who had been sent to prison many times by Kalus because he was against the laws of Kalus which prohibited the education in the kingdom.

And they also knew that Remy should be already in prison if the content of his newspaper was not true. But, what was hard for them to believe was the conversation between the king Kalus and Sunshine that was related in the newspapers mostly where Sunshine forced Kalus to make an interview on television to announce the return of the education in the kingdom in three weeks. And to release all the instructors from jail as if Sunshine was the one who ruled the kingdom.

And people were very surprised about the content of the newspapers because knowing the behavior of their king, it was impossible for their king to listen to a little girl like Sunshine, mostly a girl who was giving him the orders.

And at the same time, people were wondering why their king did not kill Sunshine and her fellows mostly that Sunshine and her fellows had protested by breaking the laws of Kalus which prohibited all kinds of demonstrations in the kingdom. But unfortunately, they could not answer this question, and for most of them the only idea that made sense in their heads was that their king had changed, and their king had become a new person.

And the whole kingdom was not only proud of their king who had decided to reopen the school in the kingdom, but they were also very proud of these brave children who were Sunshine and her fellows who had taken their courage and protested for the right to education of all children in the kingdom.

Because they knew that Sunshine and her fellows had made the history of their kingdom not only by protesting for their right to education. But mostly by succeeding to convince their king to allow the return of education in the kingdom, even if their king had the power to not accept to reopen the schools in the kingdom.

Princess Diana was very amazed by what she had read in the newspaper, and she was very proud of the courage of children who had protested for their right to education. Diana had asked her husband about children who had come to protest in the palace, but Kalus had refused to talk to her about these children.

Sunshine had become famous in the kingdom, and all the inhabitants of the kingdom had spent their day with her name in their mouths, and some people had even gone to her house to talk to her, but she had refused to see them. The next day, people were still talking about Sunshine, but the parents spent their day explaining to their children the meaning of education, and the reason why their children would go to school.

CHAPTER III

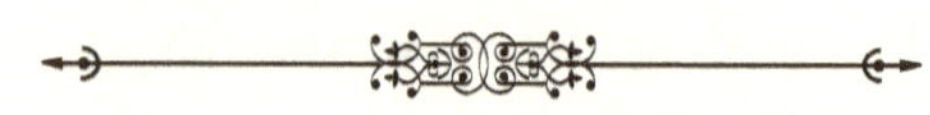

THE LIE OF THE KING KALUS AND THE WRATH OF THE CHILDREN

The days were passing and something had changed in the kingdom, and the libraries in the kingdom had reopened its doors. The school director had made a speech on television to talk about the school program, and the school director had asked parents to buy all the Superhuman book series by Thierry Kouam. Because children were going to study the books of Superhuman by Thierry Kouam like literature.

And the parents spent their time in libraries buying the books, the pencils and the school's bags for their children. And the parents had also bought the saga of the Superhuman books by Thierry Kouam for their children. The parents were spending their time teaching their children to read and write.

And it was very hard for children to read, mostly to write and the parents held their children's hands with the pencils in their children's hands and they helped their children to form the letters. And most children hated the fact that they were going to school because they hated to study, they hated to write and read mostly that their parents told them that they would read and write everyday at school.

Sunshine's parents were very surprised by the skills of Sunshine to read and write because Sunshine was able to read well and write very well without her parents's help, and they had also noticed that their daughter was very smart. And Sunshine's parents were wondering where Sunshine had learned to write and read, and they were very proud of Sunshine.

But at the same time, Sunshine's parents were very worried about her attitude because Sunshine was very strange and always thoughtful. And even worse Sunshine was not eating. And when her parents asked her why she was not eating? She answered that she was fasting. And Sunshine's parents asked her why she was fasting?

Sunshine's parents were very surprised to hear Sunshine answer that she was fasting because she wanted to be in touch with God. And Sunshine's dad asked her if the god she was talking about was Kalus? Sunshine answered her papa that Kalus was not a god, but instead a devil.

Sunshine's parents were very astonished to hear their daughter talk about fasting, and they were wondering how their daughter knew the word, "Fasting." Mostly that people had stopped fasting in the kingdom before she was born. And if people had stopped fasting, it was because the king had prohibited people from fasting, and even worse the laws of Kalus prohibited people from pronouncing the word fasting.

And the laws of Kalus also prohibited the parents to talk about everything that was related to God to their children. And Sunshine's parents were very amazed to see that their daughter was aware of everything that had happened in the kingdom before she was born.

And at the same time, they were very worried about their daughter. Because they knew that their daughter was breaking the laws of Kalus everyday. And they knew that their daughter could be killed by Kalus if Kalus knew that their daughter was fasting.

And Sunshine was fasting because she had the feeling that something worse was going to happen because she knew that Kalus and Lord had a plan. And Sunshine was praying everyday to ask God to help her find out what was the plan of Kalus and Lord.

And she was very thoughtful because she was trying to understand the reasons why Kalus had made his speech at nine o'clock, and not at eight o'clock, as they had agreed. Sunshine had thought of going to the palace to confront Kalus and to try to find out what his plan was. But she had changed her mind because she knew that she could not make Kalus talk about his plan, even if she used her magic to torture him.

Children of the kingdom were spending their last week before the back of school, and they were very eager to start school for the first time in their history. And they were very happy to know that they were going to school to realize their dream, and that they were going to meet other children of their age.

And even children who were not happy to go to school had changed their mind, and they wanted to study. And Kalus was appreciated by his people for the first since he had been crowned the king. And children were watching on television people who were working at school to make the school suitable and comfortable, and children could not wait to start school.

And Kalus had gained the confidence of the parents with the works that were being done at school. And the parents had no doubt that their children would start to study in the classrooms in a few days by watching on television the works that people were doing at school to make the school suitable, and the parents were eager to take their children to school the next week.

Sunshine and some of her fellows with whom she was at the palace were spending time together, and they were talking about the school that they were going to start in a few days. And they were trying to plan to change things in the kingdom because even if they had won their first victory against Kalus, which was the return of education to the kingdom, it was not enough for them.

And they wanted to put an end to the laws of Kalus in the kingdom. But during their meeting, they did not always agree on the way to proceed, and Asher's idea was always rejected by Aaron, and Aaron was always rude with Asher.

And except Sunshine, the rest of the people were very surprised by the way that Aaron was impolite with Asher, and they were wondering what was going on with Aaron because they knew that Aaron was a nice person. And Aaron did not answer when they asked him why he was rude with Asher.

But Sunshine knew that Aaron was rude with Asher because she had danced with Asher during the party that was organized by Aaron's mom to celebrate their victory on the return of education in the kingdom. And Sunshine had tried to talk to Aaron about his behavior towards Asher without success.

And Sunshine's friends noticed that Sunshine was always thoughtful and she was always away during their conversation, and she had also lost some weight. And when Sunshine's friends asked her what was going on with her? She lied to them that everything was fine. But they had noticed that Sunshine had a problem even if she did not want to talk about it.

The day of back to school was approaching and Sunshine's parents were very worried about her because Sunshine was still not eating and she was losing weight and looking tired. It was evening. Sunshine was having a conversation with her parents in the living room. And Sunshine's parents asked her to stop fasting and to eat because she would get sick before the back of school.

Sunshine had replied to her parents that she would not stop fasting because she was fasting for a reason. And Sunshine's father asked her why she was fasting. Sunshine answered her papa that she was fasting for the peace in the kingdom. Sunshine's dad told her that there was peace in the kingdom and that education was back in the kingdom.

Sunshine told her father that there was no peace in the kingdom because people were still living according to the laws of Kalus. David told Sunshine that she would not talk about the laws of Kalus, and that he forbade her to fight against the laws of Kalus.

And Sunshine told her papa that she would not live in the kingdom with the laws of Kalus, and that she refused to live according to the laws of Kalus. David told her daughter that children had got their right to education and that it was enough, and that she was now focused on going to school.

Sunshine told her papa that victory of the return of education to the kingdom was only the first step, and that she and her friends were going to put an end to the laws of Kalus. And that she would never live according to the laws of Kalus, and she would not hesitate to break the laws of Kalus.

Sunshine went on and said that she knew well that she was breaking the laws of Kalus by fasting, but that she was not afraid of doing it because she would never live according to the laws of Kalus, and she was ready to die to free the kingdom from the laws of Kalus.

Then Sunshine looked into the eyes of her papa and said that it was unfair to respect a law that was unfair, and that it was a right and a duty to break a law that was unfair. And that meant it was a right and a duty to break the laws of Kalus.

And suddenly, there was silence in the room, and Sunshine's parents were looking at her with surprised faces, and Sunshine's mother opened her mouth to say a word but her mouth was shaking that she was unable to pronounce a word. Then Sunshine got up from her chair and wished a good night to her parents, then she walked through her bedroom.

After a few minutes, Sunshine was walking in her bedroom and she was thinking and she was very surprised that it's been a long time she had not seen Lord, that she had not been attacked by Lord. And Sunshine was very amazed by the silence of Lord because since she was born, it was the first time that Lord spent more than seventeen days without trying to kill her mystically.

And Sunshine knew well that Lord had more good reasons to kill her now because she had succeeded in forcing Kalus to allow children to go to school. And the silence of Lord was clear for Sunshine that Kalus and Lord had a plan, and that this plan could be dangerous. And that she must do everything to stop Lord and Kalus and mostly to prevent this plan from happening because if this plan happened, it could be the end of the existence of the kingdom.

Then Sunshine understood that the one that she must stop was not Kalus, but instead Lord. And Sunshine was wondering where she could find Lord, and it was not today that she was looking for Lord's house because it's been years now that Sunshine was looking for the house of Lord without success. And Sunshine was still walking in her bedroom and her eyes were spinning, and if Sunshine's eyes were spinning, it was because she was using her magic to find the house of Lord.

After an hour, Sunshine was still looking for the house of Lord and she was looking very tired, and she was even sweating and feeling the violent headaches. And Sunshine was feeling tired and had headaches, it was because her magic was working for more than an hour now, and the fact that her magic was working had the effects on her.

Then Sunshine started to breathe loudly and she immediately stopped using her magic to look for the house of Lord because she had started feeling unwell. And it was a risk for her to continue because she could be paralyzed by her magic if she continued to use her magic when she was not feeling well.

Then Sunshine sat on the bed and she started thinking, and she did not know what to do. After a few minutes, Sunshine got an idea, and she laid down on the bed and her eyes started to spin, then the light shone into her eyes and she disappeared.

The moon was shining in the sky and the stars were shining in the clouds, and the whole kingdom was deeply sleeping. Sunshine was flying in space and she was flying in the direction of the palace, and there was the wind blowing on her face and lifting her long hair.

Then Sunshine started flying slowly as she had seen Lord who was flying while facing her, and she understood that Lord was there to prevent her from going to the palace. After a few seconds, they were facing each other.

Then Lord and Sunshine were looking at each other in the eyes, and the wind was blowing on their faces. Then Sunshine noticed that Lord's eyes were spinning and she understood that Lord wanted to fight her, and her eyes started spinning too.

Then Sunshine started feeling the effects of Lord's magic inside her, and she was feeling the violent headaches and she was feeling pains in her body too. And Sunshine was unable to fight back at Lord because she was unable to focus on herself to be able to use her magic. And Sunshine was unable to focus on herself to use her magic because she was tortured by Lord's magic.

Then Sunshine was sweating and she had even stopped using her magic, then she got an idea and she started flying away. And Lord was flying after Sunshine and he had his eyes focused on Sunshine, and Lord's eyes were spinning faster as he was looking at Sunshine. Then Sunshine stopped flying and she was turning in space, and it was Lord's magic who was making Sunshine turn. And Lord was staring at Sunshine who was turning in space with a smile on his face.

After an hour, Sunshine was still turning in the space, and she was trying to control her body without success. And she could not control her body because Lord's magic had taken control of her body. And even worse she could not use her magic because she had also lost the control of her magic.

Then Lord started to have difficulties of breathing and he was also tired because he was releasing a lot of energy from his body as he was using his magic to torture Sunshine. Then Lord turned his head away and he lifted his head through the sky and he was trying to get the energies, and there was a light coming from the sky and shining on his face.

And Sunshine started flying away as she felt that her body was no longer controlled by Lord's magic. Sunshine flew until near to a magic tree, and she stayed behind a tree's branch of this magic tree.

And Sunshine looked at Lord who was getting the energies, and she understood that Lord was getting the energies of magic to fight, but she also understood that she must do something. Then Sunshine took a deep breath and she focused her eyes on Lord, then her eyes started spinning and the bluelight started getting out of her eyes and going on Lord.

Suddenly, Lord pushed a loud scream when he felt his body that was burning and he turned his head and noticed that a blue light was shining on him. And he understood that this blue light was coming from Sunshine, and he turned his head looking for Sunshine.

Then Lord saw Sunshine behind a tree's branch of a magic tree, and he stared at her, then his eyes started spinning. But unfortunately for Lord, his magic did not have effect on Sunshine, and he was still feeling his body burning.

After a few minutes, Lord's magic still had no effect on Sunshine, then Lord changed the strategy and his eyes started spinning faster, and the yellow light got out of his eyes and went towards Sunshine. But this yellow light coming from Lord's eyes was not having effects on Sunshine, and even worse this yellow light was not touching Sunshine's body, and this yellow light was just shining on the tree's branches and tree's leaves.

And Lord's magic did not have effects on Sunshine because she was behind a tree's branch of a magic tree and she was protected by this magic tree, so Lord's magic could not reach her. And the fact that Lord's magic could not reach Sunshine meant that Lord's magic could not have effects on her.

And Sunshine was protected from Lord's magic by this magic tree because Lord's magic did not work with this magic tree, and this magic tree blocked Lord's magic to reach Sunshine. And this magic tree also absorbed the energies of Lord's magic.

And things were going worse for Lord, his body was still burning by Sunshine's magic, and he tried to fly away without success because Sunshine's magic had completely controlled his body. And Lord had even given up the fight not only because his magic did not work with the magic tree, but mostly because Sunshine's magic had drained him of his energy, and without his energy he could not use his magic to fight because his magic needed the energy to work.

Lord was tortured by Sunshine's magic, and he was sweating and looking tired. And Lord was feeling pains in his whole body and he was trying to escape without success, and he could not even use his magic to disappear. After more than an hour, Sunshine turned her head to the left and flew away, then she landed on the ground. And Lord flew through the ground too, as his body was no longer controlled by Sunshine's magic, then Lord landed face to Sunshine.

Then Lord and Sunshine were looking at each other in the eyes with their faces full of anger, and there was silence between them. And Lord was looking very tired, and there were a lot of ideas that were going on in the head of Lord. And one of these ideas was the fact that Lord wanted to fight Sunshine to make her pay for the torture she had done him a few minutes ago.

But at the same time, Lord knew that he could not take a risk to fight Sunshine because he did not have the energy of his magic in him while Sunshine had the energy of her magic. And Lord knew that Sunshine had an advantage on him, and it was impossible to fight her with the energy of her magic she had inside her body.

Then Lord broke the silence and said, "I would not congratulate you."

"Why should you?" Sunshine asked.

"You succeeded in bringing education back to the kingdom," Lord answered.

"You should congratulate me for that because I succeeded in giving children their right to education," Sunshine said.

"I would congratulate you when you would start school," Lord replied.

"Children would start school in three days," Sunshine said.

"I would congratulate you in seventy-two hours," Lord replied.

"Why not now?" Sunshine asked.

"Because a miracle can happen in three days," Lord answered.

"Which kind of miracle?" Sunshine asked.

"A miracle that can change the fate of the kingdom," Lord said.

"That miracle can prevent children from going to school, right?" Sunshine asked.

"You are very smart," Lord said.

"Thank you for telling me," Sunshine replied.

Lord smiled and said, "Congratulations!"

Sunshine cried out, "Congratulations?" looking at Lord with a surprised face, and she said, "You just told me that you can not congratulate me because the back of school is in three days, and a miracle that can prevent children from going to school in three days can happen."

"I do not congratulate the return of education to the kingdom," Lord said.

"What do you congratulate me for?" Sunshine asked.

"You just have a little brother," Lord answered.

Sunshine cried out, "What?" Looking at Lord with an amazed face.

"You just have a little brother," Lord replied.

Sunshine looked at Lord with a face empty of expression and she said, "You are crazy." And she added, "You claim to be a god, but you are even unable to know through your magic that I am the unique child of my parents."

"Your mom is pregnant," Lord said.

Sunshine cried out, "What?" And she asked, "My mom is pregnant?"

"Your mom is pregnant, and she is expecting a boy," Lord answered.

"My mom is not pregnant," Sunshine retorted.

"Your mom doesn't know that she is pregnant," Lord said.

"How is my mom pregnant, and she doesn't know that she is pregnant?" Sunshine asked.

"Your mom got pregnant a few minutes ago," Lord answered.

Sunshine looked at Lord and she opened her mouth to say a word, but her mouth was shaking so that a word could not get out from her mouth, while Lord was staring at Sunshine with his face full of smiles. Then Sunshine took a deep breath and said, "Have a good day."

"Not yet," Lord replied.

"What else do you have to say?" Sunshine asked.

"I want to make a deal with you," Lord answered.

Sunshine looked into Lord's eyes and said, "I don't even want to know what kind of deal you want to make, but I am not interested in this deal."

"Think very well," Lord said.

"I do not have to think because I would never make a deal with a devil like you," Sunshine retorted.

"I give you peace!" Lord said.

Sunshine looked into Lord's eyes and said, "I am not interested in your peace!"

"I possess the soul of the future children of this kingdom," Lord said.

Sunshine looked into Lord's eyes angrily and said, "Do not even dare to touch a child of this kingdom."

Lord burst into laughter and looked at Sunshine with a face full of smiles and said, "It's a bit late to warn me because the souls of all future children of this kingdom already belong to me, and even the soul of your little brother who was not yet born belongs to me."

Sunshine looked at Lord with a face full of anger and said, "You would never possess the soul of a child of this kingdom again."

Lord smiled at Sunshine and said, "It's too late, and there is nothing you can do to free the souls of children that I possess."

Sunshine said, "I promise you that I would free the souls of these children who were not yet born."

Lord smiled at Sunshine and said, "Twelve years ago when you were born, you succeeded to free the souls of children by turning the satanic trees that I used to control the souls of children into the magic trees." And Lord posed and he was staring with the same expression face, he took a deep breath and said, "This time, I mystically possess the souls of children in the womb of their mothers, and that means when children would be born, these children would be mine because I have the possession of their souls."

Sunshine said, "That's impossible."

Lord asked, "Why is it impossible?"

Sunshine answered, "You can not control the souls of children who were not yet born."

Lord looked into Sunshine's eyes and said, "More than twelve years ago, I got possession of children's souls only when children were born, but since you were born, you changed everything, you destroyed the satanic trees I used to mystically control children's souls. But now I changed the way to control children's souls and I decided to control children's souls from the womb of their mothers, and by this way you have no chance to free children's souls."

Sunshine looked at Lord with eyes full of anger and said, "You would possess the souls of children of this kingdom only on my dead body."

Lord smiled and said, "Think very well about my proposition of peace."

Sunshine said, "I do not need to think."

Lord said, "I think I must leave now because you will have a hard day."

Sunshine asked, "What do you mean?"

Lord answered, "You would spend the day in the hospital because all pregnant women would start feeling pains today, and these pains would come from their bellies, and these pains would be caused by the fact I possess the souls of children of the kingdom." Then Lord smiled at Sunshine and added, "The good news is the fact you would be to the hospital with your lover."

Sunshine cried out, "My lover?" looking at Lord with a surprised face.

Lord answered, "The young boy whose mom is expecting a girl." Then Lord smiled at Sunshine and said, "I do not know if you used your magic to find out that Aaron's mother is expecting a girl, or you just guessed it, but you did a great job because Aaron's mother is really expecting a girl."

Suddenly, Lord and Sunshine turned their heads to the left when they heard the rooster crowing. And Sunshine lifted her head through the sky and noticed that the moon had disappeared, while Lord turned his head around and noticed that the sun was rising. Then they turned their heads and looked at each other with silence, and the light shone in their eyes and they disappeared without saying a word.

At five in the morningSunshine was lying in her bed thinking about the conversation she had had with Lord during the night. Sunshine was very worried for two reasons, and the first reason was about the plan that Lord had to prevent children from starting school in three days, and the fact that Lord had told Sunshine that he could not yet congratulate her about the return of the education to the kingdom.

Because a miracle that could prevent children from going to school in three days could happen, and these words of Lord had just confirmed the doubts of Sunshine. And Sunshine was now sure that Lord had a plan to prevent children from going to school, and she was wondering what this plan could be.

And the second reason was the fact that Lord had told Sunshine that he now possessed the souls of children of the kingdom who were not yet born. And that he had found a way to control children's souls in the womb of their mothers.

And Sunshine was wondering if it was true that Lord really possessed the souls of children who were not yet born. Sunshine was wondering if Lord had not said that he controlled children's souls since the womb of their mothers just to hurt her or to deconcentrate her. And there were a lot of ideas that were going on in Sunshine's head, and she was wondering if Lord had not told her about children's souls that he possessed from the womb of their mothers.

Because Lord did not want her to focus on the back to school that was in three days, mostly to not focus on his plan he had to prevent children from going to school, and to focus on him and on the fact that he possessed children's souls. The real problem was the fact that Sunshine was wondering how it was possible to control the souls of children who were not yet born, and for her, it seemed impossible to do it.

Suddenly, the expression on the face of Sunshine changed and she jumped out of her bed rushing towards the door with her face full of fear, and she was hearing her mom who was yelling in pain. Sunshine got out of her room and ran towards the corridor of her parents' room, and she saw her mom who had leaned on her papa, and her parents were walking towards the front door. And Sunshine asked her father what her mother had. David told his daughter that her mother was feeling pain in her belly.

And suddenly, the expression on the face of Sunshine changed and she was looking with a face full of fear, and her heart was beating faster than the normal as she was remembering the conversation she had had with Lord a few hours ago. And Sunshine understood why her mother was feeling pain in her belly, and she was thinking what was to do.

The parents of Sunshine were looking at her with surprised faces, and they were wondering what was going on with Sunshine. And Sunshine's dad started talking to Sunshine, but Sunshine was not paying attention to her father.

Then David screamed Sunshine's name and Sunshine looked at her father. And David asked her daughter if she was alright?Sunshine answered her father if everything was fine. David asked her daughter to open the front door and take the car's key on the table and wait for her in the garage. Then Sunshine turned and left. And David continued to walk towards the front door with Sarah.

After an hour, Sunshine was walking in the waiting room of the hospital, and she was very worried about what was going on. Sunshine was hearing the screams of women in the hospital who were crying their bellies, and she was also watching women who arrived at the hospital by crying their bellies.

And Sunshine knew that all these women who were crying their bellies were pregnant. Sunshine was realizing that Lord had told her the truth that he possessed the souls of children who were not yet born. It was very hard for Sunshine to hear women who were crying, and she was thinking what to do.

Then Sunshine saw Aaron who was walking facing her, and she was not really surprised to see Aaron to the hospital because she had understood that Aaron was in the hospital because his mother was sick. And it's been almost a week that Aaron and Sunshine had not seen each other, and Aaron had taken the decision to walk away from Sunshine because he did not want to be anymore close to Asher, like Asher was also spending his time with Sunshine.

Then Aaron stopped face to Sunshine and they were staring at each other in the eyes without saying a word. Then Sunshine broke the silence and told Aaron that she was glad to see him. Aaron answered Sunshine that he was happy to see her too.

Then they started talking about the reasons why they were to the hospital, and Aaron was surprised to hear Sunshine say that she was to the hospital because her mom was feeling pain in her belly. Then they started talking, and they were very surprised to see the number of women who were arriving at the hospital by crying their bellies. And Aaron's face was full of smiles as he was talking with Sunshine, and looking at Aaron, it was obvious that he was very glad to see Sunshine.

After a few minutes, they were still talking. And suddenly, Aaron became silent and the smile that was on his face was gone, and the anger had taken the place of this smile. And Sunshine was astonished to notice that Aaron was looking nervous, and she asked Aaron what was going on, but he was not paying attention to her.

Then Sunshine turned her head through the entry door as she had noticed that Aaron's eyes were focused on the entry door, and immediately Sunshine understood why Aaron was nervous when she saw Asher who was walking towards them.

Sunshine looked at Aaron and she told him that Asher was not his enemy, but instead his brother. Aaron replied to Sunshine that Asher was not his brother but instead his enemy. And Aaron added that he did not like Asher at all. Sunshine asked Aaron for which reason he did not like Asher? Aaron looked into Sunshine's eyes and answered that she knew the reason. Sunshine took a deep breath and told Aaron that he must stop this bad behavior towards Asher, and that he wanted him to treat Asher well like Asher treated him.

Aaron replied to Sunshine that it would never happen, and that Asher would remain his enemy forever. And Aaron also told Sunshine that she was responsible if he and Asher were the enemies. Sunshine looked at Aaron with an amazed face, and she asked him how she was responsible for the fact that he was rude with Asher.

Aaron looked into Sunshine's eyes and said that she knew well what she had done to make him and Asher hate each other. Sunshine told Aaron that he was not the enemy of Asher because Asher loved him as a brother, and that he was the only one who took Asher as his enemy.

Aaron replied to Sunshine to not try to lie to him because he was not blind and he was aware of everything that was going on. Sunshine asked Aaron what she could do to make him change his behavior. Aaron answered Sunshine that he wanted her to stop seeing Asher.

And suddenly the expression on the face of Sunshine changed and she was staring at Aaron with a face full of anger. Then Sunshine looked into Aaron's eyes and told him that Asher was a brother to her, and she would never stop seeing him, and that if he could not accept that she and Asher were close, he must walk away from her.

Sunshine also told Aaron that he had the choice to walk away from her, but that if he chose to stay near to her, he must be polite with Asher. Aaron looked into Sunshine's eyes and said that he chose to walk away, and he turned and left. Sunshine was staring at Aaron who was walking away with a face full of sadness and looking at the expression on the face of Sunshine, we could see that she was hurt to see Aaron walk away from her.

And Sunshine knew well that Aaron behaved like this because he was in love with her. And that Aaron thought that she and Asher were in love together, but Sunshine also knew well that Asher was not in love with her, and she was not also in love with Asher.

Then the sadness that was on Sunshine's face turned into a smile when she saw Asher who was approaching her by dancing, and she opened her arms to Asher, and they hugged each other. And Aaron leaned on the pole and he was staring at Asher and Sunshine who had taken each other in their arms with a face full of jealousy. Then Aaron turned and left the room because it was impossible for him to watch Asher and Sunshine who were smiling at each other.

Asher and Sunshine were smiling at each other. Sunshine asked, "How did you know that I was in the hospital?"

Asher answered, "I was at your house, and your neighbours told me that you were in the hospital." Then Asher smiled and added, "I thought that you were dying, and I came to save you."

Sunshine said, "You are not a doctor."

"I hated healing people, so I was not going to be your doctor, but instead your savior," Asher said.

Sunshine laughed and said, "The kingdom does not need a savior right now, but the kingdom instead needs a doctor to heal these women who are crying."

"The kingdom needs a savior more than ever," Asher said.

"For which reason?" Sunshine asked.

"The devil is still alive," Asher answered.

Sunshine smiled at Asher and said, "You are right, the devil Kalus is still alive."

Asher looked into Sunshine's eyes and said, "If only I was born with the magic hand."

"Like Superhuman?" Sunshine asked.

"Yes, like Superhuman." Asher answered.

"What should you do with the magic hand?" Sunshine asked.

"Of course, I should kill the devil named Kalus that the kingdom has as the king." Asher answered.

Sunshine smiled at Asher and said, "It means you should use your magic hand to kill Kalus."

"Yes," Asher answered.

"Superhuman uses his magic hand to save people, and not to kill people," Sunshine said.

"Superhuman uses his magic hand to save people from the devils named Deo Caeli and Hector, and it's exactly what I should do if I had the magic hand because I should save the inhabitants of the kingdom from the devil named Kalus," Asher replied.

Sunshine smiled at Asher and said, "You are right."

Asher looked into Sunshine's eyes and said, "We were not born with the magic hands like the wizards, but at least we can make the magic spells like the wizards."

Sunshine asked, "Why do we need to make magic spells like the wizards."

"To get rid of Kalus," Asher answered.

"How are we going to use the magic spells because we are not wizards," Sunshine asked.

"We must find a way to use them," Asher answered.

Sunshine looked into Asher's eyes and said, "The wizards are people who are a little different from us, the organism of wizards are completely different from our organism because the wizards were born with the magic, and their organism work different from our organism, and it's the reason why the wizard's organism produce the magic spell that the wizards use through their magic hands."

Asher looked at Sunshine with a surprised face and asked, "It seems you know a lot about the culture of wizards."

Sunshine answered, "Yes, I know the tradition and culture of the wizards.

"How did you know that?" Asher asked.

"I read all the books in the saga of Superhuman by Thierry Kouam," Sunshine answered.

"I can not wait to read this series of books of Superhuman by Thierry Kouam," Asher replied.

Sunshine smiled and said, "Do not worry you would read all the books about the saga of Superhuman because we are going to study these books in class like literature."

Asher said, "I am sure, I would love these books."

Sunshine said, "These books are very interesting."

Asher said, "I really love the movies we watched based on these books a few weeks ago in the living room of the palace."

Sunshine said, "Yes, the movies of Superhuman are my favorite movies."

Asher said, "We watched only two movies of Superhuman, which are Superhuman 1: The Magician Boy and the Savior. And Superhuman 2: The Magician Boy and the Magic School of Wizards."

Sunshine said, "There are more than six Superhuman movies of Superhuman."

Asher cried out, "Waoooh." Looking at Sunshine with a surprised face, and he added, "I can not wait to watch all of them"

Sunshine said, "I have no doubt that you would love the rest of these movies."

Asher said, "Of course, I would love the movies of Superhuman, not only because Superhuman is my favorite actor, but mostly because the stories of these movies are great."

Sunshine asked, "What part of the movies of Superhuman 1 and 2 you loved the most?"

Asher answered, "I loved every part of these two movies I watched. But in Superhuman 1, I loved when Superhuman found out that he was a magician who was born with magic, and when he saved Luna who had the energy of his magic to the hospital."

And Asher added, "In Superhuman 2, I loved when Superhuman found out that he was a wizard, and when he arrived in the wizarding world. And mostly I loved when Superhuman was at the magic school of wizards to learn how to use and master his magic, and how to develop his magic, mostly when he faced the obstacles at the magic school of wizards."

Sunshine smiled and said, "You forgot something."

Asher asked, "What?"

Sunshine said, "The expression on the face of Superhuman when he was in his bedroom at the magic school of wizards, and he found out that his enemy Deo Caeli was still alive."

Asher smiled at Sunshine and said, "You are right."

Sunshine asked, "What is the funny part in the movie?"

Asher smiled and said, "In Superhuman 2, the funny part is where Superhuman is unconscious in the hospital bed of the magic school of wizards because he had been injured at this magic hand during the magic practice lesson. And some instructors tried to put Superhuman in the coma because they hated Superhuman. And these instructors wanted Superhuman to be expelled from the magic school because according to the law of the wizarding world and the school rule when a student was in a coma, this student is immediately expelled from the magic school because this student is considered less powerful and weak to continue his education at the magic school. But when these instructors tried to put Superhuman in the coma, these instructors were tortured and injured by Superhuman's magic."

And Asher looked into Sunshine's eyes and said, "If only we had the magic like Superhuman to torture the devil Kalus like Superhuman's magic had tortured the instructors who wanted to put him in a coma."

Sunshine smiled at Asher and asked, "Why you want Kalus to be tortured in same way that Superhuman's magic tortured the instructors who wanted to put Superhuman in a coma."

Asher answered, "Because Kalus deserves the same torture like these instructors because Kalus is mean like these instructors."

Sunshine said, "It's not a bad idea."

Asher said, "Kalus is even worse because he stole our lives and our dreams."

Sunshine looked into Asher's eyes and said, "I agree with you."

Suddenly, Sunshine and Asher were interrupted by David. And David told Sunshine that her mom was still in the emergency room and that the doctors were still waiting for the results of the blood test to know what her mom was suffering from.

Sunshine looked at her papa without saying a word because she knew what her mom was suffering from. Then David asked Sunshine and Asher to follow him, that they were going to have lunch. Then David, Sunshine and Asher walked towards the restaurant of the hospital.

After a few minutes, David, Sunshine and Asher walked into the restaurant of the hospital, and they saw Aaron and Aaron's father who were eating their lunch. And David told Sunshine and Asher that they have to go join Aaron and Aaron's father for lunch.

And Sunshine looked at her father without saying a word and looking at the expression on the face of Sunshine, she was not happy at all to spend her lunch time with Aaron. Then David, Sunshine and Asher walked till the table where Aaron and his father sat. And Aaron's father was happy to welcome David, Sunshine and Asher for lunch.

Except Sunshine who was not eating, the rest of them were eating and they were talking about the situation of the kingdom. One part of their conversation was based on women who were crying their bellies to the hospital, and another part of their conversation was based on the return of education to the kingdom which was in three days.

And during the conversation, Aaron was always rude with Asher. Aaron's father and David were very surprised to see how Aaron was rude with Asher. And Sunshine was not really astonished at how rude Aaron was with Asher, but she was uncomfortable with this situation. And David asked Aaron to change the way he talks to Asher, and to be polite with Asher.

Suddenly, their conversation was interrupted by news on television, and they had all focused their eyes on television and they were watching television with amazed faces. And the news was talking about the speech that would be made by the king at eight o'clock, and the news was asking all inhabitants of the kingdom to watch television at eight o'clock because the king had an important message for the whole kingdom.

Then Sunshine turned her head and looked at Asher with an amazed face, and Asher was looking at Sunshine too with a surprised face. Aaron was looking at Asher and Sunshine who were looking at each other with a face full of anger. David and Aaron's father were looking at Asher, Sunshine and Aaron with smiles on their faces. David and Aaron's dad had the smiles on their faces because they had understood the reason why Aaron was rude with Asher, and they had mostly understood that Aaron was in love with Sunshine.

Then Asher broke the silence and said that he hoped that the devil that the kingdom had like the king would announce the end of the laws of Kalus in the kingdom. And Aaron replied to Asher that the inhabitants of the kingdom were happy with the laws of Kalus, and that these laws of Kalus were a good thing for the kingdom.

And even worse, Aaron said that he would fight for the laws of Kalus to be maintained in the kingdom because people were happy to live according to the laws of Kalus. And although Sunshine knew that Aaron would never agree with Asher. But Sunshine did not expect to hear from Aaron that he agreed with the laws of Kalus.

Then Aaron, Sunshine and Asher started to discuss the laws of Kalus. Sunshine and Asher were sharing the same ideas about the laws of Kalus, and they were completely opposed to the laws of Kalus, while Aaron completely agreed with the laws of Kalus.

Then Aaron started to become violent with the words during the conversation and the fact that Aaron was lacking the ideas to defend the laws of Kalus was making him nervous, and his face was full of rage to see that Sunshine was against him. Aaron's papa and David were trying to calm Aaron by asking Aaron to be calm that it was just a conversation and that he did not need to be impolite when he talked, but Aaron did not listen to them.

Then Aaron did not support the fact that Sunshine always agreed with Asher, and he got up from his chair and left. Sunshine was not really surprised to see Aaron leave the table. Then Sunshine, Asher, David, and Aaron's dad started to have a conversation about the news that they had just watched on television, and they were wondering what news would be announced by Kalus at eight o'clock,.

And they were trying to guess what their king would announce at eight o'clock, and at the same time they were impatient and curious to watch television at eight o'clock, to know what news their king would announce to the inhabitants of the kingdom.

The hours were passing, and Sunshine was still in the hospital and she sat in the chair in a corridor of the hospital. And the doctors had not yet given the results of the blood test about what women who were crying with pain in their bellies were suffering from.

Sunshine was very thoughtful, and she was pensive because she was thinking about the speech that would be made by Kalus in the news at eight o'clock, and she was wondering what Kalus would announce to the kingdom.

And Sunshine was very afraid because she knew that the speech that would be pronounced by Kalus would be a disaster for the kingdom. Mostly that the souls of children who were not yet born were controlled by Lord.

Then Sunshine got up from her chair and she started walking in the hallway of the hospital without even knowing where she was going. And suddenly, the expression on Sunshine's face changed and she was looking at people who were running towards the waiting room of the hospital with an amazed face wondering what was going on. Then Sunshine heard someone say that the speech of the king would start in a few minutes, and she understood that people were running to go watch the speech of the king.

Then Sunshine started to think what to do, and she did not want to watch the speech of Kalus to the hospital, and she started turning her head and looking at the wall, and a clock on the wall grabbed her attention.

And she read 7:45 p.m., and she understood that she had only fifteen minutes to reach her home, if she wanted to watch the speech of the king on television at her home. And she also knew that it was impossible to reach her home in fifteen minutes by driving, and that it would take at least an hour to reach her home by driving.

Then Sunshine started thinking how she could reach her home in less than fifteen minutes, then she got an idea and started running towards the washroom. After a minute, Sunshine opened the door of the toilets and she got in and closed the door behind her. Then Sunshine took two deep breaths and she concentrated on herself and her eyes started spinning. After a few seconds, the light shone into Sunshine's eyes and she disappeared.

After a few minutes, Sunshine appeared in the living room of her house, and she stared at the screen of the television and her eyes started spinning, then the light shone into her eyes and the television turned on, she noticed that it was not the national channel on the television screen.

Then Sunshine focused her eyes on television's screen and her eyes started spinning and the television channel was changing, then her eyes stopped spinning when the national channel appeared on the television screen. Then Sunshine noticed that Kalus had not yet started his speech, and she turned her head and looked at the clock that was on the wall and she read 7:55 p.m.,

Then Sunshine walked till the sofa and sat and she started to watch television by waiting for the speech of the king Kalus. After a few minutes, the expression on the face of Sunshine changed and she was watching Kalus on television who sat in a chair in his palace with an astonished face.

And the first thing that Sunshine noticed about Kalus was his look, and she noticed that Kalus had shaved his beard, and also that his face was full of smiles. Also, that the look of Kalus was completely different compared to the last time that he gave the speech with a desperate look, the long beard and the face full of fatigue and sadness to announce the return of the education to the kingdom.

And Sunshine understood that Kalus was going to announce a very bad news that would be a disaster for the kingdom just by seeing the happiness that was on Kalus's face. Then Kalus opened his mouth and he announced the problem that the kingdom would have in the future, and that the kingdom would be underpopulated in the future if women did not give birth now. Especially since the kingdom had experienced a terrible tragedy in the past where many children had mysteriously lost lives.

And that was the reason why he asked women to get pregnant now because the kingdom needed births, also that the kingdom needed children who would be the future of the kingdom of tomorrow. Also, it was important to give birth now because the population of the kingdom was aging, and there were not really any younger people to replace these aging people. And the number of children who were in the kingdom now was very low, and it was the reason why women must get pregnant now and give birth to save the future of the kingdom.

And immediately, the expression on Sunshine's face changed when she heard Kalus announce that the prenatal visits for pregnant women were free and the childbirth was also free. And Sunshine was watching television with an amazed face as she was listening to Kalus who was talking about the child support for all women who would give birth this year.

And looking at the expression on the face of Sunshine, it was obvious that she did not expect the hospital to be free in the speech of the king. Sunshine was very surprised to watch Kalus on television who was talking about the money that each woman who would give birth would receive at the end of each month to take care of the newborn till when this newborn would be an adult. And Sunshine was completely lost when she heard Kalus say that women would also be paid when they would give birth because each woman who was giving birth now was saving the kingdom.

It was nine o'clock, Kalus had finished his speech. And Sunshine was walking in the living room of her house like a crazy girl, and she had understood the reasons why Kalus had made a speech asking women to get pregnant, and to give birth.

It was because Lord had found a way to mystically possess the souls of babies who were not yet born and who were the womb of their mothers. And that Kalusand Lord wanted more women to get pregnant because they needed children that they would possess their souls, and they needed children who would belong to them, and that they would be able to control and torture, also even kill like in the past.

And even if Sunshine did not expect the king Kalus to make a speech just because he wanted to ask women to give birth, she was not surprised at all about the demand of Kalus. Sunshine was very astonished about the fact that Kalus had announced during his speech that the hospital for pregnant women would be free.

And even the birth of babies would be taken in charge by the kingdom, and even all women who would give birth would receive money each month to take care of babies. And Sunshine understood that if Kalus had decided to pay women who would give birth, it meant that Kalus and Lord really needed children that they would possess their souls.

Because since Kalus had been crowned the king, he had cancelled all free services by charging them, and even worse, he had increased the taxes. And Kalus was well known for his love for the money, and he had even increased the price of all services. And Sunshine realized that if Kalus was really ready to encourage women to give birth by paying them. It meant that Kalus and Lord had a dangerous plan for the kingdom, and children who would be born now would be used for their plan.

Sunshine knew well that Kalus was the worst devil that could exist, and that he did not care about the kingdom and Kalus hated the children. Sunshine also knew well that Kalus was not interested in the welfare of the population of the kingdom. And that the only thing that Kalus cared about and interested in, was his power.

And Sunshine knew that the speech of Kalus would encourage women to get pregnant, and there was nothing she could do to prevent women from getting pregnant. But Sunshine also knew that the only thing she could do was to free the souls of babies who were in the womb of their mothers, to prevent those children who were not yet born to belong to Kalus and Lord when they would be born.

Sunshine was very worried about the souls of children who were not yet born and who were already possessed by Kalus and Lord. And she knew that she must do even the impossible to prevent the children of the kingdom who were not yet born from belonging to Kalus and Lord.

Because Sunshine knew that if children who were not yet born belonged to Kalus and Lord, it meant the future of the kingdom belonged to Kalus and Lord. And Sunshine knew that she was born with the magic and powers to save the kingdom from Kalus and Lord, and that she could not stay and watch Kalus and Lord destroy the kingdom of her ancestors.

The hours were passing, and Sunshine was walking in the living room of her house like a crazy girl and thinking how to free the souls of children who were not yet born. Then the clock on the wall caught her attention, and she read three o'clock. Sunshine turned and ran till her bedroom, and she knelt and started praying, asking God to show her the way to free the souls of children who were not yet born.

It was seven in the morning when the whole kingdom woke up with a smile on their faces. Excluding Sunshine who had not closed her eyes during the whole night, the rest of the inhabitants of the kingdom had spent a good night.

People in the kingdom had spent a great night after they had watched on television the speech of their king about the future of the kingdom and by encouraging women to give birth. And people were very proud of their king, and for them, their king had changed, and their king cared about them and the kingdom.

Except the newspaper called Kongreshow by Remy who had not congratulated the decision of the king Kalus, the rest of the newspapers in the kingdom had congratulated the decision of the king Kalus to encourage women to save the future of the kingdom by giving birth. And people spent their day talking about the decision of the king to pay women who would give birth.

And even in the hospitals, people were talking about the speech of the king to encourage women to give birth, that people were not even talking about women who were crying their bellies. And even the next day, the only conversation of people in the kingdom was about the decision to encourage women to give birth by paying them.

It was the eve of the back of school, and the parents had sent their children to bed early, and it was the first time for children to go to bed early. And the reason why the parents had sent their children to bed earlier than usual, was because children would wake up early to get ready for school. And the parents had spent the day talking to their children about how they were going to behave at school, and mostly to talk to them about new people that they would meet.

It was 1 one in the afternoon, Sunshine was walking in her bedroom like a crazy girl, and she was looking tired and weak. Sunshine was very worried not only about the souls of children who were not yet born, but mostly about the return of the education to the kingdom who was the next day.

And Sunshine was wondering what was going to happen the next day. And if the miracle that would prevent the back to school would happen. Sunshine knew that Lord had a plan to prevent the back to school, but she did not know what this plan was, and mostly that Lord had promised her that a miracle that could prevent the return to school could happen.

Sunshine was still walking in her bedroom, and her heart was beating faster than the normal and she was very afraid, and a lot of ideas were going on in her head. And the main fear of Sunshine was that Lord had a plan to kill children who were going to start school the next day. Then Sunshine walked near to bed, and she laid on the bed with her back and her eyes started spinning. After eleven seconds, the light shone into her eyes and she disappeared.

It was midnight, all the lights were turned off in the houses of the kingdom, and people were deeply sleeping in their beds. There was the moon shining in the sky, it was very cold and there was a violent wind that was blowing. Sunshine was flying in the sky, and the wind was blowing on her face and lifting her hair. Then Sunshine started flying in the space of a river, then a blue light appeared in the sky, and this blue light shone into Sunshine's eyes and she turned into a bird.

Then the bird started flying towards a big stone that was in the middle of the water, and the bird landed on the stone and this bird turned into Sunshine who was knelt on the stone, and she started praying. Sunshine was asking God in her prayer to help her to find out what the plan of Lord was, and to find the house of Lord, and mostly to give her strength to protect the kingdom and its inhabitants.

Suddenly, the waves appeared in the water, and these waves started making noises and the moon that was shining in the sky disappeared, and a rainbow appeared in the sky and the wind stopped blowing. Then the images appeared in the head of Sunshine, and she was seeing through these images a big forest with the big satanic trees, the mirrors on some of those satanic trees, and a big fire and other strange things. But there was a mirror with a red frame that was always appearing in Sunshine's head.

After a few minutes, the waves disappeared and the rainbow disappeared in the sky, then the moon reappeared in the clouds and the wind started blowing. And Sunshine was still praying, but the images had stopped appearing in her head, and a blue light shone in the sky. Then Sunshine opened her eyes and this blue shone into her eyes and she turned into the bird, then she flew through the sky.

Lord was in a huge forest full of big satanic trees and there were mirrors in some trees, and there was also a big fire that was shining in this forest. And Lord stood up and looked in a big mirror that had a red frame called the magic mirror and he was mystically communicating with this magic mirror, and he was seeing the kingdom through this magic mirror.

And Lord's eyes were changing colors as he was looking in this mirror, and he was seeing the kingdom through this mirror. And Lord was seeing people who were sleeping in their beds through this magic mirror.

Then, Lord's eyes started spinning and Sunshine's house appeared in the mirror, and Lord was seeing inside Sunshine's house and all the rooms of Sunshine's house, and there was David who was sleeping in his bed. But Sunshine's bedroom was empty, and Lord tried to find Sunshine in the whole room without success. And Lord was very surprised to not see Sunshine in her bedroom, and he was wondering where Sunshine was. Mostly that Sunshine's father was sleeping.

Then Lord got an idea and his eyes started spinning and the hospital appeared in the mirror, and he started looking for Sunshine in the hospital to know if she was in the hospital with her mom. After a few minutes, the expression on the face of Lord changed and he was looking with a worried face, and he was seeing everyone who was in the hospital, even Sunshine's mom. But Lord was very surprised not to see Sunshine at the hospital, and he was wondering where Sunshine could be.

Then Lord started to breathe deeply as he was feeling a strange smell, and he was wondering where this smell was coming from, and it was the first time that he was feeling this strange smell. Then Lord felt that this smell was becoming stronger, and he also felt that this strange smell was coming from space. Then Lord turned his head and looked through the space and suddenly the expression of his face changed and he was staring with an astonished face as he was seeing Sunshine who was flying in the space.

And Lord understood that the strange smell he felt was coming from Sunshine's body. And there were a lot of questions that were going on in Lord's head, but the main question was how Sunshine had succeeded to find the way to his house, but unfortunately Lord could not answer this question.

Then Sunshine landed near to the fire, and she turned her head and looked at Lord, and Lord was looking at her too, and there was silence between them. Sunshine could see through the expression on the face of Lord that he was very surprised to see her in his house, and she was seeing Lord who was walking through her. Then Lord stopped in front of Sunshine, and they were looking at each other in the eyes, still with the silence.

Then Sunshine turned her head and started looking around, and she was seeing the big satanic trees, and with the mirrors on some of these satanic trees. And she was not really surprised because she had seen these mirrors in her head during her prayer a few hours ago, and Sunshine noticed that all the mirrors had a black frame.

And suddenly, the mirror with a red frame attracted Sunshine's attention, and she noticed that this mirror with the red frame was the mirror that appeared in head many times when she was praying. And a lot of questions were going on in the head of Sunshine, and one of these questions was why there was only one mirror that had a red frame, but unfortunately, she could not answer this question.

Then Sunshine lifted her head through the sky, and noticed that the sky was shining with a yellow color, but she did not see the moon or the stars in the clouds. And she was wondering where this yellow color in the sky was coming from.

Then she turned her head around and noticed that the whole forest was lit with a yellow light, but she was wondering where this yellow light was coming from. Then Sunshine looked at the big fire that was burning in front of her, and the expression on her face changed as she was staring at this fire with an amazed face.

And Sunshine was wondering what was making this fire burn because she was not seeing the woods that were making this fire burn, and the fire was not in contact with the ground. So, the fire was located a little above the ground.

Sunshine also noticed that there was no smoke coming from this fire, and she understood that this fire was not natural, and that this fire was related to Lord's magic. Then Sunshine lifted her head and looked at Lord when she heard him cough. And they were looking each other in the eyes.

"Welcome to hell," Lord said.

"Thank you," Sunshine answered.

"How did you find the way to my house?" Lord asked.

"In the same way you find the way to my house," Sunshine answered.

"You did not answer my question," Lord said.

"I took the same path that you use to come to my house, to come to your house," Sunshine said.

"What are you doing here?" Lord asked.

"I came for the same reasons you came to see me," Sunshine answered.

"It means you came to visit me," Lord said.

"If when you come to my house it is to visit me, know that I have come to your house to visit you," Sunshine replied.

Lord laughed and said, "Sorry that there is no roof in my house to welcome you."

Sunshine smiled at Lord and said, "You do not have to be sorry." Sunshine added, "Do not forget that I have always welcomed you in the yard of my house, and we always talked outside when you came to visit me."

"I thought you should be asleep now," Lord said.

"I thought, I should find you asleep too," Sunshine retorted.

"A god does not sleep," Lord said.

"Why don't you sleep?" Sunshine asked.

"Because I watch over my people," Lord answered.

"Who are these people?" Sunshine asked.

"The inhabitants of the kingdom," Lord answered.

"The inhabitants of the kingdom?" Sunshine asked.

"Of course, except you," Lord said.

"I am glad to know that I am not one of your children," Sunshine said.

"Do not worry, I do not want you to be my child," Lord said.

Sunshine looked into Lord's eyes and said, "Children of the kingdom are not your people."

"Of course, they are my people!" Lord retorted.

Sunshine looked into Lord's eyes with a face full of anger and said, "A child of this kingdom would never be yours and would never belong to you."

Lord burst into laughter and looked into Sunshine's eyes with a face full of smiles and said, "I would answer this question another day."

"Why not now?" Sunshine asked.

Lord looked into Sunshine's eyes and said, "I promise you to answer your question during our next meeting." And Lord added, "You should return to your home now."

"Why do I need to return to my home now?" Sunshine asked.

Lord smiled and said, "Today, it is a great day, a memorable day in the kingdom."

"Why is it memorable?" Sunshine asked.

"Do not forget that today it's the return of education to the kingdom," Lord answered.

"Do not forget that you promise a miracle that could happen, and this miracle could prevent children from going to school," Sunshine said.

Lord smiled and started walking around the fire and said, "I understand now why you are here."

Sunshine turned her head and looked at Lord and said, "I'm curious to know the miracle that would happen."

Lord turned her head and looked at Sunshine and said, "Do not waste your time."

Sunshine started walking around and looked at Lord and asked, "What do you mean by not wasting your time?"

Lord turned his head and stared at Sunshine and they were staring at each other, and Lord said, "You could not prevent this miracle from happening."

Sunshine asked, "It means that children would not start school today?"

Lord looked into Sunshine's eyes and said, "Not only today."

Sunshine asked, "What do you mean by not only today?"

Lord smiled at Sunshine and said, "It means never."

"It means children of this kingdom would never have access to education," Sunshine said.

"You understand very well and quickly," Lord said.

Sunshine stared at Lord with a face full of anger, and said, "Children of this kingdom would go to school."

"I am the one who rules the kingdom," Lord said.

"You are nobody in this kingdom to decide if children would go to school or not," Sunshine said.

"What you did not understand in the words that I am the one who rules this kingdom?" Lord asked.

Sunshine looked into Lord's eyes and said, "You run only Kalu's life, and not the kingdom."

Lord laughed and said, "I thought you were smart."

"I am not?" Sunshine asked.

"No, you are not," Lord retorted.

"Please, can you explain to me what I did not understand?" Sunshine asked.

Lord stopped walking and looked at Sunshine and said, "You just said I run Kalus's life."

"Yes, I said it," Sunshine retorted.

"Who is Kalus?" Lord asked.

"Kalus is the king of the kingdom," Sunshine answered.

"If I run Kalus's life, and if Kalus is the king of the kingdom, it means that I am the one who runs the kingdom," Lord said.

Sunshine looked into Lord's eyes and said, "I do not care if you run Kalus's life, but you would never run this kingdom because this kingdom did not belong to Kalus."

Lord smiled at Sunshine and said, "Things would be easy for you and me if you understand that I am the one who rules this kingdom."

"Stop dreaming because you would never run this kingdom," Sunshine said.

"You have to prove to me that I am not the one who runs this kingdom!" Lord retorted.

"How?" Sunshine asked.

Lord looked into Sunshine's eyes and said, "Prevent the miracle that would occur and give children access to education."

"What is this miracle?" Sunshine asked.

"If you are really powerful and if you are really born with the magic to protect and save this kingdom, prove it now and find this miracle by yourself and mostly prevent it from occurring because in a few hours the kingdom would be a graveyard," Lord said.

"What do you mean by "the kingdom would be a graveyard in a few hours?" Sunshine asked.

Lord looked into Sunshine's eyes and said, "It means, all children who are going to school would die at six in the morning,"

"That's impossible," Sunshine said.

"You would cry the deaths of your fellows at six in the morning," Lord said.

"You can not kill my fellows because you did not control their souls because to kill them, you must control their souls first." Sunshine said.

"It's true that I can not mystically kill your fellows because I do not have the control of their souls, but I cause an accident where they can die in this accident if they are not lucky," Lord retorted.

"I do not believe you," Sunshine said.

Lord looked into Sunshine eyes and said, "I promise you that you would cry at six in the morning, and maybe all children would die in this terrible accident, may be all children would not die in this horrible accident and may be some would die and others not, but for sure that an accident would happen."

Then Sunshine continued walking around the fire with her eyes focused on Lord without saying a word, but her mind was full of thoughts, and she was thinking about the words of Lord. Sunshine was wondering if Lord was really able to cause an accident, and she knew well that although the fact that Lord did not control the souls of children, Lord was powerful enough to cause the horrible things. And Sunshine mostly knew that Lord had done everything that he had promised her to do.

Sunshine was still walking by thinking and her heart was beating faster than the normal, and her face was full of fear. And Sunshine was very afraid and she knew well that she must stop this accident that Lord was going to cause before it happens. Sunshine also knew that she had not enough time to prevent this accident from happening, but she also knew that she must do the impossible to protect children by preventing this accident from happening.

Then Sunshine turned her head and looked around and she was staring at the mirrors that were on the trees, and the expression of her face suddenly changed when a mirror with a red frame caught her attention.

And she was staring at this mirror with attention, and she remembered that this mirror always appeared in her head when she was praying. Sunshine mostly noticed that there was only one mirror that had a red frame and the rest of mirrors had the black frames. And Sunshine was wondering why among all these mirrors, there was only a mirror that had a red frame.

And Sunshine turned her head and looked at Lord, and she noticed that Lord was staring at her, and she understood that he was watching her. And Sunshine wanted to ask him why there was only a mirror with a red frame while the rest of mirrors had the black frames.

But Sunshine changed her mind, and she decided not to ask Lord this question because she knew that he would never answer this question. But she knew that there was a reason why there was only a mirror that had a red frame, and she mostly knew that Lord was watching her because he did not want her to find out the secret of this mirror with the red frame.

Then Sunshine got an idea, and she turned and started walking towards this mirror with the red frame, but she was stopped by Lord who asked her to not approach this mirror with the red frame. And Sunshine asked Lord why she could not approach this mirror with a red frame? And Lord answered Sunshine that it was a secret. Then Sunshine looked at Lord without saying a word, and Lord's answer confirmed her thoughts, and she mostly understood that she must do everything to look in this mirror.

Then Sunshine started thinking how to distract Lord and to look in this mirror with the red frame. And after a few minutes of thinking, Sunshine got an idea, and she turned around by showing her back to Lord. Sunshine closed her eyes and she took two deep breaths and concentrated on herself, then she opened her mouth and a white vapor got out from her mouth and went through the sky.

Then Sunshine closed her mouth and turned and stared at Lord who was staring at her too. And Sunshine understood that Lord had not taken his eyes off her. But Sunshine was not surprised at all to see that Lord's eyes were still focused on because Lord was watching her to make sure that she would not look in this mirror with the red frame.

Suddenly, Lord started hitting his ears to chase away the bees that made the noises in his ears. And Lord was very amazed to see the bees in his house, and it was his first time to see these bees. But it was Sunshine who had used her magic to call these bees, and it was the white vapor that had got out from Sunshine's mouth that had called these bees. And Sunshine had called these bees to distract Lord so that Sunshine looks in the mirror.

Sunshine was staring at Lord who was trying to chase the bees on him without success, then Sunshine's eyes started spinning. Suddenly, Lord started screaming because he was stung by the bees. And the smile appeared on Sunshine's face as she was using her magic to trick the bees into stinging Lord, and she loved watching Lord screaming in pain because he was stung by bees. Then Lord started running away by trying to get rid of the bees that were on him.

And Sunshine started walking towards the mirror that had a red frame as she was no longer watched by Lord. Then Sunshine stopped in front of this mirror with a red frame and looked in this mirror, but she saw nothing in the mirror except herself who was in the mirror. Then she got an idea, and her eyes started spinning and her portrait disappeared in the mirror.

And suddenly the expression on her face changed, and she was looking in the mirror with a surprised face as she was seeing the kingdom in the mirror. And she understood that Lord was controlling the kingdom through this mirror, and that he was aware of everything that was happening in the kingdom through this mirror. And she mostly understood that Lord would cause the accident that he had planned through this mirror.

Then Sunshine understood that she must destroy this mirror before Lord came back, and she took a deep breath and concentrated on herself. Then Sunshine's eyes started spinning faster than normal, and the light got out from her eyes and shone on the mirror. After a few minutes, the light was still getting out from Sunshine's eyes and shining on the mirror, and Sunshine had started to sweat.

Sunshine was losing a lot of energy that she had difficulty breathing and she was looking tired. Then Sunshine started shaking, and she was shaking not only because she was weak, but mostly because the mirror that she was trying to destroy was more powerful than her, and the power of this mirror was having effects on her.

After a few minutes, the light was still getting out from Sunshine's eyes and shining on the mirror, and the mirror started trembling. Then Sunshine started feeling the violent headaches and the mirror started breaking down. After thirteen minutes, Sunshine had finished destroying this mirror. Sunshine was feeling very tired and she understood that she must leave before Lord comes back, and her eyes started spinning, then she flew in space.

Then Lord arrived and suddenly the expression of his face changed when he noticed his magic mirror was destroyed by Sunshine, and he was staring at his magic mirror with a face full of anger. Then Lord opened his mouth and pushed a louder scream in anger, and his eyes started spinning and he flew through the space.

Sunshine was in space flying above the satanic trees, and she had difficulty flying not only because she was tired, but mostly because the satanic trees were preventing her from flying faster. Because the satanic trees had the energies that prevented Sunshine from using her magic to fly faster. And there was Lord who was flying faster after Sunshine.

After a few minutes, Sunshine felt a strange energy and she turned her head and looked around. And suddenly the expression on her face changed when she saw Lord who was flying near to her, and she was looking at him with fear on her face.

Sunshine could see the rage on the face of Lord, and she understood that she must do something to get rid of Lord, or she would be killed by Lord. Then Sunshine tried to disappear without success, and she understood that the fact that she was flying above the satanic trees was making her weak and unable to use her magic well. And Sunshine was thinking what to do.

Sunshine was looking around and she was trying to find a space that was not in contact with the satanic trees, but unfortunately for her, all the spaces were full in contact with the satanic trees. Suddenly, Sunshine felt a hand on her back, and she understood that it was Lord who was trying to grab her. Sunshine tried to fly faster, but unfortunately it was impossible because the satanic trees were preventing her from using the full potential of her magic and strengths.

And suddenly, Sunshine was pushed by Lord and she went and hit her back against a satanic tree, and she grabbed a tree branch to not fall on the ground, then she flew away, and she was trying to fly faster as she could to run away from Lord. But unfortunately,

Sunshine's hand was grabbed by Lord, and she was still trying to fly away while Lord was pulling her towards him.

Sunshine had almost lost all her strength and she was flying very slowly because she had lost her balance because she was being pulled by lord. And it was very hard for Sunshine to fly because she did not have the balance and her body was being pulled by Lord and she was trying to fight to remove Lord's hand from her hand.

After a few minutes, Lord had succeeded to pull Sunshine till him, and Lord was trying to grab Sunshine in his arms to kill her easily and Sunshine was trying to fight to push Lord with all her strength to prevent him from grabbing her in his arms. Sunshine and Lord were turning in space by fighting, but Sunshine was very weak, despite the fact that she was trying to fight to prevent Lord from taking her in his arms.

And Sunshine knew well that Lord wanted to grab her in his arms to kill her because he had an advantage on her, as he could use the full potential of his magic. Because Lord's magic was linked with the satanic trees, and she could not use the full potential of her magic because these satanic trees prevented her from using the full potential of her magic.

Lord and Sunshine were standing up in the space, and they were blowing away by a strange wind in an unknown direction, but they were not feeling this wind hitting their bodies. And they were not also feeling this wind on their faces.

And Lord had grabbed Sunshine's neck with his both hands and he was trying to kill her by squeezing her neck with all his strength, and Sunshine had grabbed Lord's hands who were on her neck and she was trying to remove Lord's hands from her neck. And they were looking at each other in the eyes, and Lord's face was full of rage while Sunshine's face was full of fear. And Sunshine was having trouble breathing because she was choking by Lord.

Sunshine understood that she was not strong enough to remove Lord's hands from her neck, but she mostly understood that she must do even the impossible to remove Lord's hands from her neck or Lord would kill her, mostly that she was already dying.

Then Sunshine removed her hands from Lord's hands, and she lifted her fingers through her eyes and she stared at her fingers and her eyes started spinning, then the light shone into her eyes and her fingernails became long. And Lord was so focused on squeezing Sunshine's neck that he was not paying attention to what was going on, and what Sunshine was doing.

Suddenly, Lord pushed a loud scream in pain, and he removed his hands from Sunshine's neck, and he was bleeding from his hands, and he was looking at Sunshine with a face full of anger because she had used her fingernails to tear his skin. Then Lord grabbed Sunshine's hand and he pulled her till him, and she was trying to defend herself from Lord. Then Lord had grabbed the two hands of Sunshine to prevent her from using her long fingernails to tear his skin.

And the wind was still directing Sunshine and Lord from an unknown direction, and they were so focused on the fight that they were not paying attention to the strange wind that was directing them. Sunshine was still trying to defend herself from Lord without success because her two hands had been grabbed by Lord.

And Sunshine could not use her feet to fight because she was suspended in the air. And Lord was thinking how to kill Sunshine, and it was not easy for Lord to find a way to kill Sunshine because he had used his two hands to grab Sunshine's hands. And he was suspended in the air, so he could not use another part of his body like his feet against Sunshine. Sunshine and Lord were looking at each other in the eyes without saying a word.

Then Lord broke the silence and said, "You would regret what you did."

"I did nothing," Sunshine replied.

"You destroyed my magic mirror," Lord said.

"I did what I was supposed to do," Sunshine retorted.

"You have no idea about the damages you caused by destroying this magic mirror," Lord said.

"I did not cause any damage by destroying this mirror," Sunshine said.

"You destroyed my magic mirror that I used to control the kingdom," Lord said.

"You should cause this accident through this magic mirror?" Sunshine asked.

"Yes, I should use this magic mirror to cause this accident at six in the morning," Lord answered.

"How were you going to cause this accident through your magic mirror?" Sunshine asked.

"I should mystically put poison in the bodies of all children who were going to school today to prevent them from going to school," Lord answered.

"How were you going to put the poison in children's bodies?"

"I should mystically put the poison in children's bodies by biting them through my magic mirror at six in the morning, to prevent them from going to school," Lord answered.

"It means you lost the control of the kingdom because your magic mirror had been destroyed," Sunshine said.

"Not really," Lord said.

"What do you mean?" Sunshine asked.

"Do not forget that I am still controlling the souls of children who were not yet born," Lord replied.

"What is important now is that children go to school today," Sunshine said.

Lord smiled at Sunshine and said, "It's true that you destroyed my magic mirror but children will not go to school."

"Why would children not go to school If you could not cause your accident to stop them from going to school anymore?" Sunshine asked.

"Because I am going to kill you now?" Lord answered.

"Even with my death, children will go to school," Sunshine said.

Lord looked into Sunshine's eyes and said, "You know well that you are the one who protects children in this kingdom, so your death would only give the path to the king Kalus to kill all children who had protested with you about the return of education to the kingdom."

Sunshine looked at Lord without saying a word, and she knew well that Lord was right because without her, children could not fight the king Kalus, and even worse children would be killed by Kalus. Sunshine understood that she must not only fight to prevent Lord from killing her, but she must do the impossible to survive not only for her, but mostly to protect the kingdom, to protect her fellows and to save the souls of children who were not yet born.

Suddenly, the expression of the faces of Lord and Sunshine changed as they were feeling a fresh air that was blowing on their faces and they were also feeling a strange feeling inside them. And Sunshine was mostly feeling that she was recovering her strengths, while Lord was feeling that he was losing his strengths. Then Sunshine turned her head and looked around and she understood that she was outside of Lord's house as she was no longer seeing the satanic trees.

Sunshine mostly understood that she was recovering her strengths because her magic was no longer in contact with the satanic trees, and she was very glad because she could now use the full potential of her magic to fight Lord. Then Lord lifted his head and looked at the sky and he saw the moon that was shining in the cloud, and he understood that he was out of his house.

And he also understood that he was out of the territory of the satanic trees, and that it was the reason why he was losing his strengths. And he mostly understood that he had lost the advantage that he had on Sunshine because his magic was no longer in contact with the satanic trees. But Lord mostly knew that there was something mysterious happening.

Then Lord looked into Sunshine's eyes and said, "Who else is here?"

"Nobody," Sunshine answered.

"Someone else is here," Lord retorted.

"Are you crazy?" Sunshine asked.

"Can you not see what is going on?" Lord asked.

"What are you talking about?" Sunshine asked.

Lord looked into Sunshine's eyes and said, "Use your brain for the first time in your life."

"Can you tell exactly what is going on?" Sunshine asked.

"Ask yourself how we got here," Lord said.

"We got here by flying," Sunshine replied.

"No, we did not fly to get here," Lord said.

"How did we get here if we did not fly?" Sunshine asked.

"The wind has led us till here," Lord answered.

"It's the same thing because that means that we used our magic to fly in the air," Sunshine said.

Lord looked into Sunshine's eyes and said, "The wind that took us here was not a natural wind."

"I do not understand," Sunshine said.

"Did you feel the wind blow on you when we were flying in the space of the satanic trees?" Lord asked.

Sunshine looked into Lord's eyes and answered, "No, I did not feel the wind blowing on me when we were in space where there were the satanic trees." And Sunshine asked, "I started feeling the wind blowing on my face when we were out of the space where there were the satanic trees."

"I have another enemy," Lord said.

"Who?" Sunshine asked.

Lord looked into Sunshine's eyes and said, "I do not yet know who that enemy is, but the only thing I know it's that this enemy is working to help you."

"To help me?" Sunshine cried out.

"It's this enemy who helped you to get out of the space of the satanic trees," Lord said.

"I do not understand," Sunshine said.

"It's this mysterious enemy who has controlled our magic by making us fly till outside of the space of the satanic trees to help you recover the full potential of your magic and all your strengths to fight me," Lord said.

"Why did this mysterious enemy help me?" Sunshine asked.

"It's obvious that this mysterious enemy wants to protect this kingdom like you," Lord answered.

"I am glad to know that I am not alone," Sunshine said.

"But it's too late." Lord said.

"What do you mean? Sunshine asked.

"I mean, this mysterious enemy can not really protect you because I am going to kill you now," Lord answered.

Suddenly, the expression on Sunshine's face changed and she was looking at Lord with a surprised face, like Lord had widely opened his mouth and he was screaming, and she was wondering what was going on with him. And suddenly, the surprise that was on Sunshine's face turned into fear when she saw a black smoke that was getting out from Lord's mouth.

Then Sunshine started coughing because this black smoke was coming on her face and she was breathing this black smoke. And Sunshine was trying to defend herself without success, and she was feeling weak because this black smoke she was breathing was making her weak.

Lord had grabbed Sunshine to prevent her from flying away, while Sunshine was trying to use her magic to fly away without success because this black smoke was making her cough and it was hard for her to focus on herself to use her magic.

Then the terror appeared on Sunshine's face when she saw Lord who had removed his tongue from his mouth and there was a long venom on his tongue that looked like the snake venom. And Lord was trying to bite Sunshine's neck with this venom on his tongue, while Sunshine was trying to defend herself. And despite the fact that Sunshine was feeling weak, she was trying to defend herself to prevent Lord from beating her.

Suddenly, Sunshine pushed a loud scream in pain, and she was bleeding from her right wrist because she had been bitten by Lord's venom on her right wrist during the fight. And Sunshine's face was full of rage, and although the fact was feeling pain, she was determined to kill Lord. Then Sunshine succeeded in removing Lord's left hand from her hand, and she tore Lord's skin with her long fingernails, and Lord yelled in pain and removed his other from Sunshine.

And Lord's eyes were focused on his left hand where Sunshine had scratched him by using her fingernails. And Lord was looking at the blood that was flowing on his hand with a face full of anger.

Then Lord lifted his head and suddenly the expression of his face changed, and he was looking with an astonished face as he was not seeing Sunshine, and he was wondering where she was. Then Lord turned his head around and saw Sunshine who was flying away. Then the light shone into Lord's eyes and he disappeared.

It was five in the morning, Sunshine was in the kitchen of her house, and she was making the bandage on her wound that was on her wrist, and Sunshine was looking tired and weak. And she was also feeling pain in her whole body, and she knew that there was poison in her body because she had been bitten by Lord's venom.

And she knew that this venom that Lord had used to bite her was a poison. But Sunshine was not really thinking about the poison that was in her body, and she was instead thinking about the mysterious enemy that Lord had talked about.

And she was wondering who this mysterious enemy was? But unfortunately, she could not answer this question. After a few minutes, Sunshine had finished making the bandage on her wound, and she walked till her bedroom. And she laid in her bed and covered her body with the blanket.

Sunshine was trying to think about the conversation she had with Lord about the mysterious enemy, but she was too weak to think, and she was feeling a strange reaction in her body. And Sunshine understood that his strange reaction in her body was the poison coming from Lord's venom that had started having effects on her. Then Sunshine closed her eyes and fell asleep.

It was six in the morning, and David was walking towards Sunshine's bedroom while singing. Then he arrived at Sunshine's door and he grabbed the door's handle and opened the door, and he walked in the room still singing with his face full of smiles. And David was singing by walking through the bed and he was staring at Sunshine who was deeply asleep in her bed with the blanket on her. Then David put his knee on the bed, and he started singing that it was time to wake up and get ready for school.

After a few minutes, David was still singing to wake up his daughter, but Sunshine had still her eyes closed, and it seemed that she was not listening to her papa sing. And David was very surprised to see Sunshine asleep at this time, mostly with the noises that he was making because she usually woke up early before six in the morning,

Then David started calling Sunshine's name with a soft voice by saying to Sunshine that today was a great day because today was the return of education to the kingdom. And that she could not miss her first day of school, or even be late for her first day of school, mostly that it would be her first time to go to school. And that it was time to wake up and get ready for school. But unfortunately for David, Sunshine did not open her eyes despite his sweet words to wake her up.

Then David started shaking his daughter to wake her up without success. And the expression on David's face was full of worry and he was worried about the fact that Sunshine was not opening her eyes. Then David pulled the blanket that was on Sunshine, and suddenly the expression of his face changed, and he was staring at his daughter with a face full of fear as he was seeing a bandage on Sunshine's wrist.

Then David started shaking his daughter by calling her with a voice full of fear. After a few seconds, Sunshine had still not opened her eyes and David put his hand on Sunshine's heart and the tears started flowing down his cheeks as he had felt that Sunshine's heart was no longer beating. Then David carried Sunshine in his arms and rushed towards the door by going to the hospital.

It was the joy in the houses of the kingdom, and for the first time, children had gotten out of the bed before 6:11 a.m., and the parents had helped some of their children to bathe and dress. And children were very eager to go to school, and they were very happy to start school for the first time in their story.

And there were a lot of questions that were going on in the head of children like who would they meet at school? What would they study at school? Who would be their instructors? And other questions. But unfortunately for children, they could not answer any of these questions.

It was seven in the morning, it was a little cold outside and the sun had not yet come out. And the streets of the kingdom were full of parents and children. And some parents had held the hand of their children, and the parents were taking their children to school for the first time. And it was a memorable day for the parents, not only because it was the first time to take their children to school, but because they had never thought to take their children to school one day.

And since education had been banned in the kingdom by Kalus, the parents had never dreamed of taking their children to school one day. And even after the king had announced the return of education to the kingdom, the parents had doubts about seeing their children go to school.

And there was happiness on the parent's faces, while the children's faces were full of worry, and the children were worried because they were a little afraid, mostly that it was their first time to go to school. And some children were still sleepy because they had woken up earlier than usual. And children were astonished to see in the streets other parents who were taking their children to school.

It was seven thirty in the morning, and the first students arrived at school and they were very surprised to see that the school's gate was still closed. And they looked around, and there was no instructor, and they did not understand what was going on because the school's director had announced in the news that the school would be opened at six thirty.

And they were wondering if they were in the right place, then they looked at the school's building and noticed that it was exactly the building they had watched on television. And the parents who had come with children told the children that they were in the right place, that the building in front of them was the school.

After a few minutes, the entrance of the school was full of the parents and children, and the gate was still closed and there was no instructor. And the parents and their children were coming more and more, and the children who were arriving were very amazed to see that the school's gate was not opened. And the children were not understanding what was going on and they were not understanding why the school's gate was still closed, and mostly that there was no instructor.

And some parents were very astonished to see that the school's gate was still closed and mostly that there was no instructor, while other parents were not surprised at all to see that the school's gate was closed. And that there was no instructor around. And these parents were not amazed to see the school's gate closed because they had already understood that the king Kalus had lied to them.

And although the fact that the parents were disappointed to know that their children were not going to start school like Kalus had promised them, they were not really surprised because they were expecting it to happen. Because they knew well that Kalus was not someone that they could trust.

It was eight in the morning, and other than Sunshine, who was not at the entrance of the school, the rest of the children were at the entrance of the school wondering what was going on and wondering why the school's gate was not yet opened. And why the school's director and other instructors were not there.

And it was very hard for children to notice that their king had lied to them, and they were not only disappointed but they were also very angry and sad. And the day that was supposed to be a memorable day for children had become their worst day.

Around thirty minutes after eight in the morning, the school's gate was still closed and no instructor had come, and the only person who had arrived was the journalist called J.P Remy to do a report on the situation that was going on. And the hope that was inside some parents of seeing the school's gate open and seeing their children walk towards the gate to go into the classrooms was gone.

And these parents had understood that their king had not only lied to them, but that the king had also lied to their children, even worse the king had played with their children. The faces of the parents and children were full of rage, and they were desperate that they did not know what to do.

It was nine in the morning, the sun was shining. The parents and children were in the sun at the entrance of the school, and they no longer expected to see an instructor or to see the school's gate open. And children were turning their heads looking around them, and they were surprised to see that there were many children.

And they were astonished to notice that the kingdom was populated by many children. And they were more astonished at the number of children who wanted to go to school but who could not go because their king had decided to ban education in the kingdom.

Sunshine's friends were wondering where she was, and they did not understand why Sunshine was not at school, and it was very strange for them. Mostly that they were with Sunshine yesterday and they had decided to meet today at school. And they knew that there was something going wrong with Sunshine, and they were very worried about Sunshine.

Asher, Mia, Ari, Isac and Nany were grouped together, and they were talking. And Asher was very angry and he was talking to his friends that they must go to the palace to fight for their rights, that they could not abandon their destiny to this devil named Kalus.

And Nany told Asher that they must find Sunshine first, that they could not go to the palace without Sunshine. And Asher replied to Nany that they did not have time to go to Sunshine's house, that they must go to the palace first to ask Kalus for explanations for the reasons why the school had not been opened.

Then Asher noticed some children who were leaving with their parents and he screamed at them by asking them not to leave, that they were going to the palace to fight for their dream, that they could not let their dream in the hands of this devil named Kalus.

And all the eyes were focused on Asher, and everyone was listening to him with attention. And Asher went on and said that they could not abandon their lives in the hands of this devil named Kalus, that the monster Kalus was nobody to control their destiny, and that they would not only fight for them, but they would also fight to save the kingdom.

Because the devil that the kingdom had as the king was not only destroying the kingdom. But this devil was also destroying their lives, the lives of their little brothers and sisters and the lives of the future generation of children of the kingdom.

Because this devil had already stolen one part of their dream, and that they must fight not only for the rest of their dream. But they must fight for the dream of their little siblings and the future generation of the kingdom.

Suddenly Asher was interrupted by the applause of a young girl with blue eyes and long gray hair named Khloe, and most children and parents followed Khloe by clapping their hands. Then Asher opened his mouth and screamed, "Education or death." And most of the children followed Asher and they started yelling, "Education or death." And the parents were very amazed to see the motivation that children had, and some parents had smiles on their faces, while other parents had the faces full of dread.

Then Asher continued his speech by using the words like devil, monster, lucifer to describe the king, and Asher even asked children to stop praying in the name of Kalus. Because Kalus was not a god but instead a monster who had stolen their dream, their lives and who had killed the kingdom.

And that this cursed devil named Kalus was not their king because they did not recognize this monster of Kalus like their king, and for that they had the duties and rights to not obey Kalus. And that they mostly had the duties and rights to break the laws of Kalus because these laws of Kalus were established by Kalus to prohibit the education in the kingdom and to prohibit the tradition, the religion and other things.

The parents and children were listening to Asher with attention, and the children were very surprised by the way Asher was talking about their king. And children were realizing that they had grown up in the lies, and that Kalus who was introduced to them like the father of the kingdom and like a god was instead a devil who had destroyed their lives.

And the parents were very astonished by the courage of Asher to describe the king Kalus like a devil, and the parents were also wondering how Asher was aware of things that had happened in the kingdom before he was born.

Then Asher was interrupted by one of the parents who tried to calm him and convince him that Kalus was a great king for the kingdom. But this parent was also interrupted by Khloe, and Khloe said that Asher was right because Kalus was worse than a devil, and that Kalus deserved the hanging because Kalus had stolen their lives, their dreams, and their future.

And Khloe added that it was time to fight for their destiny and to save the kingdom and that she was ready to die. Then Khloe yelled, "Education or death." And children followed Khloe by screaming, "Education or death."

Asher was staring at Khloe with a face full of smiles, and he was very amazed by her courage, and at the same time he admired her courage and determination to fight the devil Kalus. And Aaron was leaning on a pole alone, and he had not said a word since he had come, and Nany had tried to talk to him without success.

Then Asher, Mia, Nany, Isac, Khloe and other children decided to go to the palace. But most of the parents tried to convince children not to go to the palace without success. And children were determined to go to the palace to confront Kalus.

And some parents even forbade their children to go to the palace, but their children refused to obey them by saying that they were going to fight for their dream, their freedom and their future. Then Asher started walking towards the palace and he was followed by the rest of the children, and they were all singing, "Education or death." And Aaron was the only child who had not followed Asher. Nany and Mia had tried to convince Aaron to follow them, but he had refused. And Aaron had decided to go home.

The parents were watching with faces full of fear for their children who were walking in the direction of the palace. And the parents were afraid that their children could be killed by Kalus. And the parents wanted to follow their children, but their children refused by saying that it was only the fight of children and not the fight of the parents.

Sunshine was lying in the hospital bed and she was in a coma, and she was breathing through the oxygen mask that had been put on her. And it was the poison that was in Sunshine's body who had put her in the coma. And this poison was coming from Lord's venom like Lord had used his venom early this morning to bite her during their fight.

And despite the fact that Sunshine was in the coma, she knew what was going on through her magic, and she was very angry at Kalus. Because Kalus had lied to them, and he had not kept his promise to open the school as they had agreed and she was determined to make him pay for his betrayal.

And Sunshine was very disappointed with Aaron who had refused to follow Asher and other children. And Sunshine knew well that Aaron did not follow other children because it was Asher who was the leader of these children. Sunshine knew that the jealousy of Aaron was making him blind that he even forgot that they were all fighting for the same cause, that was the return of education to the kingdom.

Sunshine was very proud of Asher who was walking towards the palace with other children to ask the king for an explanation as to why the school was not opened. But at the same time, Sunshine was worried about Asher and other children who were walking in the direction of the palace because she knew that Kalus could send his army to kill them. And that Kalus would not hesitate to hurt these children who were walking towards the palace, mostly that she was not there to protect her friends. And Sunshine was thinking what to do.

Sunshine's parents were in the room, and they were staring at Sunshine who was in a coma lying in the hospital bed with fear on their faces. And they were wondering what had happened to Sunshine because they did not know what had happened to Sunshine like David had found her early this morning in her bedroom in the coma. And Sarah had left her hospital bedroom to come look after Sunshine, and she was very angry with her husband because if their daughter was in a coma, it was because he had not taken care of their daughter.

Then Sarah and David turned their heads through the door when they heard noises coming from this door. And suddenly the expression on their faces changed, and they were staring at Aaron with surprised faces who was walking in the room.

And David asked Aaron why Aaron was not in class? Aaron answered to David that the school's gate was not opened, and there was no instructor at school. David asked Aaron what it meant by there was no instructor at school? Aaron looked into David's eyes and said that the king Kalus had lied to them.

David cried out, "What?" With an astonished face he turned his head and looked at Sarah with his mouth open but no word was coming out from his mouth. David and Sarah were looking at each other. And looking at the expression on Sarah's face, she was not really surprised to hear that Kalus had lied to children.

Then Sarah broke the silence and told her husband that she was not surprised at all to hear that Kalus had lied to children because she already knew which devil Kalus was. And David replied to his wife that Asher and Sunshine were right to call Kalus a devil because Kalus was human without a heart.

Then David asked Aaron how Aaron knew that Sunshine was in the hospital? And Aaron answered David that he did not see Sunshine at school and he went to Sunshine's house and the neighbours told him that Sunshine was taken to the hospital early this morning.

David replied to Aaron that Sunshine was not at school because she was sick. Then David asked Aaron where Asher and other people were? Aaron answered David that they went to the palace to ask for explanations as to why the school was not opened.

David asked Aaron why he was not at the palace with his friends? Aaron looked at David without saying a word, and there was silence in the room. And David understood the reasons why Aaron was silent and why Aaron did not go to the palace. Then David looked into Aaron's eyes and told Aaron that Asher was not Aaron's enemy but instead Aaron's brother, and that Aaron must stop seeing Asher like his enemy because their enemy was the king Kalus who prohibited education in the kingdom.

And David went on and told Aaron that Aaron should not be in the hospital's room, but instead at the palace with his brothers and sisters to protest for their right to education. And that Aaron should abandon the rage he had against Asher and put this rage against the king Kalus.

David continued and told Aaron that if Aaron wanted to win Sunshine's heart, Aaron must stop acting like a child and behave like a man, and for that Aaron must stop focusing his energy on fighting Asher. Because Asher was not the problem of the kingdom, but Asher was fighting to solve the problem that was in the kingdom. And that the only problem of the kingdom was the king Kalus.

Then David took a deep breath and looked at Aaron and said that if Sunshine was not in the hospital's bed, she should be at the palace now to fight for the return of the education to the kingdom. Because the access to knowledge to the kingdom was the only thing that mattered for Sunshine now, and that she was ready to die for that. Then David looked into Aaron's eyes and said that when Sunshine would open her eyes, she would be happy to hear that Aaron was at the palace to fight for the return of education to the kingdom.

Suddenly, David was interrupted by Aaron, and Aaron looked into David and thanked David for his words, and that he was going to the palace to fight not only for his dream, but for the dream of all children of the kingdom, even for the future generation. Then Aaron turned and left the room before David opened his mouth to say a word.

Then Sarah and David turned their heads from behind when they heard the noises coming from behind, and suddenly the expression of their faces changed, and they were looking at the amazed faces at Sunshine who was looking at them too.

David and Sarah were surprised because the oxygen mask that was on Sunshine was removed, and they were wondering who had removed this oxygen mask on their daughter, mostly that a doctor or a nurse had not got in the room.

Then David asked Sunshine who had removed her oxygen mask? Sunshine answered her papa that she was the one who had removed her oxygen mask. David cried out, "What?" Looking at Sunshine with an astonished face and with the mouth opened. Then David turned his head and looked at Sarah, and Sarah was looking at her husband too, and looking at their expressionless faces, they did not believe that Sunshine had removed the oxygen mask on her.

Then David turned his head and looked at Sunshine, and he asked Sunshine why she had removed her oxygen mask? Sunshine answered her father that she was doing well. David yelled at Sunshine that it was very careless of her to remove her oxygen mask because only the doctor had the right to remove her oxygen mask. Sunshine looked at her papa and said that she removed the oxygen mask on her because she was doing well, and that she wanted to go to the palace.

David asked Sunshine why she wanted to go to the palace? Sunshine told her father that she was aware of what was going on, and that she wanted to go to the palace to join her friends to fight this monster named Kalus who had lied to them.

David asked Sunshine how she knew that her friends were at the palace? Sunshine answered David that she had heard the conversation between him and Aaron. David looked into Sunshine's eyes and said that she was not going to the palace, not only because she was sick in the hospital's bed, but also because she was punished for removing her oxygen mask.

Then Sunshine tried to convince her father that she was doing well and that she must go to the palace to meet her friends without success. Then Sarah said that she was going to call a doctor to come checkSunshine and she left the room. Sunshine was staring at her father with a silence and she was thinking about a plan to go to the palace.

Then the door opened and Sarah, a nurse and a doctor got in the room. And the doctor was very astonished to see that Sunshine was out of the coma. Then the doctor started to check Sunshine and ask her questions like how she was feeling.

Sunshine told the doctor that she was feeling well. Then Sunshine asked the doctor if she could get out of the hospital now? Doctor answered Sunshine that she could not get out of the hospital today, and that she must stay at the hospital for a few days as she would do some tests to make sure that she was really well.

Then Sunshine understood that the doctor would not let her get out of the hospital. But she knew well that she must get out of the hospital now even without an authorization from the doctor because she must go to the palace to protect her friends who were facing the king Kalus. Then Sunshine got an idea and she looked at the doctor and said that she wanted to go to the washroom.

The doctor asked the nurse to take Sunshine to the bathroom. But Sunshine refused to go to the toilet with the nurse and she told the doctor that she knew the way to the toilet and that she would go alone. Then Sunshine got out of the bed, and she rushed through the door and she opened the door and got out.

Sunshine ran till the toilet's door and she opened the toilet's door and got in the toilet, then she closed the door behind her. Sunshine walked till face to the mirror and she looked in the mirror and she took a deep breath, then her eyes started spinning and the light shone into her eyes. Then she disappeared.

Asher and other children were in front of the palace and they were screaming slogans like, "Education or death." "We want education." "Open schools." And other words. Security men were staring at children who were yelling with amazed faces. Then the gate opened and Albert, who was the right hand of the king got out of the gate, and suddenly the expression on Albert's face changed and he was looking at children who were yelling with an amazed face, and he was wondering where these children were coming from?

And Albert asked Jadis who was the head of security who were these children? Jadis answeredAlbert that these children were the kids of the kingdom who wanted to go to school. And Albert told Jadis that the king had ordered to get rid of these children who were making the noises in front of the palace.

Jadis looked at his colleagues and told them that the king had ordered them to get rid of children. Then, security men grabbed their sticks and walked towards children and they asked children to leave, and those who would not leave would be beaten with the sticks.

And some children started to walk from behind with fear on their faces, as they were seeing security men who were approaching them with the big sticks in their hands. And Asher walked towards security men and looked into Jadis's eyes and said that he and his fellows were not afraid. And Asher added that he and his fellows were ready to die for their right to education, and they were not afraid, and they were not even afraid of this devil called Kalus.

Then Mia joined Asher and she looked at security men and said that children were determined to go to school, and that there was nothing that would prevent children from going to school. And that even the monster named Kalus would not prevent them from going to school and to realize their dreams.

Mia looked into Jadis's eyes and asked him if he remembered the last time she was at the palace with her friends? Jadis answered Mia that he remembered very well. Mia told Jadis that she and her friends were those who had beaten and injured security men. And Mia added that this time, she and her friends were ready to fight.

Security men looked at Mia with surprised faces and they were surprised that they were hit and injured three weeks ago by Mia and her friends. Asher looked at security men and told them that if one of his friends was hurt, he would burn the palace with this devil inside named the king.

Then Asher turned his head and looked at his friends and told them not to run away, and not to feel any fear, then Asher screamed, "Education or death." And the rest of the children started yelling, "Education or death." And Albert stared at children who were screaming without knowing what to do and he turned and walked inside the gate.

Kalus was walking in the living room and he was tired of hearing these noises outside coming from children, and he was very angry because security men had not yet got rid of these children outside as he had ordered. Then Kalus turned his head to the left when he heard the footsteps and he lifted his hand and started rubbing his forehead by staring at Diana who was walking towards him, as he had understood that Diana was coming to question him about the noises that were outside.

Then Diana stopped face to Kalus and she looked at him and asked who these people who were making noises outside were? Kalus answered Diana that he had no idea who those crazy people who were making the noises outside were. Diana told Kalus that it seemed that these noises were coming from children's voices. Kalus replied to Diana that he had no idea. Diana told Kalus that he must get out to see what was going on.

Kalus replied to Diana that security men would get rid of these crazy people who were making noises outside. Diana looked into Kalus's eyes and said that he could not solve all the problems with violence, that he should go out and listen to these people who were yelling because there was a reason why these people were screaming.

Kalus replied to Diana that he was not going outside to listen to useless people. Diana cried out, "Useless people." By looking at Kalus with an astonished face. And she added, "You called your people useless people." Kalus looked at Diana without saying a word.

Then Kalus and Diana turned their heads through the front door as they had heard the footsteps, and they were staring at Albert who was walking towards them. Then Albert stopped facing Kalus and looked at the king and said that security men could not get rid of these children outside.

Kalus asked Albert why security men could not get rid of these children? Albert answered Kalus that there were more than a thousand children outside who were very angry and who were ready to fight. Kalus cried out, "More than a thousand children?" And looking at Albert with a surprised face. Then Kalus asked, "All these children are from this kingdom?"

"Yes, my king." Answered Albert.

"Sunshine is between these children?" Kalus asked.

"I do not know who Sunshine is," Albert answered.

Kalus said, "Sunshine is not outside because if she was outside, I should know and she should be already inside this palace with her cursed friends." Then Kalus smiled and added, "My lord told me early this morning that Sunshine was in a coma in a hospital bed and that she was dying."

Diana looked at Kalus and asked if children were not at school? Kalus looked at Diana without saying a word. Diana asked Albert if children were not at school? Albert told Diana that children were in front of the palace because they went to school, and the school was closed. And immediately, the expression on Diana changed and she looked at Kalus with a disgusted face and said, "It means you lied to children."

Kalus replied, "I had already said that education was banned in the kingdom forever."

"You are the one who had promised education to children three weeks ago," Diana said.

"It's not me who had promised the return of education to the kingdom," Kalus replied.

"Who had promised?" Diana asked.

"Sunshine," Kalus answered.

"Who?" Diana asked, looking at Kalus with an astonished face.

"Sunshine," Kalus retorted.

"Who is Sunshine," Diana asked.

"Sunshine was the cursed child of this kingdom, and she was the leader of these useless children outside." Kalus answered.

"She was?" Diana asked.

"Yes, she was," Kalus replied.

"Why was she there?" Diana asked.

"Because I am sure she is dead now," Kalus replied.

"You killed her?" Diana asked.

"My Lord killed her this morning during a fight," Kalus answered.

Diana looked at Kalus with an astonished face and asked, "Who is your Lord."

Kalus looked at Diana without answering. And Diana asked again the same question, but Kalus remained silent. Then Diana told her husband that she did not know who Sunshine was, but that he was the one who had made an interview on television three weeks ago where he had promised to the whole kingdom the return of the education to the kingdom.

Kalus looked at Diana without saying a word and he turned and walked till near the phone and he picked up the phone and called the police that he was attacked by the thieves at his palace. And Kalus ordered the police to come with the guns to get rid of the thieves who were in front of his palace and who wanted to kill him.

Diana looked at Kalus with a surprised face and she asked if he called the police against his children? Kalus replied to his wife that these cursed children outside were not his children, but instead his enemies who wanted to kill him. Diana asked Kalus what his problem was with the education in the kingdom? Kalus answered Diana that he had no problem with education, but he had the problem with the fact that children would have access to knowledge.

Diana looked at Kalus with an amazed face and asked him why he did not want children to have access to knowledge? Kalus looked at Diana without saying a word. Diana told Kalus not to forget that he had been a student, and he was even a lawyer before becoming the king of the kingdom, and they had even met at school. Diana also told Kalus that he could not deny access to knowledge to children because children were the future of this kingdom.

And denying education to children was not only a crime he was committing on children, but it was also a crime that he was committing on the kingdom because he was killing the kingdom by doing so. And Kalus looked at Diana with a face of smile while laughing at her.

And suddenly, the expression on the face of Kalus changed and he lifted his head and looked at the ceiling with fear on his face, and he was staring at the blue light that had got in the room, and that was shining in the room. Diana and Albert were looking at Kalus with surprised faces wondering what was going on, and they were worried to see Kalus who was shaking with fear. Diana and Albert had not seen the light that had shone in the room.

Then Diana asked Kalus what was going on? Kalus looked at Diana with a face full of dread and said, "She is here." Diana asked, "Who is here?" And Kalus replied to Diana that Sunshine was here. Diana asked Kalus who was really Sunshine? But Kalus did not answer Diana, and he walked through the phone.

Diana and Albert turned their heads and looked at the king who was trying to make a phone call, then the fear appeared on their faces when they saw the king throw the phone against the wall, by screaming, "She is here, she is here." "This cursed girl is still alive, this cursed girl named Sunshine is still alive and she is here. And she is the one who has spoiled the phone to prevent me from calling my army."

Diana and Albert were still staring at the king with faces full of worry and they did not understand what was going on with the king. And they were amazed to see the king who was acting like a crazy man by shouting Sunshine's name and throwing things against the wall, and it was their first time to see the king act like this.

Diana and Albert were wondering who Sunshine was, and they were watching the king who was running in the room as if he was looking for something. And they were looking at the king who was screaming Sunshine's name, and they were very afraid that the king had become crazy.

Then the king ran towards Albert and screamed at Albert to go to the police station and call the police to come protect him because he was in danger because Sunshine was in the palace to kill him. Albert asked Kalus who Sunshine was? Kalus slapped Albert and he ordered Albert to get out and go to the police station and call the police to come protect him. Then Albert ran through the door and went to call the police.

Diana was looking at Kalus with a face full of fear, and she was not recognizing Kalus, and she could see the terror on Kalus's face. And even if Diana knew that her husband was someone who was violent and who got angry easily.

Diana had never seen the fear on her husband's face, and she knew her husband like someone who was courageous and arrogant since the university where they had met. And Diana was not recognizing her husband because it was the first time he felt fear. And she was even afraid to talk to him. And she stared at her husband running through a corridor by screaming the name Lord. Then Diana turned and left the room.

Children were outside making noises, and there were Sunshine and Aaron between them. And Sunshine's friends were very proud to see her. Sunshine was quiet, and she knew that the king had sent

Albert to call the police. And she was using her magic to see what was going on.

And Sunshine was seeing three police cars that were coming towards the palace, and she was also seeing policemen with the guns in these cars. And Sunshine understood that she must do something to prevent the police from arriving at the palace. Then Sunshine's eyes started spinning, and the light got out from Sunshine's eyes and went away.

Suddenly, there were the screams in the streets and people were staring at the police cars that had crashed into a wall with their faces full of fear. And people were not understanding how all the three police cars that were on the road, left the road and went and crashed into a wall.

And all policemen, who were in the cars were injured, but luckily, no one was dead. And it was Sunshine who had mystically caused this accident through her magic because the light that had got out from her eyes had shone on the police cars and caused these accidents. Then ambulances came and took policemen to the hospital.

Children were still in front of the palace making noises, and security men were looking at children without saying a word. And security men were even afraid of these children and they were wondering if they could really protect their king if these children decided to get inside the palace because they could see the anger on the faces of these children.

Then children turned their heads from behind when they heard the car horn, and they saw a black car that was trying to get into the palace. And the driver who was in this black car continued to honk as children had blocked the entry of the palace.

And children who blocked the entry of the palace wanted to move, but Sunshine asked them to stay, and to block the entry of the palace to prevent people from getting inside the palace. And security men were just looking at children who were determined in their mission, and security men were afraid for the king because they knew that they could not protect the king against these children.

Then the doors of this black car opened, and a young girl with long hair black hair and green eyes, a young boy with short blond hair and blue eyes, and the driver got out of the car. And the young girl and young boy had carried the backpacks.

And the young girl and young boy walked till the entry of the palace, and they looked at children who were in front of the palace with surprised faces, wondering who these children were, and where these children came from. And mostly what these children were doing in front of the palace, and they mostly noticed that most of the children had carried the backpacks.

Children were also looking at this young girl and this young boy by wondering who this girl and boy were, but Sunshine knew this young girl and this young boy were Kalus's children. Then this young girl broke the silence and said, "My name is Luna."

Sunshine looked at Luna and said, "My name is Sunshine, and my friends and I are children of this kingdom and we are here because we want to go to school, we want Kalus to open schools."

Luna said, "I am the daughter of the king, and this boy near to me is my young brother named George, and we are all here in the same situation." And Luna added, "I am so happy to meet you all, not only because we are all going to be united to fight for our dream and the return of education in this kingdom, but mostly because my brother and I are going to have a new family who are you all here."

"You mean your brother and you do not go to school?" Sunshine asked.

Luna looked into Sunshine's eyes and said, "When I was a kid, I watched my mom fight my dad everyday to open school for children, and I did not know the meaning of education. But when I was nine years old, my mother explained to me what the meaning of education was, and when I understood the importance of knowledge, I joined my mom in her fight for access to knowledge in the kingdom."

And Luna went on and said, "But my father, consider me like his worst enemy since I joined my mom in her fight, and for him I am not his daughter, but a cursed daughter."

Luna added, "I thought that my father had heard my anger in the palace when three weeks ago, I watched my dad on television announcing the return of education to the kingdom. George and I were very happy because for the first time, we were going to school.

But unfortunately, when we arrived at school today, the school doors were closed, and there was no instructor. The driver, George and I stayed there till noon, without seeing anyone, and I understood that my father had not only lied to us, but he had played with us too."

Sunshine said, "Kalus lied to everyone because all my friends who are here went to school this morning, and when they arrived at school, the school's gate was closed and there was no instructor. And that's why we are all here because we want to go to school."

Luna said, "We must all get inside the palace, and take the school's keys to this man called Kalus."

"I think this is the better solution." Sunshine said.

Then Asher screamed, "Education or death." And the rest of the children followed Asher by yelling, "Education or death." Then they all ran towards the gate, they pushed security guards who were at the gate, and they opened the gate and entered the palace.

Kalus was in his private living room, and he was walking with his face full of fear, and he was walking without even knowing where he was going, and he was not even able to think. Kalus had spent hours in the magic room to try to communicate with Lord without success. And he was wondering where Lord was and looking at the expression on the face of Kalus, we could see that Kalus was very afraid.

Then Kalus turned his head through the door when he heard the noises coming from the door, and suddenly the expression face of Kalus changed, and he was looking at children who were walking towards him with a face full of terror. And Kalus was not believing what was going on, and he was turning on himself by trembling with fear, and he was seeing his own children among children who were in the room.

And suddenly, Kalus opened his mouth when his eyes met with Sunshine's eyes, and he was staring at Sunshine with a face full of dread and looking at the expression on the face of Kalus, he was not realizing that Sunshine was in the room.

And Kalus tried to talk, but his mouth and the rest of his body were shaking so that he could not utter a word. And children had their eyes focused on Kalus, and they were all surprised to see the fear on Kalus's face.

And Kalus's children were very amazed to see their papa who was trembling with fear, and it was their first time to see their father who was afraid because they knew their father was like someone with a big mouth and arrogant. And for most children who were in the room, it was their first time to be in front of their king. And there was J.P Remy in the room who was filming what was going on.

Then Sunshine broke the silence and asked Kalus if he had lost his mouth? Kalus still had his eyes focused on Sunshine and his mouth was still shaking and he was trying to talk, but a word could not get out of his mouth. Then Kalus took a deep breath and replied to Sunshine that he thought that she was dead. Sunshine replied to Kalus that she was still alive. And Sunshine asked Kalus why the school was not opened. Kalus replied to Sunshine that he was the king of the kingdom, and he had decided not to open the school today.

Sunshine told Kalus that he had promised to the whole kingdom three weeks ago that the return of the education in the kingdom was today. And Kalus replied to Sunshine that she was the one who had promised the return of education in the kingdom today and not him. Sunshine replied to Kalus that he was the one who had announced the return of the education on television and not her.

Kalus told Sunshine that she was the one who had forced him to accept the return of education in the kingdom. Sunshine told Kalus that it was an agreement. Kalus told Sunshine that did not care about the agreement he had made with her. Sunshine replied to

Kalus that he had accepted three weeks ago to open school, and he lied to everyone because he did not keep his promise.

Mia looked at Kalus and told him that he was more than a devil because he even lied to his own children. Kalus replied to Mia that he did not have children. Mia asked Kalus if Luna and George were not his children? Kalus answered Mia that he had no children, and that he did not know who Luna and George were. Luna looked at her father and said that she was so happy to know that she and her brother were not his children. And Luna added that she did not want a dad like him.

Kalus replied to Luna to get out of his palace with her fellows. Luna told Kalus that the palace was not his house, but it was the house of all inhabitants of the kingdom. And that like she and her friends were children of the kingdom, they were going to stay in the palace. The king told Luna that the palace was his house and not the house of all inhabitants.

Luna replied to Kalus that he could take the palace if he wanted, but that what they wanted was the return of the education in the kingdom. Kalus replied to Luna that there would never be a return to education in the kingdom. And that children of the kingdom would never have access to knowledge, and that education was banned in the kingdom forever.

George looked at Kalus and told Kalus that education was a duty and a right for all children, and that it was a right for children of the kingdom to go to school. Kalus replied to George that education was not a right for children. And Kalus added he was the king of the kingdom, and he had decided that children would not go to school.

George told his father that the fact his father was the king did not give the powers to his father to prevent children from their right to education. Kalus replied to his son that he [Kalus] was the king of the kingdom and he had all the powers to decide in the kingdom. And Kalus added that he even had the powers to decide who was going to live in his kingdom or not.

George told Kalus that he [Kalus] was not God to decide if people could live on their land or not. Kalus replied to George that he was god, and he had powers in the lives of people. George told Kalus that he [Kalus] was crazy, and he [Kalus] needed to see a doctor as soon as possible.

But before going to see a doctor, he [Kalus] must open the school's doors to allow children to go to school. And George also told Kalus that being the king meant taking care of his people, talking to his people, listening to his people, working for his people, respecting his people and above all loving his people and his kingdom.

Suddenly, Sunshine started clapping her hands, and said "Congratulations George, and thank you for your words." And Sunshine added, "I am sure George would be a great king for us and for our kingdom." And children followed Sunshine by clapping their hands. Mia screamed, "George is our king." And she added, "the king George."

And immediately, they all started screaming, yelling, "the king George." By clapping their hands. And Kalus was staring with a face full of surprise as he was seeing children who were clapping their hands by screaming, "the king George." With a surprised face. Then Kalus opened his mouth and started talking, but no one was paying attention to him, and there were the noises that no one could hear him.

After a few minutes, Sunshine calmed her fellows, and all their eyes were focused on Kalus. And Kalus looked at them and told them that he was the king of the kingdom, and he would be the king of the kingdom forever. And Kalus asked them to stop dreaming because George would never be the king of the kingdom.

Sunshine replied to Kalus that he was no longer the king of the kingdom because children of the kingdom had chosen their king who was George. And Sunshine added that from now on, they were going to talk with King George about the issues affecting the kingdom.

Then Sunshine looked into Kalus's eyes and said that he must apologize to the whole kingdom and especially to the children because the school was not opened. And he would also give the keys to the school to George in front of the camera of J.P Remy who was in the room with them.

And Remy would put the video on his channel and website, and the whole kingdom would watch the video. Sunshine also told Kalusnot to try to arrest Remy later, or to send his men to kill Remy. Because Remy was the journalist of the people, and Remy worked for the people and his kingdom.

Kalus stared at Sunshine and he asked her to stop dreaming because he would never give George the keys to the school. Sunshine stared at Kalus without saying a word, then her eyes started spinning. And suddenly the expression on the face of Kalus changed, and he was staring at Sunshine with a face full of fear as he was understanding that Sunshine was trying to use her magic on him by seeing her eyes that were spinning.

Then Kalus turned and tried running away, but he was blocked by Asher, George and Aaron. And Kalus was turning his head looking around trying to find a way to escape, but it was impossible for him to run away because he was surrounded by children. Then Kalus started yelling and calling for help.

Suddenly, the light got out from Sunshine's eyes and went and shone on Kalus, and Kalus started to jump. And everyone was looking at Kalus who was jumping and laughing. And Suddenly, the expression on their faces changed and they were looking at Kalus who was flying with astonished faces, wondering what was making Kalus fly.

Then Mia started laughing and she said that Kalus was acting like the instructors who were flying in the movie of Superhuman 2 by Thierry Kouam that they had watched three weeks ago in the living room of this palace.

Then children who were in the living room of this palace three weeks ago watching the movie called Superhuman 2, remembered the scene where two instructors were flying in space. Because these instructors had been projected in space by Superhuman's magic as these two instructors wanted to kill Superhuman who was sick in the hospital bed. And these children started laughing, by saying that Kalus was flying exactly like these two instructors, and other children started laughing too.

Suddenly, the expression on the faces of children changed and they stopped laughing, and some were looking at Kalus with fear on their faces like Kalus was hitting his body against the wall, while others were staring at Kalus who was bleeding on his forehead with worried faces.

But Asher and Mia were staring at Kalus with their faces full of smiles, while Sunshine and Luna were looking at Kalus with their faces empty of expression. And Sunshine's eyes were focused on Kalus, Sunshine's eyes were still spinning because she was the one who was torturing Kalus through her magic.

And no one in the room could imagine that it was Sunshine who was using her magic to torture Kalus because except Kalus, no one was seeing how Sunshine's eyes were spinning. And no one knew that Sunshine had the magic. And they were all completely lost by seeing Kalus who was flying because they did not understand how it was possible that someone who did not have the wings was flying.

Then Sunshine's eyes stopped spinning, and people pushed a louder scream of fear in the room when they saw Kalus fall on the floor. And all the eyes were focused on Kalus who was on the floor, and the hearts of most of them were beating faster than the normal as if they were going to have a heart attack. And except few of them like Sunshine, Asher, Luna and Mia, the rest of them were afraid that Kalus was dead.

Then Nany said, "I hope, the king Kalus is not dead." Asher replied to Nany and said, "I hope the devil Kalus is dead." Nany looked at Asher and asked, "How can you wish for the death of our the king?" Khloe looked at Nany and said, "Kalus is no longer our king because we have a new king who is George."

Nany replied to Khloe that even if Kalus was no longer their king, they could not wish for his death. Luna looked at Nany and said that Kalus was worse than a devil who deserved to die. And Luna added that the death of Kalus would be only a great victory for the kingdom because the death of Kalus would free the kingdom.

Suddenly, they all turned their heads towards Kalus when they heard a voice say that Kalus was getting up from the floor. And all the eyes were focused on Kalus, who was getting up from the floor with the difficulties. Then Kalus stood up, and some were looking at Kalus with the faces of sadness, while others were staring at Kalus with the faces full of smiles. And there were the wounds on Kalus's forehead, and Kalus's face was full of blood.

And Asher stared at Kalus by laughing, then Asher said that he had realized his dream and that he had always dreamed to see the devil Kalus in this position. And Asher continued and said that he had even talked about it with Sunshine a few days ago at the hospital, when Sunshine and he were talking about the movie Superhuman 2 that they had watched in the palace three weeks ago.

And Asher added that he had told Sunshine during this conversation that the best part in this movie was where the two instructors wanted to kill Superhuman who was sick on the hospital bed, but Superhuman's magic tortured these two instructors by making these two instructors' fly.

And these two instructors had flown by hitting themselves against the wall, exactly like Kalus just did. And Asher also said that the devil Kalus looked exactly like these two instructors with the wounds and blood that were on him.

Sunshine smiled at Asher and told him that she remembered that conversation a few days ago at the hospital, and that he had really realized his dream. Because Kalus looked exactly like these two instructors with these wounds and blood on him.

Mia said that it was not only Asher who had realized his dream to see Kalus hit himself against the wall because when she had watched the movie Superhuman, she had dreamed to see the monster Kalus fly like these two instructors who wanted to kill Superhuman. And children started laughing, even those who were sad were laughing.

And some who had not watched the movie were saying that they must watch this movie of Superhuman 2.

Then Sunshine looked at Kalus and said, "I told you three weeks ago in this palace not to even try to play with us. But you did not understand, and you played with us." Kalus looked at Sunshine and said, "I did not play with you." Sunshine said, "We are in this room now because you did not open the school, and it means that you played with us. Because we had an agreement three weeks ago to start school today."

And Kalus told Sunshine that he was going to open the school the next day. Sunshine replied to Kalus that he was no longer the king of the kingdom because children had chosen George like their king. And that they were going to talk with George now about the problems of the kingdom, and it's George who would open the school's doors to allow children of the kingdom to go to school. Kalus replied to Sunshine that he was the unique king of the kingdom, and that he was the only one who had the powers to rule the kingdom and to give the authorization to children to go to school.

Sunshine replied to Kalus that he was not the king of children, and he must apologize now to the whole kingdom and especially to children, then he must give the keys of school to George. Kalus looked at Sunshine and said that he was the king of the kingdom and he could not give George the keys to school and that he better to die than give George the keys to the school. And Sunshine looked at Kalus without saying a word, and there was silence in the room. Kalus was staring at Sunshine.

Suddenly, the expression on the face of Kalus changed, and he was looking at Sunshine with a face full of fear as he was seeing Sunshine's eyes that were spinning. And Kalus understood that Sunshine was going to use her magic against him to torture him again, and he opened his mouth and yelled that he would apologize.

And people were laughing at Kalus as he was screaming by saying that he would apologize, and at the same time, they were wondering what was going on with him because Kalus was acting as if he was afraid of someone or something.

And no one could imagine that Kalus was screaming because he was afraid to be tortured by Sunshine's magic. Sunshine told Kalus that he would not only apologize, but he would also give the keys to the school to King George. Kalus looked at Sunshine without saying a word, and he was still seeing Sunshine's eyes that were spinning, and he was also breathing deeply.

Then Kalus screamed by saying, "Yes, Yes, Yes, I would give the keys of school to the king George." When he saw the light shone into Sunshine's eyes because he had understood that Sunshine was ready to use her magic to torture him.

Then Kalus took a deep breath and when he noticed that Sunshine's eyes had stopped spinning. And Sunshine told Kalus that he must apologize in front of the camera and on the microphone of Remy. Kalus told Sunshine that he could not talk in front of the camera today because he had wounds on him and he was not doing well.

Sunshine replied to Kalus that he was going to talk in front of the camera today. Kalus replied to Sunshine that he needed to take a bath and clean the blood that was on him. Sunshine replied to Kalus that he was going to talk in front of the camera now in the state where he was. And Kalus looked at Sunshine and he started begging Sunshine to let him go take a shower before talking in front of the camera. And Sunshine was staring at Kalus who was begging with a face empty of expression.

And there were few people who were sad to see Kalus who was begging, while most of them were happy to see Kalus who was begging. And the children were divided on the situation of Kalus, and there were people like Nany and Isac who wanted Kalus to take a shower, while there were people like Sunshine, Asher and Luna who wanted Kalus to speak in front of the camera with the blood on him. And the children did not know what to do because some wanted

Kalus to speak in front of the camera with the blood on him, while others wanted Kalus to take a shower first.

And Nany proposed to organize a vote to decide if they wanted Kalus to speak in front of the camera with the blood on him or not. And Asher asked Nany how they were going to vote? Nany answered Asher that they would raise their hands to vote, and the first round of voting would be people who would like Kalus to take a bath before speaking in front of the camera. And the second round of voting would be people who would like Kalus not to take a bath before speaking in front of the camera.

But Luna said that she was against the vote because the vote was useless, and that the result of the vote would not change the decision that they had already made. And Luna added that Kalus was going to speak in front of the camera with the blood on him because Kalus deserved it. Then Luna posed and tears started flowing down her cheeks and all the eyes were focused on her, and they were all surprised to see Luna who was crying.

Then Luna opened her mouth and said that Kalus had not only destroyed their lives, but Kalus had also destroyed the kingdom. And she had no mercy for someone like Kalus who had destroyed her life and destroyed the lives of all the inhabitants of the kingdom. And that children of the kingdom could not write and read because the monster named Kalus had killed them by stealing their right to education. Then there was silence in the room, and they were all looking at each other with their mouths closed.

After a few minutes, Nany broke the silence and said that the tears and words of princess Luna had made her change her mind. And people who wanted Kalus to take the bath before speaking in front of camera had changed their mind after they had heard Luna say how Kalus was a nasty person who did not deserve mercy. Then Sunshine looked at George and she told George that he was the king of the kingdom, and that he was the one who was going to decide if Kalus would speak in front of the camera with blood on him or not.

Suddenly, there was silence in the room, and all the eyes were focused on George, and they were all waiting for George to speak. Even Kalus' eyes were focused on George, and Kalus's heart was beating faster than normal, but the expression on Kalus's face was full of hope.

And if Kalus's face was full of hope, it was because Kalus knew that George was a nice person with a good heart, and he was expecting George to allow him to take a shower before speaking in front of the camera.

Then George broke the silence and said that he had listened to his people very well and that he could not go against the wishes of his people, so that Kalus would speak in front of the camera with blood on him like his people had decided. Mia said, "the kingdom now has a great king named George who listens to his people." And she started to clap her hands.

And the rest of the people followed Mia by clapping their hands by congratulating George for his decision. Kalus was looking at George with a surprised face, and Kalus was very astonished to see that his own children were against him, and he was disappointed with George.

Then Sunshine looked at Remy and she asked Remy to approach Kalus with the camera and microphone. And all the eyes were focused on Remy and his colleague who were walking towards Kalus with the camera and the microphone. Then they all turned their heads towards Kalus like Remy had held the microphone up in Kalus mouth.

Then Kalus opened his mouth and he made a speech where he apologized to the whole kingdom and especially to the children about the fact that the school was not opened today. And Kalus also apologized for the fact that he had deprived the children of access to knowledge by banning education in the kingdom.

Then Kalus said that the one who was going to be in charge of education in the kingdom was George. And Kalus took the school keys from his desk drawer and gave those keys to George. Then Kalus left the room.

Then children started jumping, screaming and hugging, congratulating each other on their success against Kalus. And everyone was congratulating Sunshine for her incredible work, and they all also congratulated George like their new king, and they told George that they were proud to have him like their king. They introduced themselves trying to get to know each other. They were walking in the room, trying to talk to each other. Then Aaron stopped face to Asher and both were looking each other in the eyes without saying a word.

"I am so sorry," Aaron said.

Asher smiled at Aaron and said, "You do not have to be."

"I know I do not deserve your apologies," Aaron said.

"It's okay," Asher said.

"I have been rude to you," Aaron.

Asher walked two steps through Aaron, then he smiled at Aaron and he opened his arms and took Aaron in his arms. And Asher said in Aaron 's eyes that everything was forgotten, and they were brothers, and they had a goal to protect and save their kingdom from the devil named Kalus.

And Sunshine was not far from Asher and Aaron, and she was staring at Aaron and Asher who had taken each other in their arms with her face full of smiles. And Sunshine started walking towards them with her eyes still focused on them.

Then Asher looked at Aaron and said, "Thank you for everything,"

"I am the one who would say thank you because without you we should not be here," Aaron said.

"We both started this fight together with Sunshine and others, so we all deserve this victory," Asher said.

"You are the one who brought all these incredible people here in this room when I abandoned you at school," Aaron said.

"The importance is that you are here, and you have always been present, and today with you, we have crowned our new king named George, and George is going to give us our right to education," Asher said.

"Thank you for everything," Aaron said.

Asher smiled and said, "Take care of her,"

"Take care of who?" Aaron asked.

"Sunshine, of course," Asher.

Aaron smiled and said, "I will, I promise."

"She is not only beautiful, she is unique and brave, and she is also our hero because without her, we would not be here, we would never fight for our dreams." Asher said.

"I would do the impossible to make her happy," Aaron said.

"You must make sure that she is happy," Asher said.

"I would make sure that she always has her beautiful smile on her beautiful face, and I would take care of her beautiful heart," Aaron said.

Suddenly, Asher and Aaron were interrupted by Sunshine, and she told them that she was very happy to see them talking like this. Then Sunshine asked Asher which girl he was talking about with his brother Aaron. Asher smiled at Sunshine and told her to ask this question to Aaron because Aaron was the one who could answer this question.

Then Asher tried to walk away, but he was grabbed by Sunshine, and she looked into Asher's eyes and she thanked him for everything, mostly for his courage this morning to take children to the palace. And Asher replied to Sunshine that she did not need to thank him, and that if there was anyone to thank, it was her. Because she was the hero of this kingdom, and that without her nothing would be possible. Then Sunshine and Asher hugged each other. Then Asher walked away.

Sunshine and Aaron were staring at each other with silence. Then Aaron broke the silence, and said, "I am sorry."

Sunshine smiled at Aaron and said, "I am happy to know that you came back between us."

"I know, I hurt a lot of people, especially you with my behavior," Aaron said.

"I understood why you behaved like that," Sunshine said.

"I hope you will one day forgive me," Aaron said.

Sunshine smiled and said, "I have already forgiven you."

Aaron smiled and said, "Thank you."

"Which is the girl Asher and you were talking about?" Sunshine asked.

"How did you know that Asher and I were talking about a girl?" Aaron asked.

"We use the personal pronoun she for girls," Sunshine answered.

"I would talk to you about this beautiful girl one day," Aaron said.

"Why not now?" Sunshine asked.

"Because, I forgot her name," Aaron answered.

Sunshine smiled and said, "I would help you to remember her name."

"How?" Aaron asked.

"By remembering the words you said to describe her," Sunshine said.

Aaron smiled and said, "I listen."

"You said, you would do your impossible to make her happy, you would make sure that she always has her beautiful smile on her beautiful face, and you would take care of her heart," Sunshine said.

Aaron smiled at Sunshine and said, "It means you listened to the whole conversation between Asher and me."

"I want the name of this girl," Sunshine said.

"She is a special girl and unique, and she is the most beautiful girl I have ever seen, and I could not even imagine that such a beautiful girl could exist," Aaron said.

"Her name?" Sunshine asked.

"She has a beautiful smile, blue eyes and long blond hair," Aaron said.

Sunshine looked into Aaron's eyes with her face full of smiles and said, "You did not answer my question."

Aaron smiled and said, "I described her."

Sunshine stared at Aaron with her face full of smiles and she said, "I did not ask you to describe her, but I asked you her name."

Suddenly, Sunshine and Aaron were interrupted by a voice in the room, and they turned their heads through where this voice was coming from, and they saw George who was calling everyone to follow him in the dining room. And people started following George. Aaron smiled at Sunshine and he handed her his hand and said, "Our king George asked us to follow him."

Sunshine smiled at George and said, "You did not tell me the name of this girl, we were talking about." Aaron laughed and said, "You know well that, we can not keep our the king George waiting." Sunshine smiled and she grabbed Aaron's hand that was handed to her, and they followed other people in the dining room.

They walked in the dining room, and most of them were surprised to see how the dining room was huge and beautiful. And there were canned drinks on the table, and there were three kinds of canned drinks on the table.

George stood up near the drinks and he thanked everyone for being here, and he also thanked everyone for their courage and determination to change things in the kingdom. And that they would all work together not only to realize their dream by going to school, but also to change the kingdom by making it a better place. Then People started clapping their hands by screaming, "the king George."

Then George said that today was a great day in his life because for the first time in his life, he met his brothers and sisters. And he was going to live and work with his brothers and sisters until his last breath. And that today, it was not only the destiny of the children that had changed, but it was the destiny of the whole kingdom.

And that they were going to celebrate this moment with food and drink, and that the food would be served later. Then George said that he had ordered three kinds of drinks, then George took a canned drink from the table and the name Fortis was written on this canned drink.

And George showed this drink to everyone, and they were all reading the word, "Fortis." On this canned drink, George told them that Fortis was a Latin word that meant in English Strong, powerful, brave, valiant and courageous. That the drink called Fortis showed the courageous and strong people who they were, and they could find themselves in this drink called Fortis because Fortis was also the drink of children of their age.

And mostly by drinking Fortis, they would always have the courage, the power, the determination and the strength to overcome the obstacles and succeed in everything. Then they all started clapping their hands with a smile on their faces, and most of them were screaming, "I am Fortis."

Then George took another canned drink from the table and the name Felix that was written on this canned drink. And George lifted the canned drink by showing it to everyone, and they were all reading the name, "Felix." On this canned drink, George told them that Felix was a Latin word that meant Happy, Fortunate, Lucky, Successful, Fertile and Fruitful. That this drink called Felix showed the happy and successful people who they were because they had used their courage to change the destiny of the kingdom.

And that now they were happy with the result, and they were going to succeed in making not only the lives of all inhabitants of the kingdom better, but they were going to succeed in making the kingdom not only a better place, but a successful place for everyone.

And that they could find themselves in the drink called Felix, and that Felix was always the drink of children of their age and it was important for them to always drink Felix to keep their happiness, their smile, and their joy. Then People started to clap their hands with their faces full of smiles, and some of them were screaming, "We are Felix."

Then George introduced the last kind of canned drink called Focus, and he told everyone that Focus was an English word that meant concentration, and that it was important for them to stay focused on their dreams and on their goal to make their kingdom a better place. And that the drink called Focus was also the drink of children of their age.

Then George said that from today, they would drink only the drinks called Fortis, Felix, or Focus until the end of their lives. They all started yelling, "We are Focus." Then George said that it was time to start drinking to celebrate change in the kingdom.

Then most of the people rushed through the table to pick up a drink. And Sunshine was staring at her fellows with a face full of smiles and looking at the expression on the face of Sunshine, we could see that she was very happy. And even if Sunshine knew that the fight was not yet over because Lord was still alive, and that Lord had the control of the souls of children who were not yet born.

Then Sunshine started laughing as she was staring at Aaron who was walking towards her with two canned drinks in his hands. Then Aaron stopped face to Sunshine and he smiled at her, and he handed her a drink and she took the drink in Aaron's hand and she thanked him.

Then Sunshine noticed that Aaron was drinking the drink called Fortis, and he had given her the drink called Felix. And she asked him why he had given her the drink called Felix, while he was drinking the drink called Fortis.

Aaron answered Sunshine that he had given her the drink called Felix because Felix meant happiness in English, and that he wanted her to always be happy. And that he was drinking the drink called Fortis because he needed the courage, power and strength to be the hero of the most beautiful girl of the kingdom. And Sunshine smiled at Aaron without saying a word. Then they started talking about the situation of the kingdom.

Isac was drinking the drink called Felix, and he was staring at people who were drinking and talking. Then the facial expression of Isac changed as he was staring at Luna who was walking towards him with an astonished face. Then Luna stopped facing Isac and she handed her hand to Isac and said, "I am Luna." Isac handed his hand and shook Luna's hand and said, "I am Isac."

Then Luna asked Isac why he was alone and quiet? Isac answered that he was not alone. Luna replied to Isac that before she came, he was alone, and that since they were in the room, she had not seen him talk to someone. Isac smiled at Luna without saying a word.

Then Luna took the drink that was in Isac's hand, and she gave him her drink. Isac looked at the drink that Luna had given him, and it was the drink called Fortis. Then he looked into Luna's eyes and asked her why she had given him her drink.

Luna replied to Isac that she had given him the drink called Fortis because he needed the courage. And Isac smiled at Luna without saying a word. Then they started to talk by trying to get to know each other.

Then the day was going well for all of them, and they were eating and drinking by trying to talk to each other. Sunshine was spending her time talking to everyone to try to know each of them. Sunshine and Luna had had a good conversation, and they had mostly talked about the situation of the kingdom.

Mostly about the laws of Kalus, and how to put an end to the laws of Kalus, also about the future that they wanted for the kingdom and the inhabitants of the kingdom. Asher and Khloe were spending their time together talking trying to get to know each other. George and Mia were spending their time together talking trying to get to know each other.

It was six o'clock, except Luna and George, the rest of the children left the palace, and it was a wonderful day for them. And despite the fact that they had not started school today, they had changed the destiny of the kingdom by crowning a new king named George.

And even if they had not worn the crown on George's head, for them, George was their king. And some of them like Sunshine, Asher, Khloe George, Mia, Aaron, Nany, Isac and Luna had decided to meet the next day to talk about the situation of the kingdom and mostly about when the school would be opened in the kingdom.

It was eight o'clock, children were in their living room with their parents, and children were telling their parents their day, and mostly what had happened to the palace. And children were mostly talking about Sunshine who was their leader.

And the parents knew already that the children had not been to school because Kalus had not opened the school. And even if the parents were disappointed about the fact that Kalus had not opened the school, they were not really surprised because they knew well that Kalus was someone that they could not trust.

And at the same time, most of the parents were wondering who exactly was Sunshine that their children were talking about. And if the parents were curious to know who Sunshine was, it was not only because their children were talking about her like the hero of the kingdom.

But mostly because three weeks ago, there were pictures of Sunshine in the newspapers like the one who had forced the king Kalus to open the school's doors in the kingdom and to allow children to go to school.

But the parents were very astonished to hear from their children that they [children] had taken the school keys to Kalus and they gave these keys to George, and that George was going to open the school to allow all children of the kingdom to go to school. And the parents did not really believe in their children, when children told them that George was going to open the school against the wish of Kalus.

Because the parents knew well that a decision could not be taken in the kingdom without the authorization of Kalus. Because, Kalus had all the powers in the kingdom, and that Kalus was even more than a god because Kalus had the powers to decide who could live or not. And that Kalus had self-proclaimed himself as the god of the kingdom.

And the parents laughed at children when they heard from children that George was the new king of the kingdom, and because all children who were in the palace had named George as their king. And the parents told their children that the king was not named because the king was born.

And the parents also told children that George could not be the king of the kingdom because even if George was born prince, George was not born the king. Because the one who was born princess and queen was Luna, who was the elder sister of George.

Then the parents explained to the children that according to the tradition of the kingdom of Manitoba, the first child of the king or queen, was the future king if this first child was a son, and was the future queen if this first child was a daughter.

And that Luna was the first child of the king Kalus, and it meant that it was Luna who was the future queen of the kingdom of Manitoba. And that Luna would be crowned queen of the kingdom only after the death of the king Kalus.

And the children were very sad to hear from their parents that George could not be the king of the kingdom. But they were more sad to hear that Kalus was still the king of the kingdom, and that Kalus would rule the kingdom until his death.

And most children knew well that their hope of going to school was over because it was still Kalus who ruled the kingdom. And for children, the tradition was unfair, not only because the tradition prevented their king George that they had chosen from sitting on the throne, but mostly because the tradition had given them a monster named Kalus as their king.

And the parents also explained to their children that George could be the king of the kingdom if only Luna died without having children. And that when Luna would be alive, George would never be the king of the kingdom. And even if children wanted George like their king, they were not sad to hear that Luna was their future queen.

And for all children, George was their king, and they carried George inside their hearts as their king, and nothing was going to change even if George could be crowned the king because they had already crowned George like their king in their hearts.

And the parents were very astonished to hear from their children, that Kalus had been tortured at the palace, and that Kalus had even bled. And also, that Kalus had also asked forgiveness with the blood on him in front of the camera of the journalist named J.P Remy.

And the parents did not believe in children, and the parents told children that it was not good to lie, mostly to lie about the king Kalus, and that even if they [children] did not like Kalus, they[children] must respect Kalus because Kalus was the king of the kingdom.

Suddenly, the radio caught the attention of the parents, and they were listening to the journalist J.P Remy who was talking about what had happened inside the palace, how children of the kingdom led by a young girl named Sunshine had succeeded to take the control of the kingdom.

And that children had not only changed their destiny, but they had also changed the destiny of the kingdom. And that the kingdom had a new king named George, and George had been crowned the king by children of the kingdom, and that Kalus was no longer the king of the kingdom.

And that Kalus had even given the school keys to George. And George would open the school to allow all children of the kingdom to go to school. And Kalus had been humiliated by children. And suddenly, people in their homes rushed to turn on television and computers when they heard Remy say that there was a video of the humiliation of Kalus on his channel and on his website.

The parents were watching television with astonished faces, and looking at the expression on the parents faces, they did not believe what was going on, and they were completely lost by watching the king Kalus who was humiliated by children, and mostly by his own children.

And the parents were watching the television with their mouths open, but no word was coming out from their mouth, and looking at the expression on the face of the parents, it was as if they were dreaming. Because they had never imagined watching on television one day the god of the kingdom called the king Kalus who was humiliated by children.

Then the expression on the faces of the parents changed and their eyes opened widely as they were watching Kalus on television who was forced by children to ask forgiveness to the whole kingdom with the blood on him.

And it was like a miracle for the parents to watch on television the king Kalus who was forced by children to give the school keys to George. And the parents were realizing that everything that they had heard from their children was true.

It was 1 one in the afternoon, the parents had finished watching television, and looking at their expressionless faces, they were still not believing what they had just watched on television.

And they were wondering what had happened for the king Kalus being humiliated by children of the kingdom, and mostly by his own children. And the parents were also wondering why the security guards of the king did not prevent children from torturing Kalus. And they were wondering where the security guards of the king were.

And even if the parents were very afraid that Kalus would get his revenge on their children, the parents were very happy to watch Kalus on television who had been humiliated by children. But there was a child who had caught the attention of the parents, and this child was Sunshine, and the parents were wondering who Sunshine was.

And the parents had noticed that it was Sunshine who was the leader of the children, and the parents were very surprised by the courage of Sunshine. And the whole kingdom went to bed with the joy in them of having seen Kalus humiliated by the children.

It was three in the morning, Kalus was lying on the floor in his magic room, and he had taken refuge in his magic room since yesterday that he had left his private living room. And he still had the clothes of yesterday on him, and there was still blood on his face.

And Kalus had found refuge in his magic room without taking a shower, not only because he wanted to talk to Lord, but mostly because he was running away from Sunshine and her fellows. And Kalus had tried to talk to Lord without success, and he had spent hours calling his Lord, but unfortunately, Lord did not answer.

Suddenly, Kalus got up from the floor and knelt down when he heard the voice of Lord. And Lord asked Kalus what was going on? Kalus answered to Lord that Sunshine was still alive. Lord said that he knew that Sunshine was still alive.

And Lord added that he was surprised to see that Sunshine had succeeded to survive after she had been bitten by his venom. Kalus asked Lord if Lord was aware of what happened yesterday. Lord answered that Sunshine had destroyed his magic mirror that he was using to watch everything that happened in the kingdom.

Kalus asked Lord if it meant that since yesterday morning Lord had not watched the kingdom. Lord answered that no because he just arrived in the kingdom to check if Sunshine was dead, but that he was very astonished to find out that Sunshine was still alive, and she was lying in her bed. Kalus told Lord that Lord had made a big mistake by asking him [Kalus] yesterday early morning not to open the schools.

Lord replied to Kalus that he[Lord] came yesterday at 4:57 a.m., to ask him[Kalus] to not open the schools because he[Lord] thought that Sunshine should die before six in the morning because during his fight against Sunshine, he[Lord] had succeeded to bite Sunshine with his venom. And Lord added that he was amazed to find out that Sunshine was not dead because no human being could survive after being bitten by his venom.

Lord went on and said that the fact that Sunshine had survived to the bite of his venom meant that Sunshine was more powerful and stronger than what he had imagined. Then Lord asked Kalus what happened? And Kalus started to explain everything that Sunshine and her fellows had done.

After an hour, Kalus had finished explaining what children had done to him. And Lord told Kalus to not worry that Sunshine would pay for everything that she had done. And Lord also told Kalus to not get out of the magic room until he[Lord] ordered him[Kalus] to get out. Because Kalus was safe in the magic room, and mostly because Sunshine and her fellows could not find Kalus in the magic room. And Kalus asked Lord if it meant that they would not take the keys of school in George's hand.

Lord replied to Kalus to not worry about the school keys that were in George's hand because children would not go to school. And Lord added that when he would be alive, children of the kingdom would never have access to knowledge.

Kalus asked Lord what was the plan? Lord answered that the only plan now was to kill Sunshine as soon as possible. Kalus told Lord that this cursed girl of Sunshine was very dangerous and that Sunshine could destroy their project. Lord replied to Kalusnot to worry about Sunshine because she was no longer a threat to them and to their project.

And Lord also told Kalus that they had the control on the future of the kingdom because they already possessed the souls of children who were not yet born. And Lord added that Sunshine would never succeed to free the souls of children who were not yet born, and that even when these children would be born Sunshine would never succeed to free their souls.

Because these children would be born with the souls that belonged to Lord and Kalus. And that all the children who would be born in the kingdom in the future would belong to Lord and Kalus. Then Lord asked Kalus to stay in the magic room, that Lord was going to plan how to kill Sunshine. Then Lord left.

It was five in the morning, Sunshine was lying in her bed and she had her eyes opened and stared at the ceiling thinking. And she had not closed her eyes during the whole night, and she had spent all night thinking about Lord because she knew well that Lord would try to get his revenge for the humiliation that she and fellows had caused to Kalus.

And at the same time, Sunshine was very surprised that she had not been visited by Lord during the night, mostly after that Lord had failed to kill her and also the humiliation that children had caused to Kalus.

And for Sunshine, it was obvious that Lord had a plan, and she was wondering what plan Lord had and Sunshine was very afraid because she knew that Lord was dangerous. And that even if Lord could no longer mystically kill her fellow combatants because the souls of her friends were no longer controlled by Lord. But at the same time, Sunshine knew that Lord was powerful enough to cause troubles in the kingdom, and that even if she had destroyed the magic mirror of Lord, Lord would find a way to watch what was going on in the kingdom.

Because it was important for Lord to control the kingdom because Lord must be aware of everything that was happening in the kingdom. Sunshine also knew that it was important for Lord to control the kingdom because Lord had the control of the souls of children who were not yet born. And she was very worried about the souls of these children who were not yet born, and she was very afraid that all children who would be born in the future would be controlled by Lord.

And Sunshine knew well that if Lord controlled the souls of all the children who would be born in the future, that meant that the future of the kingdom would be controlled by Lord. Then Sunshine started thinking about how to save the future of the kingdom by saving the souls of children who were not yet born.

Suddenly, the expression of the face of Sunshine changed and she was looking with a surprised face, as she was hearing the noises, and she was wondering where these noises were coming from. Then Sunshine turned her head and looked at the clock that was on the table and she read six in the morning, and she got out of bed, and looked through the window and she was amazed to see the journalists outside of her house. And she understood that the journalists were in the yard of her house because they wanted to talk to her.

Then Sunshine went to the bedroom of her parents, and she told her father that there were journalists in the yard of the house, and that she did not want to talk to them. And David went out and asked the journalist to leave his house.

And the journalists begged David that they wanted to talk to Sunshine. David replied to the journalists that his daughter did not want to talk to them. And the journalists tried to urge David to speak to Sunshine without success. Then the journalists left without speaking to Sunshine.

The inhabitants of the kingdom woke up with the name of Sunshine in their mouths, and everyone was talking about what had happened yesterday. And they were still not realizing that the king Kalus had been humiliated by children.

And the parents were waiting for what would happen, and the parents were curious to see what Sunshine and her fellows would do. And the parents were wondering if Sunshine and her fellows would really succeed to go to school without the authorization of Kalus. And at the same time, the parents were worried about the security of their children, and they knew well that Kalus could kill their children.

And except the newspaper called Kongreshow by J.P Remy who had talked about the humiliation of god Kalus by Sunshine and her fellows, and with the photo of children in front of the newspapers. And the rest of journalists had written nothing in their newspapers about the humiliation of Kalus because they were afraid to be sent to prison by Kalus or even to be killed by Kalus.

And the whole kingdom was not really surprised to read in the newspapers of Remy the humiliation of Kalus by children because they knew that Remy was opposed to the laws of Kalus, and the way of the king Kalus to rule the kingdom.

And Remy was named the journalist of people and he was also named the voice of people or the voice of the speechless, and at the same time, Remy was the worst enemy of Kalus. And although the fact that Remy had been tortured and sent to prison many times by Kalus, Remy had never given up his fight.

The day had gone well in the kingdom. Sunshine, Luna, and other children had held the meeting in the palace where they talked about the return of education in the kingdom, and also about how to put an end to the laws of Kalus.

And they had not succeeded in deciding about the date of the return of school to the kingdom because they had not yet talked with the instructors who were going to teach them. And they had decided to meet the instructors in the coming days to talk with the instructors before announcing the date of the return of education to the kingdom.

CHAPTER IV

THE FIGHT OF SUNSHINE TO FREE THE SOULS OF FUTURE CHILDREN AND FUTURE GENERATIONS

The days were passing, and things were not going very well in the kingdom. The hospitals of the kingdom were full of women crying their bellies, and women were arriving in the hospitals everyday crying their bellies.

And the results of blood tests had shown that all these women who were crying their bellies were pregnant. But the results of the blood test had also shown that these pregnant women were doing well, and the doctors were not understanding what was causing the pain in the bellies of these pregnant women.

The whole kingdom was very worried about the situation of these pregnant women, mostly that the doctors had not succeeded to find out what these pregnant women were suffering from. And the doctors had seen nothing through the result of the blood tests and ultrasounds that they had done on these pregnant women.

And people were very afraid that the curse that had befallen the kingdom more than twelve years ago, had come back. Especially that during this period of crisis which had hit the kingdom, the pregnant women and children were those who had particularly suffered from this crisis.

Sunshine and her fellows had not yet announced the date of the return of the education in the kingdom because they were facing a big problem of lack of teachers. And the school director and instructors that Sunshine and her fellows had met to teach them had refused.

And these instructors had refused to teach children by saying that the education was banned in the kingdom by the king Kalus, and that only Kalus had the powers to authorize the return of the education to the kingdom and to open the school's doors.

The instructors had also said that only Kalus had the powers to ask them to go teach children at school because Kalus was still the king of the kingdom. And the instructors had also told children that they were amazed and proud by the courage that children had, but that they could not help children even if they really wanted because they would be killed by the king Kalus.

Kalus was still in his magic room, and since the day he had got in his magic room because he was running away from Sunshine and her fellows, Kalus had not got out of his magic room. And Kalus was feeling hungry and thirsty because he had not put something in his mouth since the days that he was in his magic room. And Kalus was also smelling bad, and there was the blood that had clotted on his face, the wounds that were on his face were not healing, but these wounds were getting worse.

And Kalus was looking tired and he was feeling pain in his body because he was spending his day and night lying on the floor. And Kalus was waiting for Lord to come and tell him if he could get out of the magic room. And despite the fact that Kalus wanted to get out of the magic room, he knew well that he could not take a risk to get out without knowing if Sunshine was still alive or not.

Because Kalus was very afraid of Sunshine and her fellows, and he knew well that Sunshine was capable of the worst. And Kalus was hoping that Lord would come soon to announce to him the good news that Sunshine was dead.

And Kalus had already planned several assassinations and horrible things in the kingdom after the death of Sunshine. And the first thing that Kalus would do after Sunshine would be buried, would be to take revenge on all children of the kingdom who had humiliated him, including his own children. And Kalus had also planned to order his security guards to kill all children who were near Sunshine and who helped Sunshine in her fight, even his own children who had not hesitated to join Sunshine.

Inside the palace, the security guards of Kalus and his personal employees were very worried about him, and they were wondering where the king Kalus was because it's been days now that they had not seen Kalus. And they were very worried about Kalus because it was the first time that Kalus was not seen in the palace for days. And Kalus had never spent a day without being seen in the palace.

And the security guards and the personal employees of Kalus knew that Kalus was not outside because it's been twelve years now that Kalus had not left the palace. And they were wondering where Kalus could be.

The security guards and personal employees of Kalus could not imagine that Kalus was in his magic room because no one in the palace knew the existence of the magic room. And Kalus's family, who were his wife and children, were not at all worried about the absence of Kalus. And they did not care about the fact that Kalus had not been seen for days now, and they were instead happy about the absence of Kalus.

And Luna had even said that she hoped that her father was gone forever, and that he would never come back. And Diana was busy with her charity across the kingdom, while George and Luna were busy with their meeting with Sunshine and other children about the change that they wanted to make in the kingdom.

It's been weeks now, nothing has changed in the kingdom, and the situation in the kingdom was going worse and worse. And the pregnant women were arriving at the hospital every day crying pain in their bellies, and the doctors had still not succeeded to find out what was causing the pain in the bellies of these pregnant women. And the real problem was the fact that there was no more room in the hospitals to keep the patients.

And the doctors had even sent home the patients who were not in serious condition because the doctors wanted bedrooms to keep pregnant women in the hospitals. And the whole kingdom was living with fear with the situation of these pregnant women, and except children, the rest of the population was afraid that the curse that had destroyed the kingdom more than twelve years ago was coming back.

Children were still at home because Sunshine and her fellows had still not succeeded in convincing the instructors to come and teach children at the school. And although the fact that Sunshine and her fellows had made an announcement in the newspapers called Kongreshow by J.P Remy that they were looking for the teachers who could teach children at school or even anyone who could teach children, no teacher had responded to this announcement.

And all the teachers and anyone who could teach were afraid of being killed on the orders of the king Kalus if they responded to this announcement to teach children. Because the whole kingdom knew well that the decision to open the schools were coming from children and not from Kalus.

Sunshine was busy with her fellows to look for instructors and people who could teach children in school, that she had almost forgotten about Lord. And despite the fact that she knew the situation of these pregnant women in hospitals, she did not have a second to think how to release the souls of the babies who were in the wombs of these pregnant women.

Because her mind was focused on how to find the instructors who could teach children at school. And the real problem was that children could not open the school without the instructors to teach them.

Kalus was still in his magic room, he was so sick that he was dying. And Lord had not yet come to see him. And Kalus was wondering why Lord had not yet come to visit him, and he was very afraid that Sunshine might have succeeded in killing Lord.

And Kalus was thinking of getting out of his magic room, but at the same time, he was very afraid of Sunshine because he knew that she was still alive. Because he knew well that Lord should have already come to announce the death of Sunshine if Sunshine was dead. Then Kalus made the decision to stay in the magic room and wait for Lord.

It was evening, Sunshine was lying in her bed and she was staring at the ceiling with her eyes opened and she was looking very tired. Sunshine and her fellows had a long day, and they had announced the return of the education to the kingdom the next day.

Sunshine and her fellows had used the newspapers called Kongreshow, the website and the television channel of J.P Remy to announce the return of the education in the kingdom the next day. And they had asked all the children of the kingdom to come to school the next day.

Sunshine and her fellows had tried to announce the return of education in the kingdom through the national television and national radio without success. The director of the national television and national radio had told Sunshine and her fellows that he could not allow them to use the national television and radio to make the announcement of the return of education in the kingdom.

Because education was still banned in the kingdom by the king Kalus. And that only the king Kalus had the powers to announce the return of the education in the kingdom through the national television and radio.

And other radios, televisions and newspapers had refused Sunshine and her fellows to use their communication channels to announce the return of education in the kingdom. And even if these radios, televisions and newspapers wanted to help Sunshine and her fellows by allowing them to announce the return of the education in the kingdom through their communication channels, they were afraid of Kalus's reaction.

And even if the owners and employees of these radios, televisions and newspapers supported the initiative of Sunshine and her fellows to open the schools in the kingdom, they could not allow Sunshine and her fellows to use their communication channels to announce the return of the education to the kingdom.

Because these owners and employees were afraid to be killed on the orders of Kalus. But Sunshine and her fellows had succeeded in making the whole kingdom aware of the return of the education in the kingdom the next day through the newspapers, television and website of Remy.

The whole kingdom was aware that the school's doors would be opened the next day and all children were very happy to start the school the next day. And despite the fact that the parents were very proud of Sunshine and her fellows who had decided to open the school the next day, the parents were divided on the idea of whether they were going to send their children to school the next day or not.

And even if the parents wanted to see their children go to school, they were afraid about Kalus's reaction, and they were afraid that their children could be killed at school on the orders of Kalus. Because the parents knew well that the decision to open the schools was not coming from the king Kalus, but this decision was instead coming from Sunshine and her fellows.

And the parents did not know what to do because their children were so eager to start school the next day. And their children had been so happy since Sunshine and her fellows had announced the opening of the school the next day.

But what Sunshine and her fellows had not said in their announcement, it was that they did not have the teachers who would teach children the next day. And the problem was that Sunshine and her fellows had not succeeded in finding a teacher who was ready to teach children.

And during the meeting of Sunshine and her fellows, Sunshine had found out that Luna could read and write. Then Sunshine decided that she and Luna were going to teach children at school. Because they knew well that all the teachers of the kingdom could not help them by teaching children at school because the teachers were afraid to be killed on the orders of Kalus.

It was 1 one in the afternoon, Sunshine was still lying on her bed and she was staring at the ceiling, but she was so thoughtful about the situation of the kingdom that she could not even sleep.

And despite the fact that Sunshine was very tired and that she wanted to get some sleep to be in good shape the next day. But, she could not because she was thinking about her mom who was still in the hospital and other pregnant women who were in the hospital crying pain in their bellies.

Sunshine knew well that the doctors could not help these pregnant women, and she also knew well that she was the only one who could help these pregnant women by freeing the souls of babies who were controlled by Lord in their wombs. And Sunshine was wondering why she had not been visited by Lord, and she was very surprised that Lord had not visited her even after the humiliation of Kalus.

And for Sunshine, it was obvious that Lord was planning something worse, and she was very worried. Then she decided to go visit Lord. Then Sunshine took a deep breath and her eyes started spinning, and the light shone into her eyes, then she disappeared.

It was midnight, Lord was in his forest and he was walking around the forest thinking how to kill Sunshine. And for Lord, it was obvious that he must kill Sunshine but he did not know how, and it's been weeks now that Lord was thinking how to kill Sunshine.

And suddenly, the expression of Lord's face changed and his face was full of smiles as he had got an idea how to kill Sunshine. Then Lord opened his mouth and said that it was time to kill Sunshine, and he lifted him through the sky and the expression of his face changed and he was staring at Sunshine who was flying in space.

And looking at the expression on the face of Lord, it was obvious that he was very surprised to see Sunshine. And he was wondering what Sunshine was doing in his forest. Then Sunshine landed near the fire and she was facing Lord. Sunshine and Lord were looking at each other in the eyes without saying a word. Sunshine broke the silence and asked, "You never sleep?"

"A god does not sleep," Lord answered.

Sunshine said, "Yes, you told me when we last met that a god does not sleep because a god needs to watch his people," Sunshine added, "I imagine that you are not sleeping because you are watching the kingdom and its people."

Lord looked into Sunshine's eyes and said, "I lost control to watch what is going on in the kingdom."

Sunshine asked, "What happened?"

Lord answered, "It seems you forgot that you had broken the magic mirror that I was using to watch what was going on in the kingdom."

Sunshine said, "Sorry, to hear that." And she added, "I had forgotten it."

"I am not stupid," Lord said.

"What do you mean?" Sunshine asked.

Lord looked into Sunshine's eyes and said, "You did not forget that you had destroyed my magic mirror. And you asked me this question because you wanted to know if I have another magic mirror to watch what is going on in the kingdom."

Sunshine said, "You are right because I asked you this question because I wanted to know if you have another magic mirror to watch the kingdom."

"Why are you not sleeping?" Lord asked.

Sunshine looked into Lord's eyes and said, "How can I sleep when I have a devil like you in my kingdom."

Lord said, "You got the school's keys, so I do not understand what you are doing here."

"Children would start school today," Sunshine said.

Lord clapped his hands and said, "Congratulations." And he added, "Today is not a great day in the kingdom, but it's a memorable day with the return of education to the kingdom." Then Lord looked into Sunshine's eyes and said, "You made history, and you wrote your name in the history of the kingdom because thanks to you children would have access to knowledge."

"I have not yet made the history of the kingdom." Sunshine said.

"What more do you want to make history?" Lord asked.

Sunshine looked into Lord's eyes with a face full of anger and she said, "Kill you."

Lord laughed and said, "Stop dreaming."

"I am not dreaming," Sunshine replied.

"You would never succeed to kill me," Lord said.

"I would, and I promise you," Sunshine said.

"I am undying," Lord replied.

Sunshine cried out, "What?" By looking at Lord with a surprised face.

"I am undying," Lord repeated.

"Undying?" Sunshine asked.

"Yes, undying," Lord answered.

"No human being is undying," Sunshine said.

"I am not a human being," Lord said.

"What?" Sunshine cried out.

"I am not a human being," Lord repeated.

"What are you if you are not a human being?" Sunshine asked.

"I am god," Lord answered.

Sunshine looked into Lord's eyes and said, "No matter who you are, I would kill you and I promise you."

Lord said, "Good luck." And Lord added, "I think you should be in your bed now because you must start school in a few hours, and it would not be a good thing to sleep in class, mostly for your first time to go to school."

Sunshine said, "It's been months now that I have not closed my eyes, and I really want to sleep."

Lord asked, "What is keeping you from sleeping?"

"The cries of pregnant women who are in the hospitals," Sunshine answered.

Lord smiled at Sunshine and said, "You can not help these pregnant women because these pain in their bellies would stop only when they would give birth."

Sunshine looked at Lord with an astonished face and asked, "Does that mean that all women who are pregnant and who would be pregnant would spend all their nine months of their pregnancy with pain in their bellies?"

Lord answered, "Yes." Then Lord looked into Sunshine's eyes with a face full of smiles and said, "Even you, you would live this situation that your mother and other pregnant women are living now because you would feel this pain in the future when you would be pregnant."

"It would never happen," Sunshine retorted.

"It means that you would never get pregnant," Lord said.

"I would get pregnant, and I would give birth to many children," Sunshine said.

"If you would get pregnant, it means you would experience this pain that pregnant women are experiencing now, and it also means that your children would belong to me," Lord said.

"No, I would not experience this pain, and no woman in this kingdom would experience these pains again, and no child in this kingdom would belong to you," Sunshine said.

"It seems you do not understand," Lord said.

"I understood that you have a dream, and your dream is that the future generation of children of this kingdom would belong to you, and also that you want to be the god of this kingdom," Sunshine said.

"It's not a dream because the future generation of children of this kingdom already belong to me, also I am already the god of this kingdom," Lord retorted.

"You are lying to yourself," Sunshine replied.

"Stop thinking that you can save the souls of the future generation of children of this kingdom," Lord said."

"I did it once, and I can do it twice," Sunshine said.

"There is a difference," Lord replied.

"What is the difference?" Sunshine asked.

Lord looked into Sunshine's eyes and said, "Twelve years ago, I did not expect a strong and powerful enemy like you to be born, and I was not prepared to face a dangerous enemy like you, and that's why your birth surprised me. And you succeeded in releasing the souls of children twelve years ago not only because I was not expecting an enemy like you, but mostly because I had used the satanic trees that were planted in front of each house of the kingdom to control the souls of children. And it was easy for you to release the souls of children by destroying these satanic trees."

And Lord added, "This time I used a different method to own the souls of children because I used to own the souls of children from the first date that children were born, but this time, I own the souls of children from the first day that a woman got pregnant. And this time when a child would be born this child would belong to me forever because it would be impossible to free the soul of a child after the birth of that child."

"Why would it be impossible to free the soul of a child after the birth of that child?" Sunshine asked.

Lord looked into Sunshine's eyes and said, "This method that I used to own the souls of children is very powerful because with this method, after seventy-seven days or exactly 1848 hours, it would be impossible to save the souls of the children again." Then Lord looked at his palm's hand and the number three appeared on his palm's hand, then he smiled at Sunshine and said, "You have exactly three hours to do the miracle."

"I do not understand," Sunshine said.

Lord started walking around the fire with his face full of smiles, while Sunshine's eyes were focused on Lord. And Sunshine was wondering what was going on with Lord, and why he was suddenly silent. Then Lord stopped face to Sunshine and looked in her eyes, and said, "I have a proposition for you."

"I do not know what your proposition is, but I am not interested," Sunshine said.

"You must listen," Lord said.

"The only good thing that you can say, it's that you must free the souls of children who are not yet born and leave this kingdom," Sunshine said.

Lord laughed and said, "Stop dreaming because it would never happen." And Lord added, "I have something better for you."

"Keep what you want to say in your mouth," Sunshine replied.

"Even if you do not want to hear what my proposition is, let me give you the hand of peace," Lord said.

Sunshine was looking at Lord with a face full of anger, and she was also looking at Lord's hand that was handed to her, and she was wondering if Lord was serious by asking her to shake his hand and to make peace with him. Then Sunshine said, "Stop dreaming because I would never shake the hand of a devil like you."

Lord smiled and said, "You won the fight by getting the return of the education in the kingdom, and I won the fight by possessing the souls of children who were not yet born." And Lord looked into Sunshine's eyes and said, "You must accept reality because the kingdom is already divided into two."

"I do not understand," Sunshine said.

Lord took a deep breath and said, "The generation of human beings who are living now, it's a good generation with a soul. But the generation who will be born in the future would be a generation without a soul because I own the souls of the generation of people who will be born in the future."

"What are you going to do with the souls of children that you want to own?" Sunshine asked.

"I would not answer this question," Lord replied.

"Why?" Sunshine asked.

Lord looked into Sunshine's eyes with silence and looking at the expression on the face of Lord, it was obvious that he was thinking. After a few seconds Lord broke the silence and said, "I did not want to tell you what my project is, but I am going to tell a part of the project because there is nothing you can do to prevent this project from happening, mostly that in less than three hours, I would be the owner of the souls of first children who would be born in the future."

"What is that project?" Sunshine asked.

Lord looked into Sunshine's eyes and said, "I have a project to create a world of vampires, and the kingdom is a part of this project, and I made a pact with the king Kalus to turn the population of this kingdom into the vampires." And Lord added, "And the most important thing to turn human beings who are not the vampires into the vampires, it's to own the souls of these human beings because by owning the souls of these human beings, it would be possible to turn them into the vampires."

Sunshine stared at Lord with an astonished face and asked, "Why do you want to own the souls of only children, and not the souls of parents."

Lord said, "It's impossible to own the souls of adults. And I can only own the souls of children who are under ten years old." And Lord added, "I can exactly control the souls of children from zero to nine years old."

"It means if you own the soul of a child of three years old, you will lose the control of the soul of this child when this child would be ten years old?" Sunshine asked.

Lord answered, "No, because once I own the soul of a child, I would own this soul forever, and even when this child would be an adult, and even when this child would die, I would still own the soul of this child." And Lord added, "At least if someone releases the souls of these children from me like you did twelve years ago. But this time, you can not free the souls of children because I already own the souls of children forever."

"The miracle can happen in less than three hours," Sunshine said.

"It's impossible for you to save the souls of these children in less than three hours," Lord said.

"Why did the king Kalus accept to turn the children of the kingdom into vampires?" Sunshine asked.

"For the power," Lord answered.

"Power?" Sunshine cried out.

"Yes, power," Lord replied.

"Kalus was born the king with all the powers and honors, so I do not understand which kind of power he is looking for," Sunshine said.

Lord laughed and said, "Power to be immortal."

"What?" Sunshine cried out.

"Kalus wants to be immortal," Lord replied.

"It means you lied to Kalus that you would give him the power to make him immortal and in exchange Kalus would allow you to turn children of the kingdom into vampires," Sunshine said.

"I did not lie to Kalus," Lord said.

"It's possible for a human being to be immortal?" Sunshine asked.

"No," Lord answered.

"How are you going to make Kalus an immortal?" Sunshine asked.

"I already changed Kalus," Lord said.

"What do you mean?" Sunshine asked.

"Kalus is no longer really a human being," Lord answered.

"I do not understand," Sunshine said.

"I have started the transformation of Kalus before you were born," Lord said.

"You have started to transform Kalus into a vampire?" Sunshine asked.

"Not into a vampire, but into a god like me," Lord replied.

"Does that mean Kalus is also immortal?" Sunshine asked.

"It's not easy to kill Kalus because Kalus has received a lot of satanic powers from me," Lord answered.

"Why did Kalus need these satanic powers?" Sunshine asked.

"Because it was the process to be immortal and to be more powerful," Lord answered.

"What is this process to be immortal?" Sunshine asked.

"One part of this process requires Kalus to mystically kill children and drink their blood by using these satanic powers," Lord answered.

"It means Kalus had mystically killed and tortured children in the past by using these satanic powers?" Sunshine asked.

"Exactly," Lord answered.

"Why ban education, tradition and religion in the kingdom?" Sunshine asked.

"Because the world of vampires has its own tradition, its own education and its own religion which are completely different from the tradition, education and religion of the kingdom of Manitoba," Lord answered.

"Does it mean you have a plan to transform the kingdom of Manitoba into the kingdom of the vampires, with tradition, education and religion of the vampires?" Sunshine asked.

"Exactly," Lord answered.

"What is the tradition, education and religion of vampires?" Sunshine asked.

"I would not answer this question because you would see what is the tradition, the religion and the education of the vampires very soon when this kingdom would be transformed into the kingdom of the vampires," Lord answered.

"I would never see it," Sunshine retorted.

"Are you going to kill yourself before I transform this kingdom into the kingdom of vampires?" Lord asked.

"No, I am not going to kill myself, but this kingdom would never be transformed into the kingdom of the vampires," Sunshine answered.

Lord looked at his palm's hand and the number two appeared on his palm's hand and he smiled at Sunshine and said, "In exactly two hours, it would be 1848 hours." And Lord added, "Right now, it's been exactly 1846 hours that I had started the process of owning the souls of the first children who would be born in a few months. And it also means that the destiny of this kingdom is going to change in two hours because the first construction to transform this kingdom into the kingdom of vampires would be done in two hours."

Sunshine was just staring at Lord with her eyes spinning without saying a word, then the light shone into Sunshine's eyes and she flew in the space. And Lord had lifted his head watching Sunshine who was flying in space with his face full of smiles. Sunshine disappeared in the space, and Lord turned his head and walked away.

Sunshine had knelt in a small desert, and she was praying with her eyes closed, asking God to help her to free the souls of children that were controlled by Lord and to protect the kingdom with its inhabitants. Then suddenly, a burst of fire appeared in her head, and she realized that it's the same fire that she had seen in the forest of Lord. She opened her eyes, and her head felt like it was spinning, then the light shone in her eyes, and she disappeared.

Lord was in his forest, walking around and with his eyes focused on the fire, looking lost in thought. Then Lord started feeling a strange smell, and he looked up the sky, and suddenly the expression of his face changed and he was astonished to see Sunshine who was flying through the forest. And Lord was wondering why Sunshine was coming back, and he was feeling that there was something going wrong.

Then Sunshine landed near to the fire, and she did not look at Lord, but she was instead staring at the fire. And there was a question that was going on in Sunshine's head, and this question was what was making this fire burn? And since the first time that Sunshine had seen this fire, she was wondering the same question and she was trying to understand what was making this fire burn without success.

And Sunshine was wondering if it was really the fire, not only because there was nothing like the woods or anything that was making this fire burn. But mostly because there was no smoke coming from this fire, and this fire did not have a smell. Because normally the fire has a smell. And Sunshine was seeing very strangely that the whole forest glowed yellow and the space of the forest was shining in yellow like if there was a yellow light that was shining in the forest.

And Sunshine knew well that the yellow light that's shining in the whole forest was coming from the fire that was burning because the flame of this fire was yellow. It was very strange for Sunshine because a simple fire like what she was seeing could not light a big forest like this. Sunshine started wondering why this fire appeared in her head when she was praying by asking God to help her to free the souls of children, but unfortunately, she could not answer this question.

And the eyes of Lord were just focused on Sunshine, and there was silence, but Lord had noticed that Sunshine was thoughtful and he knew too that she had come back for a reason. And Lord knew well that Sunshine had a plan, and her plan was to free the souls of the future children before six in the morning, and that she had probably come back for that. But Lord was not worried about this at all because in his mind, he knew that Sunshine could not free the souls of the future children, and that it was even impossible for her to find a way to try to free these souls.

"What did you forget?" Lord asked.

Sunshine looked at Lord and replied, "I forgot to ask you a question?"

"What is your question?" Lord asked.

"This strange thing that is burning like a fire, is it really a fire?" Sunshine asked.

"Yes," Lord answered.

"What is making this fire burn because I am not seeing the woods?" Sunshine asked.

"It's a magic fire," Lord answered.

"What do you mean by that?" Sunshine asked.

"The magic fire did not need the woods," Lord answered.

"What does the magic fire need?" Sunshine asked.

"Nothing," Lord answered.

"How nothing?" Sunshine asked.

"Because it's the magic fire," Lord answered.

"Can you tell me a little bit about this magic fire?" Sunshine asked.

"No," Lord answered.

"Why no?" Sunshine asked.

"Because it's my secret," Lord answered.

"Can you share this secret with me?" Sunshine asked.

Lord looked into Sunshine's eyes and said, "If I share this secret with you, it would not be a secret anymore, so I can not share it with you because I want to keep it a secret."

Then Sunshine and Lord were looking at each other without saying a word. And Lord had his eyes focused on Sunshine's eyes, and he knew well that she had something in her head, and he was keeping his eyes on her to make sure that she would not do something.

Mostly, that last time Sunshine had destroyed his magic mirror when she was in the forest, and she had succeeded in destroying his magic mirror because he was distracted. And Sunshine had taken advantage of the fact that he was distracted to use her magic to summon the bees. But this time Lord had decided to stay vigilant and careful and above all to stay focused.

Sunshine was staring at Lord by thinking what to do, and she knew that she did not have enough time because she had less than two hours to save the souls of the future generation of children of the kingdom. And if she did not succeed in less than two hours, it would be impossible for her to free the souls of these children who would be born in a few months.

And looking at the expression on Sunshine's face, it was obvious that she was very worried and afraid to not succeed, and she knew herself that if she did not succeed in releasing these souls, she would kill herself. Because she would not support seeing children of the kingdom turn into vampires just because she had failed to free the souls of these children by preventing these children from being turned into vampires.

And Sunshine knew well that Lord's eyes were focused on her because he wanted to make sure that she was not going to something, mostly that last time when she was in this forest, she had destroyed his magic mirror.

And Sunshine wanted to use her magic to summon the bees, but she knew that it would not work because Lord was going to stop her from doing that, especially since Lord's eyes were fixed on. And mostly that last time when she was in the forest, she had used her magic to summon the bees to distract Lord to be able to destroy his magic mirror.

And Sunshine wanted to use her magic, but Lord would see if she just tried to use her magic and he would directly fight her to prevent her from doing something. And Sunshine also knew well that Lord would not hesitate to fight her if she made a move or even if she turned her head away.

Then Sunshine started to think faster about what to do because she knew well that she did not have enough time to save the kingdom by preventing the kingdom of Manitoba from being turned into the kingdom of vampires.

Suddenly, Lord and Sunshine turned their heads to the left when they heard a noise coming from that side, and they were looking with surprised faces as they were hearing the cries of the bird, but they were not seeing the bird that was making these noises.

Sunshine looked at Lord and asked him if he had the birds in his house? Lord answered Sunshine that no. And Lord added that the animals did not live in his forest. Then Lord asked Sunshine if she was not the one who had used her magic to summon the bird. Sunshine answered Lord that she had not used her magic since she was in this forest.

Then Sunshine and Lord turned their heads to the right when they heard this noise of the bird coming from this side, but again they were not seeing the bird that was making noise. And they were wondering where the bird was making noises. Suddenly, Lord started turning his head looking everywhere as he was hearing the sounds of birds coming from everywhere, and these noises were not only coming from one bird, but from many birds.

And Sunshine was staring at Lord who had lifted his head in the sky looking for the birds that were making noises. Sunshine got an idea to take advantage of this situation to free the souls of the future children like Lord was distracted by the sounds of birds.

Then Sunshine looked at fire and her eyes started spinning, then the light got out from her eyes and started shining on the fire, but the light that was getting out from Sunshine's eyes and shining on the fire did not have effects on the fire. And suddenly, Sunshine started feeling her body that was burning, and she understood that it was this fire that was burning her body, and that this fire was burning her body because her magic was in contact with this fire.

Then Sunshine stopped her magic, and she took a deep breath by thinking about what to do to put out this fire, then she got an idea, and she looked at her fingernails and her eyes started spinning. Then the light got out from Sunshine's eyes and shone on her fingernails, and her fingernails became long.

Then Sunshine used these long fingernails and she tore her hands, and she started to bleed from her hands. Then Sunshine walked two steps near to the fire, and she handed her hands through the fire, and the blood was flowing from her hands and falling on the fire.

Lord had his head lifted through the sky, and he was still trying to find the birds that were making the noises because there were still the sounds of birds. Suddenly, the expression of Lord's face changed and his eyes opened wide when he saw the moon and the stars appear in the sky, and he was looking with a surprised face at the moon and the stars had appeared in the sky. And Lord was staring at the moon that was shining in the sky, and with the stars that were shining in the clouds without understanding what was going on.

And it was the first time that the moon and the stars were shining in the sky of the forest of Lord, and Lord's eyes were focused on the moon that was shining. And looking at the expression on the face of Lord, it was as if he was dreaming because he did not believe that there was the moon that was shining in his house.

And there were a lot of questions that were going on in the head of Lord, and some of these questions were, how was it possible that the moon and the stars were shining in the sky of his forest? Was it really the real moon that was shining? If it was the real moon where this moon was coming from?

And Lord was wondering about these questions because he knew well that the moon and the stars were not supposed to shine in the sky of his forest, also called his house. Because the energies of the magic fire that lit up his forest prevented the moon and the stars from shining in the sky of his forest.

And Lord was still staring at the moon that was shining in the sky as if he was watching a miracle that was happening. And the mind of Lord was completely focused on this moon in the sky that he had even forgotten about the noises coming from the songs of birds which were still occurring.

Suddenly, the expression of Lord's face changed and he turned his head around looking with an amazed face as he was seeing his whole forest that was lit by the moon that was shining in the sky. And Lord was turning on himself without understanding what was going on, and looking at the expression of Lord's face, it was obvious that he was completely lost and he was even going mad. And suddenly, the surprise that was on Lord's face turned into rage when he noticed that his magic fire had been put out by Sunshine.

And Lord was staring at Sunshine that was bleeding from her hands with a face full of rage, and he was understanding that Sunshine had used her blood to put out the fire. Then Lord opened his mouth and started screaming.

And Sunshine was staring at Lord with a face empty of expression, and she was seeing the rage in Lord's eyes and she could see the veins on Lord's neck that had come out. And Sunshine was understanding that she had hurt Lord by destroying his magic fire.

And suddenly, Lord jumped on Sunshine and threw her on the ground, and he started beating Sunshine with anger by using his hands and all his strength. Then Lord lifted Sunshine with his hand and Sunshine was bleeding from her mouth and nose, and Lord threw her away. Sunshine went and hit her body against a satanic tree and fell on the ground. And Lord walked up to near Sunshine and he stared at Sunshine who was on the ground bleeding and crying in pain.

Then Lord started to kick Sunshine with his right foot, and Sunshine was on the ground crying pain. After a few minutes, Lord lifted his left foot and he put on Sunshine and he started stomping her, by looking at her with a face full of anger.

And Sunshine was trying to remove Lord's foot from her without success because she was too weak to remove Lord's foot from her. Then Lord bent and carried Sunshine with his hand and threw her in the space, and she went and hit her body against a satanic tree and she fell on the ground.

Sunshine was on the ground and she was crying pain in her whole body, and she was bleeding, and she was trying to use magic without success. And it was impossible for her to use her magic because it was hard for her to concentrate on herself, and she could not concentrate because she was feeling extreme pains and these pains were preventing her from concentrating. And the fact that she could not concentrate, was preventing her from using her magic because she needed the concentration to use her magic.

Then Lord walked near Sunshine who was on the ground bleeding, and he bent and lifted Sunshine with one of his hands, and he looked at Sunshine with his face full of anger. And he started hitting Sunshine with his other hand. And Sunshine was so weak that she was unable to defend herself.

Then Lord stopped punching Sunshine and he stared at her, and Sunshine's face was full of blood. Then, Lord's eyes started spinning and the light got out from his eyes and shone on Sunshine. And suddenly Sunshine was pushed against a satanic tree by this light coming from Lord's eyes and she was also stuck on this satanic tree trunk by this light coming from Lord's eyes.

Lord had his eyes focused on Sunshine who was stuck on a tree trunk, and Lord's face was full of rage and his eyes started spinning and suddenly Sunshine started screaming in pain, and she was screaming pain because she was in pain all over her whole body. And she was feeling pain in her body because she was mystically tortured by Lord's magic.

Because the fact that Lord's eyes were spinning had an effect on her. And Sunshine was screaming that the tears were running down her cheeks, and the worse was that she could not defend herself. Because it was impossible for her to concentrate on herself to use her magic to fight Lord because the pain was preventing her from concentrating on herself.

After a few minutes, Lord's eyes stopped spinning. And suddenly, Sunshine stopped feeling pain in her body like Lord had stopped torturing her through his magic. And Sunshine started taking a deep breath and she was sweating.

Then Lord looked into Sunshine's eyes with the anger in his eyes and he told her that he would kill her. Then Lord asked Sunshine who was the one who was helping her? Sunshine was just staring at Lord without saying a word. Lord told Sunshine that he must kill her, then he would go find the mysterious person who was helping her and he would kill this mysterious person too.

Sunshine was just staring at Lord without saying a word, and she was wondering who was really the mysterious person who was helping her? And Sunshine knew well that she was helped by someone. Lord looked at Sunshine and told her that she had succeeded in putting out the magic fire because he was distracted by the sounds of the birds that the mysterious person who helped her had summoned.

Then Lord looked at his palm's hand and the number one appeared on his palm's hand. And he smiled at Sunshine and said that she had succeeded in destroying his magic mirror and his magic fire. But that she would never succeed to prevent him from transforming the kingdom of Manitoba into the kingdom of the vampires.

Because it's been exactly 1847 hours that he had started the process to own the souls of the future children, and in exactly an hour, it would be 1848 hours. And it meant that in an hour, he would be the owner of the souls of the children who would be born in a few months.

And that also meant that these children who would be born in a few months would be the first vampires of the kingdom. Sunshine looked at Lord with a face full of rage and said, "It would never happen." Then Sunshine took a deep breath and she was trying to focus on herself to use magic without success.

And despite the fact that Sunshine was no longer feeling pain in her body, she was unable to use her magic even if she could focus on herself. And despite the fact that Sunshine was able to focus on herself, she was unable to use her magic to fight Lord.

And Sunshine was completely lost because she was not understanding exactly what was going on, why she could not use her magic. And it was the first time that Sunshine was unable to use her magic when she was able to concentrate on herself.

Lord was laughing at Sunshine who was trying to use her magic without success, and Lord was seeing how Sunshine was making the efforts to use her magic without success. Then Lord walked two steps towards the satanic tree that Sunshine was stuck on.

And he looked into Sunshine's eyes with his face full of smiles and he told her to stop trying to use her magic, and that it was impossible for her to use her magic. Because she was stuck on a satanic tree, and on this satanic tree, it was impossible for her to use her magic because all the energies of her magic were absorbed by this satanic tree that she was stuck on.

Sunshine looked at Lord with a face full of anger and she understood why she was unable to use her magic. And immediately the anger that was on Sunshine's face turned into fear as she remembered that she had only less than an hour to save the souls of the future children. And Sunshine knew well that she was trapped on this satanic tree and that when she would be stuck on this satanic tree, she would not be able to use her magic because all the energies of her magic were absorbed by this satanic tree.

And Sunshine knew well that the only chance she had to free the souls of the future children was to find a way to use her magic. Because Sunshine knew well that she could not free the souls of the future children without using her magic.

And Sunshine started thinking about what to do and mostly how to use her magic, and Sunshine's heart was beating with fear as she was thinking. Lord had his eyes focused on Sunshine, and he could see through the expression on the face of Sunshine that she was thinking that she was trying to find a solution.

Then Lord told Sunshine to stop wasting her time to think because there was nothing that she could do to prevent him from owning the souls of the future children. And Lord added to Sunshine that everything she had succeeded to do so far was useless, like she had succeeded to open the school's doors because no child in the kingdom would go to school.

Because he was going to kill now, and when he would bury her, he would order Kalus to kill all friends with whom she was protesting for the return of education in the kingdom. Sunshine looked at Lord with a face full of rage without saying a word, then she opened her mouth and started to scream loudly to express her anger. And Lord was laughing at Sunshine who was screaming with her face full of rage.

Suddenly, the expression of Lord's face changed and he was turning his head looking around with a worried face, and he was feeling the wind that was blowing. And Lord was worried about this wind that was blowing because the wind was a poison for his satanic trees. Because the wind was natural air, and the natural air killed the evil energies that were on the satanic trees and the natural air also caused satanic trees to dry up.

And it was the first time that the wind was blowing in his forest. And Lord knew that the wind was blowing because Sunshine had put out his magic fire, and it was the energies of his magic fire that was preventing the natural phenomena like the moon, the stars, the wind, the sun, the rain and others from happening in his forest. And Lord was looking around thinking what to do to stop this wind that was blowing.

Suddenly, the wind became violent, and the worry that was on Lord's face turned into fear, as he was seeing the wind that was shaking the satanic trees. And Lord was turning his head looking around with his eyes wide opened and looking at the expression on the face of Lord, it was as if he was watching a miracle.

Lord was completely lost and he was not still realizing what was happening. Lord was not even paying attention to Sunshine who was screaming on the satanic tree. And Sunshine was still stuck on the satanic tree trunk, and she was screaming loud with her face full of anger, and there was the wind that was blowing on her face. And the wind was strongly shaking the satanic tree that Sunshine was stuck on.

Suddenly, Lord turned his head from behind when he heard a noise, then he immediately opened his mouth trying to talk but his mouth was shaking so that a word could not get out from his mouth. And he was staring at Sunshine who was lying on the ground with his face full of despair. And Lord was understanding that he was losing everything, that everything was almost over. Because Lord knew well that Sunshine had fallen on the ground because the wind had killed all the evil energies that were on the satanic tree that Sunshine was stuck on.

And Lord also knew that if the evil energies that were on the satanic tree that Sunshine was stuck on were killed by the wind, it meant that the wind had also killed the energies of the rest of the satanic trees. And it also meant that if the evil energies that were on the satanic trees were killed, that meant that these satanic trees were going to die soon because it was these evil energies that kept the satanic trees alive.

And Lord also knew that if the satanic trees died, everything would be over, his project to transform the kingdom of Manitoba into the kingdom of the vampires would be destroyed. Because he needed his satanic trees to transform the kingdom of Manitoba into the kingdom of vampires. And Lord was turning his head by looking around, staring at the satanic trees and by thinking what to do, and Lord was feeling the wind that was blowing harder and harder.

And Lord also knew that even if the wind that was blowing was natural, he knew that this natural wind was triggered by the mysterious person who was helping Sunshine in her fight. Then the smile appeared on Lord's face as he remembered that he had his satanic master tree, and that the wind could not kill that satanic master tree. Because the roots of this satanic master tree were located in the water, and this water had the powers to protect this satanic master tree in case of danger.

And Lord knew that everything was not yet over, and that he still had control of the situation. Because even if the wind killed the satanic trees that were in the forest, he could still use the satanic master tree to own the souls of the future children and to transform the kingdom of Manitoba into the kingdom of vampires.

Sunshine was trying to get up from the ground and she was looking very tired and weak. And suddenly, the moon that was in the sky caught the attention of Sunshine, and she had her eyes focused on the moon that was in the cloud. Then Sunshine noticed that the moon had started moving, and she was feeling a strange reaction inside her body.

And Sunshine was wondering why the moon that was in the sky was moving, and for Sunshine, it was like this moon was trying to send her a message. And Sunshine was curious to see where this moon was going. Then Sunshine's eyes started spinning and she flew in the direction of this moon.

Lord was still turning his head by looking around with his face full of smiles. And looking at the expression on the face of Lord, it was obvious that he was not worried about the wind that was blowing in his forest, even if he knew that this wind was a poison that killed the evil energies that were on the satanic trees. And Lord was not worried about the wind that was blowing because he knew well that the wind could not destroy his satanic master tree.

Suddenly, the expression on 'Lord's face changed when he saw Sunshine who was flying in space, and the smile that was on his face had turned into fear. Lord was staring at Sunshine who was flying in space towards the moon that was in the sky with his face full of fear and with his heart that was beating faster than the normal, like Lord had understood what was going on. And Lord knew that Sunshine was flying in space by following the moon that was moving in the sky to destroy his satanic master tree.

And Lord knew that it was this mysterious enemy who was using the moon to show to Sunshine where this satanic master tree was located. Then Lord understood that he must kill Sunshine to prevent her from destroying his satanic master tree. Then Lord opened his mouth and he screamed loudly with his face full of anger, and his eyes started spinning, then he flew in space.

Sunshine and Lord were flying in space. Sunshine was flying by following the moon while Lord was flying after Sunshine. And Lord was flying faster with his face full of anger and with his heart that was beating with fear that Sunshine could succeed in destroying his satanic master tree. And Sunshine was flying very slowly because the energies coming from the satanic trees were preventing her from flying faster. But the wind that was blowing was helping Sunshine to keep the balance in space as she was flying between the satanic trees.

Suddenly, the fear appeared on Sunshine's face when she felt the hand of Lord on her, and Sunshine knew well that Lord was trying to prevent her from going where the moon was taking her. And Sunshine was trying to run away from Lord by flying as fast as she could.

And Sunshine's heart was beating with fear as she was feeling that Lord was trying to catch her, and Sunshine was afraid that she would not succeed in saving the souls of the future children. Because she knew well that she had less than an hour to prevent Lord from turning the kingdom of Manitoba into the kingdom of the vampires.

Then Lord succeeded to take Sunshine in his arms, and they were fighting, and there was the wind that was blowing on them. And this wind that was blowing was an advantage for Sunshine because this wind was helping Sunshine to breathe easily, while this wind was an inconvenience for Lord.

Because this wind was preventing Lord from being connected to the evil energies that were on the satanic trees. And despite the fact that Lord was fighting in his forest, he did not have the advantage on the fight because the fight was very hard between them.

Then they hit themselves against a satanic tree and they fell to the ground and they kept on fighting with the anger on their faces. Then Lord grabbed Sunshine through her neck with one his hand, and he succeeded to kneel by keeping Sunshine on the ground.

And Sunshine was lying on her back on the ground, and she had grabbed Lord's hand that was on her neck with her two hands and she was trying to remove Lord's hand from her neck without success. And Sunshine had the difficulties to breath like Lord was trying to kill her by squeezing her neck.

Suddenly, Lord started feeling a violent wind that was hitting his face, and this wind made Lord lose concentration, and Lord understood that this wind was coming from the mysterious person who was helping Sunshine in her fight. And this mysterious person was using this wind to prevent him from killing Sunshine. And Lord noticed that the wind was making him lose concentration, and he got an idea, and he got up by lifting Sunshine through her neck.

And Lord was walking with Sunshine through a satanic tree, and Lord had lifted Sunshine up through her neck. And Sunshine was trying to remove Lord's hands from her neck without success. Then Lord stuck Sunshine's back on a satanic tree trunk, and he looked into Sunshine's eyes and told her that it was time for her to die. Then Lord started to squeeze Sunshine's neck with both of his hands, and Sunshine was trying to remove Lord's hands from her neck without success.

After a few minutes, Lord was still squeezing Sunshine's neck. And Sunshine had still not succeeded in removing Lord's hands from her neck, and she was breathing with difficulties. And Sunshine was losing her strengths and she was becoming weak, and she was trying to use her magic to fight Lord without success.

And she could not use her magic because she could not concentrate on herself because she was breathing heavily as she was suffocated by Lord. And she was feeling weak because the trunk of the satanic tree that she was leaning on was absorbing her strengths and energies.

Then Sunshine gave up the fight and she removed her hands from Lord's hands, and Lord looked into Sunshine's eyes how she was dying, and he started laughing by squeezing Sunshine's neck harder and harder. Suddenly, a strong wind started to blow, and Lord started losing balance, as the wind was hitting him, and the wind was shaking the satanic tree trunk which Sunshine was stuck on.

And although the wind was shaking Lord and he was trying to keep his balance, he was making the effort to keep his hands-on Sunshine's neck. And Sunshine had started to regain her strengths and she no longer had a problem breathing. And Sunshine was staring at Lord who was trying to keep his balance and who was trying at the same time to kill her by squeezing her neck. Sunshine was not fighting Lord even if she had enough strength to fight him, and he was observing Lord who was trying to kill her by thinking what to do.

Sunshine knew well that fighting Lord was not a solution, but it was instead a waste of time because she could not easily kill Lord, mostly that she only had half an hour to save the kingdom. And to prevent the kingdom from turning into the kingdom of the vampires.

And Sunshine was not worried about the fact that Lord was trying to kill her because she knew that it was going to be hard for Lord to kill her. Because the wind was preventing Lord to keep his balance and to concentrate.

Sunshine knew well that she could not use the full potential of her magic because she was stuck on the satanic tree trunk because that satanic tree was absorbing the energies of her magic. But Sunshine knew well that even if she could not use the full potential of her magic, she could use a few parts of her magic. Because the wind that was blowing harder and harder was distracting Lord, and this wind was allowing her to focus on herself.

Then Sunshine looked into Lord's eyes and noticed that Lord was not really focused because the wind was preventing him from keeping his balance. Then Sunshine got an idea, and she tried to take a deep breath, then she tried to focus on herself.

Sunshine's eyes started spinning, and Lord was focused on finding a balance that he had not even noticed that Sunshine was using her magic. Then the light shone in Sunshine's eyes and she opened her mouth and a black steam got out from her mouth and moved towards Lord's face.

And suddenly, Lord started to scream and he closed his eyes as he was feeling his eyes sting, and it was the black vapor that had got out from Sunshine's eyes that were stinging Lord's eyes. And despite the fact that Lord had his eyes closed, he still had his hands-on Sunshine's neck, and he was trying to kill her by squeezing her neck.

Sunshine had her eyes focused on Lord and she was thinking what to do, then she noticed that Lord had opened his eyes.

Then Sunshine's eyes started spinning and she lifted her hands towards her face, and the light got out from her eyes and shone on her fingernails, and her fingernails became long. Then Sunshine looked *at* Lord, but Lord's eyes were not focused on Sunshine, so Lord did not know exactly what Sunshine was doing. And Sunshine's eyes were still spinning, and the light shone in Sunshine's eyes, and Sunshine opened her mouth and the vapor got out from her mouth and moved towards Lord's face.

And suddenly, Lord opened his mouth and started to yell and he closed his eyes as the steam that had got out from Sunshine's eyes was stinging his eyes. And Sunshine handed her hands towards Lord's face and she used fingernails and tore her skin and the blood started to flow from Sunshine's hand and started to fall into Lord's mouth, like Lord had the mouth opened as he was screaming.

Then Lord started to feel something strange that was falling into his mouth, and he opened his eyes. And suddenly, the expression of Lord's face changed and he opened his eyes widely with his face full of fear as he had seen that it was Sunshine's blood that was getting inside his mouth.

Then Sunshine handed her hands towards Lord's face and she tore Lord's face by using her fingernails, and Lord's face was full of blood. Suddenly, Lord removed his hand from Sunshine's neck and she fell to the ground. And Lord was screaming by spitting on the ground.

And Lord was spitting on the ground because he was trying to remove Sunshine's blood from his mouth. And Lord was trying to remove Sunshine's blood from his mouth because he knew well that Sunshine was a human being, and the blood of a human being was a poison for him. Sunshine was lying on the ground and she was staring at Lord who was trying to remove her blood from his mouth. Then Sunshine got up from the ground and she lifted her head in the sky staring at the moon, and her eyes started spinning, and she flew in the sky.

Then Lord turned his head and immediately the expression of his face changed, and he screamed with his face full of rage, as he was seeing Sunshine who was flying towards the moon. And Lord's eyes started spinning and he flew in space. And Lord was flying after Sunshine.

After a few minutes, Lord started to become weak and he was flying slowly. And Lord was weak because he had accidentally swallowed Sunshine's blood. And it was Sunshine's blood that he had swallowed that was making him weak, and that was making him fly slowly because Sunshine's blood was a dangerous poison that was destroying him. Then Lord was getting weaker and weaker and he was flying slower and slower.

Lord's face was full of fear and his heart was beating faster than the normal as he was seeing Sunshine who was flying faster by following the moon that was moving in the sky. And Lord was realizing that everything was over, that Sunshine was going to destroy his satanic master tree. The efforts of Lord to catch Sunshine were becoming impossible because Sunshine's blood had started to affect Lord's body more and more.

And Lord had already lost all his strengths and his energy and he had more and more problems flying and breathing. And Lord was losing direction in space because he was unable to keep balance, also because he was lacking energies and strengths, and Lord's eyes were closing. Then Lord fell on the ground, and he was lying on the ground with his eyes closed like a corpse. And Sunshine was still flying by following the moon that was moving in the sky.

After a few minutes, the moon stopped in the middle of the forest. Suddenly the expression of Sunshine's face changed, and she was looking with a surprised face and with her eyes wide opened as she was seeing a tall satanic tree that was in a small hole and there was dark water in this hole. Sunshine's eyes were still focused on this satanic tree, and Sunshine was understanding that this satanic tree was the satanic master tree that Lord was trying to prevent her from destroying.

And Sunshine was also understanding that it was this satanic master satanic tree that Lord was using to control the souls of the future children, and that it was still this satanic master tree that Lord was using to practice witchcraft. Then Sunshine understood that she must have killed this satanic master tree, and she lifted her head in the sky and she noticed that the moon was moving around this satanic master tree.

And Sunshine understood that the moon was sending her message by moving around this satanic master tree, and that this message was that she did not have enough time. Then Sunshine started flying around the satanic master tree, and she had her eyes focused on the water in the hole of that tree, and she was astonished to see that the water that was in that hole was very dark. And she was wondering how to kill this satanic master tree. And her heart started beating faster as she knew that she did not have enough time.

Then Sunshine got an idea, and her eyes started spinning and she looked at her fingernails and the light got out from her eyes and shone on her fingernails. And her fingernails became long, and she tore her skin by using her long fingernails.

Then the blood started to flow from Sunshine's hands and started to fall into this hole. And After a few minutes, the dark water that was in the hole was changing color, and this dark water was becoming red because Sunshine's blood was making this dark water red. But Sunshine had started to become tired and weak because she was losing a lot of blood.

Suddenly, the expression on Sunshine's face changed and she was looking with her eyes full of fear as she was seeing something strange that looked like the snow that was falling in the hole. And Sunshine was understanding that this strange thing that looked like the snow was falling to clean her blood that was in this dark water, and to prevent her blood from killing this satanic master tree.

Then Sunshine looked in hole and she noticed that the water was becoming clear, that the strange thing that looked like the snow was cleaning her blood in the water to prevent the satanic master tree from dying. Then Sunshine's heart started beating with fear because she knew that she had only a few minutes to kill that satanic master tree. Then Sunshine turned her head and looked around, and suddenly the smile appeared on her face as she saw an arrow that was flying not far from her.

Then Sunshine flew until near to this arrow and she grabbed this arrow in her hand. And she flew until near to this satanic master tree, and she stared at this satanic master tree with her face full of rage, then she stabbed the trunk of this satanic master tree with this arrow that she had in her hand. Suddenly, Sunshine turned her head around as she had heard the noises, and the expression of her face changed and she was looking with a face full of smiles at the satanic trees that were falling on the ground.

Sunshine understood that all the satanic trees in the forest were falling because these satanic trees were mystically linked to the satanic master tree, and these satanic trees were alive thanks to this satanic master tree. And that it was this satanic master tree that was keeping all the satanic trees in the forest alive, and that it was impossible for these satanic trees to survive because the satanic master tree that was keeping them alive was dying.

After a few seconds, all the satanic trees that were in the forest had fallen, and Sunshine was astonished to notice that the forest of Lord was very big. Then Sunshine turned her head and looked at the hole, and she noticed that the water that was in the hole had dried up. And she understood that the satanic master tree was already dead, then the satanic master tree fell on the ground. And Sunshine flew away.

CHAPTER V

THE RETURN OF EDUCATION TO THE KINGDOM

It was six thirty in the morning, Sunshine was in her bathroom, and she was taking her shower, and she was very tired and weak, as she had spent her whole night fighting and as she had lost a lot of blood. Sunshine was taking her shower by thinking about Lord and about the satanic trees that she had destroyed.

And although the fact that Sunshine knew that she had saved the souls of the future children, she knew well that the fight was not over because she knew that Lord was still alive. Then Sunshine got out of the shower and she started to make the bandages on her wounds to get ready for school.

In the houses of the kingdom, there were the noises because the parents and children were arguing because the children wanted to go to school against the wishes of their parents. And the parents did not want their children to go to school because they were afraid that their children could be killed by the soldiers of Kalus.

And the parents were very worried about their children because the parents knew well that it was not Kalus who was going to open the school's doors, but it was instead Sunshine and her fellows who were going to open the school's doors.

And the parents knew well that Kalus could send his soldiers to school to kill any children who would approach the school's gate not only to get his revenge for the humiliation that children had given him in the palace a few weeks ago. But mostly because he had banned education in the kingdom. And the parents were trying to convince their children not to go to school without success, and the children were determined to go to school.

And even though the parents had even told their children it was a risk to go to school because Kalus would probably send his soldiers at school to kill all those who would approach the school's gate, the children had replied to their parents that they were not afraid to die. And children had also added that they were ready to die for their rights, and that they were going to start school today. Because it was time for them to fight for their dream, and that they were ready to die for their dream.

And despite the fact that some parents had threatened their children to punish them if they went to school, the children were determined to go to school. And children had even told their parents that they were ready to live in the streets and go to school everyday. Then most parents locked up their children in the bedrooms against their children's wishes to prevent their children from going to school.

It was seven in the morning, it was a little cold outside and the sun was rising, and the streets of the kingdom were almost empty. Because there were only a few people on the streets who were going to their work. There were some children who were leaving their home against their parents to go to school.

While some parents were in the streets running after their children to prevent their children from going to school. And children who were locked in the bedrooms were jumping out through the windows to go to school.

It was seven thirty in the morning, the streets of the kingdom were full of children who were going to school, and some of these children did not have their school's bag. Because their school's bag had been confiscated by their parents because their parents did not want them to go to school. And there were some parents who were trying to convince their children to return at home without success. Children were walking in the streets singing, "Education or death." "Power of Kids." "Children must save the kingdom."

And the children were walking on the road without even paying attention to the cars that were on the road, and children were not only walking on the sidewalk, but they were also walking on the side of cars. And despite the fact that the cars honked at children to ask children to leave on the road, children were not paying attention to the horn of cars.

And there was a huge traffic on the road that was caused by children as the children were walking on the side of cars. And some cars had stopped, while other cars were driving slowly. And there were the police who were asking the children to leave on the side of cars without success. And children were not paying attention to the policemen who were talking to them. And children were walking with the anger on their faces, by singing, "Education or death.""Power of Kids.""Children must save the kingdom."

And policemen were afraid to use the violence against children to make children leave the road because the policemen could see the rage and determination in the eyes of these children. And it was obvious that these children on the road were not afraid of anything, and that these children were ready to die.

And the opinions of the people who were in the streets were divided because most people were worried about these children who were walking on the road with the anger in their eyes. While there were a few people who were encouraging the action and the determination of these children to save the kingdom.

It was eight in the morning, Sunshine, Asher, Luna, and George were at the school's gate. And they were welcoming the children who were arriving to attend their first day of school. And the children who were arriving at school were very surprised to see the bandages on Sunshine's hands, and when they asked Sunshine why she had the bandages on her hands, Sunshine lied to them that she had fallen on the stairs early this morning. And there was the journalist named J.P Remy who was doing a report on the return of education to the kingdom.

And all the children were feeling very sorry for Sunshine, and they asked Sunshine to take care of herself because they needed her to save the kingdom, and that without her, they would never succeed in saving the kingdom. And all children who were arriving were taken in a huge classroom by Asher. And the parents who were arriving wanted to get in the gate but they were prevented by Sunshine and Luna. Sunshine and Luna told the parents that only children had the right to enter the school because only the children were the students.

And the parents told Sunshine and Luna that they wanted to get in the classrooms to watch their children because they were afraid that their children could be killed by the army of Kalus. Because Kalus could send his army at any time to kill children who had decided to break the laws of Kalus by going to school. And Sunshine replied to the parents not to worry about their children because nothing would happen to their children.

But Sunshine and Luna could see the fear in the eyes of the parents, and they understood that the parents were very afraid that Kalus could send his army to kill their children. Luna told parents that they could go home without any fear because even if Kalus sent his army, she and Sunshine would not let the army of Kalus touch a child. And the parents tried to beg Luna and Sunshine to get in the classroom to watch their children without success.

It was 8:45 a.m., all the children were sitting on the chairs in a huge classroom, and they were listening to Sunshine and Luna who were talking to them. Sunshine told children that they were going to change not only their destiny, but they would also change the destiny of their kingdom.

And that they were all going to work together to prevent the devil Kalus from destroying the kingdom. And that today was not only a great day, but it was a memorable day for the kingdom because today they were all going to start school.

Sunshine also told the children that from today, they were no longer just the children, but they were also the students because from now they were all the students. Sunshine told the students that it would not be easy, but that they would all succeed. And that they must all stay focused, and they would listen to the lessons very well, and that there were no rules, just to come to school on time and listen to each other.

And they must all back each other because they were all a family, and not to hesitate to ask a question, and not to be afraid to say a word. Sunshine also thanked all the students who were in the room who had had the courage to break the laws of Kalus and to disobey their parents to come to school.

It was nine in the morning, children were sitting on the chairs in a huge classroom, and they had the notebooks opened on the table in front of them, and all the students had held a pencil in their hand. And these children had their eyes focused on the board that was in front of them. And they were looking at Sunshine who was writing on the board. And the classroom was not full because some children had been prevented by their parents from coming to school.

And all the children had received a notebook and pencil from Luna because Luna had come to school with the boxes of notebooks, pencils, pens and books. Because Luna knew that some parents should prevent their children from coming to school by confiscating school's stuff from their children. And Luna had also brought the food and drinks to school for all the students.

After a few minutes, Sunshine had finished writing on the board, and she started to read what she had written, and the rest of the students were repeating after her. And Luna was walking between the tables to make sure that the students were pronouncing the words very well.

Then Luna asked Sunshine to stop for a bit when Luna noticed that some students had difficulties pronouncing the words very well. Then Luna started to help the students who had difficulty pronouncing the words and how to pronounce the words very well. And Luna was helping these students how to use their tongues to pronounce the words clearly.

Sunshine was watching Luna who was helping Luna who was helping the students to pronounce the words clearly with an astonished face. Sunshine was amazed by the abilities that Luna had not only to pronounce the words but to teach students, mostly that Luna had never been to school to learn how to read.

Sunshine was also very impressed by the determination that Luna had to save this kingdom and to protect the inhabitants of this kingdom from Kalus. And even if Sunshine knew that Kalus was a monster, she was not amazed by the rage that Luna had against Kalus, but she was surprised that Luna wanted to see Kalus die at any cost.

After an hour all the students were able to pronounce the words very well. And Sunshine asked the students to write the lesson that was on the board in their notebooks. Sunshine and Luna were walking between the tables to make sure that the students were taking the notes very well. And they were helping the students who had difficulty writing very well. Sunshine and Luna were also showing to the students how to hold the pencil correctly and how to form the letters well.

After more than an hour, all the students had finished writing their course, and their eyes were focused on the board. And they were looking at Luna who was writing math on the board. And looking at the expression on the faces of the students, they had no idea about the numbers that they were seeing on the board.

And they were wondering why Luna was writing the numbers on the board, and some of them were even wondering if Luna was crazy. And at the same time, they were wondering if they were the ones who were going to learn these numbers on the board.

After a few minutes, Luna had finished to write on the numbers and she turned and looked at the students, and she told them that they were going to study math, and they would learn how to use the signs, how to make the subtraction, addition, multiplication and division.

Then Luna started to explain to students how to use the signs of subtraction, addition, multiplication and division. And the eyes of the students were focused on Luna, and looking at the expression on the student's faces, it was obvious that they were not understanding the maths that Luna was explaining.

After a few minutes, Luna started to use the numbers and the signs to show to the students how to use the subtraction, addition, multiplication and the division. And some students started to understand the maths that Luna was explaining. Then Luna continued to explain more and more by making more and more examples. And the students started to understand very well, and some students had even started to love maths.

Then Luna wrote the exercises on the board and she asked the students to do the exercises in their notebooks. Sunshine and Luna were walking between the tables to check if the students were doing their exercises correctly. Sunshine and Luna were helping the students who had difficulty doing their exercises, by explaining to these students how to use the signs of subtraction, multiplication, division and addition correctly.

Sunshine and Luna had noticed that almost all the students were able to use the sign of addiction correctly. And that almost half of the students were able to use the signs of multiplication and subtraction correctly.

But most of the students were not able to use the sign of the division correctly. Then Sunshine and Luna understood that they were going to spend more time showing and explaining to the students how to use the signs of division, subtraction, and multiplication. But they would mostly work on the sign of division with the students.

After an hour, the students had finished their exercises. And it was break time, and the students had received the drink and food from Luna. There were a lot of foods and cakes and even the sweets, and there were also the juices called Fortis, Felix and Focus. The students were enjoying their break time by eating and talking between them. And there was a journalist named Remy in the classroom with his cameras who was filming since this morning.

And it was Sunshine and Luna who had asked Remy to do the report and film everything to put on his channel and website for the whole kingdom to watch and understand that it was important and necessary that the parents let the children come to school.

Sunshine and Luna also wanted the parents to understand through the video of the students in the classroom taking the lessons that would be posted by Remy on his website that it was urgent for children to go to school. And that children had already had a delay in school because children should normally start school a few years ago.

Sunshine and Luna also wanted the parents to understand through the video of students in the classroom that all children who were coming to school were safe. And that Kalus could not dare to send his army to kill the students.

Sunshine and Luna also wanted the whole kingdom to understand through the video that would be posted by Remy that they were ready to do the impossible to save the kingdom, and that they would not let the kingdom die. And that they were even ready to die to save the kingdom.

After half an hour, the students had finished their break time. Sunshine told the students that they were going to study literature and that they were going to read the book of Superhuman 1 by Thierry Kouam, then they would discuss the content of the part of the book that they would read. Then Luna walked between the tables with the books of Superhuman 1 by Thierry Kouam in her hands, and she gave a book to each student.

After a few minutes, all the students had received a book, and most of them were looking at the book cover with smiles on their faces. And they were all eager to read the book and they were more curious to know the content of the book. And looking at the expression on the faces of all the students, they were all happy to read the story of Superhuman who was a magician boy and to know the story of the wizards and the wizarding world.

Because even if Superhuman was a magician boy, Superhuman was born a wizard. And all the children had already heard the story of Superhuman, and some of them had even watched the movie Superhuman. And Superhuman was their superhero and idol.

Then the students lifted their heads and they looked at Sunshine when they heard Sunshine asked them if they were ready. And the students answered Sunshine that they were ready. And Sunshine told the students that she was going to read the book, and that each of them would open their book and they would follow the reading inside their book. And mostly that each person would make sure to follow the reading very well, and for that each of them would be able to see every word that she would be reading.

And Sunshine told them that the eyes of each of them would be focused on each word that she would be reading. Sunshine also told them not to hesitate to interrupt her by raising their hand if they were lost, and if they did not understand something or even if they had any questions.

Sunshine told the students that they were going to start by the introduction. And she asked the students to open the book on the page where the introduction was written, and that it was page three. And each student opened their book to page three.

Then Sunshine started the reading, and the eyes of all the students were focused on their book that was opened on the table in front of them. And all the students were following the reading with attention and there was silence in the room. Luna was walking between the tables to check if the students were following the reading correctly.

Luna was helping the students who were lost, and she was also answering the questions of the students. And looking at the expression on the faces of the students, we could see the joy that was on their faces and it was obvious that they were enjoying the reading.

After two hours, Sunshine had finished reading the first three chapters of the book of Superhuman 1 by Thierry Kouam. And Sunshine stopped and she told the students that they would continue the reading the next day.

And suddenly, the students reacted and said that they wanted to continue, and that they wanted to finish reading the book. Sunshine replied to the students that it was impossible to finish the whole book today because they were all already tired and that they must go home to get rest and to be ready for the next day.

And the students replied to Sunshine that they were not tired, and that they wanted to sleep at school. Sunshine smiled and replied that they could not sleep at school, and she also told them not to worry that they would read the book of Superhuman when they would come to school, and that before at the end of this year, they would read the whole books of Superhuman 1 and 2.

But the students were not satisfied and they wanted to continue the reading. And although the words of Sunshine to calm the students by telling them that they would continue the reading the next day, the students did not want to. And the students asked Sunshine to read one more chapter of the book of Superhuman.

Sunshine told the students that she could not read one more chapter because they did not have time to continue the reading. But Sunshine told the students that they were going to talk and share the ideas about the three chapters that they had read. And immediately the smile appeared on the faces of the students, and they agreed to talk about the three chapters that they had read, and they were very happy.

Then all the eyes were focused on Sunshine, and all the students were listening to Sunshine who was talking about the content of the first chapter with a smile on their faces. After a few minutes, Sunshine started to ask the questions to the students about the first chapter. And the students were raising their hands to answer, and the students were even fighting to answer, and all the students wanted to answer the questions.

And there were the noises in the classroom because many students were answering the questions at the same time. And Luna was trying to calm the students and to put order in the room without success. But at the same time, it was funny, Sunshine and Luna were enjoying seeing the students who were fighting to answer the questions.

Sunshine and Luna were very happy to see that the students really loved the education, and for Sunshine and Luna, it was a victory because they were afraid that the students should not like school, mostly that it should be the first day and the first time for children to go to school.

Then Sunshine talked about the content of the second and third chapters. And without any surprise, there was the same mood of joy in the room when Sunshine started asking questions. And all the hands of the students were raised, some students had even raised their two hands to be chosen to answer the question. And other students had even got up from their chairs to be seen very well by Sunshine, and the students were fighting to answer the questions.

And it was impossible for Sunshine and Luna to control the students or calm them because many students were talking at the same time. Sunshine and Luna were just staring at the students who were answering the questions with smiles on their faces, and the students were answering at the same time.

And the students were also giving different answers, and the students were sometimes arguing about the answers. And there were also some students who were trying to read the book to find the answers to the questions that were asked by Sunshine.

After twenty minutes, there was disappointment and sadness on the faces of the students when Sunshine announced to them that they would continue the reading of the book of Superhuman 1 by Thierry Kouam the next day.

Then Sunshine told the students that if they wanted to eat or drink something, they just needed to get up from their chairs and walk over to the dining table and take what they wanted or needed and get back to their seats. Because they were all going to listen to Luna for their last lesson.

Then the students got up from their chairs and they walked till the dining table, and some took the food and drink, while others only took the drinks and sweets. And they all returned to their seats with what they had chosen to eat, and they were eating and drinking with their eyes focused on Luna who was in front of them.

Then Luna told the students that they were going to talk a bit about the tradition and culture of the kingdom of Manitoba, that were their traditions and cultures. And that their traditions and their cultures were their history.

And that they would learn through their traditions and cultures about their ancestors, their great grandparents, who were their ancestors, who were their first ancestors who had founded the kingdom of Manitoba. And they would also learn about their different traditional dances, their traditional festivals, their rituals and their religion.

And suddenly, the students stopped eating and drinking, and they had their eyes focused on Luna. And they were listening to Luna who was talking about the traditions and cultures of the kingdom of Manitoba.

And looking at the expression on the faces of the children, it was obvious that they were interested in what Luna was talking about, and that they were happy to hear their history. And the students had smiles on their faces as they were listening to Luna who was talking about their roots, about the first inhabitants of the kingdom of Manitoba, and their ancestors.

Even Sunshine had her eyes focused on Luna, and she was very interested in the history of the kingdom of Manitoba that Luna was talking about. And Sunshine was learning a lot from Luna about the history of the kingdom of Manitoba.

And at the same time, Sunshine was very amazed to notice that Luna knew very well the history of the kingdom of Manitoba, and Sunshine was wondering how it was possible that Luna knew the history of the kingdom of Manitoba. Mostly that it was banned by Kalus to talk about the history, the traditions and cultures of Manitoba before Luna was born.

And although the fact that Sunshine knew that Luna was a princess, and that Luna had probably heard the history of the kingdom of Manitoba inside the palace, Sunshine was still not understanding how it was possible that Luna knew to read and write.

Sunshine had also noticed that Luna was very smart, and above all that Luna loved the kingdom of Manitoba with all her heart, and that Luna was ready to die for the kingdom of Manitoba. Sunshine was looking at Luna as Luna was talking about the history of the kingdom of Manitoba with passion and with love.

After an hour, Luna stopped and she told the students that they would continue to talk about the history of the kingdom of Manitoba the next day. And there were some students who wanted Luna to continue to talk about the history of the kingdom of Manitoba.

And Luna replied to these students who wanted her to continue to talk about the history of the kingdom of Manitoba that it was late to continue, but that she was going to answer the questions, if there were the students who had the questions about the history of Manitoba.

Then the students started to raise their hands and asked questions. A student asked Luna why Luna had talked about another God who was not Kalus? Luna answered this student because Kalus was not God.

And that same student asked Luna why they prayed and believed in Kalus like a god? Luna answered this student that they must all stop praying in Kalus's name like a god, and that they must also stop believing in Kalus like a god because Kalus was not a god, but Kalus was instead a monster.

After half an hour, the class was over. And the students were interviewed by J.P Remy about their first day of class. And the students were answering the questions of Remy. All the students had said on Remy's microphone that they had had a memorable day, and that this day would stay in the history of their kingdom.

And that all the children who were in the classroom had changed the destiny of the kingdom, and that Sunshine and Luna had written their names in the history of the kingdom. And that they were eager to come to school the next day, and they would come to school everyday and they would realize their dreams thanks to Sunshine and Luna.

And the students also said on the microphone of Remy that the lesson that they had enjoyed and loved the most was the reading of the book of Superhuman 1. And that the lesson that they had enjoyed less and loved less was math because the math was hard.

But that they had also loved their lesson about the history of the kingdom of Manitoba, that was a lesson on their own history. Because the lesson on the history of the kingdom had allowed them to know who they were, where they came from, who their ancestors were. And this lesson had also allowed them to know about their traditions and cultures. And mostly to know that Kalus was not their god.

And the students also said that they were surprised to find out when they were in the classroom that their teachers were Sunshine and Luna. And they had been very surprised to see that Sunshine and Luna were great teachers who had the abilities to teach very well, and that they also had been astonished to notice that Sunshine and Luna were very smart with a lot of knowledge. Then all the students thanked Sunshine and Luna not only for helping them by teaching them the lessons, but mostly for their fight to save the kingdom.

Luna was interviewed by Remy about her impression of the return of education in the kingdom, and about the first day of children in school. And Luna said on the microphone of Remy that today was a dream day because today the dream had come true.

And that today she had realized a dream that she had always fought for because she had grown up by fighting against her father who was the former the king of the kingdom named Kalus also called the devil Kalus about the access to knowledge to children of the kingdom. And that it was not easy to fight against a monster like Kalus, but with the help of Sunshine and others, they had all succeeded in opening the school, by allowing children to go to school.

And Luna also said that today was an unforgettable day for her because she had always dreamed of being a student, and sitting in a classroom with her brothers and sisters listening to the teachers.

But she had never dreamed of being a teacher because she had never imagined that she could teach her brothers and sisters without having teacher training. But that destiny had forced her to be a teacher and a student at the same time, and that it was funny to teach her brothers and sisters who were the same age as her.

Luna added that she was having a great experience being both a teacher and a student at the same time, and that she was eager to continue to work with her brothers and sisters. And that all the children of the kingdom would work together to save the kingdom.

And Remy asked Luna why she called the king Kalus the former the king of the kingdom if the king Kalus was still alive? Luna answered Remy that Kalus was no longer the king of the kingdom because the new king of the kingdom was George, and that all children of the kingdom had chosen George as their king.

Luna went on and said that all children in the kingdom should no longer abide by the laws of Kalus because King George was against the laws of the Kalus. And that the parents should let their children come to school because the laws of Kalus were not applicable to the children. And that education was a right and a duty for all the children, so that the parents had no right to kidnap their children to prevent them from going to school and to prevent their children from accessing knowledge.

Because the parents were acting exactly like the monster Kalus by preventing education to their children and the parents were stealing the lives and dreams of their children by preventing their children from going to school.

And that she wanted all children of the kingdom to come to school the next day. And she wanted all children to have access to knowledge, and for that she would always fight against all those who would try to prevent children from accessing knowledge. And she would always support children who would like to go to school.

Luna continued and said that the doors of the palace were opened to all children who wanted to come to school but who were prevented by their parents from coming to school. So children who were afraid of their parents to come to school could come live inside the palace with her and go to school every morning with her and study every evening with her.

Because the palace was the house of all the inhabitants of the kingdom. And the palace was first and foremost the home of the homeless, so that if children were afraid to be homeless or afraid of their parents, these children were welcome to the palace.

Sunshine was interviewed by Remy about the return of education to the kingdom. And Sunshine said on the microphone of Remy, and that it was incredible, and that it had finally happened.

That it was not easy, but that they had managed to take a first step because there was still a long way to go. And that it was funny and great to be a teacher and a student at the same time. And it was a good experience because she had never imagined teaching her brothers and sisters who were her fellows of the fight for the freedom of the kingdom.

Sunshine also thanked all children who had had the courage to break the laws of Kalus and to disobey their parents to come to school. And she also asked the parents to let their children come to school because all the parents who were preventing their children from coming to school were kidnapping their children, and they were preventing their children from living their lives and achieving their dreams.

And Sunshine added that the parents should stop kidnapping their children at home on behalf Kalus's laws because George who was the new the king of the kingdom had already said that the laws of Kalus were no longer applicable. And that the parents should stop being afraid of this devil named Kalus because Kalus was no longer a danger to the kingdom and to the inhabitants of the kingdom.

And that the parents must allow their children to go to school, and that the doors of her house were opened for all children who wanted to go to school and who were prevented by their parents from going to school.

So that these children who were prevented by their parents to come to school could come live with her and go to school with her. Sunshine also promised to the parents that nothing would happen to their children, and that she would never allow the monster named Kalus to hurt a child or even to send his army against a child.

Then the students left the classrooms and when they arrived outside, some students were astonished to see their parents who were waiting for them. And the children were more amazed to hear from their parents that their parents were outside of school since the morning. And the parents of some students had stayed outside of the school to protect their children who were in the classroom in case Kalus sent his army to kill children.

The parents and children started walking on their way home. And the children were talking about their first day at school to their parents. And the parents were very surprised to hear from their children that Sunshine and Luna were their teachers.

And the parents were not understanding how it was possible that Sunshine and Luna were the teachers, not only because Sunshine and Luna did not have a training to teach, but mostly because Sunshine and Luna had never been to school.

So, for the parents, it was impossible that Sunshine and Luna knew how to teach the lessons. And the parents were eager to watch on the channel of J.P Remy how Sunshine and Luna taught the lessons. And the parents were not really surprised to hear from their children that they [children] had spent a great day at school. And that it was so fantastic to be a student, to be sat in a classroom with other students, and that they had loved all the lessons, mostly the reading of the book of Superhuman 1.

And the parents were not really astonished to hear from their children that Sunshine and Luna were really the good teachers because for the parents, their children did not have the abilities to recognize the good teachers.

Because their children had never been to school, and for the parents, their children had said that Sunshine and Luna were good teachers, not only because their children had spent a good day at school. But mostly because their children loved Sunshine and Luna, mostly Sunshine who was a hero and an idol for all children.

Because for the parents, it was obvious that Sunshine and Luna could not be good teachers because Sunshine and Luna were children who had never been to school, and who had never had access to knowledge like all the children of the kingdom. And at the same time, the parents were not understanding why Sunshine had opened the doors of the school if there were no teachers to teach the students.

And for the parents, the school that their children were going to was just a waste of time because it was impossible that Sunshine and Luna, who had no knowledge, would teach something to their children. And for the parents, the children wanted to continue to go to school just because the children wanted to spend time in school playing with their friends.

And some parents had even said that Sunshine and Luna had refused them to get inside the classroom because Sunshine and Luna did not want them to see how children should spend the day in the classroom to play.

It was a great day in the kingdom, not really because it was the return of the education in the kingdom, but mostly because all the pregnant women who were to the hospital had returned home in the evening. Because the pains of these pregnant women had suddenly stopped at 5:57 a.m., the doctors had been surprised to see that the pain of these pregnant women had stopped.

And the doctors could not explain the reasons why the pain of these pregnant women had stopped. Then the doctors had released all pregnant women in the evening. After that these women had spent a day without feeling pain in their bellies. And the doctors had also made the check up on these pregnant women to make sure that they were fine before letting them go home.

It was eight in the morning, all the inhabitants of the kingdom were sitting in their living room and they had their eyes focused on the television that was in front of them. And they were all watching the children in the classroom with surprised faces. And the parents did not believe what they were watching, and they were very astonished to see Sunshine and Luna who were teaching the students.

And the parents were not really astonished to see Sunshine and Luna who were teaching, but they were surprised to see Sunshine and Luna who had the abilities to teach. And they were wondering how it was possible that Sunshine and Luna, who had never been to school, knew how to write, read, and calculate very well. And they were wondering where Sunshine and Luna had got the abilities to teach the lessons.

And looking at the expression on the faces of the parents, it was as if they were dreaming, and they were still not believing that it was Luna and Sunshine that they were watching on television teaching the students. And the parents were noticing that Sunshine and Luna were teaching very well, and they were even teaching better than the teachers who had the training.

And at the same time, the parents were very happy to see Sunshine and Luna who were working hard to change things in the kingdom, and who were determined to put an end to the laws of Kalus. And the parents were very astonished by the courage of Sunshine, Luna and other children.

And for the parents, all these children who were in the classroom were the heroes. And the parents were feeling a little cowards because they did not have the courage to fight the king Kalus when Kalus had decided to ban the education in the kingdom. But these children in the classroom had had the courage to fight the king Kalus for their rights.

But at the same time, the parents were wondering why the king had not sent his army to kill these children in the classroom. Because the parents knew that these children had broken the laws of Kalus to be in class. And the parents were very surprised that Kalus had not reacted by sending his army to kill the children who had broken his laws by going to school.

Because the parents knew well that Kalus was against education in the kingdom. And the parents were wondering why Kalus was calm. And for the parents, it was obvious that Kalus was planning something worse against the children. And the parents were very afraid because for them the worse was going to happen.

The children who had been prevented by their parents from going to school were very angry against their parents by watching on television other children who were in the classroom. And these children were determined to go to school the next day.

The parents were very afraid to send their children to school, despite the fact that the parents knew that Sunshine and Luna were good teachers. And the parents were very afraid because the parents knew well that the king Kalus was a monster, and that they could not trust Kalus. Because Kalus was a devil without a heart, who could send his army to kill their children in the classroom at any time.

But at the same time, the parents knew that it would be almost impossible to prevent their children from going to school because their children were determined to go to school. And mostly that their children had told them that they would live in the palace with Luna or they would live in Sunshine's house with Sunshine to go to school.

As the children had watched Luna and Sunshine on television said that the doors of the palace were opened and the doors of Sunshine's house were opened for all children who wanted to go to school and who were prevented by their parents from going to school.

And the parents knew well that it would be worse if their children went to live in the palace with Luna or if their children went to live in Sunshine's home with Sunshine. Not only because the king Kalus lived inside the palace and that if children went to live inside the palace the children would be close to Kalus, and it would be easy for Kalus to injure the children.

But mostly because Sunshine and Luna were the two children that Kalus probably hated the most because Sunshine and Luna were the leaders of the children. So, for the parents, all children who were near Sunshine and Luna were more in danger. And the parents went to bed thinking about what to do if they would allow their children to go to school the next day or not.

It was five in the morning, the day had not yet risen in the kingdom, and some parents were awakened by the noises of their children. And the children had already woken up to get ready for school. And the children had not closed their eyes during the whole night, and they had spent their night with their eyes focused on the clock on the wall of their bedrooms by checking the time. And the night had been very long for the children, and they had spent their night counting the hours and waiting for the day to awaken.

And the parents were staring at their children who were getting ready for school. And the parents wanted to prevent their children from going to school, but the parents were afraid that their children could run away from the houses to go and live in the palace or to Sunshine's home.

And the parents had no choice but to allow their children to go to school, as the parents did not want their children to go live in the palace or to Sunshine's home. But the parents had decided to take their children to school, and to stay in school until the end of the courses.

It was seven in the morning, the sun was rising and the streets of the kingdom were full of children who were taken to the school by their parents. And the parents who were not on the way to school with their children were lining up in front of the kiosk of the newspaper called Kongreshow to buy a newspaper.

And again, J.P Remy had broken the laws of Kalus by writing against the king Kalus in his newspapers. Because the laws of Kalus prohibited all the journalists from writing or saying something against the king Kalus.

And there were the photos of Sunshine and Luna in front of the newspapers of Kongreshow. And people were not really surprised by the content of the newspapers, but they were instead surprised by the courage of Remy to write against the king Kalus.

And people were not astonished to read in the newspapers that the kingdom was no longer ruled by the king Kalus, but that the kingdom was instead ruled by George. And that all the inhabitants of the kingdom must not be afraid to break the laws of Kalus because King George had said that the laws of Kalus were no longer valid.

The day had gone well in the kingdom, and the children had spent a beautiful day at school. Except the king Kalus who was still nowhere to be found in the palace. And the security of the king Kalus was spending their time looking for Kalus and they were not even paying attention to what was going on in the kingdom. And Kalus was still in his magic room unconscious and dying.

After the months nothing had really changed in the kingdom, children still enjoyed going to school every day. And the king Kalus had been found almost dead in his living room, and the doctors were taking care of Kalus inside his palace.

And it was Lord who had put Kalus in the living room because Lord had come to talk to Kalus, and Lord had been surprised to notice that Kalus was unconscious in the magic room. And Lord had put Kalus in the living room because he wanted the employees of Kalus to call the doctors and to take care of Kalus.

But despite the fact that everything was going well in the kingdom, Sunshine was very thoughtful. And she was thoughtful that her friends and her parents had noticed it. And when Sunshine's friends and Sunshine's parents had asked her what was going on with her, Sunshine lied to them and said that she was fine. But they all knew that Sunshine was lying to them because they had also noticed that Sunshine was looking tired, and that Sunshine had also lost appetite.

And if Sunshine was thoughtful and tired, it was because she was spending her time thinking about Lord. And she was wondering where Lord was because she had gone to Lord's forest to visit him many times, but Lord was not in his forest. And Sunshine knew well that Lord was still alive, and she was very afraid because she had no doubt that Lord was planning something.

And Sunshine was afraid that Lord could surprise her at any time, and she was afraid that she could not be ready to fight Lord, when Lord would surprise her. And that Lord could hurt the inhabitants.

But there was another problem that was preventing Sunshine from sleeping, and this problem was the fact that Sunshine was spending her nights and days thinking about the mysterious person who had helped her during the fight against Lord. Sunshine knew well that there was a mysterious person who had helped her during this fight because the arrow that she had used to stab the satanic master tree was sent by this mysterious person.

And that the wind that had blown in the forest during the fight was triggered by this mysterious person, and that this mysterious person had also shown her where the satanic master tree was through the moon that was moving in the sky. And Sunshine was wondering who this person could be, but unfortunately, she could not answer this question.

CHAPTER VI

THE CULTURAL EVENTS AND THE RETURN OF LORD WITH THE TRAGEDY AND THE CHILDREN IN A COMA

After a year of school, the students had done their first year and they were very happy to be on holiday. And even the students who had failed their first year were happy. And all the students were happy not only because they had passed or failed their year, but because they succeeded in going to school.

And all the parents were very proud of their children not only because their children had passed or failed their exams, but because their children had had the courage to break the laws of Kalus, and to go to school. The parents and children were very proud of Sunshine and Luna who had taught the students for the entire year.

Women who were pregnant had given birth, and all babies who were born were doing well. And Sunshine's mom had given birth to a son, while Aaron's mom had given birth to a daughter. And although the fact that Sunshine was very happy that women had given birth safely, she was worried about the future of the kingdom.

Because Sunshine knew that Lord was still alive, and that Lord would not stop to try to realize the project he had for the kingdom. And the worst was that Sunshine did not know where Lord was, and she was spending her time thinking about where Lord could be, and what he was planning to do.

Children were on holiday, and they had decided to break another law of Kalus by organizing cultural events. Because the laws of Kalus banned all cultural events in the kingdom. The children were determined to break the laws of Kalus to organize the cultural events despite the fact that the parents had tried to convince them to not break the laws of Kalus by organizing the cultural events. And the parents had even tried to tell Sunshine and Luna who were the leaders of the children not to break the laws of Kalus by organizing this cultural event.

But Sunshine and Luna had replied to the parents that the laws of Kalus were not applicable to children because the children did not recognize Kalus as their king. But the children instead recognized George as their king, and that the king George had said that the laws of Kalus were no longer applicable in the kingdom, and that no child should abide by the laws of Kalus.

And the parents were very worried about the cultural events that the children were going to organize because the cultural events were related to the traditions, and the king Kalus had banned the traditional events in the kingdom.

And the parents were afraid that the children would provoke the anger of Kalus by organizing the cultural events. And the parents were also afraid that the children would be killed during cultural events by the army of the king Kalus. And the parents had organized the meeting with children to beg children not to organize the cultural events without success.

In the palace, the king Kalus was doing well and he was very angry after that Luna had announced to him that the children of the kingdom had decided to break the laws of Kalus by organizing the cultural events. And Kalus had told Luna that the cultural events were prohibited in the kingdom by the law. Luna had replied to Kalus that according to king George the laws of Kalus were no longer valid, and that children of the kingdom did not care about the laws of Kalus.

And Kalus was very angry with the cultural events that children were going to organize and he wanted to send his army to arrest these children and to prevent these children from organizing the cultural events.

But at the same time, Kalus was in deep thought because he knew well that he could not take a risk to send his army against children with Sunshine who was still alive. Because he knew that things could go worse if he sent his army to arrest or kill children because Sunshine was stronger and powerful enough to kill his army.

And Kalus was not only afraid that Sunshine could kill his army, but he was mostly afraid that he could be tortured by Sunshine if he sent his army against children. And although the fact that Lord had warned Kalus to never touch a child in the kingdom or do something against children of the kingdom without his [Lord] authorization, Kalus was thinking how to prevent children from organizing the cultural events. And Kalus was very worried about the laws in the kingdom, he was afraid that the fact that the children were breaking the laws could also push the parents to break the laws.

And Kalus was very worried about the control that he was losing in the kingdom because the children had succeeded to break his laws by going to school, and the children were going to break his laws again by organizing the cultural events. And for Kalus, it was obvious that the kingdom was ruled by Sunshine and her fellows.

Because it was as if Sunshine and her fellows had the right to do whatever they wanted in the kingdom. And even worse it's been more than twelve years now that he was kept prisoner inside his palace by Sunshine, and he could not get out because Sunshine had turned the satanic trees that were planted in the kingdom into magic trees.

And Kalus was very afraid that he would never succeed in realizing his project with these children who were not afraid to break his laws. And Kalus did not know how to stop these children. But at the same time, he knew well that only the death of Sunshine was the only solution to stop these children.

And Kalus knew well that there was only Lord who could kill Sunshine and he had started to lose hope that Lord would kill Sunshine one day. And Kalus was wondering where Lord was? Because it's been months that he has not talked to Lord. And Kalus was spending his days and nights in his magic room trying to talk to Lord without success, and Lord was not replying to the calls of Kalus. And Kalus was a little afraid that Lord was dead.

The children were spending their days organizing their cultural events despite the fact that the king Kalus had given a speech asking children not to organize the cultural events. And despite the fact that the children were facing certain problems, they were determined to organize the festival events. And the children were abandoned to themselves, and the parents had refused to help children to organize their festival events.

And the children had approached the people who were previously in charge of organizing the cultural events to ask these people to help them to organize the festival events. But these people had refused by saying that the festival events were banned in the kingdom by the king Kalus, and that they could not help children to organize the festival events. Also, since Kalus was crowned the king of the kingdom, the kingdom had not organized the cultural events.

And the problem with children was that they had no idea about the cultural dances, the cultural theater and the cultural sports. And there was nobody to teach them, and the children had never even attended a cultural event because the festival events were banned by the laws of Kalus before these children were born. And it was Luna who had told about the idea to organize the cultural events during their holiday.

And children had asked the parents about the cultural dances and the cultural sports, but the parents had refused to say a word about the cultural dances and sports. And the parents had just repeated to their children not to organize these cultural events.

And Luna had told Sunshine that they could find an idea about how to organize the cultural events in the cultural house. The cultural house was the house where all the cultural events used to take place before Kalus became the king and closed this cultural house.

The children had broken the door of the cultural house, and they had found the videotapes about the cultural events that had been organized in the past. And the children were spending the days and nights watching these videotapes about the cultural events and to practice the traditional dances and sports.

And the parents were worried about the lives of children because the parents knew that Kalus could send his army to kill the children who were spending their days and nights in the cultural house to practice the cultural dances and sports.

Mostly, that the children had broken another law of Kalus by breaking the door of the cultural house. And the parents had tried to prevent their children from going to the cultural house without success.

And Kalus was aware that children were spending their days and nights in the cultural house, and he wanted to send his army to arrest these children. But at the same time, he was very afraid of Sunshine because he knew that he could be tortured by Sunshine if he sent his army against children.

The day of the cultural events was approaching and although the children were very tired, as they were spending their days and nights practicing the dances and sports to be ready for the event. And they were very eager and happy as they were waiting for the great day.

And the children were so happy because for the first time, they were not just going to attend cultural events, but they were going to practice the dances and sports of their culture. But the children were a little sad because the parents would not attend cultural events because the parents were afraid of Kalus, as the laws of Kalus banned the cultural events in the kingdom.

It was the eve of the cultural events, and Sunshine was lying in her bed and she was looking very tired. Sunshine was tired because it's been the days that she had not slept and rested because she was busy organizing cultural events. And Sunshine was staring at the ceiling and suddenly the expression on her face changed when she remembered about Lord. And Sunshine was busy organizing cultural events that she had even forgotten about Lord.

Sunshine was surprised about the silence of Lord, and she was wondering where Lord was and why he had not come to see her since the night she had destroyed the satanic trees that were in his forest. And Sunshine was very afraid because she knew that Lord was planning something worse, and she did not know what Lord's plan was. And Sunshine was very afraid and she was feeling that something worse was going to happen.

Sunshine was very worried about the cultural events that were going to take place the next day, and she had the feeling that something was going to disrupt these cultural events. And Sunshine started feeling the fear and her heart was beating faster than the normal. And Sunshine got an idea and she took a deep breath and her eyes started spinning and the light shone into her eyes. Then she disappeared.

It was midnight, Kalus was deeply asleep in his bed. Suddenly Kalus opened his eyes when he heard a voice called his name, and he looked sleepy in his eyes, and immediately the expression on his face changed. And Kalus was staring at Sunshine as if he was dreaming, and he opened his mouth and he was trying to talk but his mouth was shaking that a word could not get out.

And Kalus's eyes were still focused on Sunshine, and he was looking at her as if he was not seeing her well. Then Kalus pulled his hands off the blanket that was over him, and he started to rub his eyes. Then Kalus removed his hands from his eyes, and he looked at

Sunshine who was standing up near to his bed and staring at him too.

"Can you see now?" Sunshine asked.

"It's really you?" Kalus replied.

"Rub your eyes again, if you can not see well," Sunshine said.

"What are you doing here?" Kalus asked.

"Where is Lord?" Sunshine asked.

"You are the one who should know where Lord is because you are the one who spends your time fighting him," Kalus answered.

"Answer my question," Sunshine retorted angrily.

"I do not know where Lord is," Kalus answered.

"How do you not know?" Sunshine asked.

"It's been months that I have not heard from Lord," Kalus answered.

"When did you last hear from him?" Sunshine asked.

"It's been almost a year now that I have not heard from Lord," Kalus answered.

Sunshine was looking at Kalus without knowing what to say, but she knew that Kalus was telling the truth that he had not seen Lord in a while.

Then Sunshine opened her mouth and said, "I want you to make a speech early this morning at six in the morning, to order all the inhabitants of the kingdom to come to the cultural house to support all the children who would perform today at six o'clock,"

"What?" Kalus cried out.

"You have heard me," Sunshine answered.

"The cultural events are banned by the law," Kalus said.

"The laws of Kalus are forbidden in the kingdom," Sunshine replied.

"The laws of Kalus are still applicable in the kingdom," Kalus said.

"The king of the kingdom is George, and George had banned the laws of Kalus," Sunshine said.

Kalus looked at Sunshine and started to laugh and he said, "George would never be the king of this kingdom."

"George was crowned the king of the kingdom by the children of the kingdom," Sunshine said.

"Stop dreaming because even Luna, who was born queen, would never be queen of this kingdom, and so it's impossible that George will be the king of this kingdom," Kalus said.

Sunshine looked into Kalus's eyes and said, "I promise you that George will sit on the throne of this kingdom very soon."

"It would never happen," Kalus said.

"The real problem is that you would be dead when it would happen," Sunshine said.

"I would never die," Kalus said.

Sunshine smiled and said, "You would be surprised."

"Good luck in your dream of seeing George sit on the throne of this kingdom," Kalus replied.

"Do not forget that you would make a speech early this morning to ask all the inhabitants of this kingdom to come to the cultural house to support all children who would perform," Sunshine said.

"I would not make this speech because I am not going to break my own laws," Kalus said.

"Your laws are not applicable in this kingdom, and you are going to make this speech," Sunshine said.

"I am the king of this kingdom, and I am the one who gives the orders and not the one who receives the orders," Kalus said.

"You are not the king of this kingdom, but you are going to order the inhabitants of the kingdom to come to the cultural house today at six o'clock," Sunshine said.

"If I am not the king of this kingdom, why ask me to order the inhabitants of this kingdom to come to the cultural house at six o'clock," Kalus said.

"Because I want you to do that," Sunshine said.

"Go ask your king George to order the inhabitants of the kingdom to come to the cultural house today," Kalus said.

"I would not ask George, but I am asking you to order the inhabitants of the kingdom to come to the cultural house today at six o'clock," Sunshine said.

"I would not do that," Kalus said.

Sunshine and Kalus were looking at each other, and Sunshine's face was full of anger while Kalus's face was full of smiles. And suddenly, the expression of Kalus's face changed and the smile that was on his face turned into fear, and he was staring at Sunshine with the eyes wide opened as he was seeing Sunshine's eyes that were spinning.

Then Kalus opened his mouth to say a word, and he suddenly started to feel pain in his jaws. And Kalus wanted to scream but he was feeling pain that his mouth could not make a move or make a noise. Kalus started feeling pain in his joints and he could not even move his hands or feet. And Kalus was paralyzed. And Sunshine was still looking at Kalus with her eyes that were spinning.

After a few minutes, Sunshine's eyes were still spinning and Kalus was still paralysed and he was sweating and looking tired. Then Kalus took a deep breath like Sunshine's eyes had stopped spinning. And Kalus was looking at Sunshine by breathing deeply, and he was touching his body and making the movement with the fingers, feet, and hands to make sure that a part of his body had not been paralyzed by Sunshine's magic.

Then Sunshine broke the silence and asked Kalus if he wanted her to continue to torture him. And without any hesitation Kalus accepted to make a speech at six in the morning, to order the inhabitants of the kingdom to come to the cultural house at six o'clock, to support the children who would perform. And Sunshine told Kalus that she would be sitting in front of the television at 5:50 a.m., and she would come back to the palace if she did not watch him on television at 5:55 a.m.,

And Sunshine told Kalus that he would call the national television and the national radio at the palace. And that the journalists must be at the palace before 5:50 a.m., and he would make that speech in the news at six in the morning because she wanted all the habitants of the kingdom to watch the news before going to work.

Sunshine also told Kalus that except the hospitals, all the rest of the services in the kingdom would close at noon because today was a day to celebrate the culture. And that all those who would not come to the cultural house to support children would be punished.

Kalus was looking at Sunshine who was giving him the instructions without saying a word. After a few minutes, Sunshine asked Kalus if he had listened very well. Kalus answered her yes. Sunshine told Kalus that she wanted him to repeat everything she had said to make sure that he had not forgotten anything. And Kalus was very surprised by the request of Sunshine, and he started to hesitate because Sunshine's request was a humiliation for him, and he did not want to do that.

Because Sunshine was treating him like a child that the instructor asked to repeat the lessons to be sure that this child had understood the lessons very well. After a few minutes, Kalus understood that he did not have a choice when he saw Sunshine's eyes that were spinning, and he opened his mouth and he repeated everything that Sunshine had said.

Then Sunshine told him that he had better not to forget anything and that he must repeat everything in the news of six in the morning, and to not even try to play with her because if she did not watch him on television at 5:50 a.m., she would come back for him. Then the light shone into Sunshine's eyes and she disappeared.

It was six in the morning, all the inhabitants of the kingdom were in front of their television and they were watching Kalus who was announcing to them that except the services of the hospitals, the rest of the services would stop at noon And that all the inhabitants of the kingdom would be at the cultural house at six o'clock, to support the children who would perform. And that anyone who would not go to the cultural house to attend cultural events would be punished.

Suddenly the expression on the faces of people who were watching the television changed, and some were watching the king

Kalus with surprised faces, while others were watching the television with their mouths opened but no word was coming out. And looking at the expression on their faces, they were all surprised that the king Kalus was asking them to go to the cultural house to support the children who would perform today.

And they did not understand what was going on with Kalus because a few weeks ago, Kalus had made a speech ordering the children to stop going to the cultural house because the cultural events were banned by the laws of Kalus. And they were astonished to see Kalus who supported the cultural events that children were going to organize this evening. And although they were proud that Kalus allowed them to go to the cultural house to support the children this evening, they did not jump for joy.

And they did not jump for joy because they knew that Kalus could change his mind before six o'clock and announce to them that the cultural events were banned in the kingdom. And they would not be surprised if Kalus changed his mind after and ordered them not to go to the cultural events. Because Kalus had already changed his mind in the past about the school that he announced to open and he did not keep his promise after.

So, nothing coming from Kalus would surprise them, but they were all hoping that Kalus would not change his mind, and that they would go to the cultural house to support children this evening. Mostly since Kalus had been crowned the king of the kingdom, they had not celebrated their culture.

Children had watched the speech of Kalus on television, and there were only a few of them who were happy to hear Kalus announce that all the inhabitants of the kingdom must go to the cultural house to support the children who would perform.

And most of the children did not happily celebrate the speech of Kalus because they knew that they could not trust Kalus. And except Sunshine, the rest of the children had been surprised by the speech of Kalus, and they were wondering what had made Kalus change his mind, for that Kalus ordered the inhabitants to go to the cultural house and attend cultural events.

Mostly that Kalus had threatened to kill them a few weeks ago if they did not stop the organization of the cultural events. And even Sunshine knew that she could not trust Kalus, and that Kalus could make another speech at five in the afternoon, to ask people not to go to the cultural house, but Sunshine was ready to paralyze Kalus through her magic, if he dared to change his mind.

The hours were passing, and the children were busy organizing the event, and the rest of the inhabitants of the kingdom were talking about the speech of the king Kalus in the news this morning. And even in the streets, the people were talking about the speech of Kalus in the news and about the organization of the cultural events by the children of the kingdom. And people really wanted to attend cultural events and they were hoping that Kalus would not change his mind.

It was six o'clock, the streets of the kingdom were full of people who were walking towards the cultural house, and there were smiles on their faces as they were walking. And they were very happy that the king Kalus had not changed his mind, and they were eager to watch children perform. And all the children were at the cultural house, and George was the one who was chosen by the children to welcome the guests.

It was seven in the evening, the cultural house was full of people and the event was presented by Remy, the event was filmed by the team of Remy. And Remy said that the event would start with the speech of some children, and that everyone must get up to welcome the king George who was going to make the first speech. Then they all got up from their chairs and they started clapping their hands. Then Remy gave the microphone to George.

George looked at the guests who were in the room and he greeted them and he thanked them for coming to support the children who were going to perform tonight. And George continued and said that today was a special day for the kingdom because tonight the kingdom was resurrected from the grave because the culture that was the heart and blood of the kingdom had been killed by a monster called Kalus. But tonight, the children of the kingdom had decided to resurrect the culture and to make their kingdom alive again.

And that the children of the kingdom decided to save their kingdom against whoever would try to destroy their kingdom, and that the children of the kingdom were ready to shed their blood for the kingdom. And the children were determined to die to protect their kingdom and to prevent the kingdom of Manitoba from being destroyed by the devil Kalus. Because the kingdom of Manitoba was not a property of the monster Kalus, but the kingdom of Manitoba was an inheritance of all the people of Manitoba.

Suddenly, George was interrupted by the applause and people got up from their chairs and started to clap their hands, and there were the screams in the room who were coming from the children. Then the children started yelling, "We love the king George, the king George, our the king George." And the parents followed the children by screaming, "We love the king George, our the king, the king of our kingdom."

After a few minutes, the people were calm and George continued his speech and said that the kingdom would never die, and that the tradition, the education and the culture would never be prohibited in the kingdom by anyone again.

Because each year, the kingdom would celebrate its traditions and cultures, and all children who would be born in the kingdom would go to school. Then George thanked all children of the kingdom for their love that they gave to the kingdom each second by fighting against the laws of Kalus.

And George specially thanked Sunshine and Luna for their courage and determination to fight against the laws of Kalus, and their love to make the kingdom a better place by teaching children at school. Then George wished a great evening to everyone in the room and to enjoy the feast.

Then everyone got up from their chairs and they started to clap their hands and George left. Then Remy welcomed Luna on the stage to make her speech. And people were clapping their hands by screaming Luna's name as she was walking towards Remy with a smile on her face. Then Remy gave the microphone to Luna.

Luna looked at the people who were in the room and she greeted everyone, and she thanked them for coming to support children who would perform tonight. And Luna said that a new light had shone in the kingdom today because the kingdom was in darkness for the years, and a devil named Kalus had decided to put the kingdom in the darkness by creating the laws of Kalus. But the children of the kingdom had decided to remove the kingdom from the darkness and to turn on the light on the kingdom by fighting against the laws of Kalus.

Luna continued and said that everyone must know that the kingdom did not belong to Kalus, but the kingdom belonged to all the inhabitants of the kingdom. And that children would never leave their kingdom in the hands of a devil like Kalus.

And children would never allow a monster like Kalus to rule this kingdom. And that was the reason why the children had chosen their king named George, and all the inhabitants of the kingdom would crown George very soon as the king of the kingdom.

And that she was ashamed to be a daughter of a monster like Kalus, that it was hard to say but that the devil Kalus was her father and the father of her little brother named George. And that it was not because the devil Kalus was her father that she was going to support him and accept all the horrible things he had done since he was crowned the king and that he was still doing. And that the place of Kalus was to hell, that Kalus had no place in the kingdom of Manitoba because Kalus was not a human.

That the worst enemy of the kingdom was the devil Kalus because Kalus hated the inhabitants of Manitoba. That Kalus had not only destroyed the kingdom by banning the tradition, culture, education and religion, but that Kalus was also responsible for the deaths of thousands of children of the kingdom. Then Luna posed and she was staring at people in the room with the tears that were flowing down her cheeks. And all the eyes were focused on Luna.

Then Luna broke the silence and said that she was the heiress of the throne of the kingdom of Manitoba and she was born with the responsibility to protect the kingdom, to protect the values, the traditions and the cultures of the kingdom.

And Luna added that Kalus had never respected the values, the traditions and the cultures of the kingdom, but that Kalus had instead destroyed the values, the traditions and the cultures of the kingdom. And even worse Kalus had done the things that were completely imaginable, and that were banned by the values of the kingdom.

And suddenly, Luna stopped and she started crying and Remy wanted to remove Luna from the podium, but she refused and said that she wanted to continue. And all the eyes were focused on Luna and some of them had the tears that were flowing down their cheeks.

Then Luna took a deep breath and said that it was hard for her to make this decision that she was going to take because it would be the first time in the history of the kingdom that this decision was going to be made. And that as heiress to the crown of the kingdom, she was going to impeach Kalus, and remove the crown from Kalus's head.

And suddenly the expression of people's faces changed in the room, and they were all looking at Luna with surprised faces. Luna was staring at people and they were seeing the surprise on their faces, and Luna understood why people were surprised.

And Luna opened her mouth and said that she understood that people were surprised because she had talked about impeaching the king Kalus. And Luna told people not to worry because she was not breaking the rules of the traditions of the kingdom, but she was instead following and respecting the rules of the traditions.

Then Luna went on and said that people were surprised because they thought that it was impossible to impeach the king Kalus. Because according to the tradition of Manitoba when someone was sitting on the throne that person was the king or queen till the end of his life or till the end of her life. And it was true that according to the tradition of Manitoba when someone was crowned the king or queen, that one must rule the kingdom until death.

But that there was another rule in the tradition of Manitoba that states that when the king or queen who was ruling the kingdom was not respecting the rules of the traditions, the heir or heiress to the crown had the duty to organize the impeachment of this king or queen who was sitting on the throne with the agreement of the population of the kingdom.

And suddenly, the eyes of everyone in the room opened wide and people in the room were turning their heads and looking at each other, and some had even the mouth opened but no word was coming out.

And looking at the expression on the face of people, we could see that they were very surprised by what Luna had just said. And they could not imagine that the king could be impeached because it was their first time to hear that the king was going to be impeached in the kingdom of Manitoba.

Luna went on and said that it was very hard for her to organize the impeachment of her father and it was the first time in the history of the kingdom of Manitoba that the king was going to be impeached.

But that was also the first time in the history that the kingdom of Manitoba had a king who did not respect the traditions and the values of the kingdom. And even worse the king who banned the traditions, the cultures, the religions and the education in the kingdom.

Luna said that Kalus was not the king of Manitoba, but Kalus was instead the worst enemy of the kingdom of Manitoba because Kalus had not only broken the rules of the kingdom, but Kalus had made a pact with the devil to destroy the kingdom of Manitoba.

Then Luna posed and the tears started flowing down her cheeks and everyone was looking at Luna with a surprised face, and looking at their expression faces, they were a little lost by what Luna had said.

And they did not understand why Luna had said that Kalus had made a pact with the devil.

Then Luna took a deep breath and said that she knew what had happened in the past and that she was aware that the kingdom had lost thousands of its children after Kalus had been crowned the king. And that she knew well that children had been mystically tortured and killed in the past.

And that it was not only the parents of the kingdom who had lost their children in the past, but she and other children who were alive today had lost their big brothers and sisters. Because all the children who had died in the past were the children of the kingdom and were also her siblings.

And Luna said that the deaths of these children would not go unpunished, and that she promised to her ancestors and to all these children who had been mystically killed that the responsible for the deaths of these children would pay for it, and this responsible would pay with his life.

Because every drop of blood of these children that had been mystically drunk by the worst enemy of the history of the kingdom would be paid. Because this enemy, also called devil, would pay with his own blood and that she was the one who was going to make this devil who had drunk children's blood pay, and she promised to these children who were now with the ancestors that she was going to kill this devil who had killed them by drinking their blood. And that she would do the impossible to keep her promise. Then Luna posed.

All the people in the room had the tears that were flowing down their cheeks. And except some children, the rest of the people in the room knew that Luna was telling the truth, and there were some parents in the room who lost their children in the past because their children had been mystically killed. But most people in the room were wondering how it was possible that Luna knew about the death of these children because these children were dead when Luna was not yet born.

And even Diana, who was Luna's mom, was wondering how Luna knew about the death of these children because she had never talked about the death of these children to Luna. Andthey were all wondering who was the devil that Luna was talking about. And they were curious to know the devil who had mystically drunk the blood of children.

Sunshine was looking at Luna with a face full of tears and she knew well what Luna was talking about, and she knew well that Kalus was the devil that Luna was talking about. And Sunshine was not really surprised to hear Luna talk about the tragedy that had happened in the kingdom where children had been mystically tortured and killed. But Sunshine was instead surprised to hear Luna talk about the pact that had been made by Kalus and the devil who had mystically drunk the blood of children.

And Sunshine knew that Luna was talking about the pact that had been made by Kalus and Lord. And Sunshine was understanding that Luna had probably heard from Diana or from other people about the tragedy that had happened in the kingdom where children had been mystically killed. But Sunshine was not understanding how it was possible that Luna knew that it was Kalus who had mystically killed children and how Luna was aware of the pact that Lord and Kalus had made.

But unfortunately, Sunshine could not answer this question, but Sunshine knew that only Kalus and Lord were aware of that pact. And Sunshine knew well that Kalus and Luna hated each other, and Sunshine was wondering if Kalus had told everything to Luna during a discussion to hurt Luna. But again, Sunshine could not answer this question.

Then Luna opened her mouth and said that the devil of the kingdom was Kalus, and that she promised to the ancestors of the kingdom, to all children who had been killed by Kalus and to all the inhabitants of the kingdom that she would kill Kalus by herself.

And Suddenly, there were noises in the room, and people were talking to each other. And they were wondering if Luna was saying that it was Kalus who had mystically drunk the blood of children and who had mystically killed the children.

And looking at the expression on the faces of people in the room, they were very surprised and it was obvious that they did not expect Luna to say that it was the king Kalus who had mystically killed children. And they were still not believing what they had just heard from Luna, and it was as if they were dreaming.

And except Sunshine, the rest of the people in the room were wondering how it was possible that Kalus had mystically tortured and killed children. And it was the first time for them to hear that the king or someone had mystically tortured and killed children.

And for most of them, Luna had said that her father was the devil who had tortured and killed children because she hated her father. And for some of them, Luna was crazy because she was lying about her father.

And even if people knew that Luna was telling the truth about the fact that her father was the worst the king in the history of the kingdom, it was not possible that it was the king Kalus who had mystically tortured and killed children. And even if people knew that the torture and the death of children was mystical, they did not believe that it was Kalus who was responsible for the torture and death of these children.

Then Luna continued and said that all the first heirs of the throne of the kingdom of Manitoba were born with the magic and powers to rule the kingdom, and to protect the kingdom and its inhabitants against the evil spirits and the enemies. And it meant that Kalus was born with the powers and magic to rule the kingdom and to protect the kingdom and its inhabitants against the evil spirits and enemies.

But Kalus had never used his magic and powers that he was born with to protect the kingdom and its inhabitants, but Kalus had instead made a pact with a devil to destroy the kingdom. And Kalus had received the evil powers and evil magic from this devil, and

Kalus had used these evil powers and evil magic to mystically torture and kill children.

And that Kalus had failed in his duties as the king of the kingdom not because Kalus had destroyed the values and traditions. But even worse Kalus had invited a devil in the kingdom of Manitoba to destroy the kingdom by making a pact with this devil.

Luna went on and said that another duty of Kalus that he did not fulfill was to form the heiress to the crown. Because according to the traditions of the kingdom the first duty of the king or the queen who was sitting on the throne was to train the heir or the heiress to the crown of the kingdom on how to rule the kingdom, how to use the powers and magic to protect the kingdom and its inhabitants against the evil spirits and the enemies.

And that Kalus had not trained her as the heiress to the crown of the kingdom to show her how to rule the kingdom, to show her how to use her powers and magic that she was born with to protect the kingdom and its inhabitants against the evil spirits and the enemies.

But the worse was that her father named Kalus had not only treated her and her little brother badly, but that Kalus had tried to kill her mystically many times. Because Kalus was seeing her like an enemy for his throne, and she was the worst enemy of Kalus.

That Kalus hated all the inhabitants of the kingdom, even the children, and that she had never seen Kalus give love to someone even to his own family. She had never heard Kalus say a good word to his wife who was her mom and who was in the room listening to her, and Kalus had never looked after his son named George or carried George when George was sick.

And Kalus had never played with his kids, and that since she was born, she had never received a kiss, a hug or a gift from her father. But she had instead had the insults coming from her father, and she had never seen a good action that her father had made not to his family but to the whole kingdom.

And that everyone in the room knew well that Kalus had only made bad actions to destroy the kingdom. And that Kalus hated the kingdom and its inhabitants and that since she was born, she had never seen Kalus go outside of the palace to visit his people. And that the only thing that mattered to Kalus was his crown and throne.

And that Kalus was not a human being, but Kalus was instead a devil who hated human beings. And that Kalus was ready to burn even the kingdom and all its inhabitants to keep his crown and his throne, and it was the reason why Kalus particularly hated her. Because Kalus knew that she was an obstacle for his throne, and it was the reason why Kalus had not only tried to kill her mystically, but Kalus had also tried to destroy her powers and magic that she was born with as the heiress to the crown.

But unfortunately for Kalus, it was impossible to kill her and to destroy her powers and magic because she was protected by some of her natural powers that she was born with. And Kalus had decided to hide from her as the heiress to the throne of the kingdom all the secrets of the kingdom, and he also decided to prevent her from using her magic and powers. But she had found out by herself the secrets of the kingdom, and how to use her magic and her powers. And she had also found out the rules of the traditions.

Luna added that she thanked all the children of the kingdom who were fighting to save the kingdom, and she also thanked Remy for his courage because he was the only adult and journalist who had decided to support children in the fight against the devil Kalus.

And that Remy was a hero, and Remy was a legend and hero who had already written his name in the history of the kingdom. And that she specially thanked Sunshine for everything because Sunshine was more than a hero for the kingdom because the kingdom was still alive thanks to Sunshine.

And that Sunshine was the one who had started this fight to save this kingdom with the meeting that she had organized at her home against the wish of her parents the day of her twelfth birthday. Sunshine had changed the destiny of the kingdom and the destiny of the inhabitants of the kingdom this day with this meeting that she had organized to celebrate her twelfth birthday.

And that Sunshine was an example and that the story of Sunshine would be taught in this kingdom in schools to the children and to the future generation, and Sunshine would inspire the future generation. And that the name of Sunshine would never die because Sunshine's name would stay alive in history forever.

Suddenly, Luna was interrupted by the applause and people were clapping their hands, and some of them had smiles on their faces while others had eyes wet with tears because they were touched. And there were children in the room who were screaming Sunshine's name. And Sunshine was looking at Luna with the tears that were flowing down her cheeks.

And there were many questions that were going on in Sunshine's head like how Luna knew about everything that had happened in the kingdom, and how Luna had found out the secrets of the kingdom? But unfortunately, Sunshine could not answer these questions.

Then Luna continued and said that she would organize a meeting with all the children of the kingdom about the impeachment of Kalus, and she would follow and respect the rules of the traditions of Manitoba on the impeachment of Kalus. And she would make sure that the impeachment would happen in the rules of the traditions of Manitoba.

And she and other children of the kingdom would walk in the kingdom to get a signature of the inhabitants about Kalus's impeachment. And when they would get two-thirds of the signatures of the inhabitants of the kingdom, she would impeach Kalus on the throne of the kingdom of Manitoba.

Then Luna said that she would not lie that she hated Kalus, but that she was not organizing the impeachment of Kalus because she hated Kalus or because Kalus was a bad father for her. But because Kalus was a bad king who had destroyed the kingdom and who had used his powers to break the rules of the traditions of the kingdom. And that she was not organizing the impeachment of Kalus because she wanted to sit on the throne of the kingdom. Because she would not sit on the throne of the kingdom of Manitoba.

Then Luna posed, and she was looking at everyone and all the eyes were focused on her. And looking at the expression on the faces of people, they were a little lost because they did not understand why Luna was saying that she was organizing the impeachment of Kalus to not sit on the throne. And they were wondering if the throne of the kingdom would stay empty.

And they all knew that Luna was the heiress to the throne, and that if Kalus was removed from the throne by Luna, that meant that Luna was going to sit on the throne. And people were very confused because they were not understanding why Luna had said that she would not sit on the throne, and they were wondering if Luna meant that there would not be the king or the queen in the kingdom of Manitoba.

Then Luna continued and said that tonight she was going to make the most important decision of her life, and that this decision that she was going to make would not only change her life and her destiny.

But this decision would also change the lives of all inhabitants of the kingdom and this decision would also change the destiny of the kingdom and the history of the kingdom. Because tonight she was announcing to the whole kingdom as heiress to the crown of the kingdom of Manitoba that she was renouncing the crown and throne of the kingdom of Manitoba.

And suddenly, Luna was interrupted by the noises in the room, and the eyes of everyone had opened wide and they were all surprised by what Luna had just said. And looking at the expression on the faces of people, it was as if they were dreaming, and they were still not believing what they had just heard from Luna. It was obvious for them that they did not expect Luna to say that she was renouncing the crown and throne of the kingdom of Manitoba.

And they were all wondering if it was possible for Luna to renounce her crown because it was her destiny and she was born queen and she was born to rule the kingdom of Manitoba. And they were wondering if the traditions of the kingdom of Manitoba allowed the future king or queen to renounce the crown.

And most of them were not happy at all to hear Luna say that she was renouncing the crown, and some of them were even angry. And Luna was looking at people and she could see the disappointment on their faces as she announced to them that she was renouncing the crown and throne of the kingdom.

Suddenly, people started getting up from their chairs by asking Luna not to renounce her crown and throne because they wanted her like their queen and the queen of the kingdom. And there were the voices in the room, and people were trying to convince Luna to change her mind and not to renounce the crown of the kingdom.

Because she was destroying the kingdom by renouncing her crown. And people were also saying that they would not accept her refusal to rule the kingdom. Then Luna tried to calm people in the room without success, and she asked Remy to help her calm people. Then Remy started to calm people.

After a few minutes, there was silence in the room, and all the eyes were focused on Luna, and people were waiting for her to talk with their heart beating faster than normal. And they were all waiting for Luna to change her mind and not to renounce her crown, and mostly to accept to be the queen of the kingdom of Manitoba and to rule the kingdom.

Then Luna opened her mouth and said that she had heard the words of each of them in the room by asking her not to renounce her crown, and not to let the throne of the kingdom empty. And Luna added that not to worry because the throne of the kingdom of Manitoba would not be empty, but that she was not the one who would sit on the throne of the kingdom of Manitoba.

And that the decision not to sit on the throne of the kingdom of Manitoba was not only coming from her, but this decision was coming from the children of the kingdom of Manitoba who were an important part of the population of Manitoba, and who were mostly the future of the kingdom of Manitoba.

Because the children of the kingdom of Manitoba had chosen George as the future king who would rule the kingdom of Manitoba. And that she and other children of the kingdom had chosen George to rule the kingdom, and she was going to respect the choice of the people of Manitoba by giving to George the crown of the kingdom.

And that George had been crowned the king of the kingdom a few months ago in the palace of the kingdom of Manitoba by all the children of the kingdom including herself. And that it was the wish of the children to have George sit on the throne and rule their kingdom, and she was going to respect this choice of children by realizing it.

Then Luna was interrupted by the applause and people were staring at Luna with smiles on their faces, and people were screaming, "the king George, the king George, the king George." People were very proud of the decision of Luna to cede the throne of the kingdom to her little brother named George. And children in the room were so happy with the decision of Luna to renounce the crown and the throne of the kingdom in favor of George. And for children, their dream was coming true by knowing that George would become the next king of the kingdom.

And people were not even wondering if the fact that Luna was renouncing the crown and the throne in favor of George was not anti-traditional. And they were happy that they did not even try to know if the rules of the tradition of the kingdom of Manitoba allowed Luna to renounce her crown and throne in favor of George.

Then Luna continued and said that she was not breaking the rules of the tradition of the kingdom of Manitoba by renouncing her crown and throne in favor of George. Because there was a test also called law in the tradition of Manitoba that states that the heir or the heiress to the crown could renounce the crown in favor of his or her little brother or sister by following and respecting the rules of the traditions of the kingdom of Manitoba.

And that according to the tradition she needed to get the signature of the two-thirds of the population of Manitoba to impeach

Kalus, and she hoped she would get even more than the two-thirds of the signatures that the tradition required. And that the only way to get rid of Kalus was to sign the petition about the impeachment of Kalus.

Luna said that she would teach everything to George, she would teach and show to George how to rule the kingdom, and she would teach the secrets of the kingdom to George. And she would also transfer all her powers and magic that she was born with to rule the kingdom to George.

And she would teach George how to use these powers and magic to protect the kingdom against the evil spirits and enemies. Then Luna said that all the children of the kingdom had taken the best decision not only of their lives but also of the destiny of the kingdom by choosing George as the king of the kingdom.

And that the children had made the history of the kingdom by choosing George to rule the kingdom because George loved the kingdom and its inhabitants more than himself. And that George was ready to shed his blood and to die for the love of his kingdom and his inhabitants.

And that she had no doubt that George was going to be a great king for the kingdom of Manitoba. Then everyone in the room got up from their chair and they started to clap their hands and with the tears that were flowing down their cheeks, and they were all looking at Luna who was walking away.

Then Remy called Sunshine on the podium and people were clapping their hands by screaming Sunshine's name with their eyes focused on Sunshine who was walking towards the podium. Then Sunshine took the microphone and she looked at everyone in the room, and she thanked them all for coming to the cultural events of the kingdom.

Then Sunshine said that today was a memorable day in the history of the kingdom and that this evening would stay in the history of the kingdom. Because Luna had made the history of the kingdom of Manitoba by renouncing her crown and throne in favor of George.

And Luna had surprised the whole kingdom by giving her crown and throne to George for George to rule the kingdom as the children of the kingdom had chosen George as the king of the kingdom to rule the kingdom.

And that Luna was an example who would inspire the future generations. And the history of the kingdom of Manitoba would never forget what Luna had just done by giving her crown and throne to George for George to rule the kingdom.

And that Luna had shown to the whole kingdom the meaning of the word love by renouncing her crown in favor of George, and that Luna had renounced her crown and throne not because Luna did not love the crown and the throne.

But because Luna did not think only about herself, but because Luna thought about the kingdom, about the inhabitants of the kingdom. And Luna had renounced her crown and throne because she had understood that the inhabitants of the kingdom wanted the kingdom to be ruled by George. Because the inhabitants of the kingdom had chosen George as their king.

And Luna had decided not to be selfish and she made the hardest decision of her life, a decision that was going to change the destiny of the inhabitants of the kingdom. But also, a decision that would change the history of the kingdom by ceding her crown and her throne to George for that George rules the kingdom as the children wanted.

And that Luna had taken this decision to cede her crown and her throne to George because Luna loved her kingdom and her people. Luna had thought of the happiness of her people before thinking about her own happiness because Luna wanted to see her people happy with a smile on their faces. And suddenly, Sunshine was interrupted by the applause in the room.

After a few seconds, Sunshine continued and said that Luna had not only made history by ceding her crown and her throne to George, but she had also made history by organizing the impeachment of her own father named Kalus.

Luna did not organize the impeachment of Kalus because hated Kalus as a father, but she organized the impeachment of Kalus because Kalus was a bad king for the kingdom and the inhabitants of the kingdom. And that everyone in the kingdom witnessed that Kalus was a monster who hated his people, and that everyone in the kingdom knew how badly Kalus treated his people.

And that Luna had taken this decision to impeach Kalus because Luna loved her kingdom and her people, and the decision to impeach Kalus and to cede her crown to George was the patriotic love of Luna that she had for her, the kingdom and her people. And that Luna had just proved that she loved the kingdom more than herself, and that Luna was not afraid to give her life to protect the kingdom.

Then Sunshine went on and said that she invited all the inhabitants of the kingdom to sign the petition about the impeachment of the devil Kalus, that they would not only get the two-thirds of the signatures to impeach the devil Kalus. But they would get all the signatures of the inhabitants of the kingdom because they would all sign for the impeachment of the devil Kalus, not only because they hated Kalus but because Kalus was not the king that the kingdom needed.

And mostly because Kalus was a monster who hated the kingdom and its inhabitants, and they could not let a monster like Kalus rule the kingdom that he hated. And that if they did not sign for the impeachment of Kalus, it meant that they hated their kingdom, it meant that they wanted the devil Kalus to continue to destroy the beautiful kingdom called the kingdom of Manitoba. And they would all take their responsibilities by showing their love for the kingdom by signing for the impeachment of the devil Kalus.

Sunshine added that they all only had one land, and this land was their kingdom called Manitoba, and they all only had one history, and their history was their kingdom called Manitoba, and they all only had one home, and this home was their kingdom called Manitoba.

And that they all only had one heart, and this heart was their kingdom called Manitoba, and they all only had one blood and this blood was their kingdom called Manitoba, and they all only lived for one reason and this reason was the kingdom called Manitoba.

Sunshine said that by preventing the devil Kalus from destroying their kingdom, they were also preventing Kalus from destroying their lives and the lives of their children, and also the lives of the future generation. And that by saving the kingdom from the devil Kalus, they would also save their lives, the lives of their children and the lives of their future generation. And that it was important and necessary to sign this petition to impeach Kalus.

And that after the impeachment of the devil Kalus, they would put their king that they had chosen named George on the throne and they would also put the crown on George's head. And that she had no doubt that George would be a great king for the kingdom and its inhabitants. Because George loved his kingdom and his people, and George was ready to die for the love of his kingdom and his people. And suddenly, people started to clap their hands.

After a few minutes, Sunshine continued and said that she would like to thank all children of the kingdom who had taken their courage every morning to break the laws of Kalus by getting out of their beds to come to school.

And that she would like to say to these children that they were the heroes who had fought to save their kingdom. Because these children had proved to everyone that they were not afraid to die for their kingdom, and they had not only hesitated to break the laws of Kalus, but they had also disobeyed their parents by coming to school.

And these children had decided to come to school not only because they needed to come to school to realise their dream, but because these children had understood that they were the future of the kingdom, and that they needed to save their kingdom.

Because these children had understood that they were the future employees and employers of their kingdom, that they were those who were going to replace their parents who were getting old. And that they needed to go to school and to study well to be the future employees and employers of the kingdom and to replace the parents who were getting old.

Sunshine went on and said that the children of the kingdom had shown their patriotic love to the kingdom by breaking the laws of Kalus to save their kingdom, to mostly save the lives of the future generation.

Because the children had understood that they would not only fight for them, but they would mostly fight for the future generations of the kingdom. And the children had understood that if they did not go to school, it meant that the future generations would not go to school too, it also meant that the future generations would not be able to realize their dream.

And that the children had refused to help the monster Kalus kill the kingdom and the lives of the inhabitants of the kingdom and the lives of the future generations of the kingdom with the laws of Kalus. And the children took their courage to break these laws of Kalus not only to save the kingdom and with the values, the traditions, and cultures of the kingdom.

But also, to allow the future generations to realize their dream and to live in a great kingdom and with a great history. And that all the children who had broken the laws of Kalus were the examples for the future generations because all these children had made the history of the kingdom of Manitoba.

Then Sunshine continued and said that she would like to tell all students who had failed their exams not to get discouraged that it was okay to fail in life, and that the real problem was not to fail but the real problem was to give up after failing. And that to fail did not mean that we were not smart, but to fail meant to learn.

That the worst thing we could do after failing, was to decide to give up or be discouraged, and it was a mistake to never do. And that failing was just a normal step of life because even those we did not fail today would probably fail tomorrow.

That what was important after we had failed, was to learn from our failure, and ask ourselves some questions of why we had failed, and after we would find the answers to our questions, we would understand why we had failed and we would learn from our failure. And after that we had learned from our failure, we had gained a great lesson in our lives. Because we had learned something from our failure, and that this lesson we had learned from our failure would prevent us from failing in the future for the same reason.

And of course, we would still fail in the future but for different reasons and it was not bad to fail, but it was bad to give up and not to learn from our failure. Because what was important, it was to learn from our failures each time that we would fail.

And by learning from our failure, it would not only prevent us from failing for the same reasons in future, but it would also help us to grow up, to become a better person with a lot of courage and confidence. And it would also help us to be ready to overcome any obstacle.

Sunshine added that we would always fail because failing was the most important step in our lives, and that the only best way to learn the lesson in our lives was from failure. And that the most important thing to do, was to learn each time when we failed, and mostly to never give up. And that it was important to stay focused, and to never give up no matter what would happen, to never forget our dream, and to always fight and work hard for our dream, to work harder to become the person we want to be.

Sunshine went on and said that all children would never stop dreaming because they were the future, and that the path to reach a dream was long and hard with many obstacles. And that they would fall on the path of the dream, and some would fall many times. And the real problem was not to fall, but the real problem was to give up after falling. Because it was important to get up and to keep walking on the path of the dream after that we fell.

And that it was important to get up and to keep walking on the path of our dream each time that we fell. And it was most important to ask ourselves the question why we fell, and once we answered this question, it meant that we had learned something important that would help us to achieve our goals. And mostly to remember to never give up because it did not matter if we were not going faster on the path of our dreams, and it did not matter if we were the last on the path of our dream.

Because what mattered it was not to give up and it was to make this dream come true. And that we would not get discouraged if some people were going faster on the path of the dream than us, and we would not get discouraged if some people achieved their dream before us because what mattered was to achieve our dream too.

Sunshine added that she would like to talk to all the students who had passed their exams that she congratulated them, but not to stop working and to keep working harder because the path to achieve a dream was very long. Then Sunshine said that together they would all build their kingdom and they would make the kingdom of Manitoba great and better.

Then people got up from their chairs and they started to clap their hands with their eyes focused on Sunshine who was walking away. After the speech of Sunshine, some children like Asher, Mia and Aaron made a speech to thank all their classmates who had taken their courage to break the laws of Kalus and to disobey their parents to come to school.

And they also thanked Sunshine and Luna who were their teachers, and who had decided not to abandon the students. But who had instead decided to teach the students despite the fact that Sunshine and Luna were also the children who were going to school for their first time.

Asher, Mia and Aaron had also thanked Remy for his courage to break the laws of Kalus and to always support children in the fight to free the kingdom from Kalus's hands. Asher, Mia and Aaron had also told the parents that it was time to free the kingdom, and that all the inhabitants of the kingdom would sign the petition to impeach the devil Kalus of the throne of the kingdom.

Then Prince Diana had made the last speech to thank all children for their courage to free the kingdom. And she encouraged all the inhabitants of the kingdom to sign the petition to impeach Kalus from the throne of the kingdom of Manitoba.

Then all the people in the room moved to the stadium to watch the game. Hockey and basketball, which were the traditional sports of the kingdom, were going to be played by the boys. And the people were in the stands to applaud the children who were paying.

And the girls were standing up in the stands and they were screaming the name of their lovers to encourage their lovers who were playing. And the girls had even worn t-shirts with the number of the shirt of their lovers on it. And the girls had also written the names of their lovers on their pants.

After two hours, the games were over and the boys went to the washrooms of the cultural house to take showers and to change their dress to be ready for the dances. And the girls went to change and to be ready for the dances. And the people were still in the stands waiting for the children to come perform the dances.

After an hour, the children (boys and girls) walked on the stadium and started to perform the different dances like the ballet, the salsa and the tango which were the traditional dances of the kingdom.

And the people were in the stands, and some were sitting while others were standing up, and they were watching children who were performing with the tears in their eyes. And people were very surprised to see children who were performing very well. And looking at the expression on people's faces, they did not expect to see children perform well. Mostly because children had not been trained by the professional dancers how to dance the traditional dances of the kingdom of Manitoba.

And the people were very amazed to see that the children had succeeded in learning the traditional dances by themselves, and they were wondering how it was possible. And they were very happy of the children who had succeeded in saving the kingdom.

And they had the tears that were flowing down their cheeks as they were watching the children who were performing. And it was nostalgic to watch the children who were performing, and they were remembering their childhood. And they were remembering their childhood how they used to perform in this room through these children who were performing.

And there were smiles on the faces of the parents as they were watching their children who were interpreting the music. And looking at the expression on the faces of people, we could see that they were very happy not only to see the children who were singing very well, but they were also happy to see or to remember their childhood through these children who were performing.

And the parents were so happy that they did not believe that they were in the cultural house celebrating the cultural events. Mostly, they had lost hope to one day celebrate their culture again because since Kalus had been crowned the king, Kalus had banned all cultural celebrations.

After three hours, the children were on the dance floor and they were dancing. George and Mia were dancing together and they were looking each other in the eyes.

Mia smiled at George and said, "Congratulations, my the king."

"Congratulations?" George asked.

"You had just been crowned the king by the whole of the kingdom," Mia answered.

George smiled and said, "Thank you."

"I have no doubt that you would be a great king," Mia said.

"Why are you sure that I would be a great king?" George asked.

"Because you love your kingdom and your people," Mia answered.

"It's not enough to be a great king," George said.

"What else do you need to be a great king?" Mia asked.

"A good advisor who would be near to me and who would help me to make good decisions, who would correct me, who would not tell me things that I only want to understand but that I need to understand," George said.

"I have no doubt that you would have many people who would like to work with you," George said.

"No, I am not looking for people to work with," George retorted.

"What are you looking for?" Mia asked.

"I read a memory of my great grandfather a week ago in the library of the palace, and according to my great grandfather, a great king needed his other half who would not only take care of his heart, but who would also help him to rule the kingdom. Because only that other half can make him a great the king, and only that other half has the powers to tell him the right things, to be honest with him, to tell him things he needed to understand and to help him to make the better decision and to give him the offspring that would rule the kingdom in the future," George said.

Mia smiled and said, "It means you are looking for your other half."

"Exactly," George retorted.

Mia smiled and said, "Do not worry, I have no doubt that our king would have a choice to choose his other half. Because with all these beautiful girls in the kingdom, there would be many pretenders for our king."

"I am not looking for the pretenders," George said.

Mia looked at George with a surprised face and said, "I do not understand." And she added, "You just told me that you were looking for your other half."

"I have already found her," George said.

Mia smiled and said, "Congratulations."

"Thank you," George retorted.

"Can I know who she is? Mia asked.

"She is the one who was the first to name me the king of the kingdom," George said.

Mia smiled and asked, "How is she?"

"She has green eyes, long black hair, and a beautiful long chin," George answered.

"What is her name?" Mia asked.

"She wore a beautiful blue outfit," George said.

"You did not answer my question," Mia said.

"I forgot your question," George said.

"I asked the name of your future wife," Mia said.

George smiled and said, "I am looking into her eyes now, I have hands on her hips and she is smiling at me with her hands around my neck."

Mia smiled and said, "I want to know her name."

"I forgot her name," George said.

"How can you forget the name of the one you want to marry?" Mia asked.

"Do you really want to know her?" George asked.

"Yes, of course I want to know the name of my king's future wife," Mia said.

"As I forgot her name, I am going to kiss her," George said.

"Kiss her?" Mia cried out.

"Yes, because I forgot her name," George answered.

"Why do you want to kiss her?" Mia asked.

"Because she is the queen of my heart and because I love her," George said.

Mia smiled and said, "I did not know that my king was romantic."

George smiled and said, "Your king has a lot of secrets and qualities that you would soon find out."

Mia smiled and said, "The future wife of my king is very lucky." And she added, "You still did not tell me her name."

"I can kiss her if you want," George said.

"I am curious to know her," Mia said.

George smiled and asked, "Does that mean you allow me to kiss her?"

"Yes, you can kiss her because I want to know her," Mia answered.

Then George moved his mouth through Mia's mouth and they started kissing. Luna and Isac were dancing together, and they were smiling at each other.

Then Luna said, "You have not said a word since we are dancing."

Isac smiled and said, "I was waiting for your authorization."

"My authorization?" Luna asked.

"Yes, I was wondering if I could talk to my teacher without raising my hand," Isac said.

Luna smiled and said, "We are not in the classroom, and tonight, I am not your teacher so you are free to say whatever you want."

"I am glad to hear that I am free to talk," Isac said.

"I listen," Luna said.

Isac smiled at Luna and said, "I always lose my words when I am with you."

"Why?" Luna asked.

"There are many reasons," Isac answered.

"I want to know these reasons," Luna said.

"You are a princess, you are very strong and smart, your determination and above all your beauty," Isac said.

"What with my beauty?" Luna asked.

"You are the beautiful woman that I have never seen," Isac said.

Luna smiled and said, "Thank you." Then Luna looked into Isac's eyes and said, "I do not want you to be afraid of me, I do not want you to see me like a princess or like your teacher, I do not want you to see me like a hero, but I want you to see me like a normal person, like your friend, like your sister, like your confidence, like someone you can talk and laugh with and even cry if you want to cry."

Isac said, "Thank you."

"You are welcome," Luna said.

"Can I see you like a girl?" Isac asked.

Luna smiled and asked, "How do you want to see me like a girl if I am already a girl?"

Isac smiled and said, "I mean, like my girl."

"What do you mean?" Luna smiled by asking.

"You heard me," Isac retorted.

"I did not," Luna smiled and said.

"Why are you smiling if you did not get what I said?" Isac asked.

"I always have a smile on my face when I am with you," Luna answered.

"I noticed it," Isac retorted.

"Answer my question now," Luna said.

Isac took a deep breath and said, "It meant if I could consider you like my lover?"

Luna smiled and asked, "Are you asking me to be your lover?"

"Yes, I want you to be my lover." Isac said.

Luna smiled and said, "Your way of asking me to be your lover is very bad, so you need to convince me."

"I love you," Isac said.

"How can I be sure?" Luna asked.

"My heart is beating every time I am thinking of you, you are always in my dream, my eyes are always focused on you when you are near to me, I can not stop thinking about you, you are always in my thoughts. And you are the most beautiful, smart and above all you are an amazing human being that the world never had. Also, your beauty always makes me blind, deaf, and mute. You invaded in body, and I feel like you bewitched me." Isac said.

Luna smiled and said, "I did not know that you are a poet." And she added, "Let me answer you if I am okay to be your lover."

Then Luna and Isac were staring at each other in the eyes with their hearts that were beating of love, and with the smiles on their faces and their eyes were shining of love. Then Luna moved her head through Isac and they started to kiss. Sunshine and Aaron were dancing together, and they were looking each other in the eyes with smiles on their faces.

Then Sunshine broke the silence and said, "My father told me this morning that you must say three words to me this evening."

Aaron smiled and said, "I love you."

Sunshine smiled and said, "Four words."

Aaron smiled and said, "I love you more."

Sunshine said, "Five words?"

Aaron said, "I would always love you."

Sunshine smiled and said, "Another five words."

Aaron looked into Sunshine's eyes and said, "I would never disappoint you."

Sunshine smiled and said, "Six words."

Aaron said, "I need you in my life."

Sunshine smiled and said, "Seven words."

Aaron smiled and said, "I need you in my life forever."

Sunshine smiled and said, "You are a good talker."

Aaron smiled and said, "I am not a good talker, just that I am in love with you."

Sunshine said, "It's a pleasure to hear you say the sweet words to me, and I want to keep listening to you."

Aaron smiled and said, "We must stop talking now."

Sunshine smiled and asked, "And doing what?"

Aaron smiled and said, "Look around you."

Sunshine turned her head and she looked around, and suddenly the expression of her face changed as she was looking with joy at the couples who were kissing, and these couples were her friends. Then Sunshine turned her head and smiled at Aaron and said, "I thought your eyes were focused only on me."

Aaron said, "Yes, my eyes are focused only on you."

Sunshine asked, "How did you see what was going on around if your eyes were focused on me?"

Aaron smiled and said, "I did not see what was going on around, but I just guessed what was going on around."

Sunshine smiled and said, "I did not know that you were a magician and that you have the gift to guess things that are happening."

Aaron smiled and asked, "What is going on around?"

Sunshine asked, "What did you guess about what is happening around?"

Aaron answered, "The couples are kissing."

Sunshine smiled and said, "You guessed well."

Aaron said, "We must stop talking now."

Sunshine smiled and asked, "And do what?"

Aaron smiled and said, "Let me think."

Sunshine and Aaron were still looking in the eyes with smiles on their faces while dancing. Then Aaron moved his head to kiss Sunshine, and they were suddenly thrown on the floor by a mysterious wind that was blowing. And there were screams of fear in the room.

And they were all on the floor, and there was the wind that was blowing in the room, and no one knew where that wind was coming from. And there was fear on the faces of people on the floor and they were screaming of fear as the room was shaking and the tables and chairs were falling on them.

Sunshine was on the floor and she was trying to get up from the floor without success because she was feeling weak, and she did not understand what was going on. And she was turning her head looking around trying to understand what was going on. And Looking at the expression on Sunshine, she was completely surprised because she was wondering where this wind that was blowing in the room was coming from.

And Sunshine was still trying to get up without success, and she turned her head around as she was hearing people who were coughing. And the fear appeared on Sunshine's face as she was seeing people who were coughing and breathing with difficulty. And for the third time, Sunshine tried to get up from the floor without success. And suddenly, the light in the room went out. And there was darkness in the room and there were screams of fear coming from people in the room.

After a few seconds, the light went on and the wind had stopped blowing in the room, but there was smoke in the room, and no one knew where this smoke was coming from. And people were on the floor breathing deeply and coughing, and there were some people who were bleeding from their foreheads and noses because they had been injured by the tables that had fallen on them. And they were also feeling tired and weak, and they were trying to get up from the floor without success.

Then Sunshine and Luna succeeded to get up from the floor, and Sunshine was bleeding from her forehead. Then Sunshine and Luna started to help people to get up from the floor and they were also helping people to get out of the room. People were leaving the room as fast as they could, and they were in the yard of the cultural house and they were breathing the fresh air. And there were some people who had dizziness, and there were a few people who were even vomiting.

After a few minutes, Sunshine and Luna had succeeded in helping all people to get out, except George who was still lying on the floor. Sunshine and Luna had knelt near to George and they were shaking George who was lying on the floor.

Sunshine and Luna were surprised that George was not reacting, and they started calling George's name, but again George was not still reacting. And the fear appeared on their faces as they had understood that George was unconscious. Then Sunshine and Luna lifted their heads and they looked at each other in the eyes with their faces full of fear. And looking at their expressionless faces, we could see that Sunshine and Luna were understanding what was going on.

Then Sunshine told Luna that they must take George outside, then they carried George and walked till outside with him. And people had surrounded George who was lying on the ground still unconscious, and there were some people like Mia, Nany and others who were crying, and they were all afraid that George was dead.

People were very afraid, despite the fact that Sunshine was trying to calm them that George was not dead but that George was just unconscious. Then George was taken to the hospital.

After an hour, the waiting room of the hospital was full of children, and they were all waiting for the doctor to come tell them how George was doing. And there was panic in the waiting room, and their expression faces were full of fear, and some even had hearts that were beating faster than the normal.

And there was only Sunshine in the room who was not in panic, and looking at the expression on Sunshine's face, we could see that she was not worried about George. And we could also understand that she knew exactly what was going on.

Then a doctor walked in the waiting room, and they all rushed through the doctor. And Mia asked the doctor how George was doing? And the doctors looked at Mia without saying a word, and all the eyes were focused on the doctor. Then Luna asked the doctor how George was doing? And suddenly, there were the screams and the cries coming from children as they had heard the doctor say that George was in a coma.

Sunshine and Luna started to calm their friends by saying that George would not die. And that George would get out of the coma very soon. And it was not easy for Sunshine and Luna to calm their friends and mostly Mia who could not stop crying.

Then Sunshine succeeded in convincing her friends to go home and to get some sleep. And that they would meet during the afternoon at the hospital to see how George was doing. Then they all left the hospital.

Kalus was in his magic room and he was talking with Lord. And Kalus was so happy to hear Lord mostly that he thought that Lord was dead, as he had not heard Lord for months. And Kalus was surprised and at the same time sad to hear from Lord that they had lost everything.

That they had lost the control of the souls of children who were not yet born. Because Sunshine had succeeded in destroying the satanic master tree that should control the souls of the future children of the kingdom. And even worse that Sunshine had destroyed his forest, and it was the reason why he had disappeared during the months.

And Kalus was more surprised to hear from Lord that they must give up the plan to control the souls of the children for the moment, and they would focus on killing Sunshine. Because Sunshine was more powerful and dangerous than what they imagined, and that it would be impossible to realize their plan without having killed Sunshine first.

And Lord also told the king Kalus that he could not imagine that Sunshine could destroy his satanic master tree. And that the plan now was to kill Sunshine, before planning their plan to control the future generations.

And Kalus was astonished to hear from Lord that they had another enemy who was not Sunshine, and that this enemy was more dangerous than Sunshine. Because it was this enemy who had helped Sunshine to destroy his forest and the satanic master tree.

And that this enemy had helped Sunshine to fight him (Lord), and that it was important for them to kill Sunshine and this enemy too. And Kalus asked Lord who was this mysterious enemy? Lord answered Kalus that he had no idea about who this enemy was because this enemy was mysterious, but that this enemy was dangerous like Sunshine.

And Lord added that this enemy was even more dangerous than Sunshine because this enemy was invisible and it was impossible to fight this enemy. Because they had no idea who this enemy was. And Kalus asked Lord if Sunshine knew who this mysterious enemy was. Lord answered that he had no idea, but he had a plan to find out who this mysterious enemy was. And Lord also said that he was determined to kill Sunshine and this mysterious enemy.

Then Kalus was very astonished to hear from Lord that Luna was aware of what was going on, and that Luna even knew about the children's deaths who had been mystically killed in the past by them. And even worse that Luna had promised to take revenge for the deaths of these children.

And even worse Luna was aware of the secrets of the kingdom and she knew that she had the powers and magic. And Kalus asked Lord how Luna knew all these secrets? Lord answered Kalus that Luna had found out all the secrets by herself.

And Lord went on and said that Luna was very dangerous like Sunshine, and that it was important for them to kill Luna too. But they must focus on Sunshine first because Sunshine was their priority and that they had to kill Luna only after killing Sunshine.

Because if they killed Luna before killing Sunshine, things would be worse and Sunshine would not hesitate to make things harder or even impossible because Sunshine would try to get revenge for Luna's death at any cost.

And Kalus was angry to hear from Lord that Luna had organized his [Kalus] impeachment and that Luna had decided to cede her throne and her crown to George because the children of the kingdom had chosen George as their king.

And that Sunshine, Luna and other children were going to organize a petition to get the signature of people for his [Kalus] impeachment. And Kalus was very angry to hear that Luna was determined to get rid of him by organizing his impeachment.

And Kalus told Lord that he could not allow Luna to organize his impeachment, and for that he was going to kill Luna. That it was important for him to kill Luna, before Luna organized his impeachment. And Kalus added that Luna was even more dangerous than Sunshine because Luna knew the secrets of the kingdom, and Luna also knew the secrets of the crown and throne.

And even worse Luna knew that she was born with the powers and magic to rule the kingdom, and Luna knew that she was the heiress to the crown and that she could organize his impeachment on the basis of the rules of the traditions.

And Lord told Kalus not to worry that even if Luna was an enemy and a threat for them, Luna was weak for the moment. That for the moment Luna could not organize his [Kalus] impeachment because Luna was focused on George who was in a coma in the hospital. And that Sunshine, Luna and other children would not have the time to organize the impeachment of the king Kalus because all children were focused on George who was in a coma in the hospital.

Kalus asked Lord what had happened to George? And Lord answered that he had mystically attended the cultural event, and he watched the whole event and he heard everything that was said during the event. Then he caused a disaster and he put George in a coma to prevent children from organizing the impeachment of Kalus. Because with George in a coma, the whole kingdom would be focused on the situation of George who was in a coma.

And Kalus told Lord that Lord had done a great job by putting George in a coma, but that Lord should instead kill Sunshine and Luna because the real enemies were Sunshine and Luna. And Kalus added that even if George was also an enemy, George was not dangerous and George was not a powerful enemy, and that George could not do something without Sunshine and Luna.

Lord replied that it was impossible to kill Luna and Sunshine, and it was also impossible to kill other children of the kingdom. Because he[Lord] had lost the control of the souls of children like Sunshine had succeeded in freeing the souls of children.

And Kalus told Lord that Lord should instead put Sunshine and Luna in a coma because even with George in a coma, Sunshine and Luna would not stop. And that the only way to stop all the children was to put Sunshine and Luna in a coma.

Lord replied that he tried to put Sunshine and Luna in a coma, but he failed to do that because Sunshine and Luna were protected by their powers and magic. And Lord added that the only solution he had to stop the children, especially Sunshine and Luna, was to put George in a coma.

And Lord went on and said that he had chosen George to put in a coma because George was the one that children had chosen as their king, and George was the most beloved by the children. And that by putting George in a coma, all the children would be deconcentrated on the impeachment of the king Kalus, and children would be focused on George with the fear that their king George would die.

Kalus told Lord that Lord should not only put George in a coma, but Lord should put all the children in a coma. Except Sunshine and Luna who could not be put in a coma, like Sunshine and Luna were protected by their powers and magic.

And Kalus added that because if all the children were put in a coma, the whole kingdom should be in fear now, and the parents should be crying their children with the fear that their children would die.

And Kalus also said that with all children in a coma, Sunshine and Luna would lose their strengths and their courage to continue the fight because Sunshine and Luna should be focused on children in a coma. Lord replied to Kalus that it was not a good idea to put all the children of the kingdom in a coma because with all the children in a coma, it would only give the anger, the strengths and the determination to Sunshine and Luna to fight.

Because the only thing that mattered for Sunshine and Luna was the safety of the children, and that if all the children were in a coma, things would only go worse because Sunshine and Luna would have more determination to fight to free the kingdom.

And Lord added that the only thing to do now was to find out who was the mysterious enemy who was helping Sunshine in her fight. Kalus told Lord that he was very tired to be at home, that since more than twelve years that Sunshine had kept him prisoner in his palace, he had not got out.

And Lord told Kalus that it was time for him [Kalus] to get out and to make the speech to seduce the inhabitants of the kingdom and to get the confidence of the people because Sunshine and Luna who were becoming dangerous.

And Lord added that the love and confidence of the inhabitants of the kingdom were on Sunshine and Luna, and it was time to change that. Because if Sunshine and Luna went out now to ask the inhabitants to sign the petition for the impeachment of Kalus, the inhabitants of the kingdom would not hesitate to sign this petition.

And Lord went on and told Kalus what Kalus would do when Kalus would get out of the palace and how Kalus would behave. Lord also told Kalus that Kalus would say that Luna was a liar, and that she had lied to the whole kingdom about the secrets of the kingdom.

Then Lord told Kalus that the first thing he [Kalus] would do when he [Kalus] would get out of the magic room, was to call the journalists to make a speech that all the inhabitants of the kingdom would watch.

And Lord told Kalus what Kalus would say in his speech. Then Lord told Kalus that he was going to give him [Kalus] the magic that would protect him [Kalus] against the magic trees that were outside. And Lord added that Kalus must stay in the magic room because Kalus was going to receive the power and the magic that would protect him against the energies of the magic trees that were outside.

And Lord told Kalus that a white smoke would appear in the magic room, and Kalus would breathe this white smoke for three hours, and that Kalus would spend three days without taking a shower. Because if Kalus took a shower before three days ago, the power and magic that Kalus would receive would not be effective.

Suddenly, the magic room was filled with white smoke, and Kalus started coughing as he was yearning for this white smoke. And after a few minutes, Kalus started to sweat, and he was shaking. And after an hour, Kalus started to feel a strange reaction in his body and his stomach was turning. And Kalus was feeling tired and weak, he was breathing with a lot of difficulty. After more than two hours the white smoke had disappeared in the room, and Kalus got up and left the magic room.

CHAPTER VII

THE IMPEACHMENT OF THE KING KALUS, AND LUNA SHOWS HER POWER AND MAGIC TO THE WHOLE KINGDOM

It was noon, the children were in the waiting room of the hospital, and their faces were full of sadness and the eyes of some of them were wet with tears because the doctor had just informed them that George was still in a coma.

And looking at the expression on the faces of children, we could see that they were really afraid that George would die. And even Sunshine who knew that it was Lord who had mystically caused the disaster that had happened early this morning during the event was afraid about the situation of the kingdom.

And Sunshine knew that it was Lord who had put George in a coma to scare the inhabitants of the kingdom. And Sunshine knew that Lord had mystically attended the event, and that Lord was aware of everything that was said during the meeting. And that if Lord had decided to put George in a coma, it was because Lord wanted to prevent them from organizing the impeachment of Kalus.

Because Lord knew that with George in a coma, the whole kingdom would be focused on George's health, and children would be affected. And Sunshine was realizing that Lord had paralysed the kingdom by putting George in a coma.

And even if Sunshine knew well that Lord could not kill George because the soul of George was not controlled by Lord and that everything would be fine, Sunshine could not help but be worried because she knew that Lord was in the kingdom. And that with the Lord in the kingdom, the worst could happen at any time, and that Lord had the powers to put all the children of the kingdom in a coma. Then Sunshine started to think about what to do, and mostly where she could find Lord.

Then Sunshine turned her head through her right as she had heard her name that was called by Luna, then Sunshine looked at Luna and she noticed that Luna's eyes were focused on the television that was in the room.

Then Sunshine turned her head and looked at the television. And suddenly the expression of her face changed, and she was watching the television with a surprised face as she was watching Kalus on television who was giving a speech in the garden of the palace.

Sunshine was amazed to hear Kalus said that he was aware of everything that was said in the cultural house last night, and that he wanted to inform the whole kingdom that Luna was not his daughter, that Luna was not his child, and that everything that was said by Luna was lies.

And that Luna was not the heiress to the crown and the throne of the kingdom. And that Luna had no idea about the secrets of the kingdom, and that Luna did not know herself the traditions and the cultures of the kingdom.

And that in the traditions of the kingdom of Manitoba, the one who was sitting on the throne was going to die on the throne. And that the impeachment of the king or a queen did not exist in the traditions of Manitoba because the king or queen reigned for life in the traditions and cultures of Manitoba. And Kalus went on and said that Luna hated him and she also hated this kingdom because she was not a child of this kingdom.

And that Luna wanted the throne of the kingdom, but unfortunately for her, she was not his daughter, and she could have the throne of the kingdom. And Luna would never have the throne and crown of the kingdom.

And that Luna was a curse for this kingdom, and that Luna was responsible for all the curses and the bad events that had happened in the kingdom because Luna was not accepted by the ancestors of the kingdom. And that Luna had lied by saying that she was born with the powers and the magic because Luna had no power, and she had no magic. And that Luna was born with nothing exceptional, and she was born without power or magic.

And that Luna was the only responsible for the disaster that had happened early this morning during the cultural events, and that Luna was also the only responsible if George was in a coma. Because this disaster that had happened early this morning during the cultural event was the wrath of the god, and that god of the kingdom was angry because god had heard Luna say that she was going to organize the impeachment of the king Kalus.

And Kalus added that there were two devils in the kingdom who were Sunshine and Luna, and that he wanted all the inhabitants of the kingdom to stop listening and following Sunshine and Luna. Because Sunshine and Luna were the cursed girls and the curses for the kingdom. And that all the parents would prohibit their children from walking with Sunshine and Luna because Sunshine and Luna were in the kingdom to destroy the kingdom.

Then Kalus said that he prohibited all the inhabitants of the kingdom to sign the petition about his impeachment that would be organized by Sunshine and Luna. And that he would send his army outside, and that all the children who would be outside would be arrested or killed by his army.

And that all people who would be in contact with Sunshine and Luna would be arrested or killed by his army, and that even all those who would be seen near Sunshine and Luna would be arrested. Then Kalus said that he was going to visit his dogs and he got up from his chair and left.

And all the children in the room had still had their eyes on the screen of the television, then they turned their heads and they looked at each other with their mouths closed and with surprised faces. And looking at the expression on the faces of children, they were completely lost and they were still not realizing what they had just heard from Kalus's mouth.

And it was obvious for children that they did not expect the speech of Kalus, mostly the words that were pronounced by Kalus. And some of them opened their mouths to speak, but their mouths were shaking that a word could not get out.

Then Isac walked near Luna, and he took Luna in his arms, and Isac said in Luna's ear that he loved her and to never forget it, and that he would always be with her and that she would never be alone. And Isac also told Luna that he knew well that she was the heiress to the crown and throne of the kingdom. And mostly that she was a blessing not only for him, but also for the kingdom and its inhabitants. And Luna thanked Isac for his words and she kissed him.

Then all the children went and they hugged Luna and Sunshine by giving their support to Luna and Sunshine. And the children told Luna and Sunshine that they were all a family, and that they knew that Kalus was lying because Kalus was afraid of them.

And children also said that they would always be together and that they would not stop and they were ready to die to free the kingdom from Kalus's hands. Then Sunshine and Luna thanked their friends for their support.

Then Remy and his team walked in the waiting room of the hospital, and Remy went and he told the children that he had watched on television the speech of the devil Kalus. And Remy also told children that he would always be with them no matter what would happen, and that he knew that the devil Kalus was a liar, and that Kalus was afraid.

And the children thanked Remy for his support. Then Luna asked Remy if he had the camera with him. And Remy answered that yes, that he had the camera. And Luna told Remy that she wanted to make a speech that he would post on his website and on his television channel so that the whole kingdom would watch and listen.

After a few minutes, Luna was in front of the camera talking on the microphone, and she was saying that she was happy to hear that she was not the daughter of the devil Kalus. And that herself she did not want to be the daughter of a monster like Kalus, and that she knew that she was not the daughter of the monster Kalus.

But she knew that she was the daughter of the kingdom and that she was the heiress to the crown and the throne of the kingdom of Manitoba. And that she would prove to the whole kingdom that she was the heiress to the crown and the throne.

Luna went on and said that the only liar in the kingdom was the devil Kalus, and that the only true thing that was said by the monster Kalus, was the fact that the monster Kalus had mentioned that she was not his daughter. Because of herself, she did not want to be the daughter of a monster like Kalus. But all the rest of things that were said by Kalus were lies, and that these words were said by Kalus because Kalus was afraid of the impeachment.

And that Kalus knew well that the traditions of the kingdom of Manitoba allowed her as the heiress to the crown and the throne of the kingdom to organize his impeachment because he broke the rules of the tradition.

And Luna continued and told the whole kingdom not to be afraid of the words of Kalus because Kalus would do nothing, and that Kalus had already lost the control of the kingdom. And that Kalus was already a dead man. And Luna also told the whole kingdom to be ready to sign the petition about the impeachment of Kalus.

After Luna's speech, all Luna's fellows who were in the waiting room of the hospital made a speech together in front of the camera to support Luna and Sunshine. And the children also said that they would not stop walking with Sunshine and Luna because Sunshine and Luna were their family. And that they were not afraid of the devil Kalus, and that they were ready to die with Sunshine and Luna to save the kingdom of Manitoba.

After the speech of children, the princess Diana who was in the waiting room of the hospital made a speech in front of the camera to support the children, and she told the whole kingdom that even if it was hard to accept, Luna and George were the children of Kalus. And that Luna and George had only one father, and this father was their genitor who was Kalus.

And that Kalus and Luna were father and daughter even if they hated each other. And that Luna was the daughter of Kalus, and Luna was also the heiress to the crown and the throne of the kingdom of Manitoba.

Diana added that even if Kalus was her husband, Kalus was a bad king, and that the whole kingdom must put their fear aside and support the children in their fight to get rid of Kalus. And that the whole kingdom must follow children, and the whole kingdom must help children to get rid of Kalus by signing the petition about the impeachment of Kalus.

Diana also said that Sunshine and Luna were not the curses for the kingdom of Manitoba, but Sunshine and Luna were instead the blessing for the kingdom of Manitoba. Because Sunshine and Luna were the light of the kingdom, and the kingdom were grateful to have Sunshine and Luna among its children.

Diana also said that the whole kingdom must listen to Luna and mostly trust Luna because even if it was not a secret that Luna hated Kalus for many reasons. Luna was unable to break the rules of the tradition of the kingdom to get rid of Kalus.

And that the whole kingdom must trust Luna when Luna says that the tradition of the kingdom of Manitoba allowed her (Luna) to organize the impeachment of Kalus because Kalus had broken the rules of the tradition.

After Diana's speech, Sunshine made her speech in front of the camera, and she told the whole kingdom that it was time to free the kingdom and its inhabitants by putting an end to the laws of Kalus. And for that the whole kingdom must sign the petition about the impeachment of Kalus.

Sunshine also told the whole kingdom not to be afraid because Kalus would do nothing, and that Kalus was using his army and the threats because Kalus was seeing his end, and that Kalus knew well that his reign was over. And that she would never allow Kalus to hurt an inhabitant of the kingdom. Then Sunshine asked the whole kingdom to get ready because she and her fellows would be out the next day to ask the children to sign the petition about the impeachment of Kalus.

Then the children started to plan how to organize the impeachment of Kalus. But Mia, Isac and Nany were against this plan for the moment because they wanted George to be out of the coma and to recover before planning Kalus's impeachment.

But Sunshine and Luna had succeeded in convincing Mia, Isac and Nany that it was time to get rid of Kalus, and that they could not wait for George to come out of the coma to continue with their fight. Because they did not know when George would get out of the coma. Then the children spent the rest of the day planning how to free the kingdom by getting rid of Kalus.

It was evening. And all the inhabitants of the kingdom were in their living room, and they had watched the speeches of Kalus, Luna, children, Diana and Sunshine. And they had not been surprised at all by the speeches of Luna, children, and Sunshine.

But they had been very surprised to hear from Kalus's mouth that Luna was not his daughter and that Luna was not the heiress to the crown and throne of the kingdom of Manitoba and that Luna was born with no power and magic. Mostly that Luna had lied about the secrets of the kingdom because Luna did not know the secrets of the kingdom.

And despite the fact that the whole kingdom had watched the speech of Diana and that they had heard Diana say in her speech that Kalus and Luna were father and daughter. And that Kalus was the genitor father of Luna, the whole kingdom had started to have doubts on Luna as the daughter of Kalus.

Because for the inhabitants of the kingdom, Kalus could not say that Luna was not his daughter just because he hated Luna. And for the people even if Kalus was a monster, a bad father and a bad king, Kalus could not reject his own children, even if he hated his children because his children had joined Sunshine and other children to fight him.

And for the people there was a reason why between the two children of Kalus who were Luna and George and who were recognized by the whole kingdom as his children, Kalus had said that Luna was not his child, and he did not say that George was not his child.

And the whole kingdom knew that Luna and George hated Kalus for many reasons, and also that Kalus hated Luna and George too. But Kalus did not say that George was not his child, despite the fact that he hated George the same way he hated Luna.

And it was obvious for the whole kingdom that if Luna was not the child of Kalus, it meant that princess Diana had cheated on Kalus, or maybe Luna had been adopted by Kalus and Diana. And the whole kingdom knew that they could not really trust Diana because Diana was a mother and Diana would always support her children as a good mother. So even if Luna was not the daughter of Kalus, the princess Diana could not confess it.

And for the inhabitants of the kingdom, if Luna was not the daughter of Kalus, it meant that Luna was not the heiress to the crown and the throne. And it also meant that Luna knew nothing about the secrets of the kingdom, and it also meant that Luna had lied about the rules of the traditions that states about the impeachment of the king or queen, but it mostly meant that Luna had lied to the whole kingdom.

And it was obvious for the inhabitants of the kingdom that Luna wanted to get rid of Kalus and give the throne to George because Luna knew herself that she was not the daughter of Kalus. And that she was not the heiress to the crown and the throne of the kingdom.

And it was obvious for the inhabitants of the kingdom that the fact that Luna was not the daughter of Kalus, meant that Luna was not the heiress to the crown and the throne of the kingdom, it also meant that Luna was born with no power and magic.

And the inhabitants of the kingdom knew well that each future the king or queen who was the heir or the heiress to the crown and the throne of Manitoba was born with the powers and magic. Because in the tradition of Manitoba the heir or the heiress to the crown and to the throne showed the power and magic that he or she was born with to the whole kingdom before thirteen.

And the whole kingdom was very surprised because Luna was already thirteen. And she had never shown to the whole kingdom the powers and magic that she was born with as the heiress to the crown and the throne of the kingdom.

And the fact that Luna was thirteen and she had never shown the whole kingdom the powers and magic she was born with, was just an evidence that Luna was not the daughter of Kalus and she was not also the heiress to the crown and the throne.

Because in the history of the kingdom, all the heirs and heiresses to the crown and the throne had shown their powers and magic to the whole kingdom before their thirteen, and before becoming the kings and queens of the kingdom.

And even Kalus had shown his magic and the powers to the whole kingdom when Kalus was only nine years old during an event that was organized by Kalus's father who was the former the king of the kingdom. And Luna was the only one who had never shown her powers and magic as the heiress to the crown and throne to the whole kingdom.

And even if Kalus was hated by the whole kingdom, the inhabitants of the kingdom had decided not to sign the petition of his impeachment. Because, for the inhabitants, Luna had lied to them, and Luna had lied to them that she was the heiress to the crown and the throne. But Luna had also lied to them that the tradition of the kingdom allowed her as the heiress to the crown and throne to organize the impeachment of Kalus because Kalus had broken the rules of the traditions.

And even if the parents knew that Sunshine and Luna were fighting to free the kingdom, the parents were very worried about the safety of their children. And the parents knew that the worst could happen at any moment, and that Kalus would not hesitate to kill children just to keep his throne and crown, mostly that children wanted to get rid of him.

And the parents were very afraid because the children had declared war on Kalus. And the parents spent their whole night thinking how to prevent their children from seeing Sunshine and Luna. Mostly that Kalus had said in his speech that he would send his army outside to arrest or kill all children who would be seen with Sunshine and Luna.

It was eight in the morning, the weather was good, and the sun was shining outside. And there were some people in front of the kiosks of newspapers who wanted to buy the newspapers.

And except the newspaper called Kongreshow that had supported children and Diana by encouraging people to sign the petition for the impeachment of Kalus. While the rest of newspapers had called people not to sign the petition of the impeachment of

Kalus because Luna was a liar and she was not the heiress to the crown and the throne of the kingdom.

And that Luna had no idea about the secrets of the traditions of the kingdom because she was not the daughter of the king Kalus. Sunshine and Luna were especially insulted by almost all the journalists in the newspapers. And Luna was treated like an adulterous daughter by some newspapers. And that Luna wanted to destroy the kingdom.

And even if the journalists did not like the king Kalus, the journalists did not support the children in their fight to free the kingdom because the journalists thought that Luna was a liar, and that Luna was not the heiress to the crown and the throne of the kingdom.

And the streets of the kingdom were not really full of people as usual. And if the streets of the kingdom were not full of people as usual, it was because most of the people had decided not to go to work and to stay at home.

And between the people who had decided to stay at home, most of them were the parents. And the parents had decided to stay at home because the parents wanted to prevent their children from going out to meet Sunshine and Luna. And other people had decided to stay at home because they were afraid to be arrested or killed outside by Kalus's army.

In the houses of the kingdom, there were the noises and the children were crying because they were prevented by their parents from going outside. The children were very angry and the children were telling their parents that they would go outside and that they were not afraid of the army of Kalus. And the children also told their parents that they would not stop seeing Sunshine and Luna because Sunshine and Luna were not only their friends and their teachers, but Sunshine and Luna were their families.

And the children also told their parents that they were not going to grow up with a devil named Kalus like the king of their kingdom, and that they refused to have their kingdom ruled by the devil Kalus.

And the parents told the children that Luna had lied to the whole kingdom that she was the heiress to the crown and the throne.

Because Luna was not the daughter of Kalus, and like Luna was not the daughter of Kalus, she could not be the heiress to the crown and the throne of the kingdom. And the children replied to their parents that it was a good thing that Luna was not the daughter of the devil Kalus because the monster Kalus did not deserve a child like Luna.

The children continued and said that it was good to hear that Luna was not the daughter of the monster Kalus. Because the good thing was the fact that Luna did not have the blood of the devil Kalus in her body.

But the fact that Luna was not the daughter of the monster Kalus did not mean that Luna was not the heiress to the crown and the throne of the kingdom. Because for them, the only heiress to the crown and the throne of the kingdom was Luna.

And the children also said that no matter what would happen, they would always be with Luna in the good and bad moments. Then children told their parents that no one would stop them to free the kingdom from the hands of the devil Kalus, and they were ready to die to free the kingdom.

It was nine in the morning, and the streets of the kingdom were full of the children who were walking in the direction of the palace for their meeting with Luna and Sunshine. And despite the fact that the parents had asked their children not to get out of the houses, the children had refused to listen to their parents.

And some children had run away from their houses when their parents were distracted, and other children had got out of the houses through the windows of their bedrooms because their parents had locked up the doors.

Luna and Kalus were in the living room arguing, and there were tears that were flowing down Luna's cheeks, and Luna was asking her mother to Kalus. Because Luna's mom had been arrested by Kalus's men on the orders of Kalus.

And if Kalus had decided to arrest Diana, it was because Diana had given a speech in front of the camera of Remy to say to the whole kingdom that Kalus was a liar, and that Luna was the daughter of Kalus, and mostly that Luna was the heiress to the crown and the throne of the kingdom.

And Kalus had been very angry with the speech of Diana not only because Diana did not support him as a wife must support her husband, but mostly that Diana supported Luna and Sunshine. And even worse Diana had asked the whole kingdom to sign the petition about the impeachment of Kalus. And for Kalus, Diana was not only an enemy, but Diana was even worse than Sunshine and Luna because Kalus considered Diana like a traitor.

And Kalus looked into Luna's eyes and said, "You would never see your mom again because your mom is a traitor."

"What do you mean by I would never see my mom again?" Luna asked.

"I would kill your mom tonight," Kalus answered.

"Do not even dare," Luna said.

Kalus smiled and said, "I would kill your mom in front of you tonight, and after I would kill you."

Luna walked two steps in front of her father and she looked into Kalus's eyes and said, "If you touch only a hair of my mom, I will not only kill you, but I would burn you."

Kalus looked into Luna's eyes and said, "I would kill you and your mom tonight."

Luna looked at Kalus angrily and said, "I promise you that I will kill you."

Kalus smiled and said, "Do not waste your time because you can not kill me."

Luna said, "I promise to the whole kingdom that I would kill you, and I would keep my promise."

Kalus smiled and said, "You can not kill me because I am stronger and powerful than you."

Luna looked at Kalus and said, "It's what you think."

Kalus said, "Even if we hated each other, do not forget that I am your dad."

Luna said, "The fact that you are my dad did not mean that you know all my powers."

Kalus said, "I know all your powers."

Luna looked into Kalus's eyes and said, "You know most of my powers as I know most of your powers."

Kalus looked into Luna's eyes and said, "I have the powers that you do not know."

Luna looked into Kalus's eyes and said, "I am aware of your satanic powers."

Kalus said, "I would use these satanic powers to kill you."

Luna looked into Kalus's eyes angrily and said, "Look into my eyes very well because when I would be killing you, and when you would be dying, I would be staring into your eyes with these eyes that I am staring at you now."

Kalus smiled and said, "Good luck."

Then Kalus turned and started to walk towards the door, and Luna was following Kalus by asking him where he had kept her mom prisoner. But Kalus was still just walking without paying attention to Luna. And suddenly the expression on Luna's face changed when she noticed that Kalus was getting outside of the palace.

And it was the first time for Luna to see her father get out of the palace because since she was born, she had never seen her father leave the palace. And Luna knew well that her father could not get out of the palace because the magic trees that were outside prevented her dad from getting outside.

Because the magic trees that were outside were preventing her father from getting out because the satanic magic that was in her father's body could not work with the energy coming from these magic trees. And Luna knew well that the energy coming from the magic trees could kill a human being who had the satanic powers in the body like her father.

And Luna was wondering what was going on? Why was her father getting outside of the palace knowing that he had the satanic powers in his body? And Suddenly Luna understood that her father was getting outside of the palace because her father had received from Lord the powers and magic that could protect him from the energy coming from the magic trees that were outside.

Sunshine and her fellows, also with Remy and his team, were walking towards the gate of the palace. And Sunshine was surprised to see the cars that were parked outside of the palace, the cars were parked as if Kalus was going somewhere.

And Sunshine knew well that Kalus could not go somewhere because the satanic powers that were in his body prevented him from getting out of the palace. Because these satanic powers could not work with the energy coming from the magic trees that were outside. Then Sunshine noticed that the gate was pushed by someone, then Sunshine saw the bodyguards of Kalus come out of the gate.

And suddenly, the expression on Sunshine's face changed when she saw Kalus get out of the gate, and Sunshine was looking at Kalus with a surprised face. Sunshine was wondering what Kalus was doing outside, then she remembered that the speech that Kalus had made yesterday was in the garden of the palace. And Sunshine understood that Kalus had received more power and magic from Lord.

Sunshine also understood that Lord had given more powers and magic to Kalus to get out the palace because Lord had understood that the things were going worse. And that Kalus was losing the control of the kingdom, with children who were calling the inhabitants of the kingdom to sign the petition for the impeachment of Kalus. Lord had given more powers to Kalus to allow Kalus to get out of the palace and to gain the confidence of people by preventing people from signing the petition for the destitution of Kalus.

Then the surprise that was on Sunshine's face turned into worry when she saw Luna walk outside of the gate with eyes wet with tears. And Sunshine was looking at Luna with a worried face and she asked Luna what was going on? Luna replied to Sunshine that Kalus had kidnapped Diana. Immediately, the expression on Sunshine's face changed and she turned her head and looked at Kalus with the expression on her face full of rage, and Kalus was staring at Sunshine with a face full of smiles.

Then Sunshine asked Kalus where Diana was? And Kalus replied to Sunshine to find Diana by herself. And immediately, Sunshine's eyes started spinning, and Kalus was staring how Sunshine's eyes were spinning with the smiles on his face. And looking at the expression of Kalus's face, we could see that the magic of Sunshine did not have effect on him. After a few minutes, magic of Sunshine had still no effect on Kalus, then Sunshine's eyes stopped spinning.

And Sunshine was still staring at Kalus who was laughing at her, and Sunshine understood that her magic had no effect on Kalus because Kalus was more powerful. And Sunshine understood that she needed more concentration for her magic to have an effect on Kalus. Then Kalus turned and started walking towards the car. And Sunshine was breathing deeply by trying to focus on herself with her eyes still focused on Kalus who was walking through the car.

Then Kalus got in the car and the bodyguard closed the car's door, and the driver got in the car, then a light got out from Sunshine's eyes and went towards the car. The driver started the car's engine, and suddenly the expression of Kalus's face changed when he noticed a light shone in the car, and he was looking with the fear on his face.

And the car's engine stopped and the driver was trying to restart the car's engine without success. Then Kalus understood that the light that had shone in the car was coming from Sunshine, and that it was light that had stopped the car's engine.

Suddenly, Kalus started feeling hot in the car and he was also breathing with difficulty, and he looked at his clothes and he noticed that his clothes were wet with sweat. And Kalus understood that Sunshine was killing him through her magic.

Then Kalus opened the car's door and he got out, and the expression of faces of all those who were outside changed and they were looking at Kalus with surprised faces. And they were all astonished to see Kalus who was sweating, and except Sunshine and Luna, the rest of the people were wondering what was going on with Kalus.

And Sunshine's eyes were focused on Kalus, and she was looking at Kalus with her eyes that were spinning, and Kalus's eyes were also focused on Sunshine. And Kalus was trying to make his eyes turn to fight Sunshine back, but unfortunately for him, he was so weak that he could not make his eyes turn.

And the fact that Kalus was so weak and unable to make his eyes turn was because Kalus was less powerful than Sunshine. And the fact that Sunshine was more powerful than Kalus was preventing Kalus from using his own magic because Kalus's magic was dominated by Sunshine's magic.

Then Kalus started to feel tired and weak, and there was the sweat that was running down Kalus's body as if someone had thrown the water on him. Then Kalus tried to run away without success, and he could not run because he could not move with his feet, and he could not even lift his foot. And it was as if his feet were glued to the ground. Then Kalus started screaming while scratching his body because he was feeling something that was stinging in his body.

And the children and people who were outside were focused on Kalus. And all the children had smiles on their faces as they were staring at Kalus who was acting as if he was crazy, and it was funny for them to look at Kalus scratch his body. And suddenly the expression on the faces of some children changed and they were staring at Kalus with surprised faces as they were seeing Kalus who was removing his clothes by screaming in pain.

And everyone who had their eyes focused on Kalus was wondering if he was really crazy. And no one could imagine that it was Sunshine who was torturing Kalus. But looking at the expression on the face of Luna, it seemed she knew what was happening to Kalus.

And Kalus already removed the costume that was on him, and he had only his panty on him, and he was still scratching his body by yelling in pain. Then children pushed a loud scream when they noticed that Kalus was trying to take off his panties.

And immediately, Kalus was grabbed by his bodyguards, and his bodyguards grabbed Kalus's hands to prevent him from removing his panty. Then Kalus screamed at his bodyguards to release Diana from the jail. And two of Kalus' bodyguards rushed towards the gate, and the rest of the bodyguards had grabbed Kalus to prevent Kalus from removing his panties. And the bodyguards tried to take Kalus inside the palace, but they were surprised to notice that the feet of Kalus could not move off the ground.

And the bodyguards even tried to carry Kalus without success. And the bodyguards were very surprised to notice that they were unable to lift Kalus from the ground because the feet of Kalus were glued to the ground.

And the bodyguards did not understand what was going on, and children had noticed that the bodyguards were trying to carry Kalus without success because Kalus's feet were glued to the ground. And except Luna, the rest of the people were not understanding what was going on, and they were not understanding why Kalus's feet were glued to the ground.

Mostly that Kalus had taken off his clothes, even his pants a few minutes ago, and they had all seen how Kalus had lifted his feet off the ground to take off his pants. And no one could imagine Kalus's body was controlled by Sunshine's magic, and that every gesture or move of Kalus was guided by Sunshine's magic.

Then the two bodyguards who had gone to release Dina from the jail walked out of the gate with Diana, and these bodyguards were walking towards Kalus with Diana. And the bodyguards had held Diana's hands. And Kalus shouted at the bodyguards to let Diana's hands and walk away. Then Luna ran and hugged her mom as the bodyguards had walked away from Diana.

Then Sunshine's eyes stopped spinning, and she turned her head and walked away. And suddenly Kalus turned and started running towards the gate. And children were looking at Kalus who was running by getting inside the gate with the panties on him by laughing.

Then Luna walked near Sunshine and she looked into Sunshine's eyes and said, "Thank you." Sunshine asked, "Thank you for what?" Luna answered, "For releasing my mom from the torture of the devil Kalus." Sunshine said, "I do not understand." Luna said, "If you had not come to save my mom, the monster Kalus would have killed my mom."

Sunshine and Luna were looking at each other in the eyes. And there were a lot of questions that were going on in her mind, and one of these questions was the fact that Sunshine was wondering if Luna knew who she (Sunshine) was.

But unfortunately for Sunshine, she could not answer this question. Then Luna told Sunshine that they should go inside the palace to organize their meeting. And Luna asked other children to follow her inside the palace. Then all the children walked towards the gate of the palace.

After a few minutes, the children were sitting in the living room. Luna and Sunshine were giving small notebooks and pens to each person. Then Sunshine stood in the middle of the room and all the eyes were focused on her.

And Sunshine said that they were going outside for the impeachment of the devil Kalus, and that they would use these notebooks to take the name and the signature of people. And that all those who would like to sign for the impeachment of the devil Kalus would write their names in these notebooks and they would sign near to their names.

Sunshine went on and said that they would walk together, and they would always be a group, and that they would walk near each other because they would defend themselves in case they were attacked by Kalus's army. Because Kalus would not hesitate to send his army against them, and that they must be careful. And that today, they were going to war against Kalus.

Then Asher got up from his chair and he screamed, "It's time to free the kingdom." And the rest of the people got up from their chairs and they screamed, "It's time to free the kingdom." And they all started to clap their hands by screaming. Then they all walked towards the door by holding the notebooks and pen in their hands.

After a few minutes, the children were walking in the streets, and they were approaching people that they were seeing in the streets to get the names and signatures about the impeachment of Kalus. But unfortunately for children, things were not going as well as they had expected. Because people in the streets were refusing to sign for the petition about the impeachment of Kalus.

And people were saying that they could not sign the petition about the impeachment of Kalus because Luna had lied to the whole kingdom that she was the daughter of the king Kalus and the heiress to the crown and the throne of the kingdom.

And that Luna could not know the secrets of the traditions of the kingdom of Manitoba because she was not the daughter of the king Kalus, and like Luna was not the daughter of the king Kalus, she could not be the heiress to the crown and the throne of the kingdom.

And like Luna was not the heiress to the crown and throne of the kingdom, it meant that Luna was not born with the power and magic and she had no idea about the secrets of the traditions of the kingdom. And that it also meant that Luna had lied to them that the tradition allowed her to organize the impeachment of the king Kalus.

After three hours, the children were walking downtown and they were still trying to get the signature of people without success. And the children had not even got a signature, and they were still rejected by people for the reason that Luna was a liar. And the children were not discouraged and they were determined to make people sign for the impeachment of Kalus.

And the children were still approaching people by trying to convince people to sign for the impeachment of Kalus without success. And the children were very surprised by the attitude of people, and the children did not understand how people could still trust a devil like Kalus after all the worse things that Kalus had done.

The children were walking in the middle of downtown and a big bus parked near to them. Then the children stopped walking and they turned and looked at the bus. And suddenly the expression on the faces of children changed when they saw the bus's door open and the soldiers got off the bus.

And some children were staring at soldiers who were getting out of the bus with fear on their faces, while other children like Sunshine, Asher, Khloe, Isac, Aaron, Mia and Luna were staring at the soldiers who were getting out of the bus with the anger on their faces, as they had understood that Kalus had sent his army to kill them.

Then Sunshine asked her fellows to stay behind her, like Sunshine had seen the soldiers who were approaching them with the guns in their hands. And some children were shaking with fear, by seeing the soldiers who were walking towards them with the guns.

And Luna asked everyone to stay behind Sunshine and her. And Asher refused and said that it was men who would protect women, and not women who would protect men. Luna turned her head and looked at Asher and she told Asher that it was good to try to protect women but that women could also protect men in case of danger.

Then Aaron and Isac joined the idea of Asher and they said that they were not going to stay behind women, and that they wanted all women to stay behind them because they were going to protect women, and that it was their responsibility as men to protect women.

Luna replied to Aaron and Isac that men without the guns could not protect women against the crazy soldiers who had the guns. And Asher asked Luna how women without the guns were going to protect men against the crazy soldiers who had the guns. Luna replied to Asher that women had the powers and magic to protect men.

And Asher asked Luna which power and magic that women had to protect men. Luna answered to Asher to watch very well what was going to happen now. Then Luna turned her head and looked at Sunshine.

And Luna told Sunshine that she was going to prove to the whole kingdom that she was not a liar, and that she was well the heiress to the crown and the throne of the kingdom of Manitoba. And Sunshine smiled at Luna without saying a word, and Sunshine had understood the message of Luna, and Sunshine knew very well what Luna was going to do.

Luna was staring at the soldiers who were walking towards her with her face full of rage. And there were people around who were looking at the soldiers with faces full of fear, and some people were even crying by begging the soldiers to not kill children. Then Luna lifted her right hand through the sky and a blue light shone in her eyes and a stick appeared in her hand.

Then Luna started walking towards the soldiers with this stick in her hand. And suddenly, the expression of the faces of people changed and they were all looking with surprised faces at Luna who was fighting against the soldiers.

And except Sunshine, the rest of the children were completely lost because they did not understand what was going on. And the children had their eyes focused on Luna who was using a stick to fight the soldiers, and the children were wondering if the young girl who was fighting against the soldiers with a stick was really their friend named Luna, or she just looked like Luna.

And the children were saying that if that young girl was their fellow named Luna, where Luna had taken the stick that she was fighting with, and where Luna had learned to fight? But unfortunately for the children, they could answer this question.

And the children and other people who were watching the fight were very astonished to see how Luna was very strong, and how she was beating the soldiers by using her stick. Then the eyes of people widened when they saw Luna who was jumping by using her stick.

Luna was jumping by leaning on the stick and she was hitting the soldiers with her feet each time when she was jumping. Luna was also hitting the soldiers with her stick, and there were many soldiers on the ground who were bleeding because these soldiers had been injured by Luna's stick.

And the soldiers were trying to shoot Luna without success, and the bullets coming from soldiers's guns were blocked by Luna's stick. And people were very amazed to see how Luna was using her stick to block the bullets and to prevent the bullets from touching her.

And after a few minutes, Luna had won the fight and all the soldiers were lying on the ground. Then Luna saw another bus parked not far from her, and she saw the soldiers get off the bus with the guns, and the soldiers were walking towards Luna with the guns pointed at her.

Then Luna looked at her stick and the light got out from her eyes and shone on her stick and her stick turned into a sword. And Luna pointed her sword at the soldiers who were walking towards her. And a light got out from Luna's sword and went towards the soldiers.

And suddenly, there were the screams of fear, and people had lifted their heads through the sky and some were looking with their eyes full of fear, while others were looking with surprised faces as they were seeing the soldiers who were flying in the space.

And it was the light that had got out from Luna's sword and went towards the soldiers that had pushed the soldiers in the space. And the soldiers went and fell on the ground. And people were staring at the soldiers who were crying in pain on the ground.

Then Luna looked at the sword and the light got out of her eyes and shone on the sword and the sword turned into a stick, and Luna got on that stick and she flew in space. And people had lifted their heads through the sky and they were all looking at Luna who was flying on the stick with surprised faces.

And people were watching Luna who was flying on the stick in space with their mouths opened and it was as if they were watching a miracle. And there were the cameras that were filming Luna who was flying on her stick.

And suddenly, people shouted, "Waooooh." When they noticed that the stick that Luna was flying on, had turned into a big hawk and Luna was flying on the hawk. And except Sunshine, the rest of the children were wondering how Luna was doing all these incredible things, and they did not understand how it was possible.

And it was the first time for the children to see what Luna was doing. And looking at their facial expressions, we could see that they were not believing that what they were watching with their eyes was possible and true.

Although the parents were watching with astonished faces, it was not new for them what Luna was doing. Because the parents knew that Luna was showing to the whole kingdom that she was the daughter of the king Kalus, and that she was also the heiress to the crown and the throne of the kingdom of Manitoba.

And that she was born with the power and magic, also that she knew the secrets of the traditions and that everything she had said during the cultural events was true. But the parents were very amazed by the way that Luna was showing her powers and magic to the whole kingdom. And they were amazed because Luna was doing it very well, and she was incredible.

And for the parents who had watched the spectacle where the former heirs and heiresses to the crown and the throne had shown their powers and magic to the whole kingdom, Luna was the one whose spectacle was amazing.

And the parents could see through the spectacle of Luna, that Luna was more powerful than the former heirs and heiresses. Because Luna was doing things that the former heirs and heiresses did not do.

And there were a huge noises, and people who were watching Luna show her magic were making a lot of noises that people who were in the malls, in the offices, in the cars, and even those who were walking in the streets were running towards the place where Luna was doing her spectacle to watch Luna show her magic to the whole kingdom.

Then people watched how the hawk that Luna was on was flying towards the ground. And suddenly the expression of their faces changed and they had their mouths opened as they had seen the hawk turned into a horse.

And people were watching Luna who was riding the horse. Then Luna raised her left hand and a sword appeared in her hand, and she raised her right hand and a fighting shield appeared in her hand.

Luna was on the horse and the horse was walking with her and Luna had lifted her sword and her fighting shield. Then people started clapping their hands by screaming, "Princess Luna, princess Luna, Princess Luna, the heiress to the crown and the throne of our kingdom."

And even the soldiers who were on the ground had got up from the ground and they had their eyes focused on Luna and their faces full of smiles as they were watching Luna who was showing her magic to the whole kingdom.

And the soldiers were also applauding Luna by screaming her name and by screaming, "Our princess Luna save us, save our kingdom and save our future generation. Princess Luna, we would work for you from today, you are the heiress to our crown and throne."

Then three cars parked not far from people and Kalus got off in one of these cars and he was surrounded by his bodyguards. And Kalus was watching what was going on with a face full of anger, as he had understood that Luna was showing her magic and power to the whole kingdom. And mostly that Luna was proving to the whole kingdom that she was the heiress to the crown and the throne of the kingdom, and that she was born with the power and magic.

And Kalus also knew that Luna was proving to the whole kingdom that she was not a liar, and that everything that she had said was true. And mostly that she knew very well the secrets of the tradition.

Also, she had not lied when she had said that one of the rules of the tradition of the kingdom authorized her as the heiress to the crown and the throne to organize his impeachment because he had broken the rules of the traditions.

Kalus was very furious by what was happening, and he was more angry by seeing people who were applauding Luna. And looking at the expression on the face of Kalus, it was obvious that he did not expect to see Luna show her power and magic to the whole kingdom.

And Kalus had got out of the palace to make a campaign to seduce the inhabitants, and to show to the whole kingdom that he was a good king and that he loved the kingdom and its inhabitants. And that Luna and Sunshine were those who wanted to destroy the kingdom.

And Kalus's eyes were focused on Luna who was flying in space and although the fact that he was furious, he was surprised at the same time by what Luna was doing. And he had noticed that Luna was very powerful and talented. And Kalus was very amazed by the powers of Luna, and he was wondering how it was possible that Luna knew how to use her powers, mostly that Luna had not been trained by him to show how to use her powers.

And Kalus was mostly wondering how Luna had found out that she was born with the power and the magic because he had never told Luna that she was born with the power and magic. And even worse he had tried to destroy the power and the magic of Luna without success.

And Kalus was understanding that he had lost the control of the kingdom, and that his seduction campaign that he had got out of the palace to do would not work. Because no one would listen to him or even trust because Luna had just shown to the whole kingdom that she was the heiress to the crown and the throne of the kingdom.

And Kalus was very furious because Luna had just destroyed his campaign of seduction of the inhabitants of the kingdom by proving to the whole kingdom that she was not a liar, but that the liar was him.

Suddenly, the expression of the Kalus's face changed and he was looking at children with the full of fear as he was seeing the children who were giving the pens to the people. And people were writing in the notebooks.

And Kalus was understanding that people were writing their names and signing near to their names in these notebooks. And Kalus knew well that the fact that people were writing their names in these notebooks meant that people were signing for his impeachment.

And Kalus's heart was beating faster than normal as if he was going to have a heart attack as he was watching people who were fighting to sign for his impeachment. And Kalus was very thoughtful that he was trembling with fear, and he was thoughtful because he was thinking how to stop people from continuing to sign the petition of his impeachment.

And suddenly Kalus opened his mouth and he was trying to talk but his mouth was shaking so that he could not pronounce a word, and Kalus had his eyes wide open. And looking at the expression on the face of Kalus, we could see that he was completely lost, and he did not believe that he was watching his own soldiers who were signing for his impeachment.

And Kalus was completely downcast by seeing his own army who was in charge to protect him and to protect the laws of Kalus sign the petition for his impeachment. And seeing his own army signing for his impeachment, Kalus was understanding that it was the end of his reign.

Because his own army that was supposed to prevent people from signing for his impeachment were instead signing for his impeachment by encouraging people to sign for his impeachment too. And for Kalus, it was a betrayal to see his own army who was working against him.

Then Kalus turned his head and looked at his bodyguards and he told his bodyguards to take the notebooks that were in the children's hands and to prevent people from continuing to sign for his impeachment.

And Kalus's bodyguards walked till the crowd, and the bodyguards tried to take the notebooks that were in children's hands by trying to prevent people from continuing to sign for the impeachment of Kalus. But the bodyguards were beaten by the population, even the soldiers were beating the bodyguards.

Kalus was watching his bodyguards who were on the ground bleeding without knowing what to do. And Kalus was seeing the population with the help of his soldiers who were hitting and punching his bodyguards. And Kalus was feeling weak because he was unable to save his bodyguards.

Then expression of Kalus's face changed and he was looking with an astonished face as he was seeing the children who were running towards him, and he was wondering why the children were running towards him. And the driver of Kalus asked Kalus to get in the car that children were coming to kill him (Kalus).

But Kalus did not listen to his driver, and his eyes were still focused on the children who were running towards him. And the driver of Kalus was trying to convince Kalus that they must run away before these children catch them, and that these children would not hesitate to kill him (Kalus).

And again, Kalus did not listen to his driver, but suddenly the expression on Kalus's face changed and he was looking with a face full of fear as he was seeing some of these children who were picking up the stones on the ground. And Kalus understood that the children would not hesitate to kill him with these stones that they were picking up on the ground.

Then Kalus turned and rushed towards the car's door as he had understood that he was in danger, and Kalus was trying to open the car's door when he felt the stones hit his head and back. And Kalus removed his hands from the car's door and he covered his head with his palm's hands by trying to protect his head from the stones that children were throwing at him. And Kalus was screaming at his driver to help him open the car's door.

The driver tried to rush towards Kalus to help Kalus open the car's door. But the driver noticed that it was too late and that he(driver) could not help Kalus, as the driver had noticed that children were already near to Kalus.

Then the eyes of the driver opened widely when the driver saw the children jump on Kalus and throw Kalus to the ground. And the driver was astonished to see the king Kalus on the ground who was being beaten and hit by the children.

Then the fear appeared on the face of the driver when he saw some children who were running towards him. The driver immediately opened the car's door and he got in the car, then he drove away as the driver had understood that these children were running towards him to beat him.

Kalus was on the ground and he was bleeding from his mouth and nose, as he was being beaten and kicked by the children. Then a police car parked near the children and the policemen got out of the car, then policemen started preventing the children from continuing to beat and kick Kalus.

After a few minutes, policemen had succeeded in removing Kalus in the hands of the children, and Kalus was put in the car by the police, and Kalus was taken to the palace by the police. And the children were very proud to have beaten the king Kalus because it was their dream to one day beat the king Kalus, and they had just made their dream come true by beating the king Kalus. Then the children continued their day collecting the signatures of people about the impeachment of Kalus.

It was six o'clock, Kalus was knelt in his magic room, and he was calling the name of Lord. And suddenly the fear appeared on Kalus's face as he had noticed that the room was shaking and he was turning his head looking around wondering what was going on. And Kalus was also feeling a strange smell in the room and it was the first time for him to feel this strange smell.

Then he heard a voice say, "I am here."

"It's you, Lord?" Kalus asked.

"Yes, it's me," Lord answered.

"Why did I feel the room shake and why am I feeling this strange smell?" Kalus asked.

"I got the new powers, and that's why the room started shaking when I appeared and it's also the reason why you are feeling a strange smell," Lord answered.

"What do you mean you got the new powers?" Kalus asked.

"I am more powerful," Lord answered.

"Why did you get more powers?" Kalus asked.

"For Sunshine," Lord answered.

"For Sunshine?" Kalus cried out.

"Yes, for Sunshine because it's time to kill her," Lord replied.

"I am so happy to hear that Sunshine is going to die," Kalus said.

"I got these new powers to kill Sunshine, so I would use these new powers to kill Sunshine," Lord said.

"I have been tortured and humiliated today by Sunshine, Luna and children," Kalus said.

"I am aware of everything that has happened today," Lord said.

"The children almost killed me," Kalus said.

"I know," Lord replied.

"I want to get my revenge on Sunshine, Luna and the children," Kalus said.

"You can get your revenge on Luna and the children, but not on Sunshine," Lord said.

"Why not on Sunshine?" Kalus asked.

"Because Sunshine is more powerful than you, you can not kill Sunshine," Lord said.

"I was very surprised that even with the new powers I got from you, I was not able to fight Sunshine when I got out of the palace because I was tortured and humiliated by Sunshine today," Kalus said.

"I had warned you to never fight Sunshine because no matter how many powers you would get, you can not kill Sunshine," Lord said.

"Sunshine is a real curse, but the one I can not wait to kill it's Luna," Kalus said.

"Be patient, you will kill Luna, but for now we must think how to kill Sunshine first," Lord said.

"Think how to kill Sunshine?" Kalus asked.

"Yes, think how to kill Sunshine," Lord answered.

"You just told me about your new powers, you have to kill Sunshine," Kalus said.

"Yes, I have the new powers to kill Sunshine, but I need to find out something about Sunshine first," Lord said.

"What do you need to find out about Sunshine?" Kalus asked.

"I need to find out the weaknesses of Sunshine," Lord said.

"Why do you need to find out the weaknesses of Sunshine?" Kalus asked.

"I just need only one of the weaknesses of Sunshine to kill her," Lord said.

"Why do you need one of the weaknesses of Sunshine to kill her?" Kalus asked.

"Because it would be easy to killSunshine by knowing what her weakness is," Lord answered.

"How easy would it be?" Kalus asked.

"Because I would use one of the weaknesses of Sunshine to kill her," Lord answered.

"Sunshine has weaknesses?" Kalus asked.

"Although the fact that Sunshine was born with the powers and magic, she is a human being," Lord replied.

"I do not understand," Kalus said.

"All human beings have weaknesses, so even Sunshine has weaknesses," Lord replied.

"I would have liked to know only one of the weaknesses of Sunshine," Kalus said.

"The only chance to kill Sunshine it's to know only one of her weaknesses," Lord said.

"I hate this cursed girl named Sunshine, mostly that this morning I have been tortured and humiliated by her," Kalus said.

"Why have you been tortured and humiliated by Sunshine?" Lord asked.

"Because I had kept Diana prisoner," Kalus answered.

"Why did you keep Diana prisoner?" Lord asked.

"I have kept Diana prisoner because Diana had betrayed me by saying that Luna was the heiress to the crown and the throne of the kingdom. And Diana had asked the whole kingdom to sign the petition of my impeachment," Kalus answered.

"I understand," Lord said.

"I thought you were aware of that," Kalus said.

"It's hard for me to know everything that is going on in the kingdom since the day Sunshine destroyed my magic mirror," Lord said.

"I understand," Kalus said.

"It's impossible for me to watch everything that is happening in the kingdom without this magic mirror," Lord said.

"It means that this magic mirror that had been destroyed by Sunshine was your eyes," Kalus said.

"Yes, my magic mirror that had been destroyed by Sunshine was my eyes, and it means that Sunshine had destroyed my eyes. Because if my magic mirror had not been destroyed by Sunshine, I should use this magic mirror to find out the weaknesses of Sunshine," Lord said.

"How your magic mirror should help you to find out the weaknesses of Sunshine?" Kalus asked.

"I should watch Sunshine through this magic mirror twenty-four hours on twenty-four hours every day, and I should follow Sunshine through the magic mirror everywhere Sunshine should be. And I have no doubt that I should find at least one of the weaknesses of Sunshine through the magic mirror if the magic mirror had not been destroyed by Sunshine," Lord answered.

"I understand," Kalus said.

"Are you the one who released Diana from the jail?" Lord asked.

"Sunshine did not give me the choice," Kalus replied.

"I know that Diana had been released from the jail because you had been tortured by Sunshine, but I want to know if it's Sunshine who had opened the prison door to Diana?" Lord asked.

"No, it's my bodyguards who had opened the jail's door to Diana," Kalus answered.

"Why Sunshine did not open the jail's door to Diana?" Lord asked.

"I have no idea but maybe Sunshine did not know where Diana was kept prisoner," Kalus answered.

"Where Diana was kept prisoner?" Lord asked.

"In the basement of the palace," Kalus answered.

"How is this prison built in the basement?" Lord asked.

"This prison is built with steel," Kalus answered.

"I just found one of the weaknesses of Sunshine," Lord said.

"What is it?" Kalus asked.

"The steel," Lord answered.

"Steel?" Kalus cried out.

"Yes, because if Sunshine's magic could see a place built with the steel, Sunshine should go release Diana from the prison by herself," Lord said.

"I understand why Sunshine tortured me until I ordered my bodyguards to release Diana," Kalus said.

"I am going to kill Sunshine now," Lord said.

"How would you use Sunshine's weakness to kill her?" Kalus asked.

"I would use the steel to kill Sunshine," Lord answered.

"Sunshine's magic can not protect her from the steel?" Kalus asked.

"No, Sunshine's magic can not protect her from the steel because Sunshine's magic can not react with the steel," Lord answered.

"I am glad to hear that Sunshine will die in a few hours," Kalus said.

"Do not get out of the palace until I announce to you the death of Sunshine," Lord said.

"I can not take the risk to get out of the palace for the moment, not only because the children have almost killed me today, but mostly because there is nobody to protect me for the moment. Because my own army betrayed me and my soldiers are supporting the fight of children, and my bodyguards have been injured by the population today," Kalus said.

"Go to bed now, and if you feel any danger just come and stay in this magic room," Lord said.

"Good luck, Lord," Kalus said. Then Kalus got up and left the magic room.

It was nine o'clock, the inhabitants of the palace were in their living room, and they were all talking about Luna who had shown her magic and powers to the whole kingdom this afternoon.

And people who had not had the chance to watch Luna show her powers and magic downtown had watched the television channel of Remy to see how Luna had shown the powers and magic she was born with to the whole kingdom. And everyone had been amazed by the way that Luna had shown her powers and magic to the inhabitants of the kingdom.

And people who had watched the former heirs and heiresses show their magic to the whole kingdom had noticed that Luna had performed differently from the former heirs and heiresses. And that the spectacle of Luna was as if it was a miracle not only because Luna had done the incredible things but because Luna had done things that they could not imagine that it was possible.

And she had also done things that the former heirs and heiresses had not done. And they had enjoyed watching Luna show the powers and magic that she was born with to the whole kingdom.

And the people knew that Luna had decided to show her powers and magic to the whole kingdom. Because Luna wanted to prove to the whole kingdom that she was not a liar and that she was well the heiress to the crown and the throne of the kingdom of Manitoba.

And the whole kingdom knew now that Luna was not a liar, and that Luna was well the heiress to the crown and throne of the kingdom of Manitoba. And the whole kingdom knew now that everything that was said by Luna during the cultural events was true, and that the only liar of the kingdom was Kalus.

And the whole kingdom knew that Kalus was a liar, and they hated Kalus and for them, Kalus was a disgrace to the kingdom, the worst king in the history of the kingdom. And for the whole kingdom, Kalus did not deserve to be the king of the kingdom of Manitoba, not only because Kalus was a bad king.

But mostly because Kalus was not a human being because a human being could reject his child for the power, like Kalus had rejected Luna for the power. And the whole kingdom was very proud of Sunshine, Luna and the rest of children who were fighting to free the kingdom from the Kalus's hands. And the whole kingdom had enjoyed watching the children beat Kalus.

And the people who had refused to sign the petition of the impeachment of Kalus were very sad after they had watched Luna show her magic on the television channel of Remy, and they had decided to sign the petition of the impeachment of Kalus the next day. And all the people who were downtown and who had watched Luna show her magic to the whole kingdom had signed the petition for the impeachment of Kalus.

And for the first time, the children had the support of their parents and even the support of the army of Kalus. And the children were very proud because the whole kingdom was with them, and there was no doubt for the children that Kalus would no longer be the king of the kingdom in a few days.

And the children knew that in the next few days, they would have enough signatures to impeach Kalus. And the children also knew that all the people who had refused to sign the petition of the impeachment of Kalus would change their mind after watching Luna show her magic to the whole kingdom on the television channel of Remy.

It was 1 one in the afternoon, except Sunshine, the whole kingdom was deeply asleep and it was a great day for everyone, and the whole kingdom had gone to bed with the joy on their faces because they had watched Luna show her magic to the whole kingdom. Sunshine was lying in her bed, her eyes opened and she was thinking about what had happened today, especially about how Luna had proved to the whole kingdom that she was the heiress to the crown and the throne of the kingdom.

And today, Sunshine had found some answers to the questions she had about Luna. AndSunshine was understanding a lot of things about Luna, and she was understanding that Luna was able to teach the students because Luna was born with magic and powers. And that Luna was using her powers and magic to teach the students. Sunshine also understood that it was Luna's magic who had allowed Luna to find out the tragedy that had happened in the kingdom before Luna was born.

And Sunshine was very happy not only because she and her fellows had the support of the whole kingdom, but mostly because she had a potential fellow named Luna who had the powers and magic. And Sunshine knew that with the powers and magic of Luna, she and Luna would be able to fight Lord and Kalus.

Then Sunshine started wondering if the mysterious enemy who was helping her to fight Lord was Luna? And Sunshine was trying to understand if the mysterious enemy who had helped her in the forest during her fight against Lord was Luna. But unfortunately, Sunshine could not really answer this question.

Suddenly, Sunshine started to feel the violent headaches and she was sleepy. Then the eyes of Sunshine closed, and she fell asleep without even turning off the light. After an hour, Sunshine was deeply asleep, and she was dreaming and she was seeing Lord in her dream who was talking to her. And they were having a conversation and Lord was asking Sunshine how to control her powers. Suddenly, Sunshine opened her eyes and she was feeling very tired and she had headaches.

And Sunshine was wondering what was going on, and she did not remember anything. Then Sunshine started breathing deeply, as she was feeling a strange smell, and she was wondering where this strange smell was coming from.

Then Sunshine remembered that she had just seen Lord in her dream, and she understood what was going on. Then Sunshine laid on the bed with her back and her eyes were focused on the ceiling, then her eyes started spinning. Then the light shone in Sunshine's eyes and she disappeared.

After a few minutes, Sunshine was standing up facing Lord in the yard of her house. Sunshine and Lord were looking at each other in the eyes, and Sunshine's face was full of anger while Lord's face was full of smiles. Sunshine was seeing some scars on Lord's face, and she was not very surprised about these scars on Lord's face because she had injured Lord during their last fight in the forest.

But Sunshine was instead astonished by the strange smell she was feeling coming from Lord's body, and it was the first for her to feel this strange smell coming from Lord's body. And Sunshine was understanding through this strange smell coming from Lord that Lord had got the new powers and that Lord was more powerful.

Then, Lord broke the silence and said, "It's been a long time."

"What do you want?" Sunshine asked.

"I missed you and I am glad to see you again," Lord said.

Sunshine looked at Lord with a face full of anger and said, "Stop coming in my dream."

Lord smiled and said, "It was the only way I found to let you know that I was outside waiting for you."

"Do not dare to possess my body again," Sunshine said.

"You have a great soul and it would be a pleasure to share your soul with you," Lord said.

Sunshine looked into Lord's eyes with her face full of anger and she said, "You would regret if you dared possess my body again."

"I am not afraid of you," Lord said.

"Try to possess my body again and you will see what I am able to do," Sunshine said.

"You would do nothing to me because I am immortal," Lord said.

Sunshine looked into Lord's eyes and said, "I promise you your death soon."

Lord smiled and said, "It's your own death that will happen in a few hours."

"Everything that had been promised to you by me had happened," Sunshine said.

"I know that you had done everything that you had promised to me like the return of the education in the kingdom, like you saved the souls of the future generation of the kingdom, and like you destroyed my forest that was my home," Lord said.

"You forgot something," Sunshine said.

"What?" Lord asked.

"That George is the king of the kingdom," Sunshine said.

Lord smiled and said, "George has not yet been crowned the king."

Sunshine said, "I have promised you that George would be the king, but that you would not have the chance to see George sit on the throne with the crown on his head because you would be dead at that moment."

"The one who is dying in a coma now is George and not me," Lord said.

"I know you are the one who had put George in a coma," Sunshine said.

"I can put all the children of this kingdom in a coma, and even yourself," Lord said.

"It's true that you can put all the children of this kingdom in a coma, except me," Sunshine said.

"Even yourself I can put you in a coma," Lord said.

"You just tried it less than an hour ago, but you failed," Sunshine said.

"I did not try, but I am going to put you in a coma if you do not obey me," Lord said.

"Do not be stupid because I would never obey to you," Sunshine said.

"Kalus would establish a law in the kingdom in two days, and I do not want you to fight against this new law, and I want you to convince Luna and your fellows to accept this new law," Lord said.

"I thought you were just crazy, but I just noticed that you are not only a crazy man, but you are also a brainless man to think that I would obey you and I would stay quiet and watch the devil Kalus destroy this kingdom," Sunshine said.

"I warn you not to dare to fight against the law that would be established by Kalus," Lord said.

"I do not know what this law is, but I promise you that I will fight against this law," Sunshine said.

"How do you want to fight against a law that you do not even know the content of?" Lord asked.

Sunshine looked into Lord's eyes and answered, "Because nothing coming from a devil like you and from a monster like Kalus can be good for the kingdom."

"I have warned you," Lord said.

"What is this law about?" Sunshine asked.

"You would find out when this law would be out," Lord answered.

"I promise you that no one would respect this law," Sunshine said.

"I would put you in a coma if you tried to oppose this law," Lord said.

"Stop dreaming, you can not put me in the coma because you tried to put me in the coma when you possessed my body an hour ago, and you failed." Sunshine said.

"I did not try," Lord said.

Sunshine looked into Lord's eyes and said, "When you possessed my body an hour ago, you made me fall asleep, and during my sleeping, you tried to put me in a coma. But you failed because you could not control my powers, and I saw you in my dream when I was sleeping, and you were trying to put me in the coma by controlling my powers, but you failed."

Sunshine added, "The only chance for you to put me in the coma it's to control my powers, and it's the reason why you asked me in the dream how to control my powers, but I did not tell you how to control my powers and I immediately opened my eyes. So, you can not control my powers so it's impossible for you to put me in a coma."

Lord said, "It's true that I can not put you in a coma, but you can not fight alone."

"What do you mean?" Sunshine asked.

"I would put all the children of this kingdom in a coma, if you dare to fight against the new law of Kalus," Lord answered.

"I would not be alone because Luna and I would fight against this new law of Kalus," Sunshine said.

"Luna?" Lord cried out.

"You know well that you can not put Luna in the coma because Luna was born with the powers and magic," Sunshine answered.

"Luna is not an enemy for me because I can kill Luna at any time," Lord said.

"You must kill me first before killing Luna," Sunshine said.

"Luna is useless," Lord said.

"Do not forget that it's Luna who organizes the impeachment of the devil Kalus, and that thanks to Luna, things would change in this kingdom. And in a few days, Kalus would no longer be the king of this kingdom," Sunshine said.

"I know all the powers and magic of Luna, and I know what Luna is able to do, and I also know all the strengths of Luna, so Luna is not a problem," Lord said.

"You think you know all the powers of Luna," Sunshine said.

Lord said, "All the heiresses and heirs of this kingdom born with the same powers and magic, so Luna was born with all the powers and magic that Kalus was born with." And Lord added, "And the fact that I know all the powers and magic of Kalus means that I know all the powers and magic of Luna, and I also know the strengths of Luna. So, I can stop Luna at any time."

"What are you waiting to stop Luna because Luna would make people sign for the impeachment of Kalus?" Sunshine asked.

"The impeachment of Kalus would not happen," Lord answered.

"There are only two solutions for Kalus," Sunshine said.

"Which are these two solutions?" Lord asked.

"The impeachment or the death," Sunshine answered.

"Neither of these two solutions would happen," Lord said.

"Do not forget that you are a loser," Sunshine said.

"I am a god and not a loser," Lord retorted.

Sunshine looked into Lord's eyes and said, "You failed all your promises and you were not even able to prevent children from going to school, you were not able to possess the soul of the future generations and you lost the control of the kingdom."

"The war is not yet over," Lord retorted.

"The war is over," Sunshine said.

"Who is the winner?" Lord asked.

"The children," Sunshine answered.

Lord laughed and said, "Do you know why I came back?"

"To try to possess the souls of the children again," Sunshine answered.

"No, but to kill you," Lord said.

"I am not surprised to hear about that because it's not a secret for both of us. I am your worst enemy and you have been trying to kill me since I was born," Sunshine said.

"You would be dead in a few hours," Lord said.

"I can see that you got more powers to kill me," Sunshine said.

"Exactly," Lord retorted.

"Where were you after I had destroyed your forest?" Sunshine asked.

"I would take you to where I live now since you destroyed my forest, also called my house," Lord said.

Then Sunshine and Lord were looking at each other in the eyes without saying a word. And suddenly the expression of Sunshine's face changed and she was looking at Lord with a face full of fear as she was seeing Lord's hands that were turning into the wings of the bird. Then Sunshine started turning her head around with her eyes focused on Lord who was flying around her.

And suddenly, Sunshine pushed a loud scream of fear as she was carried by Lord. Lord was flying in space with Sunshine that he had grabbed with his left wing. After a few minutes, Lord disappeared into space with Sunshine.

CHAPTER VIII

THE BAN ON BIRTHS IN THE KINGDOM BY THE KING KALUS AND THE INVASION OF THE KINGDOM BY MONSTERS

It was seven in the morning, and the streets of the kingdom were full of people who were going about their occupations, and almost everyone had a newspaper in their hand. And for the first time since the existence of the laws of Kalus, the journalists had taken their courage to break the laws of Kalus.

And all the journalists had praised the children in their newspapers especially Sunshine and Luna. And the journalists had also encouraged the fight of the children to free the kingdom. And the journalists had also given their support to children, and the journalists had encouraged the whole kingdom to sign the petition for the impeachment of Kalus.

And the journalists had also apologized to Luna for insulting her yesterday in their newspapers that she was not the daughter of

Kalus, and that she was not the heiress to the crown and the throne of the kingdom.

And people were very surprised to read in the newspapers the journalists who were supporting the children and encouraging the whole kingdom to sign the petition for the impeachment of Kalus.

It was nine in the morning, the children of the kingdom were in the living room of the palace, and they were waiting for Sunshine to go in the streets and to get the signature of people about the impeachment of Kalus. And the children were very surprised that Sunshine was not there yet because Sunshine was always the first person to come to the meeting.

And Aaron said that they must go to Sunshine's house because Sunshine would probably be sick. And other children agreed to go to Sunshine's house to see if Sunshine was doing well or not. Then Nany said that they have to wait for Luna to come, and together they would go to Sunshine's house.

Then Luna walked in the living room and she told her friends that the breakfast was ready. But all of them told Luna that they did not have the appetite and that they were eager to go out to get the signature of the people about the impeachment of Kalus. And Aaron told Luna that they were going first to Sunshine's house to see if Sunshine was doing well.

Luna looked at Aaron and she opened her mouth to talk but Luna's mouth started shaking that she could not pronounce a word. And looking at the expression on the face of Luna, it was obvious that she was thinking about what to say.

And Luna was thinking of what to say because she knew what was going on with Sunshine, and Luna could not tell the truth to her friends about where Sunshine was, and Luna was thinking about a lie to tell her friends. And all the eyes were focused on Luna. And they were all wondering what was going on with Luna, and why Luna's mouth was shaking?

Then Isac asked Luna if she was doing well? Luna looked at Isac and she took a deep breath, then she said that she was doing well. And Luna added that she spoke with Sunshine this morning, and that Sunshine would not come today because Sunshine had the headaches, but that Sunshine would come the next day.

And Nany said that they must go to visit Sunshine like Sunshine was sick. But Luna replied that during her conversation with Sunshine, Sunshine told her they must go outside to get the signature of the people about the impeachment of Kalus because the only thing that mattered now was to free the kingdom.

Mia said that they must go to greet Sunshine and that it was important for them to know if Sunshine was doing well or not. Luna said that when she talked with Sunshine, she proposed to Sunshine to come visit her (Sunshine), but Sunshine refused and Sunshine said that she(Sunshine) was just tired and she(Sunshine) wanted to be alone and to rest a little bit.

Luna added that it would be a good idea to leave Sunshine alone because Sunshine must probably be very tired, mostly that it's been more than a year that Sunshine was fighting day and night for the freedom of the kingdom. But some of them said that it was important for them to go see if Sunshine needed something or if Sunshine needed to see the doctor.

Luna said that Sunshine was not at home alone, and that if Sunshine needed to see a doctor, Sunshine's parents would call a doctor or would take Sunshine to the hospital. And Luna added that Sunshine would be happy if they all go out to get the signatures of people about the impeachment of Kalus.

Because the only thing that mattered to Sunshine, it was to free the kingdom and that they must go in the streets now to make people sign for the impeachment of Kalus. And that they could not lose a second because they must free the kingdom as soon as possible before the devil Kalus finishes destroying the kingdom.

And Asher supported Luna's idea by saying that they must go out to finish the fight they had started, and that they must let Sunshine get rest and they would see Sunshine the next day. And that what mattered now was to free the kingdom, and that they could not stop fighting just because Sunshine wanted a day to get rest.

And Asher also said that Sunshine would not be happy if they did not go to the streets to make people sign for the impeachment of Kalus because what mattered for Sunshine was not her health, but it was the freedom of the kingdom. And that Sunshine was the first person to start with this fight, and Sunshine would be very glad that they were in the streets to get the signatures of people about the impeachment of Kalus.

Then Mia said that there was no reason to stop the fight, and that they must let Sunshine get rest and continue the fight today without Sunshine. Because what was important now was to get rid of Kalus, and that each second that was passing, the kingdom was in danger with the devil Kalus on the throne of the kingdom.

Mia also said that they must go to the streets to make people sign for the impeachment of Kalus not only for them and inhabitants of the kingdom, but especially for George and Sunshine who were sick. And that George would be happy when he would get out of the coma to see that they had succeeded to continue the fight and that they had liberated the kingdom when he was in the coma.

Then Asher got up from his chair and said that they were going to the streets to continue their fight and to get the signature of people about the impeachment of Kalus. And the rest of the children got up from their chairs and they all left the palace. And the children spent their day walking in the streets of the kingdom to get the signatures of people.

And it was a great day for the children because all the people that the children had approached in the streets had accepted to sign the petition about the impeachment of Kalus. And people were even fighting to sign the impeachment of Kalus.

And the children had almost got the percentage of the signatures they wanted to impeach Kalus. And they had planned to go to the streets the next day to get the rest of the signatures that they needed to impeach Kalus.

It was midnight, there was the moon that was shining in the sky of a desert. And there was a small hut built with the steels in the middle of this desert, and Sunshine was lying in the hut. Sunshine was lying on the ground with her eyes closed and there was a sword in her belly and she was bleeding from her belly because she had been stabbed in her belly with a sword. And Sunshine had her eyes closed and she was not breathing and it was as if she was dead.

And there was a big hawk with Luna on it that was flying in the space of the desert, and the hawk was flying towards the hut. Then the hawk landed not far from the hut and the light shone into Luna's eyes and the hawk turned into the horse and Luna handed her hand in space and a long sword appeared in her hand. Luna was on the horse and she had grabbed the sword in her hand, and Luna's face was full of anger and the horse was running towards the hut.

Then the horse stopped near to the hut and Luna got off from the horse with her sword in her hand, and she rushed towards the hut. Luna put her sword on the hut and suddenly the sparks of fire started shining between the sword and steels that had been used to build the hut.

Then the hut fell down and Luna rushed towards Sunshine with her face full of fear as she had seen the sword in Sunshine's belly. Then Luna knelt near Sunshine and she looked at Sunshine with her heart beating faster than the normal as if she was going to have a heart attack. Then Luna put her palm's hand on Sunshine's heart to feel if Sunshine's heart was still beating.

And suddenly the fear appeared on Luna's face as she had felt that Sunshine's heart was no longer beating. And there were the tears that were flowing down Luna's cheeks with the fear that Sunshine was probably dead. Then Luna looked at Sunshine without knowing what to do, then she started shaking Sunshine by calling Sunshine's name, but unfortunately for Luna, Sunshine was not reacting.

Then Luna got an idea and she removed the sword that was in Sunshine's belly and there was a wound on Sunshine's belly. Then

Luna laid her own sword on Sunshine's belly and Luna's sword had covered Sunshine's wound.

And Luna's eyes were focused on the sword that was laid on Sunshine's wound, then Luna's eyes started turning and the light got out from Luna's eyes and shone on the sword that was on Sunshine's belly. Suddenly, a white smoke appeared between Sunshine's belly and the sword, and this smoke appeared where Sunshine's wound was located.

And Luna was staring at this white smoke that was coming from Sunshine's wound with a face full of hope that Sunshine would open her eyes. And suddenly the hope that was on Luna's face turned into fear as she saw that this white smoke coming from Sunshine's wound had turned into a black smoke.

And Luna was understanding that the black smoke was coming from Sunshine's wound because there was poison in Sunshine's body. Luna also understood that the poison that was in Sunshine's body was coming from the sword that had been used to stab Sunshine.

Luna also knew that the poison that was in Sunshine's body was being destroyed and that it was the reason why the black smoke was coming out from Sunshine's wound. But Luna was afraid that Sunshine would not survive and that even if the poison was completely destroyed in Sunshine's body, Sunshine would not survive. And Luna was afraid that she had arrived too late to save Sunshine, and that the poison that was in Sunshine's body had already killed Sunshine.

Suddenly, Luna turned her head and looked at Sunshine as she had heard Sunshine cough. Then the smile appeared on Luna's face as she had noticed that Sunshine had opened her eyes. And Luna rushed near Sunshine's head, and she asked Sunshine if Sunshine was doing well?

Sunshine opened her mouth to talk but Sunshine was feeling tired and weak that she could not pronounce a word. Then Luna removed the sword that was on Sunshine, then Luna noticed that Sunshine's wound was healed. And Luna understood that the poison that was in Sunshine's body had been completely destroyed.

Then Luna helped Sunshine to get up from the ground, and Sunshine leaned on Luna, and they both walked till near to the horse, and Luna helped Sunshine to get on the horse, then Luna got on the horse too.

And the horse started running, then the light shone into Luna's eyes and the horse turned into the hawk and the hawk started flying through space. And suddenly, Lord appeared near the hut that had been destroyed by Luna and immediately the expression of Lord's face changed.

And Lord was looking at the hut had been destroyed with a surprised face, and mostly he was not seeing Sunshine, and he was not understanding what was going on. And looking at the expression on the face of Lord, we could see that he was completely lost, and Lord started to turn his head around by trying to look for Sunshine.

Then Lord lifted his head through the sky and suddenly the expression of his face changed and he opened his mouth to talk but no word was coming out from his mouth. And Lord's eyes were focused on Sunshine and Luna who were on the hawk in space.

And Lord was wondering what Sunshine and Luna were doing on the hawk, and Lord was not believing that he was watching a hawk that was flying with Sunshine and Luna. And there were a lot of questions that were going on in the mind of Lord.

And Lord was wondering how Luna had found Sunshine? How did Luna know that Sunshine was in this desert? How was it possible that Sunshine was still alive? How could Sunshine have survived the poison that was on the sword that he had stabbed her with? And who had saved Sunshine?

And Lord started wondering if it was Luna who had really saved Sunshine or if it was the mysterious enemy who had saved Sunshine. But for Lord it was obvious that it was not Luna who had saved Sunshine but instead the mysterious enemy.

And for Lord, it was obvious that Luna had found Sunshine alive, and that it was not Luna who had saved Sunshine because Luna was not powerful enough to save Sunshine. And Lord was very furious because he had not found the identity of the mysterious enemy who had saved Sunshine.

Then Lord saw Sunshine and Luna disappeared in the space, and he turned and looked where he had left Sunshine lying dead on the ground, and he saw two swords on the ground, and he walked till near to these swords.

Then Lord knelt near the swords and looked at the two swords and he noticed that one of these swords was his sword that he had used to stab Sunshine with. Then Lord looked at the other sword, and he was wondering where this sword was coming from, and what this sword had been used for.

Then Lord took this sword from the ground and he looked at this sword by trying to find out where the sword was coming from? And who had used this sword? Then Lord smelt this sword to find out who owned this sword, but unfortunately, he failed to find out who belonged to this sword through the scent.

And Lord was very surprised because he did not understand why it was hard for him to find out who owned this sword. Then Lord got an idea and his eyes started spinning, and the light got out from his eyes and shone on the sword that he had held in his hands, and a name appeared on the sword.

And suddenly, the expression of Lord's face changed and he was looking at the name that had appeared on the sword that he had in his hands with an amazed face, and he had his mouth opened and he was trying to speak but no word was coming out from his mouth.

And Looking at the expression on the face of Lord, it was obvious that he was not believing what his eyes were seeing on the sword. Then Lord took a deep breath and he cried out, "Luna?"

And Lord was staring at the name of Luna that was written on the sword that he had held in his hand with an astonished face. And Lord was not believing that it was Luna's name that he was reading on this sword.

And it was hard for Lord to believe that the sword belonged to Luna, and Lord did not understand what was going on. And Lord was wondering if this sword really belonged to Luna. And Lord knew well that if this sword belonged to Luna, it meant that Luna was the mysterious enemy.

Then Lord put his tongue on the sword, and he used his tongue to make sure that the sword was really coming from Luna. And Lord had found out that this sword belonged to Luna through his tongue because he had tasted Luna's magic on this sword.

And Lord was able to discover Luna's magic on this sword because Lord knew all the magic of Kalus. And Lord knew well that Kalus and Luna had the same powers and magic. And for Lord it was obvious now that Luna was the mysterious enemy who had spent the time to help Sunshine to fight him.

And at the same time, Lord was very surprised not only because he had never imagined that Luna could be the mysterious enemy who was helping Sunshine to fight him and who had just saved Sunshine. But mostly because he could not imagine that Luna was powerful enough to help Sunshine to fight him and to save Sunshine.

And Lord was wondering if Luna and Kalus really had the same powers and magic. And it was obvious for Lord that if Kalus and Luna had the same powers and magic, it meant that he did not know all the powers of Kalus, and that Kalus had lied to him. Then Lord got up from the ground and he was determined to find out the truth about the powers and magic of Luna. Then the light shone into Lord's eyes and he disappeared.

It was three in the morning, Sunshine was lying on Luna's bed with her eyes open, and she was talking with Luna who sat on the bed. And Sunshine was very tired and weak. And Luna apologized to Sunshine for not coming in time to save her(Sunshine).

And Luna also told Sunshine that she was the one who was using her powers and magic to help her (Sunshine) to fight against Lord. And Sunshine understood that Luna was the mysterious enemy who was helping her in her fight against Lord. And Sunshine was very surprised to know that this mysterious enemy was Luna.

And Sunshine thanked Luna for saving her and to help her to fight against Lord. Then Sunshine asked Luna how Luna knew that Sunshine was the one who was fighting Lord. Luna answered that when she found out that she was born with the powers and magic, she learned to know how to use her powers and magic. Then she found out about the secrets of the traditions and about the duties of Kalus as the king, and she was astonished to find out that Kalus had broken all the rules of the traditions.

Then Luna added that she tried to understand why Kalus had broken all the rules of the traditions, and she was shocked to find out that Kalus had made a pact with a devil named Lord. And she also found out that there was a young girl who was fighting to save the kingdom, and she started to use her powers to help this young girl to fight Lord, but she did not know that this young girl was Sunshine.

Luna said that she found out that this young girl was Sunshine the day that they had started the class, when she saw the bandages on Sunshine's hands. Because she knew through her magic that the young girl who was fighting Lord had been hurt during this night during her fight against Lord, and when she saw these wounds on Sunshine's hands, she understood that Sunshine was the one who was fighting Lord.

Luna went on and said that she was not really surprised to find out that Sunshine was the one who was fighting Lord because she already had the doubts that Sunshine was born with the powers and magic. Because she had noticed that Kalus was afraid of Sunshine, and she had also felt that Sunshine was different since the first day that she had met Sunshine.

Sunshine smiled at Luna and she thanked Luna for everything, mostly for her courage. And Luna also thanked Sunshine for everything, mostly her courage to fight Lord. Then Sunshine said that during her conversation with Lord last night, Lord told her about a new law of Kalus that would be established in the kingdom.

And Lord did not tell her what this law would be, but Lord warned her not to fight against this new law and to encourage people to accept this law. Then Luna and Sunshine spent the rest of the night thinking of what this new law could be, and they were very afraid, but they were determined to fight against this new law.

It was eleven o'clock, an hour before noon, and the sun was shining in the kingdom. And the children were in the waiting room of the hospital with fear on their faces because their friends named Aaron had been taken to the hospital this morning.

And Aaron had been hit by a car an hour ago when the children were in the streets to get the signatures of people about the impeachment of Kalus. And despite the fact that Aaron was not injured and that he was not feeling any pain when he was taken to the hospital, the children were very worried. And Sunshine knew that Aaron's accident was caused by Lord.

Then Mia saw the doctor, and she told her fellows that the doctor was coming and they all turned their heads and looked towards where Mia was looking. And their hearts started beating faster than normal as they were seeing the doctor who was approaching them.

And Sunshine had her eyes focused on the doctor who was approaching, and Sunshine had the feeling that Aaron was not doing well. Then the doctor stopped facing the children, and the doctor was looking at the children in the eyes while the children were staring at the doctor in the eyes. And there was silence, and the children were waiting for the doctor to talk.

Then Asher broke the silence and asked the doctor how Aaron was doing? The doctor answered that he did not have good news about Aaron. Asher looked at the doctor and asked, "What do you mean by you do not have the good news about Aaron?" The doctor took a deep breath and answered that Aaron was in a coma.

And suddenly, there were the screams of children, and some of them like Nany, Khloe and others had tears that were flowing down their cheeks. And looking at the expression on Sunshine's face, we could see that she was not surprised at all to hear that Aaron was in a coma. And Sunshine knew well that it was Lord who had put Aaron in a coma. Then the doctor said that he was sorry and he turned and left.

Then Sunshine and Luna started to calm their friends by telling their friends that Aaron would be alright. And most of them did not have the morals, and they were all worried not only about Aaron who was in a coma, but also about George who was still in a coma.

And most of the children were very afraid about the tragedy that was going on, and for them the fact that Aaron and George were in the coma, it was a tragedy. And Nany even said that they must take a break about the fight. And Sunshine replied to Nany that no, that they could not take a break about the fight, and that it was time to get rid of Kalus.

Sunshine added that she knew that it was hard for everyone to keep fighting with George and Aaron who were in the coma, but that by stopping the fight, would not make George and Aaron get out of the coma. And that by stopping the fight now was not the solution.

Because if they stopped the fight now it would be the worst decision of their lives, not only because they were already close to the victory but mostly because they were allowing the devil Kalus to continue to destroy the kingdom. Sunshine said that they already got almost the number of signatures they needed to impeach Kalus, and they just needed some signatures again, and that they could get these signatures in less than an hour.

Then Sunshine continued and said that it meant that tomorrow Kalus would no longer be the king of the kingdom. Because they would get these signatures in less than an hour, then they would impeach Kalus today before midnight.

And suddenly, Sunshine stopped talking and she was feeling a strange smell, and Sunshine was breathing deeply. And she was the only one who was feeling this strange smell. And everyone was looking at Sunshine with worried faces wondering what was going on with her.

And Asher asked Sunshine if she was alright? But Sunshine did not answer Asher. Then Sunshine turned her head through where this strange smell that she was feeling was coming from. And immediately the expression on her face changed when she saw Lord.

And she was looking at Lord who was walking towards the back door with an amazed face. Then Sunshine looked at Luna and she asked Luna to continue her(Sunshine) speech that she was coming. Then Sunshine turned and left.

Sunshine was walking towards the back door and she was following Lord who was walking in front of her. Sunshine was very surprised to see Lord in the hospital, and she was more surprised to see Lord during the day because she knew well that Lord hated the light of day.

Then Sunshine got out and she saw Lord who was leaning on a pole. And Sunshine walked till near to Lord and she was looking in the eyes of Lord with a face full of anger, while Lord was looking staring at Sunshine with a face full of smiles.

Then Sunshine broke the silence and said, "Do not waste your time because you would not stop us."

"Us?" Lord cried out.

"My fellows and I," Sunshine answered.

"Your fellows are useless because I can put all your fellows in a coma now," Lord said.

"Even if you put all my fellows in a coma, Luna and I would not stop the fight," Sunshine said.

"Luna is not a potential enemy," Lord said.

Sunshine looked into Lord's eyes and said, "Luna is the one who saved me."

"I know that you are still alive thanks to Luna," Lord retorted.

"If Luna saved me, it means that Luna is a potential enemy for you," Sunshine said.

"I know all the powers and magic of Luna," Lord said.

"It's what you think," Sunshine said.

"It's not what I think, I know all the powers and magic of Luna," Lord retorted.

"If you knew all the powers and magic of Luna, you should find out that Luna was the mysterious enemy who helped me to fight you," Sunshine said.

"I know that the mysterious enemy is Luna," Lord said.

"You found out that Luna is the mysterious enemy this morning when you saw me and Luna on the hawk," Sunshine said.

"It's not this morning that I found out that Luna is the mysterious enemy," Lord said.

"I did not know that you were a liar," Sunshine said.

"I am not a liar," Lord retorted.

Sunshine said, "If you knew that Luna was your mysterious enemy, you should have tried to kill Luna a long time ago." And Sunshine went on and said, "It's this morning that you found out that Luna was your mysterious enemy when you saw me and Luna on the hawk. Because I saw you when I was on the hawk."

And Sunshine added, "If you knew that Luna was your mysterious enemy, you should try to kill Luna to stop Luna from continuing to help me fight you. And if you knew all the magic of Luna, you should have known a long time ago that Luna was your mysterious enemy."

Lord looked into Sunshine's eyes and said, "The good thing it's that I know how to kill you."

"You really do not have the chance because you found out how to kill me when it was too late," Sunshine said.

"You would not have the chance to be saved by Luna next time," Lord said.

"There would not be next time because you would never have the chance to try to kill me again," Sunshine said.

"I know how to kill you," Lord said.

"You think you know how to kill me," Sunshine said.

"I do not think so, but I know how to kill you," Lord said.

"I know the strategy you had used to try to kill me this morning, so I know how you would try to kill me, and that means that I know how to protect myself from you." Sunshine said.

"I am here to make a deal with you," Lord said.

"I am not interested in your deal," Sunshine said.

"The new law is already out," Lord said.

"Kalus is no longer the king of this kingdom because me and my fellows got the signatures that we needed to impeach the devil Kalus, so this new law of Kalus is illegal and nobody would respect this law." Sunshine said.

"I am here because I want you to convince the whole kingdom to accept this new law of Kalus, and I would not put your fellows in the coma, but I would also take Aaron and George out of the coma." Lord said.

Sunshine looked into Lord's eyes and said, "You can put the whole kingdom in a coma if you want, but I promise you that I am going to fight against this new law of Kalus. And even if I do not yet know the content of this new law, I would fight against this new law."

And Sunshine added, "You can put the whole kingdom in a coma, I am not afraid about that because I know that you can not kill them because you do not control their souls. So, I am not afraid because even if I am alone, I will keep fighting you until you die." Then Sunshine turned and left.

The children were still in the waiting room of the hospital, and they had all their eyes focused on the television and they were watching the king Kalus who was talking on television with surprised faces. And some of them even had their mouths opened but no word was coming out from their mouths.

And looking at the expression on their faces, it was obvious that they were not believing what they were hearing from Kalus, and they were completely lost. Then they turned their heads and looked at each other with fear on their faces, and some of them opened their mouths to talk but their mouths started shaking so that they could not pronounce a word.

Then Sunshine joined her fellows and Sunshine was surprised to see that all her fellows had faces full of fear and sadness. And

Sunshine asked what was going on? But none answered Sunshine. And Sunshine asked again what was going on? And everyone looked at Sunshine without answering her question. And Sunshine asked if Aaron and George were doing well? Asher answered Sunshine that Aaron and George were still in the coma. And Sunshine looked at Asher and she understood that something worse had happened.

Then Sunshine asked Asher about what was going on? Asher took a deep breath and he told Sunshine that the devil Kalus had just banned the births in the kingdom, and that all the pregnant women must have abortions. And that the doctors must perform abortions on all pregnant women who were in the hospital now, and that the pregnant women who were at home must go to the hospital to have anabortion.

And that all the babies who would be born from today would be killed, and it did not matter if these babies were born to the hospitals or at homes, and that women would stop getting pregnant for the moment. Also, all the doctors and people who would help the pregnant women to give birth would be killed. And that the births would start again in the kingdom only when he(Kalus) would give the order to women to give birth.

And that Kalus also said that all the birth services in all the hospitals of the kingdom would be closed. And that all women who had given birth almost a year ago without paying the birth costs of the hospital must go to Kalus's bank to pay these fees.

And if a woman did not pay this birth costs to the Kalus's bank, her child would be killed by Kalus's army. And that all these new reforms were the new laws of Kalus, and that the whole kingdom must respect the new laws of Kalus. And that anyone who would not respect the new laws of Kalus would be killed.

And that Kalus also added that his new army was already outside, and his new army would visit all the hospitals and houses of the kingdom to find the pregnant women. And that he had given the right and order to his new army to kill all pregnant women, all new babies and all people who would not respect the new laws of Kalus.

So that if a pregnant woman did not want to die, this pregnant woman must have an abortion today. And that before midnight, all pregnant women should already have an abortion because he did not want to see or hear that there was a pregnant woman in this kingdom after midnight.

Sunshine said, "Please, tell me what is going on."

"I just told you what is going on," Asher retorted.

"Please stop joking," Sunshine said.

"I am not joking," Asher replied.

"Are you serious?" Sunshine with a surprised face.

"Yes, I am," Asher replied.

Then Sunshine looked at Asher with an astonished face wondering if she was not dreaming, then she turned her head and looked at her other fellows and she noticed that all her fellows were surprised like her. AndSunshine was also seeing the fear on the faces of her fellows, and she was understanding through the expression of her fellow's faces that she was not dreaming and that everything that was told to her by Asher were not the jokes.

Sunshine understood that the new laws of Kalus that were told to her by Lord were to prohibit the birth of children in the kingdom. And Sunshine was completely lost and she did not even know what to say.

And despite the fact that Sunshine knew that there was a new law of Kalus, and that she knew that the new law of Kalus was not going to improve the situation of the kingdom. Sunshine did not expect that the new laws of Kalus would ban births in the kingdom.

And looking at the expression on Sunshine's face, we could see that she was still not realizing what was going on. And it was obvious that Sunshine was completely lost, and she was not understanding how the two devils who were Lord and Kalus had got the idea to ban the births in the kingdom and mostly to force all pregnant women to have an abortion.

And there was a question that was going on in the head of Sunshine, and this question was why Lord and Kalus had decided to ban the births in the kingdom? But unfortunately, Sunshine could not answer this question.

Then Nany broke the silence and said that they must go to the streets now and get the rest of the signatures they needed to impeach Kalus. And Nany added that there was no time to waste. Luna looked at Nany and said that there was no time to go to the streets to get the signatures, and that the only thing they must do now was to gain on time. Asher asked Luna how they would gain on time?

Luna answered Asher that they must kill Kalus. And Luna added that they must go to the palace now and kill Kalus because only the death of Kalus would solve all the problems of the kingdom, and only the death of Kalus would put an end to the laws of Kalus. And mostly only the death of Kalus would save the future babies by preventing pregnant women from having an abortion.

Sunshine looked at Luna and said that it was true that only the death of Kalus would solve the problems that were going on in the kingdom. And that it was also true that only the death of Kalus would put an end to the laws of Kalus. But it was not easy to kill Kalus because Kalus was a powerful man who was protected by his powers. Luna looked at Sunshine and said that it was true that it was not easy to kill Kalus, but that Kalus was not immortal.

Sunshine replied to Luna that it was true that Kalus was not an immortal, but that it must take them the time to kill Kalus, and they did not have this time now because all the pregnant women of the kingdom were in danger. Asher asked Sunshine what the solution was?

And Sunshine answered Asher that the only solution that they had now was to save all the pregnant women of the kingdom. Asher asked Sunshine how they were going to save all the pregnant women? And Sunshine answered that they would take all the pregnant women of the kingdom with them. And that they would put those pregnant women in a safe place and they would watch over those pregnant women to prevent the army of the devil Kalus from killing those pregnant women.

Asher told Sunshine that it was a good idea, but that they could not keep the pregnant women with them because there was not a doctor between them. And Asher added that it was risky to keep the pregnant women with them without a doctor who could take care of the pregnant women in case of need because the pregnant women could need a doctor at any time. Sunshine replied to Asher that they would not keep the pregnant women without the doctors because they would find the doctors who would take care of the pregnant women.

Then they looked at each other without saying a word. And Luna asked if there was someone who had something to say because they must start now if there was nobody who wanted to talk. Mia asked where they would keep the pregnant women and how they would take the pregnant women with them? Khloe answered that she had a big house and that her living room was huge and that they could keep the pregnant women in her house. And Sunshine said that they would use the car to take the pregnant women with them, and they would keep the pregnant women in Khloe's house.

Asher told Sunshine that they needed a car and a driver. And Sunshine answered Asher that they did not need a driver because she could drive, and that they would steal any car in the street because they did not have money and time to go buy a car.

And Luna said that she could drive too. And Nany asked Sunshine and Luna how it was possible that the children of thirteen years old could drive because the legal age to drive was eighteen. Sunshine answered that her father had taught her to drive when she was eleven. And Luna said that her mom had taught her to drive when she was twelve years old.

But Sunshine and Luna had lied when they said that it was their parents who had taught them to drive because Sunshine and Luna could drive through their magic and powers. So, Sunshine and Luna would use their magic to drive. Nany said that it was illegal to drive at thirteen and it was also illegal to steal the car in the street.

And Sunshine replied to Nany that it was true that stealing was not good, but that they were in a situation that they must save the lives of future babies of the kingdom. And that they could not stay and watch the monster Kalus kill the future babies of the kingdom, just because they could not steal a car in the street.

Sunshine added that it was not the moment to think about if what they were doing was legal or not because if they wanted to do only the things that were legal, they should never fight against Kalus and fight against the laws of Kalus because even the laws of Kalus were legal.

And that it was the moment to do only the right things and it did not matter if these things were legal or not. Because the only thing that mattered now it was to save the lives of the future babies by preventing pregnant women from having an abortion.

Then they all agreed with Sunshine. Sunshine said that they would start to search the pregnant women in the hospitals, and they would take all the pregnant women who were in the hospitals with them first. And that they must start to search the pregnant women who were in the hospital where they were.

And suddenly, they turned their heads towards the left when they heard the voices called the name of Sunshine. And they saw the journalist Remy and his team who were walking towards them. And Luna said that it was a good thing that Remy was there with his cameramen because she would give a speech to the whole kingdom asking the doctors not to perform the abortions on the pregnant women. And to tellpregnant women not to feel any fear and especially not to take any pill that could cause them to have an abortion.

Then Remy and his team stopped near the children. And Luna asked Remy if she could make a speech to the whole kingdom through his television channel. And Remy answered Luna that yes, and that his television channel was live, so that people who were watching his television channel now would watch everything that he would film. Then Remy asked Luna if she was ready? And Luna answered yes.

Then Remy held the microphone to Luna's mouth and Luna said that she was talking to the whole kingdom not only like the heiress to the crown and throne of the kingdom, but mostly like a human being. And that the new law of Kalus was not only illegal because Kalus was no longer the king of the kingdom to make the decision, but mostly because the traditions of Manitoba prohibited abortions.

So that it was illegal to perform abortion, and that all people who would perform abortions on pregnant women would be charged with murdering babies. And that all pregnant women who would have an abortion by themselves would also be prosecuted for murdering babies.

And Luna added that Kalus was no longer the king of the kingdom because the children of the kingdom had already got enough of a signature to impeach Kalus. And that Kalus had neither the power, nor the right to make a decision in this kingdom. And that all the doctors of the kingdom and the pregnant women must know that the abortion was illegal and anti-traditional.

And Luna told the doctors that their work was to save the lives and not to kill the lives, so that if a doctor performed the abortion on a pregnant woman, this doctor would be killed too. And Luna told the whole kingdom not to worry because everything would be fine.

And Luna continued and said that no woman would go to the bank of Kalus to pay the birth costs, that they (women) did not pay when they had given birth a few months ago because Kalus was no longer the king of the kingdom.

So all the new reforms of Kalus were illegal. And that according to the traditions of the kingdom the births should be free, so that the devil Kalus was the only king in the history of the kingdom who had stolen money from the parents by making the parents pay the birth costs.

And Luna ended her speech by asking the whole kingdom to stay quiet and that nothing would happen to them, and no one would be injured or be killed by Kalus's army. Because she and her fellows were outside to protect the whole kingdom and all the inhabitants of the kingdom.

Then Remy held the microphone toSunshine's mouth and the camera was focused on Sunshine. And Sunshine said that she was talking to the whole kingdom, and that the whole kingdom must know that all the laws of Kalus were illegal.

And that this new law of Kalus that forced the doctors to perform abortions on pregnant women was not only illegal, but it was also anti-traditional like Luna had said. And that people would not only stop listening to Kalus, but they would also stop respecting and following the laws of Kalus. Because Kalus was no longer the king of the kingdom because they had already got enough signatures to impeach Kalus, so that all the decisions that would be taken by Kalus were illegal.

And Sunshine added that no one had the right to perform abortions on the pregnant women. Sunshine told the pregnant women not to worry because she and her fellows were on their way to save them, and that she and her fellows would take them and keep them to a safe place, and there would be the doctors who would take care of them. Then Sunshine ended her speech by asking the whole kingdom not to feel any fear, and mostly not to respect the laws of Kalus and to take care of all pregnant women who would be near to them.

Then Sunshine looked at her fellows and said that they must start to look for the pregnant women in this hospital where they were. And they would search all the bedrooms of the hospital and each woman that they would see, they would ask this woman if she was pregnant, and that they would also ask women who were working in the hospital because women who were working in the hospital could also be pregnant. Then Sunshine said, "Let's go."

And Sunshine turned and she started to walk towards a hall, and she was followed by her fellows and Remy, also the cameramen. Then some children started feeling unwell, and suddenly there were the screams coming from children and they were all looking with fear on their faces, as they were looking at two of their friends who had fainted.

Except Sunshine and Luna, the rest of the children were looking at their friends who were lying on the floor with their eyes closed like corpses. And the children were afraid that their friends who were on the floor were dead. And the children were wondering why their friends had fainted? And what had happened? But unfortunately, they could not answer these questions.

Except Sunshine and Luna who knew that it was Lord, who had put their friends in the coma. Sunshine and Luna knew that Lord had put their friends in the coma to discourage them and to prevent them from continuing their fight to save the pregnant women.

And Sunshine was understanding that she and her fellows were mystically followed by Lord. And Sunshine knew that Lord would not stop and she also knew that Lord would put all her fellows in the coma if she and her fellows did not give up the idea to fight against the new laws of Kalus.

And Sunshine knew well that she would not give up the fight, and that she was determined to protect the pregnant women and the future babies. And even if Sunshine knew that only she and Luna could only be the ones who could continue the fight because the rest of her fellows could be put in the coma at any time by Lord.

Sunshine was determined to protect the offspring of the kingdom, but Sunshine was also very worried about her fellows who were in the coma, and about her fellows who could be put in the coma by Lord. And even if Sunshine knew that Lord could not kill her fellows, she was thinking how to prevent Lord from continuing to put her fellows in the coma.

Then the doctors and the nurses arrived and they checked the children who were on the floor. And suddenly the children yelled when they heard the doctors announce that these children who were on the floor were in a coma.

Except Sunshine and Luna who were not surprised by the announcement of the doctors. And the children were watching their friends who were taken to the emergency by doctors with their faces full of fear and sadness. And some had even the tears that were flowing down their cheeks.

Then Sunshine looked at her fellows and she told her fellows that what they were living right now was a tragedy, and that it was hard for all of them to see their fellows in the coma. Sunshine added that she was afraid and worried about what would happen, and she did not want one of them to go into a coma again. And for that she and Luna would continue the fight, and the rest of them would return home and get rest.

And suddenly Sunshine was interrupted by Asher who told her that he was not going home, and that he would continue the fight. And Sunshine replied to Asher that he could not continue the fight because it was risky, and that he could get in a coma too. So that it was important for him and others to go home and get rest.

And Asher told Sunshine that he was not afraid to get into a coma, and he did not even care to die. And that he was ready to die to save his kingdom and to protect all the habitants of the kingdom. So that he would not go home and that he would continue the fight, and no one would prevent him from continuing his fight to save his kingdom.

Mia joined Asher's idea and said that she would not go home and that she was ready to die for her kingdom. And Mia added that she had more motivation to fight for the freedom of this kingdom since George got into the coma, and that it was important to continue this fight not only for her and the kingdom, but mostly George and all their friends who had got in the coma during the fight. Mia continued and said that some of them were already in the coma, and that her eyes just saw two of them got into the coma.

So that even in the name of those who were in the coma, she could give up the fight because it would be like betraying those who were in a coma. And that she was ready to join her fellows who were in the coma, and she was even ready to die to save this kingdom. And that nothing would stop her because she was ready to die during the fight and if she did not die during the fight, she would fight until the victory of the freedom of the kingdom.

And Khloe said that she was not going home, and that she would continue the fight. And that the new laws of Kalus gave her more motivation and more reasons to fight. Because as a woman, she refused to stay and watch a devil like Kalus kill the future babies by forcing the pregnant women to have abortions.

And Khloe continued and said that she was a woman, and that if she did not die during this war, she would carry a baby in her womb in the future. And she would not be happy if there was a stupid law that forced her to kill her baby by forcing her to have an abortion. And that for the love of her the kingdom and for the love of all the babies who were in the wombs, she would fight until her death or until the victory.

Suddenly, Asher started clapping his hands by smiling at Khloe, and the rest of the people followed Asher by clapping their hands. And Asher screamed, "The freedom of the kingdom or the death." And the rest of them followed Asher by screaming, "The freedom of the kingdom or the death." And Sunshine's fellows told Sunshine that they would not go home, and that they would continue to fight and that they were ready to die to free their kingdom. Then the children started screaming, "The freedom of the kingdom or death."

Sunshine and Luna were staring at their fellows with faces full of smiles, and they were seeing the determination on the faces of their fellows. And although the fact that Sunshine was worried about the fact that Lord could put her fellows in the coma, she was also very happy to see that her fellows were determined to die in the name of the kingdom.

Then Sunshine opened her mouth and said that they were all going to continue their fight, and that they would fight until the victory or until death. And the children screamed by clapping their hands, and by yelling, "The victory or the death."

And suddenly the expression on everyone's face changed, and they were looking with astonished faces, as they were seeing a long sword that was flying towards Luna. And it was Luna who had made this sword appear through her magic.

Then Luna grabbed the sword in her hand, and she started walking towards her fellows and all the eyes were focused on her. And they were all wondering what Luna was doing, and some of them were a little bit afraid that Luna was going to use this sword to kill them.

Then Luna stopped near to Sunshine and she held the sword horizontally, by showing the sword to Sunshine, then Luna looked into Sunshine's eyes and Luna asked Sunshine to put her two palm's hands on the sword. And Sunshine put her two palm's hands on the sword.

And suddenly, the expression on the faces of everyone changed and some were looking with fear on their faces, while others were looking with astonished faces as they had all seen a blue light get out from the sword and shone on Sunshine. And they were all wondering what was going on? What Luna was doing? and Why was Luna doing this?

Then Luna continued and she stopped near to Nany with the sword that had held horizontally by showing the sword to Nany. Then Luna looked into Nany's eyes and she asked Nany to put her two palm's hands on the sword.

And Nany looked into Luna's eyes with fear in her eyes, and Luna told Nany not to feel any fear, and to put her two palm's hands on the sword. And Nany lifted her two hands and she was trying to put her hands on the sword, but her whole body was trembling so that her palm's hands could not touch the sword.

And all the eyes were focused on Nany, and everyone could see that Nany was very afraid to touch the sword. And most of them were understanding the reaction and the fear of Nany to touch the sword because themselves they were afraid to touch the sword.

Mostly that they had all seen the light get out from the sword and shone on Sunshine when Sunshine had touched the sword. And

Nany had not yet touched the sword because her hands were shaking and her palm's hands could not touch the sword.

And Sunshine told Nany not to be afraid and to touch the sword. And Nany was trying to approach the sword with her hands, but her whole body was shaking and she was breathing deeply, and her hands had stopped near the sword. And she was looking at the sword with her heart beating faster than normal, and she was very afraid to touch the sword.

Then Asher walked near to Luna and he told Luna that he wanted to touch the sword. Luna smiled at Asher and she showed the sword to Asher, and she asked Asher to two his two palm's hands on the sword. And Asher looked at the sword that was held horizontally by Luna.

Then Asher put his two palm's hands on the sword and a blue light got out from the sword and shone on Asher. And all the eyes were focused on Asher and they were trying to see the reaction of Asher, and they were trying to know if the light that had shone on Asher had a particular reaction on him. But they were all surprised to notice that Asher had no particular reaction.

Then Mia walked up to near Luna, then Mia told Luna that she wanted to touch the sword. And Luna showed the sword to Mia, and Luna asked Mia to put her two palm's hands on the sword. And Mia put her two palm's hands on the sword that was horizontally held by Luna.

And a blue light got out from the sword and shone on Mia when Mia touched the sword. And people looked at Mia to see the reaction of Mia, and again, they were astonished to see that Mia had no particular reaction. And Isac asked Mia which reaction she felt when the light that got out from the sword shone on her? Mia answered Isac that she felt no reaction.

Then Luna walked till near to Isac with the sword and she showed the sword to Isac. Then Luna smiled at Isac and she asked Isac to put his palm's hands on the sword. And Isac put his two palm's hands on the sword that was horizontally held by Luna. And a blue light got out from the sword and shone on Isac when Isac touched the sword.

Then after Isac, the rest of the children approached Luna to touch the sword without any fear. After a few minutes, they had all touched the sword, and the blue light had shone on each of them when they touched the sword. Then Asher asked Luna why she had made them touch the sword and why the blue light had shone on them when they touched the sword.

Luna answered Asher that she had made all of them touch the sword because she wanted to protect them against the bad energies. Luna added that the blue light that had shone on them would protect them against the bad energies, when they would be attacked by the monsters.

Asher asked Luna if there were monsters in the kingdom? Luna answered Asher that the new army of Kalus were the monsters. And that was the reason why she had used her powers coming from this magic sword that they had touched to protect them against the new army of Kalus.

And Suddenly the expression on the faces of most of them changed, and some of them were looking at Luna with fear on their faces. And Nany asked Luna if the new army of Kalus were the real monsters? Luna told Nany not to worry about the monsters that they would see during the fight because these monsters could not hurt them or kill them because they were all protected by the blue light that had come out from the magic sword and shone on them.

And Luna added that not to worry if they felt a strange reaction in their bodies later. Because the blue light that had shone on them would have a strange reaction in their bodies when they would fight the monsters.

Because the bad energies coming from the monsters would try to take possession of their bodies. But the good energies coming from the blue light that had shone on their bodies would mystically fight the bad energies to prevent the bad energies from getting possession of their bodies. And that it would be a normal reaction to feel a strange reaction in their bodies during the fight.

Nany told Luna that Luna did not answer the question about if the new army of Kalus were the real monsters or not? Luna looked at Nany and answered that Nany would find the answer to this question later, but that it was time to go save the whole kingdom, especially the pregnant women.

Then Sunshine said that they must go and search all the rooms in the hospitals to find the pregnant women. And Sunshine added that not to forget to ask all women that they would meet if these women were pregnant. Then Sunshine and her fellows started walking towards the stairs by singing, "The freedom of our kingdom or death." And there were people in the hospital who were looking at the children with amazed faces, and people were very surprised by the courage and the determination of the children to save the kingdom.

Then the children started to walk in the rooms of the hospital looking for the pregnant women, and every woman who was seen was asked by the children if this woman was pregnant. And the doctors and nurses were surprised to see the children got in the rooms looking for the pregnant women.

And although the doctors and nurses were astonished to see the children in the rooms without authorization, the doctors did not call the security on the children. And the doctors and nurses were very proud of the children.

Then a nurse told children that there were three pregnant women in this hospital today, and these three pregnant women had disappeared after the speech of Kalus on the new laws of Kalus that force pregnant women to have an abortion.

Sunshine asked the nurse where were these pregnant women? And the nurse answered that she had no idea because it's been hours that the security of the hospital was looking for these pregnant women. And the nurse added that she was worried about these pregnant women because one of these pregnant women was going to give birth tonight or tomorrow, and two others had come to the hospital for their visit.

And suddenly, the expression on Sunshine's face changed and she was looking at the nurse with fear on her face. And Sunshine asked the nurse if Kalus's army was in the hospital? And the nurse answered that she had no idea. And the nurse added that it was hard to control everyone entering and leaving the hospital since Kalus had announced the new laws of Kalus because many people were entering the hospital looking for their relatives.

Then Sunshine took a deep breath and she concentrated on herself and she was trying to use her magic to find these three pregnant women. While Luna was giving the instructions to the nurse how to protect all pregnant women who would come to the hospital or who would be seen at the hospital.

And Luna also told the nurse that no pregnant woman would have an abortion in the hospital. And suddenly Luna was interrupted by Sunshine who asked for directions to the basement of the hospital.

And the nurse told Sunshine that they needed to take the elevator to reach the basement. Sunshine told the nurse that they could not all get on the elevator, and that there was no time to waste because they only had a few seconds to reach the basement.

Asher looked at Sunshine and said, "Let's run." Sunshine replied, "Great idea, Asher." Then Sunshine started running towards the hall, and she was followed by her fellows. And the nurse was looking at the children who were running with an amazed face by wondering if these children were not crazy.

After a few minutes, the children were climbing down the stairs by going to the basement of the hospital. And suddenly some of them stopped as they had heard the screams, and they were looking with fear on their faces.

And Sunshine said that these screams were the screams of despair, and that it was these pregnant women who were calling for help. And Sunshine added that they have to run. Then they started climbing down the stairs as fast as they could as if they were running.

After a few seconds, they were running in the hallway of a basement, following the direction of the screams that they were hearing. And they were running towards a door, and Sunshine's eyes started spinning as she was staring at the door by running, and the door opened.

And suddenly the expression of their faces changed and they were running faster with their faces full of fear, as they were seeing a pregnant woman who was lying on the floor and there were two other pregnant women who were trying to help the one who was lying on the floor. And the children were running with their eyes focused on these pregnant women that they did not try to know about who had opened the door.

Then Sunshine and her fellows stopped near these pregnant women, and the first thing that they noticed was that the pregnant woman who was lying on the floor was about to give birth. And Sunshine said that they have to take all these pregnant women with them.

And one of the pregnant women said that they could not leave the basement because they could be killed with their babies in their wombs if they refused to have an abortion. And Sunshine told the pregnant women that they would not have an abortion because she and her fellows would protect them, and that nothing would happen to them.

Then Sunshine told her fellows that some of them would carry the pregnant woman who was lying on the floor, while others would help the other two pregnant women to walk. Then the pregnant women refused to leave because they were afraid to be killed by Kalus's army if they were seen by Kalus's army, mostly if they were seen with children (Sunshine and her fellows) by Kalus's army.

Because Kalus hated the children, and the children were the worst enemies of Kalus, mostly that Kalus had already warned that everyone who would be seen with the children would be arrested or killed. But Sunshine succeeded in convincing these pregnant women that she and her fellows would protect them from Kalus's army. Then Sunshine and her fellows took these pregnant women with them.

After a few minutes, the children were walking as fast as they could with these pregnant women towards the emergency room of the hospital. And the pregnant woman who was carried by the children was crying in pain.

And the children were yelling by calling for help. But none was paying attention to the screams for help coming from the children, and all the nurses and doctors who were in the hall were just staring at the children without doing anything to help the children. The doctors and nurses were afraid to be killed by Kalus's army if they helped the children and the pregnant women.

Then Sunshine saw an empty rolling bed in the hallway, and she told her fellows that they would lay the pregnant woman that they were carrying in this empty rolling bed. Then they walked near this empty rolling bed and they laid this pregnant woman on this empty bed.

And there were also the wheelchairs in the hallway, and Sunshine asked her fellows to help the other two pregnant women to sit on these wheelchairs. Then Sunshine said that they must push the bed and the two wheelchairs until the emergency and they would stay with these pregnant women no matter what would happen.

Then they started to push the bed on which the pregnant woman was lying, and the two wheelchairs where the two other pregnant women were sitting towards the emergency. And there were people in the hall of the hospital who were just staring at the children with worried faces.

And these people were not worried about the children, but they were instead worried about these pregnant women who were taken to the emergency by the children. Because these pregnant women were taking a risk to go to the emergency because the children could fail to protect these pregnant women and the doctors could perform abortions on these pregnant women.

Then the children saw the doctors and the security who were walking towards them. Mia said that she hoped these doctors would help them. Then the security and doctors stopped face to face with the children. The doctors and the children were looking each other in the eyes.

Then one of the doctors broke a silence and introduced himself like the doctor Thomas, and that he was the director of the hospital. And the doctor Thomas added that he would like to talk with the children. Sunshine replied to the doctor that the children did not have time to talk, and that the pregnant woman who was lying on the bed needed help.

Thomas took a deep breath and said, "The doctors would help these pregnant women to have abortions."

"What?" Luna cried out.

"The new laws of Kalus require all the hospitals of the kingdom to perform abortions on pregnant women," Thomas said.

Luna looked in Thomas's eyes and said, "I want you as the director of this hospital to help and protectall the pregnant women who would come to this hospital. And you would make sure that the abortion would not be performed in this hospital because if the abortions were performed in this hospital, all staff working in this hospital would be sent to jail." And Luna added, "The director of this hospital and all those who had performed the abortions by killing the babies in the wombs, would be killed too."

Thomas looked at Luna and said that, "The new laws of Kalus banned the births in the kingdom."

"Kalus is no longer the king of this kingdom, and the new laws are anti-traditional because the traditions of Manitoba banned the abortions." Luna said.

Thomas said, "Kalus is still on the throne of the kingdom, and we must respect the decisions of Kalus."

Luna looked into Thomas's eyes and said, "I am the heiress to the throne and crown of this kingdom, and I order you to help this pregnant woman lying on the bed to give birth."

Thomas looked into Luna's eyes and said, "No woman would give birth in this hospital, so you would take these pregnant women to another hospital."

Luna looked into Thomas's eyes and said, "This woman would give birth in this hospital and you are the one who would help this woman to give birth. So, you are the first doctor who would give an example to the members of your staff, to the other doctors of this kingdom by helping this woman to give birth."

"The birthing service is closed and the doctors and nurses responsible for helping women to give birth have been dismissed after the speech of Kalus to ban the births in the kingdom." Thomas said.

"You are going to open the birthing service of this hospital now, and you are the one who would help this woman to give birth," Luna said.

"I would not open the birthing service, and I would not allow a woman to give birth in this hospital, so I would not help a woman to give birth," Thomas said.

Luna looked at Thomas with a face full of rage and said, "Think well."

"I do not have to think," Thomas retorted.

And suddenly there was silence between them. And the eyes of everyone were focused on Luna, and they could all see the rage on Luna's face. Then a woman joined them and she introduced herself as Doctor Michelle.

And Doctor Michelle looked with a worried face at the pregnant woman who was lying on the bed and crying in pain. And Doctor Michelle said that this pregnant woman on the bed could not stay in the hall of the hospital, and that they must take this pregnant woman to the delivery room and help this pregnant woman to give birth.

And Doctor Thomas looked at Doctor Michelle and said that the births were banned in the kingdom by the king Kalus, and that the hospital would not help this woman to give birth. And that the only thing that the hospital could do for pregnant women, it was to preform abortions on pregnant women.

And Doctor Michelle told Doctor Thomas that as a woman and as a mother, she refused to perform abortions on the pregnant women. And Doctor Thomas looked into the eyes of Doctor Michelle and he told Doctor Michelle that she was fired from the hospital.

Luna looked at Doctor Thomas, and she told him that no one would be sacked, and no pregnant woman would have an abortion. And Luna asked Doctor Thomas to push the bed where this pregnant woman was lying to the delivery room.

And Doctor Thomas looked at Luna with a surprised face and asked her if she was crazy? Then Doctor asked the security to kick out from the hospital the children, and to take the pregnant women to a room and he would perform abortions on these pregnant women.

Then the security men started walking towards the children. And some children were walking from behind as they were seeing the security men who were walking towards them with the big and long sticks that security men had held in their hands. Sunshine and Luna had their eyes focused on security men, and the eyes of Sunshine and Luna were spinning.

Suddenly, there were the screams of fear coming from the children. The children and other people who were in the hall were looking at the security men who were flying in space with astonished faces. And suddenly the expression on their faces changed, and the surprise that was on their faces turned into fear, as they were staring at the security men who were hitting their bodies against the walls.

And there was blood on the walls because the security men had been injured on their faces. Then Luna turned her head and looked at Doctor Thomas and her eyes started spinning. And suddenly Doctor Thomas flew in space and he started hitting his body against the wall.

And there were people who were watching what was going on, and even the cameraman was filming. And most of them had fear on their faces, while others like Asher and Mia had smiles on their faces. And they all thought that the security men and Doctor Thomas were tortured only by Luna, as they all knew that Luna had the magic.

And no one could imagine that the security men and Doctor Thomas were also tortured by Sunshine, as they did not know that Sunshine had the magic, and as they were not seeing how Sunshine's eyes were spinning. And only Luna knew that the security men and Doctor Thomas were also tortured by Sunshine.

Isac's eyes were focused on Doctor Thomas who was bleeding, and he was thinking how to save Doctor Thomas. Then Isac started screaming Luna's name to prevent her from killing Doctor Thomas and security men. Then Nany joined Isac, and they were begging Luna to stop.

Suddenly, the security men and Doctor Thomas fell on the floor. And Luna turned and she looked at Remy and she told Remy that she had a message for all the doctors and nurses of the kingdom. And Remy walked until near Luna with the microphone and he held the microphone near Luna's mouth.

And Luna said that her message was for all the hospitals of the kingdom. And that all the doctors and nurses who would refuse to help a pregnant woman would be tortured by her, as she had just tortured Doctor Thomas who had refused to help the pregnant woman who was laid on the bed.

And that if a pregnant woman died in a hospital, or if a baby died in a hospital or even if the abortion was performed in a hospital, all people working in this hospital would be killed by her. And even the security working in this hospital would be killed by her.

And Luna added that no one had the right to refuse to take care of a pregnant woman. And that if the new laws of the devil Kalus were enforced in a hospital, the director of this hospital would be killed, and all people working in this hospital who had applied the new laws of the devil Kalus would be killed too.

Luna continued and said that Doctor Thomas, who had refused to help this woman lying on the bed to give birth, was going to take this woman to the delivery room and he would help this woman to give birth in front of the camera, and everyone must watch the birth of this new baby. And that Doctor Thomas would be killed by her if he continued to refuse to help this woman to give birth.

Then Luna turned and looked at Doctor Thomas who was standing up with his face full of blood and there were the wounds on his face too. And Luna told Doctor Thomas to push the bed where the pregnant woman was lying until the delivery room.

Then Doctor Thomas walked near to the bed without saying a word and he started to push the bed towards the delivery room. And children followed the nurses and doctors in the delivery room with the two pregnant women who were sitting in wheelchairs.

After a few minutes, the children were in the delivery room of the hospital, and they were watching Doctor Thomas, Doctor Michelle and the nurses who were helping this pregnant woman give birth. And the cameraman was filming what was going on. And there were the fears on the faces of some children while the hearts of other children were beating faster than the normal, as they were all hearing this woman who was yelling in pain as the doctors were asking her to push harder.

Suddenly, the smiles appeared on the faces of the children when they heard the cries of a baby. And The children turned their heads and they saw a little boy who was carried by Doctor Michelle. And they had all their eyes focused on the baby who was crying. Then Doctor Michelle took care of the newborn.

After a few minutes, the baby was given to his mom called Julia. And Julia thanked all the children and the doctors and also nurses who had taken care of her, and who had helped to give birth. And Julia said that she would like to name her son George like the king of the kingdom. And Julia added that she chose the name George for her son to thank all the children for their fight to free the kingdom and to save the kingdom and the future of the kingdom.

Julia went on and said that she would be happy if she could give the name of every child of this kingdom to her son, but that it was impossible. And that she had chosen to name her son George because George was chosen by the children as the king of this kingdom.

And the children clapped their hands and they thanked Julia for naming her son George. Mia told Julia that George would be happy when he would get out of the coma to know that a son was born when he was in the coma, and that this son had been named George like him.

Then Sunshine told Julia to get ready that they must leave now, and they would go to a safe place with all the pregnant women. Then Sunshine also said she would like some volunteers like the doctors and nurses to come with them.

Because they would need the doctors and nurses who would help the pregnant women in case that there would be a pregnant woman who would need the doctors to give birth or for something else. And Doctor Michelle and two nurses told Sunshine that they were coming with her. Then everyone was surprised when they heard Doctor Thomas say that he was coming too.

All the eyes were focused on Doctor Thomas, and they were very astonished to see that Doctor Thomas had changed his mind. Because a few minutes ago, Doctor Thomas wanted to apply the new laws of Kalus in the hospital by performing the abortion on Julia.

Then Doctor Thomas broke the silence and he apologized for his behaviour he had a few minutes ago. And that he was very sorry, if he wanted to perform the abortion on Julia to kill baby George. And the excuses of Doctor Thomas were accepted by the children. And Sunshine accepted that Doctor Thomas joined them. Then they all left the hospital.

After a few minutes, Sunshine and her fellows were getting out of the hospital, and they were hearing the screams of fear coming from the streets. And they could also hear how people were running. And they were wondering what was going on outside, and they could not see what was going outside because they were walking in the yard of the hospital, and the yard of the hospital was surrounded by high walls.

Then the children got out of the gate, and suddenly the expression on their faces changed. And except Sunshine and Luna, the rest of the people were looking with the faces full of terror. And some of them were even shaking with fear, and the hearts of others were beating faster as if they were going to have a heart attack.

As they were all seeing the monsters in the form of skeletons who were walking towards the hospital with the swords and shields in their hands. And there were people in the streets who were running away as fast as they could by yelling in fear because they were afraid of the monsters. Some people were even falling to the ground.

And the children had their eyes widely opened as they were staring at the monsters. And looking at the expression on the faces of the children, it was obvious that they were not realizing that they were seeing the monsters with their eyes.

And it was their first time that they were seeing the monsters with eyes because they had always watched the monsters on television. And there were a lot of questions that were going on in their heads. And some of these questions were, were they really the real monsters? If it was the real monsters where these monsters, where these monsters came from? Were the monsters in the kingdom? Why were these monsters walking towards the hospital? But unfortunately, they could not even answer one of these questions.

Then some children started walking from behind as they were seeing the monsters who were approaching. And Nany asked, "It's the real monsters?"

Luna looked at Nany and answered, "Yes, it's the real monsters."

"Where these monsters come from?" Nany asked.

"The devil Kalus has the satanic powers to make the monsters appear," Luna answered.

"How?" Nany asked.

"The devil Kalus woke up the monsters from their graves through his satanic powers," Luna answered.

"Why Kalus woke up the monsters?" Nany asked.

"To kill us," Luna answered.

"Kill us?" Nany cried out.

"Yes, to kill the children of the kingdom," Luna replied.

"Why kill all the children of the kingdom?" Nany asked.

Luna looked into Nany's eyes and said, "The monsters are the new army of Kalus. So Kalus is using the monsters to fight the children because the children are the enemies of Kalus. And Kalus knew well that the only chance he has to enforce his new laws in the kingdom it's to kill the children first."

"What are we going to do now?" Nany asked.

"We are going to fight the monsters," Luna answered.

"Fight the monsters?" Nany asked.

"Yes, we must fight the monsters," Luna answered.

"How?" Nany asked.

"Just watch what is going to happen," Luna answered.

Then Luna handed her hand and her eyes started spinning, then there were horses that were running towards Luna, and the swords, helmets and the shields that were flying towards Luna. And the children were staring at the horses, the swords, the helmets and the shields with amazed faces. And the children knew well that the horses, the swords, the helmets and the shields were to fight the monsters.

And most of them were wondering if they were really going to fight the monsters, mostly that they had never fought the monsters in their lives. And that they did not even know how to use the horses, the shields, the helmets and the swords to fight.

Then Luna turned and she looked at her fellows and she told them not to feel any fear, and that she knew that they had never fought, and she also knew that they had never used the horses, the shields, the helmets and the swords to fight.

But not to worry because it was easy to fight the monsters, and that the blue light that had shone on them a few hours ago coming from her sword that they had touched would give them strength. Luna added that this blue light that had shone in their bodies would not only give them strength, but this blue light would also protect them and give them courage.

But that did not mean that they could get injured or get killed by the monsters, and that they must be careful because the monsters were very dangerous. And Luna continued and said that only she and Sunshine would start the fight, and the rest would watch the fight and see very well how she and Sunshine fight.

Asher said that he wanted to start the fight too. Luna replied to Asher that it was important to protect the new baby and the two pregnant women who were with them. Because the mission of the monsters was to kill the children, the pregnant women and all the babies who would be born after that the devil Kalus had banned the births in the kingdom.

And Luna went on and said that she and Sunshine would go fight the monsters, and the rest would stay near to the pregnant women and the baby to protect them in case the monsters approached the pregnant women and the baby to kill them. And that everyone could not join the fight because some must stay to protect baby George and the two pregnant women.

Suddenly, Luna was interrupted by Nany who said that the monsters were close. And Luna turned and she looked at the monsters that were already near to them. Then Luna looked at Sunshine and asked, "Are you ready?" Sunshine answered, "There is no more time to lose."

Then Sunshine and Luna rushed towards the horses that were near to them, and they got on the horses. Then Sunshine and Luna handed their hands through the space and they grabbed the helmets, the shields and the swords that were flying in the space. And they wore their helmets on their heads, and they grabbed the sword in their hands and they led the horses towards the monsters.

And the eyes of the children were focused on Sunshine and Luna who were fighting the monsters. And the children were very surprised to see how Sunshine and Luna were fighting.

Sunshine and Luna were sitting on their horses and they were fighting with the rage on their faces, and they were using their swords to cut the heads of the monsters. And they were using the shields to protect themselves against the monsters. And Remy was doing the report on the fight and the cameraman was filming what was happening.

All the offices of the kingdom were empty, people had returned to their homes after hearing that there were monsters in the streets. And most of the inhabitants of the kingdom were in their living room and they were watching on television what was going on with the fear on their faces.

They had hearts that were beating with fear as they were watching on television Sunshine and Luna who were fighting against the monsters. And they were very amazed by the courage of Sunshine and Luna to fight against the monsters. And they were all very worried about their lives, and it was their first time to see the monsters in the kingdom. And they were wondering where the monsters were coming from?

In the street, Sunshine and Luna were still fighting the monsters, and they had already killed a lot of monsters, but there were still many monsters. And despite the fact that Sunshine and Luna were fighting with determination and rage, they were feeling tired. And the eyes of the children were still focused on Sunshine and Luna who were fighting the monsters. And the children could see that Sunshine and Luna were already tired.

Then Asher rushed towards the horse that was near to him, and he got on the horse, and he lifted his head through the space and he saw the helmets, the shields and the swords that were flying in the space. Then Asher handed his hand and he grabbed a helmet, a shield and a sword, then he wore the helmet on his head and he led the horse towards the monsters.

Suddenly, the expression on the faces of the children changed and they were looking with fear as they were seeing the monsters who were coming towards them. Then Mia, Isac and Khloe rushed towards the horses and they got on the horses, and they lifted their hands through the space and they grabbed the shields, the helmets and the swords.

And they wore their helmets and they grabbed the swords in their hands. Then they led the horses towards the monsters and they started fighting the monsters. Asher, Mia, Khloe and Isac were fighting with a lot of difficulties, and they had the difficulty to use the swords correctly.

Then Sunshine told Luna that they must fight near their fellows because they must protect their fellows in case of danger. And Luna said that she was moving near Mia, Isac and Khloe. And Sunshine started leading her horse near Asher. And Isac saw Luna who was leading her horse while fighting against the monsters. Then Isac started to lead his horse towards Luna as fast as he could to help Luna, like Luna was surrounded by the monsters.

Then Isac pushed a loud scream of anger when he saw Luna who had been stabbed in her leg by a monster. Then Isac started fighting with anger, and with all his strength. And Isac was fighting by trying to reach Luna. After a few seconds, Isac was fighting near Luna.

And despite the fact that the children were looking tired, they were fighting with a lot of energy. And the children were not really feeling this fatigue in their bodies because the blue light that had shone in their bodies coming from Luna's word was giving them the energy and strength.

After a few minutes, the fight was over, and the children had killed all the monsters. Then Sunshine checked to see if all her companions were doing well. And Sunshine noticed that Luna had been injured, and Sunshine said that they must take Luna to the hospital. But Luna refused and Luna said that she was fine. But Isac told Luna that he was worried about her, and that it was important to see a doctor with her wound.

And Luna told Isac that she could not see a doctor now because there was no time to go see a doctor now because they must find all the pregnant women of the kingdom before the army of Kalus finds these pregnant women. Because if the army of Kalus found the pregnant women before children, the army of Kalus would kill the pregnant women.

And Isac told Luna that there were no more monsters because they had already killed all the monsters. And Luna told Isac that the monsters could appear at any time. Then Sunshine told her fellows that they must find a bus because they needed a bus to go find other pregnant women. Then the children, Julia, the pregnant women, the doctors and nurses started walking in the street.

And the children were looking for a bus. Then Sunshine saw a bus that was parked in the street. And Sunshine told her fellows that they were going to use this bus that was parked in the street. Then they started walking towards the bus, and Sunshine's eyes were focused on the bus and her eyes were turning. Then they reached the bus, and Sunshine opened the bus's door and everyone got on the bus.

Then Sunshine took the wheel and she used her magic to start the engine and she drove away. Then the children spent the rest of their day looking for pregnant women. Sunshine and Luna were using their magic to look for the pregnant women. And through their magic, they could see where the pregnant women were hiding.

And the children were fighting the monsters each time when they were facing the monsters. And the children were fighting the monsters to protect the pregnant women and newborn because the monsters were always appearing to kill pregnant women with the newborn. It was evening, Sunshine and her fellows took all the pregnant women that they had found to Khloe's house.

It was midnight, Kalus had knelt in his magic room, and he was trying to talk to Lord without success. And Kalus was calling Lord but unfortunately, Lord was not answering. And Kalus had started to be worried about the fact that Lord was not answering because it's been more than an hour that he was calling Lord without success. And mostly that he had an appointment to talk with Lord.

And suddenly a voice said, "You betrayed me."

"Lord?" Kalus cried out.

"Yes, it's me," Lord answered.

"How I betrayed you?" Kalus asked.

"You did not tell me the truth about the powers and magic of Luna," Lord answered.

"I told you the truth about the powers and magic of Luna thirteen years ago when Luna was born," Kalus said.

"No, you did not tell me the truth," Lord said.

"What do you mean?" Kalus asked.

"You had told me that you had the same powers as Luna," Lord said.

"It's true," Kalus said.

"I know all your powers, but I do not know all the powers of Luna because Luna has the powers that I do not know." Lord said.

"It's true that Luna has three powers that you do not know," Kalus said.

"Why did you not tell me about these three powers of Luna?" Lord asked.

"Because of myself, I have no idea about these three powers of Luna," Kalus answered.

"How do you not know these three powers of Luna, if you have the same powers as Luna?" Lord asked.

"I was born with twenty-one powers like Luna because all the heirs and heiresses to the crown and the throne of the kingdom were born with twenty-one powers. But between those twenty-one powers, only eighteen were identical and three were completely different." Kalus answered.

"I do not understand," Lord said.

"I know eighteen powers of the twenty-one powers of Luna, like Luna knows eighteen of my twenty-one powers because these eighteen powers are the same, but the rest of the three powers are different," Kalus replied.

"It means all the heirs and heiresses to the crown of the kingdom were born with twenty-one, and eighteen of these twenty-one powers were the same for all the heirs and heiresses. And the rest of the three powers were different," Lord said.

"Yes," Kalus answered.

"Which are the eighteen powers between the twenty-one who are identical?" Lord asked.

"The eighteen first powers are the same for all the heirs and heiresses, and the rest three last powers are completely different." Kalus answered.

"Can you have an idea about the last three powers of Luna?" Lord asked.

"No, I have no idea about the last three powers of Luna," Kalus answered.

"I understand everything now," Lord said.

"What do you mean?" Kalus asked.

"Luna is the mysterious enemy," Lord answered.

"What?" Kalus cried out.

"Luna is the one who always helps Sunshine to fight me," Lord said.

"How did you find out that Luna is the mysterious enemy?" Sunshine asked.

"Sunshine had been saved by Luna when Sunshine was dying," Lord answered.

"Did you see how Luna saved Sunshine?" Kalus asked.

"Yes," Lord answered.

"I must kill Luna now," Kalus said.

"Luna is even more dangerous than Sunshine because if Luna had not saved Sunshine, Sunshine should be in her grave now," Lord said.

"Sunshine and Luna are the two cursed children of this kingdom," Kalus said.

"We need a new plan because we are losing the fight against Sunshine and Luna right now," Lord said.

"How are we losing the fight against Sunshine and Luna?" Kalus asked.

"The children had succeeded in killing all the monsters. And the children are looking for the pregnant women now," Lord answered.

"We must send other monsters to the children," Kalus said.

"No, because the monsters are not the solution," Lord said.

"What is the solution?" Kalus asked.

"I have to think about something else," Lord answered.

"I am wondering how these children got the courage to fight the monsters," Kalus said.

"Sunshine and Luna gave motivation to their fellows," Lord said.

"How can we stop these children?" Kalus asked.

"Only death can stop these children," Lord answered.

"I thought that with their fellows in the coma, they should be discouraged," Kalus said.

"It's impossible to put all the fellows of Sunshine and Luna in a coma," Lord said.

"Why is it impossible?" Kalus asked.

"I use my own energy to keep the children in the coma, so I will feel weak, and less powerful if I put all the fellows of Sunshine and Luna in the coma," Lord said.

"I understand why you can not put all the fellows of Sunshine and Luna in the coma," Kalus said.

"A woman called Julia gave birth to a baby called George yesterday," Lord said.

"I would kill this baby named George, Julia, and all those who had helped Julia to give birth," Kalus said.

"Julia, George and those who had helped Julia to give birth are with the children now. And it's the children who had saved Julia," Lord said.

"These children are more dangerous than what I have imagined," Kalus said.

"The only solution is to kill Sunshine and Luna," Lord said.

Then Lord and Kalus spent the rest of the night talking about the situation of the kingdom. And to find how to stop the children, and mostly how to kill Sunshine and Luna. Lord and Kalus were also very worried about the fact that the new laws of Kalus were not enforced by the inhabitants of the kingdom.

Lord and Kalus were also thinking how to kill all the pregnant women who were in the kingdom now. Because Lord knew well that he must prevent these pregnant women from giving birth. Because if all these pregnant women gave birth, the worst would happen. And it would be his end and the end of Kalus, also the end of their project to turn the kingdom of Manitoba into the kingdom of vampires but it would be mostly the victory of the children.

CHAPTER IX

THE FIGHT BETWEEN LUNA AND KALUS AND THE BIRTH OF THE SAVIOR

It was five in the morning, the inhabitants of the kingdom were still in bed deeply asleep. And they were suddenly awakened by the cold that was entering the house. And people got out of the beds and they were astonished to see that it was raining outside.

Because it was summer, and they had never seen the rain during the summer. And there was darkness in the room, and they tried to turn on the light to look for the blankets, but unfortunately, there was no light.

And there were also people who wanted to drink water, but they noticed that there was no water. And some people were using the torches to look for the blankets, while other people were trying to get ready to go to their daily occupation. And people were very surprised to notice that their cell phones and home phones were not working.

And they checked their phones, and they noticed that everything was fine and that their phones were charged. But they were still not understanding why their phones were not working. And it was the first time that they had this problem, that their phones were not working, that they could not make a phone call.

Then some people approached the door to get out, but the expression on their faces changed when they opened the door. And they were looking at the weather outside with amazed faces and they were seeing the storm outside. And they immediately closed the doors and they returned to the beds, and they covered their bodies with the blankets.

Sunshine and her fellows were in the living room, and they had spent their whole night in the living room because the pregnant women had slept in the bedrooms. And the children were feeling very cold and they were looking very tired because they had spent their whole night talking about the situation of the kingdom. Except Sunshine and Luna, the rest of the children were very surprised to see that there was a storm outside, and that there was neither light nor water.

Sunshine and Luna were very worried not only about the storm that was outside, but mostly about the cold that was getting inside the houses, about the fact that there was neither light nor water. Sunshine and Luna knew that the storm that was outside was triggered by Lord and Kalus to prevent people from getting out of their houses.

Sunshine and Luna also knew that the inhabitants of the kingdom could not live without light and water. Because without light and water, people would die of thirst and starvation because they would not be able to make food because the cooker worked with the light in the kingdom. And people would not even be able to drink tea or coffee or even take their breakfast because there was no light and water.

Sunshine and Luna were mostly worried about people who were in the hospital, and especially people who were in the emergency rooms. Sunshine and Luna did not have the powers to bring back the light and the water in the kingdom.

So, only Kalus and Lord could use their powers to bring back the light and water. Sunshine knew that she could not let the kingdom in the darkness, mostly with pregnant women and people who were sick in the hospitals. Because they would need light and water to do everything, mostly if there was a pregnant woman who wanted to give birth.

Then Sunshine got up from her chair and she started walking in the living room thinking what to do. And Sunshine was very afraid not only because there was neither light nor water in the kingdom, but mostly because there was still a pregnant woman who was missing.

Sunshine and Luna had seen eleven pregnant women through their magic, but they had succeeded in finding only ten. And Sunshine knew well that there was still a pregnant woman somewhere in the kingdom, and she was worried about this pregnant woman. Because this pregnant woman would be killed by Lord if Lord found this pregnant woman before the children. And Sunshine was using her magic to try to find this pregnant woman without success.

Then Sunshine walked till the door and she opened the door and got out. Sunshine was in the veranda and she was staring at the storm with a face empty of expression. And looking at the expression on Sunshine's face, we could see that she was completely lost, and she did not know what to do, and it seemed that she had lost control of the kingdom. And for the first time, Sunshine did not know what to do, and she was unable to find a solution on what was going on.

Then Sunshine turned her head on her left when she heard a noise, and she saw Luna who was looking through the sky. Sunshine was looking at Luna with an amazed face wondering what was going on, as she was seeing Luna who was looking through the sky with a face full of fear. And Sunshine was wondering why there was fear on Luna's face.

Then Luna turned her head and looked at Sunshine and said, "the kingdom is in danger."

"What?" Sunshine asked.

"People are prisoners in their houses," Luna answered.

"What do you mean?" Sunshine asked.

"People could not get out of their houses because there are the microbes in the spaces," Luna answered.

"What are the microbes?" Sunshine asked.

"The microbes are worse than the poisons because the microbes can kill and paralyse people," Luna answered.

"I do not understand," Sunshine said.

"The microbes are used only when the kingdom is attacked by the enemies, and the microbes are used to kill the enemies," Luna said.

"Who used the microbes?" Sunshine asked.

Luna looked into Sunshine's eyes and said," Only the current king or the current queen has the power to use the microbes. And the microbes could only be used when the kingdom was invaded by the enemies." And Luna added, "The whole kingdom must be notified a week not to get out of their houses, and to make enough errands and to get enough stuff, before the microbes are being used."

"The microbes had already been used in the kingdom?" Sunshine asked.

"Yes, the microbes had been used three times in the history of the kingdom when the kingdom had been invaded by the enemies," Luna answered.

"Why did Kalus use the microbes?" Sunshine asked.

"To control the kingdom, and to prevent people from getting out of their houses," Luna answered.

"Why Kalus did not warn people that he was going to use the microbes?" Sunshine asked.

"Kalus does not care about people, he does not care that people die," Luna answered.

"Kalus is a real devil without a heart, and this Kalus is able to burn the whole kingdom just to keep his power and his throne," Sunshine said.

"Kalus sent the microbes outside to kill the children," Luna said.

Sunshine looked into Luna's eyes and said, "Especially you and me."

"Not you and me, but our fellows," Luna said.

"I do not understand," Sunshine said.

Luna looked into Sunshine's eyes and said, "Kalus knew well that the microbes could not kill you and me because we were born with the powers and magic, and we are protected by our powers. But Kalus knew that our fellows were not born with the powers, and that he could kill our fellows by using the microbes."

"I understand," Sunshine said.

"Kalus wants to kill our fellows to make us weak and to push us to give up the fight," Luna said.

"What can we do now?" Sunshine asked.

"We must get rid of these microbes in space," Luna answered.

"How?" Sunshine asked.

"We must go to the sacred forest to find the leaves of a tree called Baoba to get rid of the microbes," Luna answered.

"How would we use the leaves of Baoba to get rid of the microbes?" Sunshine asked.

"When we would burn the leaves of Baboa, the microbes would run away. Because the microbes could not live or survive with the scent coming from the leaves of the tree called Baoba. Because these leaves of Baoba contain the poison that kills the microbes," Luna answered.

"There is still a pregnant woman that we have not found," Sunshine said.

Luna said, "I know, but we must get rid of the microbes first because even if we found this pregnant woman now, we could not get in the storm with her because she would be killed by the microbes if we get in the storm with her when the microbes are still in the space."

"Are you going alone to the sacred forest?" Sunshine asked.

"No, I am going with you," Luna answered.

"How about these pregnant women in the house?" Sunshine asked.

"I can not go alone because I can be attacked on the road by Lord and Kalus," Luna answered.

"I have a solution," Sunshine said.

"Which solution?" Luna asked.

"I can lock the house's door through my magic to prevent someone from entering and leaving the house," Sunshine answered.

Luna smiled at Sunshine and said, "It's a good solution."

Then Sunshine turned and looked at the house, and her eyes started spinning, and the light got out from her eyes and shone on the house. Then Sunshine looked at Luna and said that they must leave now. Then they walked to the car, and they got in the car. And Luna touched the wheel with her hands, and the light got out from her eyes and shone on the wheel, then the engine of the car started and she drove away.

After an hour, Sunshine and Luna were still driving on an empty road. Luna asked, "Why did you not kill Kalus?"

"Because Kalus is mystically protected by Lord," Sunshine answered.

"Does that mean we would never free the kingdom?" Luna asked.

"It's since I was born that I have been trying to kill Kalus without success," Sunshine replied.

"We will never free the kingdom, if we do not kill Kalus," Luna said.

"I am stronger and more powerful than Kalus, but I always failed to kill him," Sunshine said.

"We must find a solution to get rid of Kalus," Luna said.

"It would be not easy, but it's not impossible," Sunshine said.

"We must get rid of Kalus as soon as possible, and it's the only way to save the kingdom," Luna said.

"We must start to find the weakness of Lord because the only solution to kill Kalus, it's to kill Lord first," Sunshine said.

"I hate this devil called Lord," Luna said.

"I hate Lord more," Sunshine said.

"Why did Lord and Kalus ban births in the kingdom?" Luna asked.

"I have no idea," Sunshine said.

Suddenly, Luna pushed a loud scream of fear, like the car had started to shake. Luna had difficulties controlling the wheel and Luna had lost control of the car. And suddenly, Sunshine and Luna were trembling with cold because the cold was getting on the car.

Luna looked at Sunshine and said that the car was attacked by the bad spirits. And Sunshine said that there were the satanic trees around, and that these evil spirits were coming from the satanic trees. Then Luna and Sunshine started to freeze, and it was impossible for Luna to control the wheel of the car.

Sunshine noticed that the car was losing the direction of the road, and she put her hand on Luna's hand that was on the wheel. And Sunshine's eyes started turning, and a red light started shining between Sunshine's hand and Luna's hand, like Sunshine had put her hand on Luna's hand that was on the wheel. And this red light was getting out from Sunshine's body to get into Luna's body, and Sunshine was giving a part of her energy to Luna to help Luna to control the wheel and the warm Luna's body.

Luna had regained control of the car and she was driving without any problem, and she was also feeling less cold, as she was receiving the energy from Sunshine. But Sunshine was feeling more and more cold, as she was transferring a part of her energy to Luna. Then Luna looked at Sunshine and said, "I think you must stop transferring me, your energy because I can drive with what you already give me. And you need the energy to stay warm." And Sunshine removed her hand from Luna's hand.

Despite the fact that the car was still attacked by the evil spirits, Luna was driving as fast as she could. And suddenly, Sunshine and Luna pushed a loud scream and they were looking with their faces full of fear, as they were seeing a big stone that was flying in space and coming through the car. Then Sunshine opened the car's door and she started to try to get on the roof of the car.

And the cold was getting inside the car more and more. And Luna asked Sunshine where Sunshine was going? Sunshine answered

Luna not to worry and just focus on driving. Luna told Sunshine that it was dangerous what she(Sunshine) was trying to do. And Sunshine replied to Luna that they did not have a choice, and they must take the risk.

Then Sunshine reached the roof of the car, and a violent rain was falling on her and she was shaking with cold. And Sunshine's eyes were focused on the big stone that was flying in space coming through the car.

Then Sunshine took a deep breath and she pointed her both hands through this stone. Sunshine's eyes started spinning, and a red light got out from both of her palm's hands and went through the stone that was coming through the car. And this red light coming from Sunshine's palm hands was shining on the stone. And Sunshine was shaking more and more as if she was going to fall.

And Sunshine was shaking more because she was losing more energy as her magic was in contact with the stone. And Sunshine was trying to break the stone to prevent the stone from hitting the car. And the light that was coming from Sunshine was slowing the speed of the stone, and the stone was flying very slowly by shaking. And the red light that was shining on the stone was making the stone tremble, and this red light was trying to break the stone.

And Sunshine was feeling more and more cold, and weak and she was also losing her strength. But Sunshine was trying to be focused on the stone that was in space. Then Sunshine started screaming and her face was full of anger and there were the veins that were coming out around her neck.

And the light was getting out more and more from Sunshine's palm hands and going through the stone, and the stone was shaking more and more. Then the stone stopped moving, and the stone was just turning in space. And the stone was becoming more and more weak, and the light that was shining on the stone was preventing the stone from moving and was making the stone weaker. Then the stone fell on the ground and collapsed.

Then Sunshine saw a big tree trunk that was flying in space and coming towards the car. And Sunshine pointed her both hands towards this tree trunk and a red light started getting out from her palm's hands and going through this tree trunk. And this tree trunk started shaking as this red light coming from Sunshine's hands were shining on this tree trunk. And this tree trunk started flying slowly as this red light was preventing this tree trunk from flying faster.

Then Sunshine started yelling and her face was full of anger, then the light was getting out of her palm's hands faster and faster and going through the tree trunk. Then Sunshine turned her hands to the left and this tree trunk went and fell in the forest that was on the left side of the road.

And Sunshine started breathing deeply, and she was feeling tired and weak. And Sunshine was still standing up on the car's roof in the cold and the rain was falling on her. And she did not get in the car because she wanted to protect Luna and herself in case that another obstacle appeared. Because by staying on the car's roof, she could easily prevent an obstacle from happening.

Suddenly, the expression on Sunshine's face changed and she was looking with an astonished face as she was seeing the sun in front of her. And Sunshine was wondering why it was raining where she was, why there was the sun a few meters from her. And Sunshine was trying to understand, but it was impossible for her to find an explanation.

Then Sunshine started feeling less cold as the car was approaching the sun, and she lifted her head through the sky and she noticed that the sky was blue, while since she had left the house the sky was dark.

Then Sunshine started feeling the sun that was hitting her skin, and her dress was getting dry. Sunshine turned her head around and she was seeing the forest with the tall trees, and she also noticed that the rain had not fallen in this forest. Then the car stopped and Luna got out of the car, and Luna asked Sunshine to get out of the car.

And Sunshine jumped from the car's roof and landed on the ground. Then Sunshine and Luna started walking by talking.

"Where are we?" Sunshine asked.

"In the sacred forest," Luna answered.

"Why is it not raining in the sacred forest?" Sunshine asked.

"Because the rain is not natural," Luna answered.

"What do you mean?" Sunshine asked.

Luna looked at Sunshine and said, "Only the natural rain could fall in the sacred forest. And it's not raining in the sacred forest because the rain that it's falling on the kingdom is not natural, and this rain was triggered by Lord and Kalus."

"Why Lord and Kalus could not make the rain fall in the sacred forest?" Sunshine asked.

"Because, the sacred forest is protected by the ancestors of the kingdom, and only the natural events could happen in the sacred forest," Luna answered.

"How did you know the existence of the sacred forest?" Sunshine asked.

"I found out about the sacred forest when I read the secret book about the secrets of the traditions and culture of the kingdom," Luna answered.

"People have the right to come to the sacred forest?" Sunshine asked.

"People used to come to the sacred forest to find the certain herbs, the tree's bark, and tree root that they used to make the traditional remedy with," Luna answered.

"Why People stop coming here?" Sunshine asked.

"Because the devil Kalus prohibited people from coming here," Luna answered.

"Who takes care of this huge sacred forest?" Sunshine asked.

"Nobody because everything in this sacred forest is sacred and natural," Luna answered.

"Who cut the herbs in this sacred forest?" Sunshine asked.

"We do not have the herbs in this sacred forest because all the herbs of this forest are used for the remedy," Luna answered.

"Since the existence of this forest nothing has changed?" Sunshine asked.

"Yes, everything in this forest is still the same since the existence of this forest, the herbs do not get old and the trees do not die," Luna answered.

"This sacred forest is very big," Sunshine said.

"Yes, this sacred forest is very huge because there is a place that only people who are born with the powers like the king, the queen and heir or the heiress to the crown can visit," Luna said.

"Why is there a place that only the members of the royal family who have the powers could visit?" Sunshine asked.

"Because this place in the sacred forest is dangerous, and the worst could happen at any time, and mysterious things could happen, and people need the powers to cut the herbs in this place. And also, only the powerful people could get the tree's leaves, tree's roots and tree's bark in this place of the sacred forest. And everything in this place like the trees, the herbs, the river, the sand and others were used only in case that the kingdom was in danger and when the kingdom needed to be saved," Luna answered.

"Why do you say this place is in the sacred forest?" Sunshine asked.

"Because we are walking in the place of the sacred forest where only the powerful people can walk," Luna answered.

"But I am not an heiress to the crown," Sunshine said.

"It's true that you are not an heiress to the crown, but you are born with the natural powers, so you can walk in this part of the sacred forest because you have the natural powers in you," Luna said.

"It means all those who are born with the natural powers could walk in this place of the forest," Sunshine said.

"Yes," Luna replied.

"How about Kalus, who has two different kinds of powers in him that are the satanic powers and the natural powers?" Sunshine asked.

"Kalus has stopped coming into this sacred forest since the day that he had received the satanic powers from Lord. And if Kalus came into the sacred forest with the satanic powers in his body, he would be paralysed or he would die. Because the spirits that are in the sacred forest could only accept the natural powers," Luna answered.

Then Sunshine and Luna got inside a small hut, and there were two small beds and the stuff in the hut. And Sunshine asked Luna why there was a hut in the sacred forest? And Luna answered Sunshine that the hut was built by the first king in the history of the kingdom.

Luna added that the tradition of Manitoba required the current king to come and spend a weekend in the sacred forest at least once a month. Sunshine smiled at Luna and said it meant George would come to the sacred forest at least each month to spend a weekend. Luna said that it was not easy to be the king or queen of Manitoba because being the king or queen of Manitoba meant making a lot of sacrifices, by following and respecting the tradition.

Then Sunshine and Luna picked up two small bags that were on the ground, and they left the hut. Sunshine and Luna were walking in the forest while talking. After a few minutes of walking, they stopped under a big tree, and Sunshine was staring at this tree with an amazed face and looking at the expression on the face of Sunshine, it was obvious that it was her first time to see such a big tree.

Then Sunshine looked at Luna and asked Luna why the tree that was in front of them was bigger and taller? Luna answered Sunshine that they were under the tree called Baoba, and that it was the bigger and taller of the sacred forest.

And it was the most powerful tree in the forest, and the leaves, the roots and bark of Baoba tree could be used to cure all kinds of sicknesses and also to get rid of the bad spirits and the monsters, and even to protect the kingdom in case of danger. Sunshine asked Luna how they were going to get the leaves of Baoba's tree? And Luna answered that she would use her magic to get the leaves of Baoba's tree.

Then Luna lifted her two hands through the sky and her eyes started spinning, and the fingers of her nails became long, and the light started getting out from her fingernails and going through the tree. And the tree's branches started shaking, and the tree's leaves started falling to the ground.

After a few minutes, Luna lowered her hands, and the tree's leaves stopped falling. Then Sunshine andLuna picked up the tree's leaves that were on the ground and they put these tree's leaves in the bags they had. Then they walked to where they had parked the car, and they got in the car. Then Sunshine drove away.

After an hour of driving, the car started shaking. Sunshine told Luna that the car was attacked by evil spirits. And Luna replied that she was not surprised because they were no longer in the space of the sacred forest. And Luna added that the bad spirits got their energies from the satanic trees that were planted on the sides of the road.

Sunshine said that after the death of Kalus, they must destroy these satanic trees. Luna said that these satanic trees were planted by Lord and Kalus to prevent people from going to the sacred forest. And that it was necessary to destroy these satanic trees before people started going to the sacred forest after the death of Kalus.

Because the bad spirits coming from these satanic trees would kill people who would try to reach the sacred forest if they did not destroy these satanic trees before people started going to the sacred forest.

Suddenly, Sunshine pushed a loud scream of fear, as she was seeing the road that was split in two, and Sunshine's eyes started spinning. And the light got out from Sunshine's eyes and the car flew into space.

Sunshine told Luna that the evil spirits had destroyed the road, and that there were big holes on the road, and that they could not drive on the road. Luna said that she hoped that they would not get into an accident. Sunshine said that they would need a lot of energy to drive in space because the car needed a lot of energy to stay in space.

And Luna replied that she would transfer her energy to Sunshine, to help Sunshine to keep the car in space. And Sunshine replied to Luna that Luna would need her(Luna) energy to fight outside. Luna asked Sunshine what Sunshine meant? And Sunshine replied to Luna to look in front of her. And suddenly the expression on Luna changed and she was looking with fear on her face, as she was seeing the monsters that were flying in the space. And these monsters were flying towards the car.

Then Luna's eyes started spinning and she opened the car's door, and she flew in space. Then Luna was flying through the sword and shield that were flying in space, and it was Luna who had made this sword and shield appear in space through her magic.

Then Luna grabbed the sword and the shield in space, and she started flying towards the monsters who were flying through the car. Then Luna started to fight the monsters by using her sword, and the rain was falling more and more with a huge storm.

And despite the fact that Luna was fighting in the rain and in the cold, she was very strong and she was succeeding in keeping her balance in space by fighting. And there was a strong wind that was blowing more and more and it was also raining more and more, this wind was blowing to weaken Luna and mostly to prevent Luna from fighting and from having a balance in space.

And the monsters were trying to reach the car but it was not easy for them because Luna was fighting the monsters to prevent them from reaching the car. And the monsters wanted to reach the car not only to destroy the car to prevent Sunshine and Luna from reaching downtown. But mostly to destroy the leaves of the tree that were in the car. And these monsters were sent by Kalus not only to kill Sunshine and Luna, but mostly to destroy the leaves of tree Baoba that were in the car.

Because Kalus knew that Sunshine and Luna would use the leaves of this tree to get rid of the microbes that were in space. And if Sunshine and Luna succeeded in getting rid of these microbes in space, it meant that Lord and Kalus would lose control of the kingdom, and the children would regain control of the kingdom.

And the children could continue to look for the missing pregnant woman if the children succeeded in regaining the control of the kingdom. And this missing pregnant woman was very important for Kalus and Lord, and it was important for them to find this missing woman before children.

Because if this missing pregnant woman was found by the children, it would be the end of the Lord and Kalus. Because this missing pregnant woman had something that Lord and Kalus were looking for. And it was important for Lord and Kalus that this pregnant woman did not give birth, so Lord and Kalus were looking for this pregnant woman to kill her.

Sunshine was still driving in space, and she was looking tired and weak because she was using a lot of her energy to drive in space. And the fact that Sunshine was using a lot of the energy of her magic was making her weak and tired.

And Sunshine wanted to land on the ground, but it was impossible because there were not only huge holes on the ground, but the road was also divided. Then Sunshine looked at Luna who was fighting against the monsters, and the expression of her face changed and she was looking with fear on her face as she was seeing Luna who was surrounded by the monsters.

Then Sunshine understood that she must do something not only to help Luna, but mostly to get rid of the monsters. Then Sunshine opened one of the bags that was near her, and she took the tree's leaves that were inside that bag.

And Sunshine stared at these tree's leaves and her eyes started spinning. Then, the light got out from her eyes and shone on these tree's leaves, and the fire appeared on these tree's leaves. Sunshine was staring at these leaves that were burning, then she opened the car's door and she threw the leaves outside.

These tree's leaves were flying in space by burning, and these tree's leaves were flying towards the monsters. And these tree's leaves were flying in the rain, but the falling rain had no impact on these tree's leaves and the falling rain could not put out the fire that was on these tree's leaves.

And if the rain did not have an impact on these tree's leaves or if the rain could not put out the fire on these tree's leaves, it was because the rain was not natural. And these tree's leaves were more powerful and stronger than the falling rain. And suddenly the monsters started to become weak and the monsters were flying with the difficulties.

And it was the smoke coming from these tree's leaves that was making the monsters weak and this smoke was also preventing the monster from flying faster. Because the smell coming from this smoke was a poison for the monsters, and this smell was preventing the monsters from breathing.

Then some monsters started to fall to the ground because they could not fly anymore, while other monsters were trying to run away because they could not fight anymore. And because they could not only breath but they had also lost all their strength.

Then Luna flew up to the car, and she got in the car. And Luna told Sunshine that Sunshine got a great idea to use the tree's leaves to get rid of the monsters. Sunshine looked at Luna and she saw the small wounds and the blood on Luna's face and Sunshine understood that Luna had been injured by the monsters. Sunshine told Luna that Luna had been very brave to fight against these monsters.

Luna smiled at Sunshine without saying a word, then Luna put her hand on Sunshine's hand that was on the wheel. And there was a blue light that was shining between Sunshine's hand and Luna's hand. And this blue light was coming from Luna's body and getting in Sunshine's body and this blue light was a part of Luna's energy.

And Luna was giving a part of her energy to Sunshine to allow Sunshine to be more powerful and stronger, and to allow Sunshine to drive faster. And suddenly, the car started to go faster, and it was Luna's energy in Sunshine's body who was helping Sunshine to drive faster.

It was noon, the streets of the kingdom were empty, and there was no car on the road, and the offices, the shops, and the malls were closed. It was still raining, and there was a huge rain and a storm that was hitting the kingdom and a strong wind was blowing.

Except Sunshine and Luna who were outside, all the inhabitants of the kingdom were in their house, and most of them were still in their beds with the blankets on them. And most of them had still not eaten since this morning, and those who had eaten had eaten the cold food because there was still no light and water.

And for most people, it was the end of the kingdom because it was the first time that they were living in this situation. And mostly that since Kalus had been crowned the king, the kingdom was getting worse and worse with the horrible events, like the death of the children in the past, the torture of the children, the monsters that had appeared in the kingdom, and the kingdom in the darkness today without light.

There were the leaves of the tree called Baoba that were burning by flying in the sky. Despite the fact that it was raining, there were the tree's leaves that were burning in the sky by flying. The rain had no impact on these tree's leaves that were burning because this rain was not natural.

So as this rain was not natural, this rain could not put out the fire that was on these tree's leaves. And the microbes that were in space were running away and some were dying. Because it was impossible for the microbes to live or to survive with the smell coming from the burning tree's leaves. Because the tree's leaves were the poison for the microbes, and the smoke coming from these tree's leaves prevented the microbes from breathing.

Sunshine and Luna were driving in the streets of the kingdom, and they were throwing the tree's leaves through the windows of the car's doors. Sunshine and Luna were using their magic to put fire on these tree's leaves before throwing these tree's leaves outside, and these tree's leaves were flying through the sky to kill the microbes that were in space.

And the storm was over, the wind had stopped, but the rain had not stopped but it was raining very slowly. And the reason why the storm and the wind had stopped was because there were no more microbes in space. Because the storm and the wind were hitting the kingdom thanks to the microbes. So it was the microbes who had allowed the storm and wind to hit the kingdom.

And the storm and wind had stopped because there were no more microbes in the spaces. And it was also the reason why it was raining slowly because it was the microbes who had helped the rain to be stronger by giving the strength to the rain.

In Khloe's house, everyone was worried about Sunshine and Luna because since this morning that Sunshine and Luna had left the house, they had not come back. And people had tried to open the door without success.

And the children had even tried to break the door without success, and they wanted to break the door to get out to look for Sunshine and Luna. And the children were afraid that maybe Sunshine and Luna had been killed outside by the monsters.

Then Asher turned his head towards the door when he heard a noise coming from the door. And suddenly the expression on his face changed and he was looking at Sunshine and Luna who were walking in the room with a smile on their faces.

And everyone in the house was very happy to see that Sunshine and Luna were still alive. Asher asked Sunshine and Luna where they were? Luna answered to Asher that she and Sunshine went to the sacred forest to find the tree's leaves to make the remedy.

And Asher asked Luna if there was someone who was sick? Luna answered Asher that no one was sick for the moment and that she hoped that no one would be sick, but that it was not safe to stay with the pregnant women without remedy because these pregnant women could need the remedy at any time. Asher asked Luna if the tree's leaves that were in the bag that she had held in her hand were the remedy? Luna answered yes. Then Luna asked Asher how the pregnant women were doing?

And Asher answered that so far, the pregnant women were doing well, just that they were very tired and hungry, and that pregnant women had not eaten since this morning. Because there was no light and no water to make them something to eat. And Luna replied to Asher that she would be back and that she was going to the kitchen.

Then Luna started walking towards the kitchen. Sunshine was talking with a pregnant woman who was sitting in the living room. And Sunshine was trying to know how this pregnant woman was doing. Then Sunshine saw Luna who was walking towards the kitchen, and Sunshine told this pregnant woman that she would be back. Then Sunshine turned and walked towards the kitchen.

Luna was walking in the kitchen thinking and she was very nervous, and her face was full of rage. Then Luna turned her head towards the door as she had heard the footsteps and she was looking at Sunshine who was walking towards her. Sunshine looked into Luna's eyes and said that she imagined that Luna was nervous about the situation of pregnant women who had not eaten since this morning.

And Luna replied to Sunshine that there were not only the pregnant women who had not eaten since this morning, but that there were also the babies who were in the wombs of these pregnant women. Because the babies who were in the wombs of these pregnant women were in danger, like these pregnant women who carried these babies in their wombs had not eaten since this morning, and these pregnant women had not even drunk the water.

And Luna went on and said that there were also all the inhabitants of the kingdom who had not probably eaten and drunk water. And there were women who were breastfeeding the babies in the kingdom, and who may not have breastfed their babies since this morning because they had not eaten to breastfeed their babies.

And there were also people who were sick in the hospital beds who may not have taken their medication since this morning because they did not eat food and because there was no water to take the medication. And Luna added that she was the one who was using a part of the energy of her magic to keep people who were in the coma in the hospitals alive.

Sunshine asked Luna what they could do because they did not have the power that could turn on the light in the kingdom. Luna looked into Sunshine's eyes and said that she had the solution.

Sunshine replied to Luna that the only solution they had was to kill Kalus, but that the only way to kill Kalus, was to kill Lord first, and they did not know yet how to kill Lord. Luna replied to Sunshine that she had another solution. And Sunshine asked Luna what was this solution? Luna answered that they would talk about it when she would be back.

Then Luna tried to walk towards the door, but Sunshine asked Luna to wait. And Sunshine walked towards Luna, then Sunshine stopped face to Luna and she handed her two hands to Luna by looking into Luna's eyes without saying a word. Then Luna handed her hands and she grabbed Sunshine's hands as she had understood why Sunshine had handed the hands.

Then Sunshine's eyes started spinning and there was a blue light that was shining between Sunshine's hand and Luna's hand. And this light was coming out from Sunshine's body and getting inside Luna's body. And Sunshine was giving a part of the energy of her magic to Luna to make Luna more powerful and stronger because Sunshine knew that Luna was going to confront Kalus.

After a few minutes, Sunshine and Luna walked into the living room. Luna told her fellows that she would be back and she walked towards the door before one of her fellows opened her mouth to say a word.

And Isac asked Sunshine where Luna was going? Sunshine answered Isac that Luna went to look for a technician who could fix the light. Isac asked Sunshine where Luna could find a technician with the bad weather that was outside.

Sunshine told Isac not to worry that Luna knew someone who could solve this problem of light in the kingdom. But Sunshine had just lied to Isac because she could not tell Isac that Luna had gone to fight Kalus because Kalus was responsible for the fact that there was neither light nor water in the kingdom. Then Abraham, who was the grand dad of Khloe came and sat with the children and he started talking about the history of the kingdom to the children.

Kalus was sitting in his living room alone, and he was thinking about how to kill Sunshine and Luna. Then Kalus turned his head towards the door as he heard footsteps. And suddenly, the expression on Kalus's face changed and he was looking with an astonished face as he was seeing Luna who was walking towards him.

Then Kalus got up from his chair and started walking towards Luna with his eyes focused on Luna. Then Kalus stopped face to Luna and they were looking at each other in the eyes with their faces full of rage with the silence.

After a few seconds, Luna broke the silence, "I want light and water in the kingdom now."

"I want all the pregnant women of the kingdom and the baby called George who was born yesterday," Kalus said.

"Why do you want the baby called George and all the pregnant women of the kingdom?" Luna asked.

"It's personal," Kalus answered.

"Why did you ban all the women from giving birth?" Luna asked.

"It's personal," Kalus answered.

"Why did you make a pact with the devil called Lord?" Luna asked.

"I have another vision for my kingdom and my people," Kalus answered.

"Which vision?" Luna asked.

"I want to turn this kingdom into the kingdom of a vampire and create the kingdom of vampires with a population of vampires. And I want to stay immortal," Kalus answered.

"Even the vampires die," Luna said.

"Yes, even the vampires die, but I would be the god of the vampires also called the king of the vampires and the god of the vampires does not die," Kalus said.

"Do not you see that it's time to give up?" Luna asked.

"Give up?" Kalus cried out.

"It's obvious that you have failed to transform this kingdom into the kingdom of the vampire, and it's also obvious that you have failed to turn the population of this kingdom into the vampires," Luna replied.

"I did not fail because my vision and my dream would be realized soon," Kalus said.

"Stop dreaming because this kingdom would never be the kingdom of vampires, and the population of this kingdom would never be the vampires," Luna said.

Kalus looked into Luna's eyes and said, "I am so sorry for you because you would be in your grave when this kingdom would be turned into the kingdom of vampires. And when this population would be turned into vampires."

"Do not be stupid, do not you see that even your own army has abandoned you," Luna said.

"I still have my army," Kalus said.

"The monsters?" Luna asked with a surprised face.

"The monsters are better and stronger than the human beings. And the monsters are the future army of this kingdom," Kalus said.

"Are you crazy?" Luna asked with an astonished face.

"I am not, and the monsters can protect the kingdom better than human beings," Kalus said.

Luna said, "The monsters can not share the same space with human beings." And Luna added, "Everyone ran away a day ago when you made the monsters appear in the kingdom to kill children."

"I would use the monsters like the army and the police of this kingdom when this kingdom would be turned into a vampire kingdom. And when the population would be turned into vampires.

And the vampires and the monsters can share the same space because the vampires are not afraid of the monsters," Kalus said.

"It's your right to dream, and I can not prevent you from dreaming," Luna said.

"I am not dreaming, but I am telling you what is going to happen," Kalus said.

"I am not here to listen to your dream of the future that would never come true," Luna said.

"Why are you here?" Kalus asked.

"I am here because I want the light and the water in the kingdom," Luna answered.

"I want all pregnant women, and the newborn called George," Kalus retorted.

"I am not here to negotiate with you or to beg you," Luna said.

"If you want light and water in the kingdom, you must give me all the pregnant women of the kingdom and the newborn called George," Kalus said.

Luna said, "The inhabitants of this kingdom are not only in the darkness, but they are also dying of hunger and thirst because since this morning no one in this kingdom had put the cooking pot on the fire." Luna added, "And there are people who are dying in the hospital now because their oxygen masks have stopped working because there is no light. And there are people who have not taken their medicines since this morning because they have not eaten, and because there is no water."

"Give me all the pregnant women and the newborn named George if you want to save all these people who are dying now," Kalus said.

"Stop asking for the pregnant women and George because I would never give you them," Luna said.

"It means that there would never be the light and water in the kingdom," Kalus said.

"Of course, there would be the light and the water in the kingdom," Luna said.

"You do not have the power to bring back the light and the water in the kingdom," Kalus said.

"It's true that I do not have the power to bring back the light and the water in the kingdom, but you have this power to do that," Luna said.

"But I would not bring back the light and the water in the kingdom until you give all the pregnant women and this baby called George," Kalus said.

"I am curious to know what you want to do with these pregnant women and the baby George," Luna said.

"I would kill them," Kalus answered.

"Why kill them?" Luna asked.

"I would not answer this question," Kalus said.

"You have three minutes to bring back the light and water in this kingdom," Luna said.

"You would beg me when people would start dying," Kalus said.

"Nobody would die," Luna said.

"These pregnant women would start to die of hunger and thirst soon," Kalus said.

"You have two minutes," Luna said.

"Stop wasting your time," Kalus said.

"You have only a minute," Luna said.

"Do not be stupid because I am immortal. And even Sunshine, who is more powerful and stronger than you, did not succeed in killing me," Kalus said.

Suddenly, the expression on Luna's face changed, and she was looking with a face full of rage and her eyes were spinning. And Kalus was staring at Luna and he was understanding the reason why Luna's eyes were turning, and Kalus's eyes started spinning too. Then there were two swords that were flying in the space, and they handed their hands through the space and each of them grabbed a word. Then they started walking towards each other.

And they started fighting with their faces full of anger. The fight was very hard and Kalus was fighting with a lot of anger and determination and he was trying to kill Luna. But Luna was fighting with technique and she was trying to avoid Kalus's sword, and she was also stronger than Kalus. After a few minutes, Kalus started to sweat, and she was very tired. And Kalus was fighting by moving from behind, while Luna was having an advantage in the fight.

Suddenly, Kalus pushed a loud scream and his sword fell on the floor, and there was the blood that was flowing from his hand. And Kalus had been injured by Luna. Then Kalus tried to bend to pick up his sword on the floor, but Luna pointed her sword on Kalus's belly to prevent him from bending to take the sword. Luna and Kalus were looking at each other in the eyes without saying a word, and there was the sword that Luna had pointed on Kalus's belly.

Then Luna broke the silence and said, "I have my sword on your belly."

"You can not kill me because I am immortal," Kalus replied.

"You are bleeding," Luna said.

"You have been lucky to hurt me," Kalus said.

"If you are bleeding, it means that you can die," Luna said.

"I am immortal," Kalus retorted.

"Stop lying to yourself," Luna said.

"I have the satanic powers in me that make me immortal," Kalus said.

"Your satanic powers could not even help you to beat me, your satanic powers only helped you to kill children and drink children's blood," Luna said.

"I can kill you," Kalus said.

"How are you going to kill me if you can not even beat me?" Luna asked.

"I can kill you by using my satanic powers," Kalus answered.

"If you could kill me, I should be in my grave now because the only dream you have it's to kill me," Luna said.

"It's true that the only dream I have it's to kill you, and today it's my lucky day," Kalus said.

"Your lucky day because you are going to kill me?" Luna asked.

"Yes, my lucky day because I would realize my dream to kill you now," Kalus answered.

"Rather your unlucky day," Luna said.

"It's time for you to go to hell to meet all the children I had mystically killed and drank their blood," Kalus said.

Suddenly, Kalus's eyes started spinning and a sword flew near to him, and he grabbed this sword. Then Kalus and Luna started fighting with the anger on their faces, but Luna was still stronger than Kalus.

Kalus had some difficulty fighting because he was feeling pain on the hand which he had grabbed the sword to fight with, as he had been injured on this hand a few minutes ago by Luna. And despite the fact that Kalus was feeling pain in his hand, he was fighting with a lot of determination, and he was trying to stab Luna or to cut Luna's head without success.

After a few minutes, the fight was still going on. Kalus was sweating and he was feeling that he was losing the fight, and he had the difficulties to protect himself against Luna's sword. Because Kalus had been injured by Luna's sword for the second time on his hand and he was losing a lot of blood. Then Kalus's eyes started spinning, and a shield flew near to Kalus, and he grabbed this shield and he started to protect himself against Luna's sword still by fighting Luna.

Suddenly, Kalus pushed a loud scream of pain, Luna had stabbed him in his stomach with her sword, and there was the blood that was flowing from Kalus's belly, then Kalus threw his sword and his shield on the floor. And Kalus was looking at Luna's sword that was in his belly, then he grabbed Luna's sword and he removed Luna's sword from his belly, and he threw Luna's sword on the floor. And there was the blood that was flowing more and more from Kalus's belly as he had removed Luna's sword that was in his belly.

Then Kalus put his left palm's hand on the wound that was on his belly, and his eyes started spinning and there was a light that was shining between Kalus's palm hand that was on his belly and his belly. And Kalus was trying to use his magic to stop blood and to heal the wound that was on his belly without success. Because this light that was shining between Kalus's belly and his palm's hand was to stop the blood and to heal Kalus's wound that was caused by Luna's sword.

After a few minutes, Kalus had still not succeeded in using his magic to stop the blood and to heal the wound. And he started to understand that Luna's sword that had stabbed him contained a powerful poison. And that his magic could not stop the blood or heal the wound that was on his belly because his magic did not have the antidote of the poison that was on Luna's sword that Luna had used to stab him with.

Luna was staring at Kalus with a face empty of expression, like Kalus was trying to heal his wound through his magic. But although the fact that Luna was showing no signs through her facial expression, there was the rage inside her, as she was remembering all the horrible things that had been done by Kalus to the inhabitants of the kingdom. especially the children who had been killed by Kalus.

Luna was looking at Kalus how he was trying to use all the potential of his magic to heal his wound without success because the light that was shining between Kalus's belly and Kalus's palm hand that was on his belly was changing the color. And this light was changing the color because Kalus was trying to use all the potential of his magic to heal the wound that was on his belly.

Then Luna broke the silence and said, "I thought that you were powerful enough to heal that wound on your belly or to even to stop this blood that is flowing from your belly."

Kalus looked at Luna and said, "This is proof that I am immortal because you stabbed me in my stomach with a sword that contained the poison, but I am still alive and I am feeling well. And despite the fact that I am losing a lot of blood, I am breathing well and I am fine."

"I thought that your satanic powers could heal this wound on your belly or at least stop this blood that is flowing on your t-shirt and on your pants," Luna said.

"My satanic powers keep me alive, and I am immortal thanks to my satanic powers," Kalus retorted.

"I am wondering how you are going to live with these wounds on your belly and on your hand, and with the blood that is flowing from your belly and your hand?" Luna asked.

"What matters is the fact that I am immortal," Kalus answered.

"Your satanic powers are useless if these satanic powers could not even prevent you from looking like a vampire," Luna said.

"A vampire?" Kalus cried out.

"You have a dream to turn this kingdom into a vampire kingdom and to turn the population of this kingdom into vampires, andI just made your dream come true. But the only problem is that you are the only vampire of this kingdom, and you would stay the only vampire of this kingdom, and you are a real vampire with these wounds on you and this blood that is flowing from your wounds," Luna answered.

"I am not a vampire," Kalus said.

"Try to get out of this palace, you would see how everyone would run away from you by screaming Kalus is a vampire," Luna said.

"I am not a vampire," Kalus repeated.

Luna said, "Look at you in the mirror, you would see what a vampire looks like." Luna added, "It's better for you to die than to live like a vampire who would scare people, and that everyone would run away when they will see you. No one would stay near you or even talk to you because you are a vampire."

"Stop calling me a vampire," Kalus said angrily.

Luna said, "I call you a vampire because you are a vampire. And I would not stop calling you like this because the whole kingdom would call you a vampire." And Luna added, "I do not understand why you do not want to be called a vampire because you are the one who have the dream to turn this kingdom into a vampire the kingdom and to turn the population of this kingdom into vampires."

"Of course, that this kingdom would be a vampire kingdom and the future generations of this kingdom would be the vampires, and I would be the god of the vampires," Kalus replied.

"If you would be the god of the vampires, it means you would be a vampire too," Luna said.

"No, I would be just a god, and I would be called the god of the kingdom of vampires," Kalus said.

"I understand now," Luna said.

Then Kalus turned without saying a word to Luna, and he started walking away. Luna had turned her head and she was staring at Kalus who was walking towards the huge mirror that was in the living room, and she was wondering why Kalus was walking towards the mirror.

Then Kalus stopped in front of the mirror, and he was staring at himself in the mirror. And suddenly the expression of Kalus's face changed and he was looking in the mirror with a strange face as he was seeing the wound that was on his belly in the mirror.

And Kalus noticed that the wound that was on his belly was very well seen, that this wound was like a hole, and there was the blood that was still flowing from his wound. And Kalus was understanding that he must do something to heal this wound because he could not live with this wound because people would run away from him by seeing this wound on his belly.

And this wound on his belly made him look like a vampire with the blood that was flowing from this wound. And Kalus knew well that he could not heal this wound, but he knew well that Luna could heal this wound, not only because this wound was caused by Luna. But mostly because Luna's magic could heal the wounds that were caused by the poison, and also because Luna's magic contained the antidote.

Then Kalus turned and he started to walk towards Luna, looking at Luna with a face full of anger. Then Kalus stopped face to Luna and he looked into Luna's eyes and he asked Luna to heal the wounds that were on his hands and his belly. Luna replied to Kalus that she would not heal these wounds.

And Luna also told Kalus that he had better die because if he was going to live, he would live with these wounds. And suddenly the rage appeared on Kalus's face, and his eyes started spinning and the light got out from his eyes and went and shone on Luna, and this light pushed Luna in the space. And Luna went and hit her back against the wall.

Luna was on the floor and she was crying her back, and she saw Kalus who was walking towards her. Then Luna got up from the floor, and she was staring at Kalus who was approaching her, and she also noticed that Kalus's eyes were spinning.

And Luna tried to use her magic to fight Kalus, but suddenly a light shone on Luna and this light was coming from Kalus's eyes, and this light pushed Luna away and she went and hit her back against the television that was in the room, and she fell on the floor. And there was the blood that was flowing from Luna's hand, and she had been injured by the television's screen because the television had been broken as she had fallen on the television.

Then Luna saw Kalus who was walking towards him, and she got up from the floor and she tried to use her magic, but unfortunately, she had difficulty using her magic. And suddenly, the light shone on Luna, and this light projected Luna into space, and Luna went and fell on the table. And Kalus continued to torture Luna, and Luna had difficulty to use her magic.

And Luna was not understanding why she was unable to use her magic. And Kalus was torturing Luna by asking Luna to heal his wounds, but Luna had replied to Kalus that she would rather die than to heal his wounds. And despite the fact that Luna was feeling pain in her whole body, she was trying to resist Kalus by trying to fight back Kalus, even if she had difficulty using the full potential of her magic.

Luna was lying on the floor and she was almost unconscious, and she was feeling the violent headaches because she had just fallen to the floor with her head because she had been projected in space by Kalus's magic, and she fell with her head. Luna had her eyes closed and it seemed that she was a little unconscious because she was trying to remember what was going on.

And suddenly, Luna started to remember something strange, and she was remembering how Sunshine was giving her a part of the energy of her magic(Sunshine's magic) in the kitchen of Khloe's house.

And immediately Luna remembered that she was fighting against Kalus in the living room of the palace, and that she had the difficulties to use the full potential of her magic. Luna understood that she had difficulty using the full potential of her magic because her magic contained the energy of Sunshine's magic, and the problem was that she did not know very well how Sunshine's magic worked.

And Luna started to think how Sunshine's magic worked because she could not use the full potential of the magic that was in her body, if she did not know how Sunshine's magic worked. Because the energy of Sunshine's magic was mixed with the energy of her magic. Then Luna remembered that during her conversation with Sunshine in the sacred forest, Sunshine told her that she(Sunshine) needed to take a deep breath and concentrate on herself (Sunshine) to use her magic (Sunshine's magic).

Then Luna opened her eyes and she got up on the floor and she saw Kalus who was walking towards her, and she also noticed that Kalus's eyes were spinning. Then Luna took a deep breath and she concentrated on herself.

And suddenly, Luna's eyes started spinning and a blue light got out from her eyes and went towards Kalus, and at the same time there was a red light that was getting out from Kalus's eyes and going towards Luna.

Then the two lights, the light coming from Luna's magic and the light coming Kalus's magic met. And these two lights were fighting because the light coming from Luna's magic was trying to reach Kalus' body, while the light coming from Kalus's magic was trying to reach Luna's body.

And the blue light coming from Luna's magic was trying to prevent the red light coming from Kalus's magic to reach Luna's body, while the red light coming from Kalus's magic was trying to prevent the blue light coming from Luna's magic to reach Kalus's body.

Luna and Kalus were standing up, and they were looking at each other with their faces full of rage, and they were focused on the fight of their magic, and they were trying to keep concentration. And it was important for them to stay focused on the fight because they needed to be focused on staying in contact with the light that had got out of their eyes.

Luna and Kalus were feeling the reaction of the fight of the lights coming from their magic in their bodies. And suddenly, Kalus started to breathe deeply, and he started to sweat, and he started to shake a bit and he also had difficulty keeping his balance.

And Kalus had the difficulty to keep his balance because the red light that had got out from his eyes was losing the fight, and this red light was pushing by the blue light that had got out from Luna's eyes. And Luna had more balance and she was more focused on the fight because the blue light that had got out from her eyes was having the advantage over the fight.

Then Kalus was trembling more and more, and he was sweating more and more, and Kalus was losing his strength, and he was feeling weak. And he did not have enough strength to fend to the blue light that was approaching him.

And despite the fact that Kalus was no longer able to fight and to push this blue light coming from Luna's magic, he was trying not to give up the fight. While Luna was more and more strong, and she was no longer affected by the effect of the fight because she had taken the advantage of the fight through the blue light that had got out from her eyes.

The blue light that had got out from Luna's eyes was going towards Kalus, while the red light that had got out from Kalus's eyes was trying to prevent this blue light from reaching Kalus without success. And Kalus had started to feel the reaction of this blue light on him.

Suddenly, Kalus was projected into space by this blue light because this blue light had shone on him. And Kalus went and hit his body against the cupboard that was in the living room, and he fell to the floor. Kalus was on the floor and he was crying his back, and he saw Luna who was walking towards him, and he noticed that Luna's eyes were spinning.

And Kalus was trying to get up from the floor when a light got out from Luna's eyes and shone on him, and this light projected Kalus into space. And Luna lifted head and she looked at Kalus who was in space and Luna's eyes started spinning, and Kalus started to turn in the space.

Then Luna started to walk still with her eyes focused on Kalus and her eyes were still turning as she was walking, and Kalus was flying in the direction that Luna was walking through. And Kalus had lost the control of his body because his body was completely controlled by Luna's magic, then Kalus started rolling on the ceiling.

Then Kalus started to scream in pain because he was flying and hitting his body against the walls of the living room. The walls of the living room were red with blood, and this blood was coming from Kalus because Kalus's face was full of wounds as he was hitting his body against the walls.

After a few minutes, Kalus went and hit his body against the wall and he fell to the floor. Kalus was sitting on the floor and he had leaned his back against the wall, and he was breathing with a lot of difficulty, and he was unrecognizable because his face was full of blood and wounds.

And there were also some places on his face like his forehead and his left eye that had swelled, and he had even lost one of his teeth, and the blood was also flowing from his mouth, and he was feeling pain in his whole body. And Luna was walking towards Kalus.

Then Luna stopped face to Kalus and she told him that the kingdom needed the light and water. And Kalus opened his mouth to talk and he had the difficulty to talk, but he managed to tell Luna that he would not give the light and water to the kingdom until she and her fellows gave him all the pregnant women and newborn called George.

And suddenly, the expression on Luna's face changed and she was looking at Kalus with a face full of anger, and her eyes started turning. Then Kalus started yelling in pain, and he was feeling pain in his whole body, and he was mostly feeling pain in his joints.

Then Kalus tried to move his hands without success, and he tried to move his feet without success, and he was no longer feeling pain. And he was also not feeling any sensation in his body, and he was no longer feeling his whole body except his mouth.

And Kalus understood that his whole body was paralysed by Luna's magic, and that except his mouth that was not paralyzed. Luna was staring at Kalus with a face empty of expression and she told Kalus that she did not paralyze his mouth because she wanted him to keep talking, and she did not paralyze his brain because she wanted him to keep thinking to be able to use his magic and powers.

Then Luna told Kalus that the kingdom needed the light and water. And Kalus replied to Luna he knew that she did not paralyze his brain and his mouth because she needed the light and water in the kingdom. Because she knew well that he needed to use his brain to trigger his power that could bring light and water in the kingdom, and that if his brain was paralyzed, he could no longer use his power that could give the light and water in the kingdom.

Because she knew that most of his powers were located in his brain, as most of her powers were located in her brain too. And Kalus added that he knew that Luna was stronger and powerful like that because she had the energy of Sunshine's magic in her body because he had experienced some tortures coming from Sunshine's magic.

And Kalus went on and told Luna that he was not afraid and that she could keep torturing him. And she could even paralyse his brain and his mouth, but that he would not give the light and water to the kingdom. And that he would give the light and water to the kingdom only when the children of the kingdom would give him all the pregnant women of the kingdom and the newborn called George.

And that it's only when he would receive all these pregnant women and newborn called George and when he would kill all these pregnant women and the baby named George that he would give light and water to the kingdom.

Then Kalus continued and said that he was not worried about himself because he was immortal, and that he had all his time because he could live without water and light. And that it was the population of the kingdom who needed the light and water because this population could not live without light and water.

Because people needed light to make food because in the kingdom, all the cookers worked with the light, and it was impossible for people to live without drinking water. And that especially the pregnant women could not live without eating food and drinking water because these pregnant women needed to feed their babies who were in their wombs.

Then Kalus added that the pregnant women would be the first to die because it would be impossible for the pregnant women to survive in this situation without eating food and drinking water.

And Kalus told Luna that he was immortal and that he knew well that he could be tortured by her, but he was not afraid of that because he also knew well that he could not be killed by her or even by someone else. And that she could continue to torture him, and she could even put him in the coma, but that he would not give the light and water to the kingdom.

Luna was staring at Kalus by thinking what to do, she knew well that she could not kill Kalus because the life of Kalus was protected by Lord, and that the only solution to kill Kalus was to kill Lord first.

And Luna knew also that she could not put Kalus in the coma and she could not also paralyse Kalus's brain because by putting him in the coma or by paralysing his brain, he could no longer use his magic to give the light and water to the kingdom.

Mostly that Kalus was the only one who had this power to give the light and water to the kingdom because between the three powers of Kalus that were different from her three powers. One of these three powers of Kalus could prevent the inhabitants of the kingdom from having the light and water.

And Kalus had used this power to cut the light and water in the kingdom and only himself could bring back the light and water to the kingdom through this power. And Luna was thinking what to do, and she was trying to find a solution that could force Kalus to give the light and water to the kingdom.

And Luna knew well that she did not have enough time because the kingdom needed the light and water as soon as possible because people were probably dying now. And Luna also knew that she was faced with her responsibilities as the heiress to the crown and the throne of the kingdom to save the kingdom.

And it was unthinkable for Luna to give the pregnant women and the newborn called George to Kalus for that Kalus killed them. Because the goal of the fight was to save the kingdom and to protect all the inhabitants of the kingdom and mostly not to allow Lord and Kalus to kill an inhabitant of the kingdom.

The hours were passing, and Luna was still thinking and she was a little scared because she did not know what to do. Then Luna got an idea to make a deal with Kalus. And Luna was thinking to heal the wounds of Kalus that were caused by her sword for that Kalus gives the light and water to the kingdom.

And Luna knew well that Kalus could accept her deal because Kalus could not heal his wounds that were made by her sword. Because her sword contained the poison, and Kalus's magic did not contain the antidote to heal these wounds, and only her magic had the antidote to heal these wounds. And only Luna's magic contained the antidotes to the poisons because between the three powers of Luna that were different from the three powers of Kalus, one of these three powers of Luna contained the antidotes.

And it was the reason why only Luna could heal the wounds of Kalus that were made by her sword because the sword that she had stabbed Kalus with, contained the poison. And it was also the reason why Luna had succeeded to save Sunshine when Sunshine had been stabbed with a sword that contained the poison by Lord. And Luna was still thinking if it was a good idea to make a deal with Kalus.

After a few minutes, Luna gave up the idea to make a deal with Kalus because Kalus was a devil who had destroyed the kingdom. And Kalus had no right to prevent the inhabitants of the kingdom from having light and water.

And Luna knew well that Kalus was born with these powers to protect the kingdom and not to destroy the kingdom. And Luna also knew all the powers that Kalus was born with were to protect the inhabitants of the kingdom, even his power that he had used to cut the light and water in the kingdom.

And that Kalus was born with this power that he could use to cut the light and water in the kingdom because in case of danger Kalus could use this power to cut the light and water in the kingdom. And this danger was only if the kingdom was invaded by the enemies because if the kingdom was invaded by the enemies, Kalus had the right to cut the light and water to prevent the enemies from staying in the kingdom.

But Kalus had no right to prevent the inhabitants of the kingdom from having light and water, and it was even against the values of the tradition of the kingdom that the king torture his own people, and it was also anti-traditional to prevent his people from having the light and water.

And although the time was passing and that Luna was extremely worried about the inhabitants of the kingdom, mostly pregnant women and women who were breastfeeding their babies, also people were sick in the hospitals or at home. And Luna was still thinking, and she had already given up the idea to negotiate with Kalus.

Suddenly Luna got an idea, and she looked at Kalus and her eyes started spinning, and a light got out from her eyes and went and shone on Kalus. And suddenly Kalus felt a strange reaction in his body, and he was feeling his feet and hands, and he was feeling that he was no longer paralyzed, and he was no longer feeling pain. But there were still the wounds that were made by Luna's sword on Kalus.

And Kalus was very surprised that Luna had stopped his pain, and he was more surprised that Luna had made him feel his feet, his legs and his hands. But Kalus knew that Luna had an idea, that Luna did not stop his pain because she loved him, and he was wondering what this idea could be.

Then Kalus asked Luna why she had stopped his pain? Luna answered Kalus that she had stopped his pain because he wanted him to follow her. Kalus asked Luna where they were going? Luna answered Kalus that he must follow her without asking the questions. And Kalus told Luna that he would not follow her without knowing where she would take him.

Luna told Kalus that he had the choice to get up from the floor and walk by himself to follow her, or she would use her magic to drag him or to make him fly. And Kalus replied to Luna that he was the king of the kingdom, the one who gave the orders, and not the one who received the orders.

And that he would not follow her. Luna told Kalus that she was nice to give him a choice, and that now he would follow her in her own way. Then Luna's eyes started turning, and Kalus started to fly in space. Luna started walking towards a hallway with her eyes focused on Kalus, and Kalus was flying in space by following Luna.

After a few minutes of walking, Luna stopped near a wall and her eyes stopped turning, then Kalus fell on the floor near to her. Then Kalus got up from the floor and he was standing up, and both Luna and Kalus were looking at each other in the eyes.

And looking at the expression on the face of Kalus, he was a little worried and his heart was beating faster than normal. And there were a lot of questions that were going on in his mind, like why Luna had taken him to this corridor? How did Luna know the existence of this corridor? Why did Luna stop near this wall? What Luna was trying to do? And what Luna knew about this corridor? But unfortunately, Kalus could not even answer one of his questions, but he was very afraid.

Then Luna broke the silence and asked, "Do you know why I took you here?"

"Do not waste your time," Kalus answered.

"This is your private hallway, and you could not even imagine that I knew the existence of this corridor," Luna said.

"You have no idea what secret this corridor contains," Kalus said.

"I am not stupid because I took you in this corridor because I know exactly what this corridor means for you and I also know about the secret of this corridor" Luna said.

"How did you know the existence of this corridor? Because no one in this palace even your mom does not know the existence of this corridor," Kalus asked.

"Do not forget that I am the heiress to the crown and the throne of this kingdom," Luna answered.

"Even if you know about the secret of this corridor, there is nothing you can do against me," Kalus said.

Luna put her left palm's hand on the wall that was near to her and she looked into Kalus's eyes and said, "This wall that I had put my palm's hand on it, it's the door of your magic room also called your secret room, and it's in this magic room that you talk with Lord, and all your satanic powers are stocked in this magic room, and you can not live without these satanic powers."

Kalus smiled at Luna and said, "Do not be stupid because you can not open this door."

"If I was you, I would not be sure," Luna said.

"It's impossible for you to open this door because you do have the satanic powers, and only someone who has the satanic powers can try to open this door," Kalus said.

"Have a good journey to hell," Luna said.

Then Luna turned and she looked at her palm's hand that was on the wall, and her eyes started spinning, then a blue light shone between her palm's hand that was on the wall and the wall. And Kalus had his eyes focused on Luna palm's hand that was on the wall and he was staring at the blue light that was shining between Luna palm's hand and the wall with a worried face.

Then Luna took a deep breath and she concentrated, and she turned her palm's hand that was on the wall, and the wall started to open as if it was a door. And there was a white smoke coming out from the room through this wall that was opening as the door.

Suddenly, there were the screams coming from Kalus who was begging Luna to close this door, that she was killing him. And Kalus told Luna that he was using his magic to give the light and water to the kingdom, but Luna was not paying attention to the cries of Kalus.

Then Luna lifted her head and looked at the ceiling as she noticed that the light was shining, and she noticed that the bulbs were on and that Kalus had effectively given the light to the kingdom. But despite the fact that Kalus had given the light to the kingdom, Luna did not close the door of the magic room and the smoke was still getting out.

Kalus was still crying by begging Luna to close this door because she was killing him, and that he had already given the light and water to the kingdom. Luna turned her head and she looked at Kalus and she was staring at Kalus who was begging her to close the door of his magic room with a face empty of expression.

And Kalus was telling Luna that he was her father, and that a daughter could not kill her father, and that it was a curse for a child to kill his father, and that even if Luna hated him, she could not kill him because he was her father. And Luna was just staring at Kalus who was becoming weak with the anger in her eyes.

And looking at the expression on the face of Luna, we could see that she was not feeling any pity or compassion for Kalus, but that she was instead disgusted by Kalus. And Kalus was becoming more and more weak, that he had even lost all his strength. And Kalus was trying to talk without success because he was so weak that he could not make a movement with his mouth or even make a gesture. Then Kalus fell to the floor like a dead body with his eyes closed. Luna was staring at her father who was lying on the floor like a corpse with a face empty of expression.

And Suddenly the expression of Luna's face changed when she saw Lord who had appeared near to Kalus, and she was looking at Lord with an astonished face. Lord had knelt near Kalus, then Lord had put his left palm's hand on Kalus's heart and there was a red light that was shining between Lord palm's hand and Kalus's heart.

And this red light was shining to keep Kalus alive, and Lord was trying to continue to make Kalus's heart beat through that red light. Then Lord felt that Kalus was dying and he put his right palm's hand on Kalus's nose, and there was a yellow light that was shining between his palm's hand and Kalus's nose. And this yellow light was helping Kalus to breathe because this yellow light was getting inside the nostrils of Kalus to help Kalus to stay alive because this yellow light was like the air for Kalus.

Then Lord looked at Luna and said, "Please, there is the light and water in the kingdom." And Lord added, "I just got your fellows out of a coma."

Luna looked into Lord's eyes and said, "If this devil named Kalus succeeded to survive, tell him that I would be back for him, and that I would keep the promise that I had made to the whole kingdom to send him to hell."

Then Luna took her hand off the wall, and she turned and walked away. Lord carried Kalus and he got in the magic room with Kalus and he closed the door of the magic room. Kalus was lying on the floor of the magic room, and Lord was trying to take care of Kalus to keep Kalus alive as he could. Luna was walking in the yard of the palace towards the car, then Luna got in the car and she drove away.

People had got out of their beds and they were in the kitchen, and they were making food, and they were very happy that the light and water had come back. And in the hospitals, everyone was fine, even people who were in a coma were still alive and were doing well. Luna was walking in the hallway of the hospital where her fellows were hospitalized, and she was using her magic to find the rooms where her fellows were hospitalized.

Then Luna stopped in front of the door and she opened this door and she got in the room, and she saw George who was lying in the bed with his eyes closed and with the oxygen mask on him. Luna walked until near the bed and she took off the oxygen mask that was on George and George opened his eyes. And George was looking at Luna with a surprised face and he asked Luna where he was? Luna answered George that they would talk later, and that he must get out of the bed because they must leave.

Then George got out of the bed, and he wanted to change his clothes to remove the hospital's dress that was on him and wear his clothes, but Luna told him that they did not have enough time. Then George took the bag that contained his clothes, then Luna and George left the room.

Then Luna went to the rooms of her fellows and took off the oxygen masks that were on her fellows. Then Luna and her fellows left the hospital against the wishes of the doctors who had tried unsuccessfully to prevent Luna from getting her fellows out of the hospital.

There were more people in Khloe's house, and some parents had joined their children to Khloe's house because they were worried about their children, as they had not seen their children since yesterday that their children had left home.

Women were in the kitchen making food and the children were in the living room with the fathers. The fathers and children were sitting on the carpet that was on the floor and some of them had crossed their feet. And the children were listening to the stories that were told by the fathers.

Then Sunshine turned her head towards the door when she heard the noises coming from the door, and suddenly the expression of her face changed and she was looking with a smile on her face, as she was seeing Luna and her fellows who were getting in the room.

Then Sunshine pushed a yell of joy and she got up from the floor and she rushed through the door as she had seen Aaron who was getting in the room. Then Sunshine hugged Aaron, and the children got up from the floor with smiles on their faces and they went and welcomed their friends. And the parents were looking at the children with smiles on their faces. The parents that their children were in the coma were very happy to see that their children had gotten out of the coma and that their children were doing well.

Then Abraham looked at Luna and he thanked Luna for the light and water. And Luna smiled at Abraham and she told him that he did not have to thank her because it was her duty to make sure that all the inhabitants of the kingdom had the light and water.

Abraham asked Luna where she found the technician? Luna looked at Abraham with an astonished face and she asked Abraham which technician he was talking about? Abraham replied to Luna that Sunshine told them that she(Luna) went to find the technician who could fix the light.

And Luna smiled at Abraham as she understood why Sunshine had told Abraham and other people that she(Luna) went to look for the technician. Then Luna had her mouth opened and her mouth was shaking as she was trying to find the words, and Luna was trying to find the words because she was thinking what to say to Abraham.

And Luna was thinking what to say to Abraham because she could not tell the truth that it was Kalus who had used his magic to prevent the inhabitants of the kingdom from having light and water. And all the eyes were focused on Luna, and some of them were wondering if Luna had lost her tongue as they had noticed that Luna was searching the words.

Then Luna took a deep breath and said that she knew a technician who worked at the palace, and that it was this technician who had fixed the light. Abraham smiled at Luna and he understood that Luna was not telling the truth. Then Abraham asked Luna to come and sit near to him and that he had a story to tell her.

And Luna replied to Abraham to give her a few minutes because she must talk with Sunshine first. Then Luna turned her head around and looked around and she did not see Sunshine, then she asked where Sunshine was. And Khloe told Luna that Sunshine had left with Aaron. And Khloe added that Sunshine and Aaron were talking in the corner of the corridor. Then Luna said that she would be back and she turned and left.

Sunshine and Aaron were kissing in the corner of the corridor. Then Sunshine stopped kissing Aaron and she turned her head as she had felt a hand on her shoulder, then the smile appeared on her face as she was staring at Luna who was staring at her.

And Sunshine made a joke to Luna by asking Luna to go see Isac, that Isac was alone. Luna replied to Sunshine that Isac was fine. Then Luna told Aaron that she was so sorry to disturb his romantic moment with Sunshine. Then Luna asked Aaron if she could talk to Sunshine in private? Aaron smiled at Luna and answered that yes. Then Aaron left.

Sunshine looked into Luna's eyes and asked, "How did it go with Kalus?"

"We will talk about Kalus later," Luna answered.

"Why didLord release our fellows from the coma?" Sunshine asked.

Luna answered, "We must talk about Lord and Kalus later."

"I am going outside now to look for this missing pregnant woman," Sunshine said.

"I came to talk about that missing pregnant woman," Luna said.

"I was waiting for you to come before I went outside," Sunshine said.

"We have to go now," Luna said.

"We can not go together," Sunshine said.

"Why can't we go together?" Luna asked.

"You must stay here with these pregnant women, we can not abandon these pregnant women not only because Lord and Kalus could come here and kill them, but because these pregnant women can need help at any time," Sunshine said.

"You are right, I must stay," Luna said.

Then Khloe came and she told Sunshine and Luna that the food was ready. Sunshine replied to Khloe that they were coming. And Khloe left. Then Luna looked at Sunshine and she told Sunshine that Sunshine needed the powers to go outside. Then Sunshine handed her two hands towards Luna, and Luna also handed her two hands and she grabbed Sunshine's hands.

And there was a light that was shining between Sunshine's hands and Luna's hands and this light was coming from Luna's body to get inside Sunshine's body. And this light was a part of the energy of Luna's magic that she was giving to Sunshine, and Luna was also giving back the energy of Sunshine's magic that she had received a few hours ago when she went to the palace to fight Kalus.

After a few minutes, Sunshine told Luna that she had enough energy in her body, and that Luna could not give her(Sunshine) all the energy of her(Luna) magic. Then Luna removed her hands from Sunshine's hands. Then Luna looked into Sunshine's eyes and said, "It's time to go." And Luna added, "Good luck." Then Sunshine and Luna walked until the living room and they noticed that everyone was eating.

Then Abraham asked Sunshine and Luna to serve themselves at the dining table. Sunshine told Abraham that she would eat when she would be back, and she walked towards the door before Abraham opened his mouth to say a word.

Then Asher got up and started walking towards the door, but he was stopped by Luna. And Luna asked Asher where he was going? Asher answered that he was going to join Sunshine. Luna told Asher that Sunshine went out to look for something, and that Sunshine would be back soon. Abraham looked at Luna and he asked her what Sunshine went out to look for? Luna looked at Abraham without saying a word, then Luna said that the food was smelling good.

And Abraham smiled and he told Luna that she could eat, but that they would talk later. Luna smiled at Abraham without saying a word, and she walked towards the dining table to save herself the food.

Sunshine was driving in the streets of the kingdom and she was looking for this missing pregnant woman, and she was using her magic to look for this pregnant woman. And Sunshine could see through her magic that this pregnant woman was in pain somewhere, but her magic was unable to locate the exact place where this pregnant woman was.

And Sunshine had seen the shadow of Lord in the cloud, and she knew that Lord was following her. And Sunshine knew that Lord was following her because Lord was also looking for this missing pregnant woman. And Sunshine was very worried about the pregnant woman, and Sunshine was afraid that the worst could happen and that this pregnant woman could die with her baby in her womb.

After two hours, except Abraham, the rest of the parents were sleeping in the bedrooms. Abraham was sitting in the living room with the children, and the children were listening to the history of their kingdom that was told by Abraham. And the children were very happy to hear the story of their ancestors and their kingdom.

Abraham had a pencil and notebook in front of him, and he was drawing how the first inhabitants of the kingdom dressed, and he was also drawing the first houses that were built in the kingdom. And Abraham had also drawn the first school and the first church of the kingdom, and he had also drawn the first palace of the kingdom.

And the children were amazed to see how their ancestors used to dress, and how people dressed in the past.

And the children were also astonished to notice that their ancestors had lived in the small houses that looked like the huts. And Abraham also told the children that a few centuries ago, there was no hospital, no doctor, no pharmacy and no medicine. And people were treated to the traditional remedies that were made with the tree's leaves, the tree's barks and the tree's roots.

And Abraham went on and said that a few centuries ago, there were no cookers, light and water in the houses. Mia asked Abraham how people lived in the past without light, water and cookers? And Abraham answered Mia that people used river water, and people used the lamps and the kitchen were outside of the houses and people cooked with the wood fire.

Then Aaron turned his head towards the door as he had heard a noise, and the smile appeared on his face as he was looking at Sunshine who was walking in the room. And everyone had their eyes focused on Sunshine. And Asher asked Sunshine where she was? Sunshine answered Asher that they would talk later.

And Asher asked Sunshine why she could not talk now. Sunshine replied to Asher that she wanted to talk to Luna in private. Asher told Sunshine that she would not talk to Luna in private, and that if she wanted to talk to Luna, she must talk to Luna in front of everyone because they were all concerned by the fight.

Sunshine walked near to Asher and she sat on the carpet and she looked at Asher and she told Asher that she was so sorry about her behaviour, and that she apologized if her behaviour made him and others think that they were not concerned by the fight.

And Sunshine added that everyone was involved in the fight, and that they were all fighting together to save their kingdom, and that it was together that they would all succeed to save their kingdom. And that the fact she wanted to talk to Luna in private did not mean that the rest of the people were not involved in the fight.

And suddenly, Sunshine was interrupted by Abraham, and Abraham told Sunshine that he was very surprised by her talent because she was a great leader, and that he was very surprised by the way she just talked to Asher and to the rest of the members of the group.

And Abraham also told Sunshine that he was very proud of her and he was also proud of the rest of the members of the group for their courage and determination to save this kingdom. And Abraham went on and said that he was especially proud of Luna who had decided to make the dream of the children of the kingdom come true by giving her crown and her throne to George, and to make George the king of the kingdom, as the children had wished to have George as the king of the kingdom.

Abraham added that the children had been very brave because the children had succeeded where the parents had failed. Because the children had had the courage to fight the king Kalus to save the kingdom, despite the fact that the children had been threatened with death by Kalus.

And the children had fought the king Kalus against their parents' will. And that the children had succeeded where the parents had failed because the parents had not even had the courage to fight Kalus. And the parents had accepted the laws of Kalus without even fighting, while the children had decided to ban the laws of Kalus in this kingdom.

Suddenly, Abraham became calm, and he was looking with a sad face. And the children were staring at the sadness that was on Abraham's face, and some children like Sunshine, Luna, Khloe and George were understanding why Abraham was sad, while others were not understanding why Abraham was sad.

Then Sunshine broke the silence and told Abraham that the children did not want to see him sad. Luna told Abraham that she did not want to see the sadness on his face, and that he wanted him to continue to tell them the stories of the kingdom.

Abraham told Luna that it was hard for him to see how the kingdom had been destroyed by Kalus, and that he had wished to die rather than to live the reign of Kalus. George told Abraham not to worry because the kingdom would be rebuilt and that the children were determined to build the kingdom and to make the kingdom great again.

Suddenly, a drawing in the notebook that was opened in front of Abraham caught the attention of Sunshine. And Sunshine asked Abraham if he was the one who had drawn this drawing in the notebook. And Abraham answered Sunshine that he had drawn these drawings in the notebook to show to children how in the past people lived.

Then Abraham showed some drawings to Sunshine and he told her that these drawings were the first houses and first school of the kingdom. Sunshine looked at Abraham and asked him if he knew the map of the kingdom. And Abraham answered Sunshine that he knew the map of the kingdom as well as he knew well that his name was Abraham.

Sunshine asked Abraham how many bridges did the kingdom have? Abraham answered Sunshine that the kingdom had three bridges. Luna looked at Abraham and asked if the kingdom did have two bridges?Abraham replied to Luna that the kingdom had three bridges, just that Kalus had closed the road that led to the third bridge.

Luna asked Abraham why Kalus had closed this road? Abraham told Luna that he had no idea that only Kalus could answer this question. And Abraham added that Kalus had not only destroyed the kingdom, but Kalus had also destroyed the history of the kingdom like the traditions, the cultures and the values of the kingdom.

Because Kalus had not only closed the schools and the churches, but Kalus had also closed the museums and all the places that were related to the traditions and culture of the kingdom. And even worse Kalus had banned people from going to the rivers, and he had closed all the roads that led to the rivers.

And Kalus had even destroyed the statues of all the former kings of the kingdom. Even the statues of the heroes who had fought during the wars of the kingdom to free the kingdom when the kingdom had been invaded by the enemies. And even worse, Kalus had destroyed the status of the founding fathers of the kingdom.

Then Abraham stopped talking, and there were the tears that were flowing down his cheeks. And the children were staring at Abraham with the sadness on their faces, and they were trying to calm Abraham. And George told Abraham that the kingdom would be rebuilt with its traditions, cultures and values.

And George went on and said that as the king of the kingdom, he would rebuild all the statues that had been destroyed by Kalus, and he would also build the statues of all the children who were fighting now to free the kingdom. And he would not only reopen all the museums, but he would also reopen the roads and the places that were related to the tradition and cultures.

And George went on and said that he would also build a museum that would represent the history of the children who were fighting now to free the kingdom. Because the future generations would know that he and his fellows had fought to free the kingdom, when the kingdom was destroyed by a devil called Kalus.

And George continued and said that as the king of the kingdom, he would make sure that not only the traditions and the culture of the kingdom would be taught in school. But he would also make sure that the history of the children who were fighting now to save the kingdom would be taught in school because he and his fellows would inspire the future generations.

Because the future generations would be ready to fight if one day the kingdom was attacked by the enemies, even if these enemies were the inhabitants of the kingdom. Then George said that they would make sure that their stories would live forever, and that their stories would never die.

Because their stories would not only inspire the future generations, but their stories would give courage and strength to the future generations. And that the patriotic spirit would be taught not only in school but also in the kingdom.

And the future generations would be able to take the example of Sunshine, Aaron, Luna, Isac, Asher, Khloe, Mia, Nany, and others. And the future generations would be able to fight whoever would try to destroy the kingdom even if this person would be the king or the queen of the kingdom.

Suddenly, George was interrupted by Mia who was clapping her hands, and the rest of them followed Mia by clapping their hands. And Abraham was staring at the children as they were clapping their hands for George with a smile on his face. And looking at the expression on Abraham's face, we could see that he was very proud of these children.

Then Abraham opened his mouth and he told them that he was very proud of them, and that he had no word to describe these moments that he was sharing with them. And that they were all the angels coming from heaven to save the kingdom and to save the inhabitants of the kingdom.

And Abraham added that he had no doubt that George would not only be a great king for the kingdom, but George would also be the greatest king that the kingdom had ever had. And the children told Abraham that they were very proud to have him, and that he was not only the grandfather of Khloe but he was also the grandfather of all the children of the kingdom.

And that was the reason why they wanted him to be happy, and they would make sure that he would always be happy. And Abraham told children that he was already happy thanks to them. And George told Abraham that he needed Abraham to rule the kingdom because Abraham would not only be the minister of traditions and culture of the kingdom, but Abraham would also be his advisor.

Suddenly, there were the screams of joy in the room, and they were all clapping their hands, and they were congratulating Abraham on his appointment as the minister of the tradition and the cultures of the kingdom and as the advisor of the king George.

Abraham thanked George for this nomination and he told George that it was a great pleasure to serve his kingdom, and that it was a dream that was coming true to serve his kingdom. And Abraham added that he would work with all his strength and his energy, and he would also put his heart to rebuild this kingdom. And to make the kingdom great again and a better place.

Then each child congratulated Abraham on his nomination by giving a hug to Abraham. And the children also thanked George for the nomination of Abraham. Then Sunshine asked Abraham if Abraham could draw the three bridges of the kingdom. And Abraham answered that yes, that he could draw these three bridges.

Then Abraham picked up the pencil and he started to draw the first bridge. All the children had their eyes focused on the bridge that Abraham was drawing. And Sunshine was looking at this bridge which was being drawn by Abraham with attention, and she was trying to see if it was the same bridge that she was seeing through her magic.

Then Sunshine asked Abraham if he could draw the second bridge as she had noticed that the bridge that Abraham was drawing was not the bridge that she was seeing through her magic. Abraham told Sunshine that he had not yet finished drawing the first bridge. And Sunshine replied to Abraham that she knew, but that she wanted him to draw the second bridge.

And Abraham told Sunshine that he would finish the first bridge later so that the rest of people could see how this bridge looks. Then Abraham started to draw the second bridge, and everyone had the eyes focused on the second bridge that Abraham was drawing. And Sunshine's eyes were focused on the second bridge that Abraham was drawing.

After a few minutes, Abraham was interrupted by Sunshine, and Sunshine asked Abraham if he could draw the third bridge, as she had noticed that even the second bridge was not the bridge that she was looking for.

And except Luna, the rest of the children turned their heads and they looked at Sunshine with surprised faces, as they were not understanding why Sunshine was asking Abraham to draw the third bridge like Abraham had not yet finished to draw the second bridge.

And Asher told Sunshine that Abraham had not yet finished drawing the second bridge. And Sunshine replied to Asher that she knew that Abraham had not yet finished drawing the second bridge but that she wanted to know what the third bridge looked like.

Abraham told Sunshine that he could finish drawing the second bridge, then draw the third bridge. Luna told Abraham that there was no more time, and that it was important to draw the third bridge, and that he would finish the second bridge later.

And suddenly, except Sunshine, the rest of the children were looking at Luna with astonished faces wondering what was going on. And looking at their expressionless faces, we could see that they were completely lost. But some of them had understood that Sunshine and Luna were hiding something from them.

And Asher asked Luna what was going on? Luna answered Asher that nothing was going on. Asher asked Luna why she told Abraham that there was no more time. Luna answered Asher that she was curious to know what the third bridge looked like. Asher told Luna that Abraham could finish drawing the second bridge, and draw the third bridge because there were people who wanted to see what the second bridge looked like.

And Asher added that Abraham had not finished drawing the first bridge because Abraham had been interrupted by Sunshine who asked Abraham to draw the second bridge. Then George, Mia, Aaron, Nany and others joined Asher's idea and they told Luna that they wanted Abraham to finish drawing the second bridge, then Abraham would draw the third bridge.

Then Luna and Sunshine looked at each other without saying a word, and looking at their facial expressions, we could see that they were worried about what was going on, and that they did not know what to do.

Then Luna looked at Asher and she told Asher that it was important that Abraham draw the third bridge because she really wanted to see what this third bridge looked like. Asher replied to Luna that there were people in the room who really wanted to see what the first and second bridges looked like. Luna told Asher that she would explain the reasons why she wanted Abraham to draw the third bridge later, but that it was important that Abraham draw this third bridge first.

Asher told Luna that they had time to listen to the reasons why she wanted Abraham to draw the third bridge first. Isac looked at Asher and Isac asked Asher to stop asking questions to Luna. And Isac added that Abraham could draw the second bridge and the first bridge later. Asher replied to Isac that Abraham could draw the third bridge later. Isac told Asher that it was not fair that Asher prevented Abraham from drawing the third bridge that Sunshine and Luna wanted because the idea to draw the bridges was Sunshine's idea.

Asher told Isac that what was not fair was the fact that Sunshine and Luna were hiding things from them. Isac told Asher that Luna had promised to talk about what was going on later, but that it was important that Abraham draw the third bridge now. Asher told Isac that Luna can talk about what was happening now.

Isac told Asher that they could save time and allow Abraham to draw this third bridge. Asher told Isac that Luna could prevent them from wasting their time by telling them what was going on. Isac replied to Asher that nobody could force Luna to talk now, and that Luna had the right to talk when she would feel ready to talk.

Suddenly, the conversation between Isac and Asher was interrupted by Abraham. And Abraham told Isac and Asher to calm down. And Abraham added that Isac and Asher were both right but that they were not going to argue because they were all a family who were fighting for the same goal, and that this goal was to save the kingdom. Then Abraham became silent and he looked at Isac without saying a word, and everyone had their eyes focused on Abraham and they were all wondering why Abraham was staring at Isac.

Then Abraham broke the silence and said that thought that Isac was mute. And everyone burst into laughter as they had all understood why Abraham had said that he thought that Isac was mute. Asher told Abraham that Isac only talked when Isac needed to protect Luna. Luna asked Asher to stop bothering Isac.

Abraham replied to Luna that Asher was right because since yesterday that they had come home, he had not heard the voice of Isac, and he had even tried to make Isac talk without success. And Abraham went on and said that Isac talked now just because Isac wanted to defend and protect Luna because Isac should not open if Luna and Asher were not arguing. And Abraham also said that it was not the first time he saw Isac protect Luna.

Asher asked Abraham how Abraham knew that Luna was always protected by Isac? Abraham answered that a few days ago, when the kingdom was invaded by the monsters, he watched on television how the children were fighting against the monsters. And Abraham added that this day, he watched on television how Luna was surrounded by the monsters, and he watched how Isac came with a face full of anger to save Luna, and he mostly watched the fear on Isac's face when Luna had been injured by the monsters.

Asher told Abraham that Luna and Isac were in love. Abraham told Asher that Asher had forgotten to mention that he(Asher) and Khloe were in love, also that George and Mia were in love, and that Sunshine and Aaron were in love. And they were all looking at Abraham with amazed faces by wondering how Abraham knew that. And Asher asked Abraham how Abraham knew that? Abraham answered that he had the eyes, and that he had been a teenager too. And they all laughed in the room.

Then Abraham asked all the children if they all agreed that he started to draw the third bridge. And Asher answered that he agreed, then the rest of the children said that they agreed too. Abraham looked at the children and said that they were amazing, and that they were a good family. Then Abraham took the pencil and he started to draw the third bridge. And all the eyes were focused on Abraham like Abraham was drawing the bridge.

After a few minutes, the expression of Sunshine's face changed and she was looking at the bridge that was drawn by Abraham with a surprised face as she was noticing that the bridge that was drawing by Abraham was the bridge that she was seeing through her magic. And Sunshine was using her magic to find where the bridge was located as Abraham was drawing.

Suddenly, Abraham was interrupted by Sunshine who asked Abraham if he knew where the bridge was located. Abraham looked at Sunshine and said that this bridge that he was drawing had been built when he was fourteen. And Abraham added that his father and grandfather were between the employees who had built this bridge, and that it was his grandfather who was the architect of this bridge.

Sunshine asked Abraham if Abraham knew the road that led to this bridge? Abraham answered Sunshine that he was taken by his dad and granddad every morning to work on the construction of this bridge. And Abraham added that his childhood friends and he had also helped to build this bridge by carrying the stones and picking up the sand and gravel.

Sunshine asked Abraham if he could draw the path that led to this bridge. Abraham answered Sunshine that he could take her on the path that led to this bridge, just that they could not reach the bridge because half of the path to the bridge was closed. Sunshine told Abraham that no, that they did not need to go there, just that she wanted him to draw the path that led to this bridge.

Then Abraham started to draw the path that led to this bridge. Sunshine's eyes were focused on the drawing of Abraham, and at the same time Sunshine was using her magic to find where the road was located. Then something caught Sunshine's attention on the drawing of Abraham, and Sunshine noticed that Abraham was drawing a huge wall.

And Sunshine asked Abraham if the bridge was located behind the wall? And Abraham answered that yes, that the wall had been built by Kalus to prevent people from going to the bridge. And Abraham added that there were many walls that had been built on the orders of Kalus to prevent people from going to the bridge, and there was also a small tunnel under the bridge. And that it was impossible to reach the bridge.

Sunshine cried out, "A tunnel?" Abraham answered, "Yes, a tunnel." Then Sunshine asked Abraham if this tunnel was built in steel? And Abraham answered that yes, that this tunnel was built in steel. Then Sunshine became silent, and she was understanding why her magic was unable to locate this missing pregnant woman. And she was also understanding why she was seeing just the bridge and not the tunnel. And Sunshine could not see this tunnel because this tunnel was built in steel, as her magic could work with the steel.

Suddenly, Sunshine got up from the floor and she said that she would be back. Aaron asked Sunshine where she was going? Sunshine answered Aaron that she would be back soon. Then Sunshine rushed towards the door.

Aaron, Asher, George and others got up from the floor and they rushed towards the door to follow Sunshine. But they immediately stopped near the door as they saw a long sword that was flying in front of them, and this sword was preventing them from getting out of the house.

And looking at the expression on their faces, we could see that they were a little surprised by this sword that was flying in front of them, but they were not afraid. And if they were not afraid, it was because they knew that this sword was coming from Luna's magic, and that Luna had used this sword to prevent them from following Sunshine. AndSunshine had already left.

Then Asher tried to grab the sword to remove the sword in front of them. But unfortunately for Asher, he was unable to grab the sword because the sword was sliding into Asher's hand. And the children who were close to Asher were astonished to see that Asher was unable to grab the sword.

Then George and Aaron tried to grab the sword, but unfortunately, they were unable to grab the sword because the sword was sliding into their hands. And George said that it was Luna who was preventing them from grabbing the sword through her magic. Then they all turned and they stared at Luna who was staring at them with a smile on her face.

Then they all walked until the carpet, and they sat on the floor, and they looked at Luna. Then Asher asked Luna why she used the sword to prevent them from going out? Luna answered Asher that it was not safe to go out. Asher replied to Luna that Sunshine was outside.

Luna told Asher that Sunshine just had the chance to get out before the sword appeared in front of the door. Asher asked Luna where Sunshine went? Luna answered Asher that not to worry, that Sunshine would be back. Asher told Luna that he wanted to know what was happening. Luna answered Sunshine that they were all fighting against Kalus and Lord to save the kingdom.

Nany asked Luna who was Lord? Luna answered that Lord was the devil who had given the satanic powers to Kalus to destroy the kingdom. Nany said that she wanted to know a little more about Lord. Then everyone had their eyes focused on Luna as she was talking about Lord.

It was nine o'clock, the streets of the kingdom were empty, and the whole kingdom was in their houses. There was darkness outside, there was neither moon nor stars in the sky. And there was Sunshine on the road who was driving faster and she had put her foot on the accelerator. And she was driving towards the third bridge of the kingdom with her face full of worries, and looking at the expression on Sunshine's face, we could see the fear on her face.

And Sunshine was afraid not only because Lord was outside looking for this pregnant woman too because she had seen Lord's shadow appear near to her car many times, she knew that she was followed by Lord. But Sunshine was mostly afraid because she could see through her magic that this pregnant woman was dying.

Sunshine was driving as fast as she could with her foot still on the accelerator, and with her heart that was beating faster than the normal. And there was a question that was going on in Sunshine's head. And this question was why Lord was interested in this pregnant woman? But unfortunately, Sunshine could not answer this question. But Sunshine had noticed that Lord was paying attention to this missing pregnant woman, and that Lord had not even tried to fight her to get other pregnant women who were in Khloe's house.

And for Sunshine, it was obvious that this missing pregnant woman was very important for Lord. AndSunshine was trying to understand without success why between all these pregnant women, only this missing pregnant woman was important for Lord.

But Sunshine knew that this pregnant woman had something different from the rest of the pregnant women, and that it was the reason why Lord was interested in her. But Sunshine did not know what this pregnant woman had that was different from the rest of the pregnant women. And she was thinking about what could be the thing that could make this missing pregnant woman different from other pregnant women.

Suddenly, Sunshine took her foot off the accelerator as she had seen a big wall in front of her, and she had understood that this wall was built to prevent people from reaching the bridge. And Sunshine's eyes started spinning, then the light got out from her eyes and shone in the car, then the car flew in space.

Sunshine was driving in the space, and she was amazed to see the walls that were built on the orders of Kalus to prevent people from going to the bridge. Sunshine was wondering why Kalus did not want people to go to this third bridge. Why was this third bridge important for Kalus that he built the walls to prevent people from reaching this bridge? But unfortunately, Sunshine could not answer this question.

Then Sunshine landed on the road with the car as she had crossed the space of the last wall. Sunshine had her foot on the accelerator and she was driving towards the bridge as fast as she could, and she was seeing a part of the bridge and she was also seeing the tunnel in front of her.

After a few seconds, Sunshine was driving in the tunnel, then she suddenly took her foot off the accelerator and she put her foot on the brake as she had seen two people who were lying on the ground. Then Sunshine stopped the car and she got out of the car and rushed towards these two people on the ground.

Then Sunshine saw a pregnant woman and an old man who were lying on the ground. Then Sunshine knelt near this pregnant woman and she started to shake this pregnant woman, but unfortunately this pregnant woman was not reacting. Then Sunshine put her palm's hand on the heart of this pregnant woman, and she felt the heart of this pregnant woman was still beating, then Sunshine understood that this pregnant woman was still alive, but that she was unconscious.

Then Sunshine got up and she ran until near the man who was lying on the ground. Then she knelt on the ground and she put her hand on the heart of this man, and she felt that his heart was still beating. Sunshine took a deep breath by looking at the sky and she was happy that this woman and man were still alive.

Then Sunshine got up from the ground and she ran to her car and she got in the car, then she drove until near to this pregnant woman and she stopped the car's engine. Then Sunshine got out of the car and she ran till this man, and she knelt near to this man and she started shaking this man by asking this man to open his eyes.

But unfortunately, this man was not reacting, and Sunshine's heart was beating faster than normal, as she was shaking this man, and we could even feel the fear in Sunshine's voice. And Sunshine was afraid because she knew that Lord could appear at any time, as she knew that Lord was outside looking for this pregnant woman too. And Sunshine knew that if Lord appeared, the worst could happen, and she could fail to protect this pregnant woman and Lord could kill this pregnant woman.

After a few minutes, Sunshine was still shaking this man, but unfortunately for Sunshine, this man was still not reacting. Then

Sunshine got an idea and her eyes started spinning, then a light got out from her eyes and shone on this man. Suddenly, this man felt a strange reaction in his body, and he opened his eyes, then the expression of his changed as he had seen Sunshine, and he was looking at Sunshine with a face full of fear.

And Sunshine looked into his eyes and told him not to be afraid because she had come to help him. And this man asked where his wife was? Sunshine answered this man that his wife was lying on the ground, and that he must get up from the ground and help her to put his wife in the car.

But that man refused and he told Sunshine that his wife and him would not leave because Kalus had decided to kill their baby. Because his wife was pregnant and that the new law of Kalus forced all pregnant women to have an abortion.

Sunshine looked into the eyes of this man and she said that her name was Sunshine. And immediately, that man cried out, "Sunshine?" And the expression on his face had changed and he was looking at Sunshine with an amazed face. And this man added, "It's really you?" Sunshine answered, "Yes, it's really me."

Then this man raised his both hands and he rubbed his both eyes, then he removed his hands from his eyes he looked at Sunshine with a face full of smiles. And he told Sunshine that he was sorry, just that he was so afraid that he did not recognize her, and that he watched her on television many times, and that he was very proud of her and her fellows about children's fight to save the kingdom.

Then this man handed his hand to Sunshine and said, "I am John." Sunshine shook John's hand and she told him that they must leave now. John told Sunshine that he could not leave because he must stay with his wife. Sunshine told John not to worry because his wife and him were safe with her. But John refused and told Sunshine that his wife and him had decided to die with their baby in the womb of his wife.

And after three minutes, Sunshine had finally succeeded in convincing John. Then John got up from the ground and he followed

Sunshine who was walking towards his wife. Then they stopped near John's wife and they both carried John's wife and they laid John's wife on the back seat of the car.

Then Sunshine and John got in the car, and Sunshine drove away. Sunshine was driving faster, and there was silence in the car. And John had his eyes opened, then the expression on John's face changed and he was looking with fear on his face as he was noticing Sunshine who was driving towards the wall.

Then John turned his head and looked at Sunshine and he told Sunshine that there was a wall in front of them. Sunshine turned her head and looked at John without saying a word, and her eyes started spinning. But despite the fact that John was staring at Sunshine, he was not noticing that Sunshine's eyes were spinning. Then the light got out from Sunshine's eyes and shone on John, and John immediately fell asleep.

Then Sunshine put her foot on the accelerator and she was driving faster towards the wall, then her eyes started spinning and the light got out from her eyes and shone in the car. Then the car flew in the space, and Sunshine was driving in the space.

Suddenly, the expression on Sunshine's face changed and she was looking with a face full of fear, as she was seeing a car that was coming towards her, and she knew that it was Lord who was in that car.

Then Sunshine wanted to land on the ground to run away from the car that was in space, but it was impossible for Sunshine to land on the ground. Because there were walls that had been built on the orders of Kalus to prevent people from going to the bridge.

Then Sunshine noticed that the car that was in space was already near to her car, and she turned the steering wheel of the car to the left to avoid an accident. Then Sunshine put her foot on the accelerator and she was driving faster, and she had her eyes focused on the mirror that was in the car, and she was seeing through the mirror of her car Lord in his car chasing her.

Sunshine was very worried and she knew that the worst could happen, and that Lord could kill John's wife who was in the car because Lord was looking for John's wife. And suddenly the expression on Sunshine's face changed and she was looking in the mirror with a surprised face as she noticed that Lord's car had disappeared. And Sunshine was turning her head and looking through the car's windows wondering where car's Lord was.

Suddenly, the fear appeared on Sunshine's face when she saw Lord's car that was coming in front of her car, and Sunshine noticed that both cars were going to crash. Then Sunshine's eyes started spinning and the light got out from her eyes and shone in the car.

Then Sunshine's car flew in the direction of the sky, and Sunshine was still in space and she knew that it was very dangerous because the car was very high in space. Sunshine knew that it was dangerous that the car was very high in space not only because it was risky if an accident happened, but mostly because John and his wife could have difficulties breathing.

Then Sunshine started to think how to get rid of Lord, and she suddenly felt that her car was hit by something from behind. And Sunshine looked in the mirror that was in the car, and she noticed that Lord's car was hitting her car from behind. Then Sunshine understood that she would do everything possible to avoid an accident in space because an accident in space was extremely dangerous and John's wife could die or lose her baby.

Then Sunshine's eyes started spinning and she pressed the accelerator and the car was going faster, and she had her eyes focused on the mirror. And Sunshine was thinking what to do as she had noticed that Lord was chasing her car with his car.

Sunshine was trying to find the ideas to get rid of Lord without success. Suddenly, the expression on her face changed as she was looking through the car's window with fear on her face, as she was seeing Lord who was driving near to her. Then Sunshine pressed the accelerator with all her strength and her eyes were spinning faster and the car was going faster.

And Lord's car was going faster, and both cars were at the same level and they were still driving in space. And they were driving as fast as they could as if they were doing the car's race to see who was going to be the winner.

After fifteen minutes, both cars were still racing. And Sunshine was not really focused on the wheel because she could not stop thinking about how to get rid of Lord. And Sunshine wanted to land on the ground as she had already crossed the place where the walls were built.

But Sunshine knew that she could not land on the ground with Lord who was driving near to her because Lord could easily cause an accident if she tried to land on the ground. And Sunshine knew that if an accident was caused by Lord, the worst could happen because John or John's wife or even the baby that was in the womb of John's wife could die. Or even worse the accident could cause John's wife to miscarry.

Then Sunshine started to feel that the car was losing the balance, and she looked in the mirror. And suddenly the expression of her face changed and the fear appeared on her face, as she was seeing through the mirror Lord was hitting the back's door of her car with his car. Sunshine's heart started beating faster than normal, and she was very worried about John's wife who was lying in the back seat because the car's Lord was hitting the back door of her car.

And Sunshine was afraid that Lord could cause an early delivery or even a miscarriage to John's wife like Lord's car was hitting the car's door where John's wife was. Then Sunshine started thinking what to do, and she knew well that the car could not go faster than the car was going now.

Because she could not increase the speed of the car anymore because the car was now traveling at its fastest speed. And Sunshine could no longer use the magic to make the car go faster because the car was going right now with all the potential of her magic.

After a few seconds of thinking, Sunshine decided to fight Lord because for Sunshine, the only solution was the fight. Because

Sunshine knew that if she did not fight, Lord would kill her or he would kill John's wife. But Sunshine knew that she would be careful when she would be fighting Lord because she knew that she must avoid that Lord hit the back door of her car during the fight because John's wife was lying in the back's seat.

Then Sunshine turned the steering wheel and she turned her car, and her car was face to Lord's car, then she put her foot on the accelerator. And suddenly, the anger appeared on Sunshine's face, and she was driving towards Lord's car, while Lord was driving towards Sunshine's car and there was also anger on Lord's face.

Suddenly, the two cars crashed, then both Sunshine and Lord started fighting with their cars, and they were hitting their cars. Lord was trying to hit the back door of Sunshine's car without success because Sunshine was fighting with great intelligence, and Sunshine was hitting the car's Lord by avoiding that Lord hit the back's door of her car with his car.

After a few minutes, Lord and Sunshine were still fighting in space by using their cars, and both cars were destroyed. But Lord's car was completely destroyed while only the front of Sunshine's car was destroyed. Then Lord noticed that his car was all destroyed and he understood that it was impossible to continue to fight by using his car.

Then Lord got an idea, and he broke his car's door with his elbow and he got out of the car, then he flew towards Sunshine's car. Sunshine was seeing Lord who was flying towards her car, and she started to turn the steering wheel to the right, as she had understood that Lord was coming to kill John's wife who was still lying in the back seat.

Then Sunshine pressed the accelerator and she drove away, and she had her eyes focused on the mirror that was in the car. And Sunshine was seeing through the mirror Lord who was chasing her car by flying. Then Sunshine started thinking what to do, and she was very worried about what was going to happen, and she was very afraid that Lord could catch the car and kill John's wife.

And Sunshine knew well that she could not get out of the car to fight Lord because if she got out of the car, the car would not keep its balance in the space. And the car would fall to the ground, and John's wife and John would die.

Then Sunshine was trying to find a solution, and suddenly the expression on Sunshine's face changed. And she was looking in the mirror with the terror on her face, as she was seeing Lord who was already near to the car. Then Sunshine tried to drive faster, but it was impossible because she was already driving at the fastest speed of the car. And she was already using all the potential of her magic to drive the car.

Suddenly, Sunshine's heart started beating faster with fear, as she was feeling her car was shaking, and she was seeing through the mirror that Lord was trying to open the back's door of the car. And Sunshine was very afraid that Lord would succeed in opening the back's door of the car because she knew that if Lord opened this door, he would kill John's wife who was lying in the back's seat.

Then Sunshine started to think about what to do, and it was impossible to fight Lord because she could not get out of the car, and it was impossible to fight Lord by using her car. Because Lord had an advantage on her because Lord could move in space by flying, so she could not use the car to hit Lord.

Then Sunshine looked in the mirror as she had heard a noise, and she started breathing deeply and her whole body was trembling with fear, as she had noticed that Lord had broken the window of the car door. And Sunshine noticed that Lord was trying to send his hand through the car's window to kill John's wife.

Then Sunshine started to think what to do as she had noticed that Lord's hand was in the car, and that he was trying to pull John's wife out of the car. Then Sunshine got an idea and her eyes started spinning, and the car started shaking, and it was Sunshine who was using her magic to shake the car.

And Sunshine was making the car shake because she wanted to prevent Lord from killing John's wife or from pulling John's wife out of the car. Sunshine was still driving in space by thinking what to do, while Lord still had his hand in the car. And Lord had the difficulties to grab John's wife because Lord did not have the balance like the car was shaking.

Sunshine had her eyes focused on the mirror and she was seeing Lord who was trying to grab John's wife without success. Then Sunshine understood that she must get rid of Lord because she would never reach home if she did not get rid of Lord.

Sunshine also knew that it was risky to continue to drive in space because Lord could succeed in killing John's wife, like Lord had his hand in the car. Sunshine also knew well that the only solution to get rid of Lord was to fight Lord, but she knew that she could not fight him in space because she could not get out of the car. Then Sunshine got an idea, and she took her foot off the accelerator, and the car started flying towards the ground.

After a few seconds, the car landed on the ground, and Sunshine opened the car's door and got out of the car. Then Sunshine looked at Lord and she noticed that Lord had sent his two hands through the car's window, and he was trying to kill John's wife by pressing the neck of John's wife. Then Sunshine's eyes started spinning as she was looking at Lord.

And suddenly, Lord pushed a loud scream as he had felt a strong pain in his body, and he pulled his hands out of the car's window. Then Lord turned and looked at Sunshine and he noticed that Sunshine's eyes were spinning. Then Lord opened his mouth to talk but unfortunately, he was pushed into the space by the light that had got out from Sunshine's eyes. Then Lord went and fell to the ground.

Then Sunshine started walking faster towards Lord, and her eyes were spinning, and Lord was trying to get up from the ground, and he saw Sunshine who was staring at him. Then Lord started to yell in pain, and he was torture by Sunshine's magic.

And despite the fact that Lord was feeling pain in his whole body, he was trying to concentrate to use his magic to fight Sunshine, but it was impossible for Lord to use his magic. Because he was feeling extreme pain in his whole body that he could not concentrate to use his magic to fight Sunshine.

Because Lord needed to concentrate first to trigger his magic to fight, but the pain coming from Sunshine's magic was preventing him from concentrating on triggering his magic. Lord was staring at Sunshine by yelling in pain, and he did not know what to do, and it was impossible for him to use his magic. But Lord had felt that the pain that he was feeling was very strong, and that it was his first time to feel the stronger pain like this.

And Lord was very surprised by this pain coming from Sunshine's magic because it was the first time that he was feeling the strongest pain like this coming from Sunshine's magic. And Lord was wondering where Sunshine had got more powers and magic, and if she had really got more powers and magic where she had got these powers and magic from? And Lord was very astonished by the powers of Sunshine because it's been more than a year that he was fighting Sunshine, and this was the first time that he was unable to use his magic to fight Sunshine.

Lord was still tortured by Sunshine, and he had started to sweat, then Lord got an idea and he turned and gave his back to Sunshine, and he was still feeling the same pain, and he was still trying to use his magic without success.

And Lord had turned by giving his back to Sunshine because he had thought that by giving his back to Sunshine, he would be able to concentrate to trigger his magic to fight as his eyes should no longer be in contact with Sunshine's eyes. And Lord was completely lost, and he did not understand what was going on because although the fact that his eyes were no longer in contact with Sunshine's eyes, he was still unable to concentrate to use his magic.

Then, Lord turned and looked at Sunshine. And immediately, the expression on the face of Lord changed and his face was full of fear as he noticed that Sunshine's eyes were spinning faster than usual. And Lord understood that Sunshine was more powerful and stronger because she had the energy of Luna's magic in her body. And

Lord also understood that he could not fight Sunshine and that he was too weak to fight Sunshine.

Because the energy of Luna's magic that was in Sunshine's body was making Sunshine more powerful and stronger because it was as if Sunshine was using two magic that were her own magic and Luna's magic to fight him. Sunshine was still torturing Lord by thinking what to do because she knew that she could not kill Lord, and she also knew that she could not spend her whole night to torture Lord.

Because it was useless to spend the entire night to torture Lord, mostly that she must take John's wife to Khloe's home for that the doctors and nurses take care of John's wife. Sunshine knew that it was risky to stay outside with John's wife not only because Lord could finally succeed in killing John's wife, but mostly because John's wife could finally die because John's wife was already unconscious.

But Sunshine knew that the only solution to take John's wife to Khloe's home, was to get rid of Lord. Then she got an idea, and her eyes stopped turning. Then Lord took a deep breath as he had felt that the pain had gone, and he looked at Sunshine and he noticed that Sunshine's eyes had stopped turning. And there was the sweat that was running down Lord as if it was the water.

Lord was still on the ground and he was staring at Sunshine and he was looking tired and he was also breathing deeply with the sweat that was running down his clothes. And Lord was wondering why Sunshine had stopped torturing him, but he knew that Sunshine had stopped torturing him because she had another plan.

Because he knew well that Sunshine had not stopped his pain because Sunshine had taken a pity on him. Because Lord knew that Sunshine hated him like he hated her, and that Sunshine wanted him dead like he wanted her dead. And Lord was wondering what Sunshine's plan could be? But unfortunately, he could not answer this question.

Then Lord started thinking what to do, he got an idea to trigger his magic to fight Sunshine like Sunshine had stopped using her magic, but he gave up this idea because he knew well that he could not win a fight against Sunshine.

Because Sunshine was more powerful and stronger than him like Sunshine had the energy of Luna's magic in her body. Then the smile appeared on Lord's face like Lord had got a new idea, and this new idea was to fight Sunshine and kill her, and Lord had just remembered that the weakness of Sunshine's magic was steel, and that he could turn into steel to fight Sunshine.

And Lord knew well that if he turned into the steel, Sunshine would not be able to use her own magic to fight him because Sunshine's magic could not react with the steel. And like Sunshine would not be able to use her own magic to fight, that meant that Sunshine would be able to use only the energy of Luna's magic that was in her body to fight him.

And Lord knew well that Sunshine would not win a fight against him by fighting him by using only the energy of Luna's magic that was in her body (Sunshine's body) because Luna was not powerful and strong enough. And the fact that Luna was not stronger and powerful enough meant that the energy of Luna's magic that was in Sunshine's body was not stronger and powerful enough.

And it also meant that it would be impossible for Sunshine to use that energy of Luna's magic to protect John's wife because the only chance for Sunshine to protect John's wife was to beat him. But like Sunshine could not beat him by using only the energy of Luna's magic meant that he had the power not only to kill John's wife but also to kill Sunshine.

And Lord started to laugh as he had understood that he was going to put an end to the fight now by killing Sunshine and John's wife. Then Lord got up from the ground with his face full of smiles. Lord and Sunshine were staring at each other with silence. And Sunshine had a face full of anger, while Lord had a face full of smiles. And Sunshine was a little amazed to see the smile on Lord's face, and she was wondering why Lord was smiling? But unfortunately, she could not answer this question.

Then, Lord broke the silence and said, "I want this pregnant woman in the car."

"Why do you want this pregnant woman?" Sunshine asked.

"I must kill her," Lord answered.

"Why do you want to kill her?" Sunshine asked.

"Because she must not give birth," Lord answered.

"Why must she not give birth?" Sunshine asked.

"When I would kill her, I would tell you the reasons why I have killed her," Lord answered.

"It means that you would never tell me the reasons why you want to kill her," Sunshine said.

Lord smiled at Sunshine and asked, "You mean I would never kill her?"

"You understood me well," Sunshine answered.

"I would kill both of you now," Lord said.

"Stop dreaming," Sunshine said.

"I would kill you first, then I would kill this pregnant woman with her baby in her womb," Lord said.

"Why did you not try to kill other pregnant women because there are many pregnant women in Khloe's house?" Sunshine asked.

"Because other pregnant women are not really important," Lord answered.

"Is it only this pregnant woman in the car who is important?" Sunshine asked.

"Only this pregnant woman in your car is important and special for me, and it's the reason why she would not give birth," Lord said.

"Why ban all pregnant women of the kingdom from giving birth if only one pregnant woman is special?" Sunshine asked.

"All the pregnant women of the kingdom are banned from giving birth because it's important not to take any risks," Lord answered.

"Which risk?" Sunshine asked.

"Because I can be wrong about the pregnant woman who must not give birth," Lord said.

"It meant that there is only a pregnant woman that you do not want her to give birth, but like you do not want to take a risk by mistaking the pregnant woman that you do not want to give birth, you and Kalus chose to ban all pregnant women to give birth by forcing them to have the abortions," Sunshine said.

"It's exact," Lord replied.

"What makes you think that this pregnant woman in the car is the right pregnant woman that you do not want her to give birth to?" Sunshine asked.

"I have the feeling that the pregnant woman in the car is the right one," Lord answered.

"What about if you are mistaken and that she is not the right one?" Sunshine asked.

"Do not worry, I have a plan," Lord answered.

"What is this plan?" Sunshine asked.

"When I would kill you and that pregnant woman in your car, I would go to Khloe's house and I would kill the rest of the pregnant women, and of course it would be a pleasure to kill your fellows," Lord answered.

"You forgot Luna," Sunshine said.

"I would invite Kalus to kill Luna because Kalus's dream is to kill that cursed girl named Luna," Lord said.

"You would not be able to kill all these people in Khloe's house without killing Luna first," Sunshine said.

"Luna is useless, Luna is not an enemy, and Luna is not powerful enough to fight me," Lord said.

"I tortured you a few minutes ago with the energy coming from Luna's magic, and you were not even able to defend yourself because you were focused on crying pain like a baby," Sunshine said.

"You succeeded to torture me because you were using your magic and the energy of Luna's magic," Lord said.

"It means that you can not kill me because you are too weak to fight me when I have my magic and the energy of Luna's magic in my body," Sunshine said.

Lord stared at Sunshine and said, "Do not forget that I know your weakness."

"Do not forget that I told you that you found my weakness when It was too late for you to use it against me," Sunshine said.

"I would turn into steel now, and you would not be able to use your magic to fight me because your magic could not react with the steel. Then I would kill you because you would not succeed in fighting me with only the energy of Luna's magic that is in your body. And when you would be dead, I would kill this pregnant woman in your car," Lord said.

"Good luck," Sunshine said.

Then Lord smiled at Sunshine and his eyes started turning. And Sunshine was looking at Lord as his eyes were spinning with a face empty of expression, then Sunshine noticed that Lord had turned into a steel man.

Sunshine's eyes started spinning as she was staring at Lord who was walking towards her, and Sunshine's heart was beating faster than normal because she was trying to use the energy of Luna's magic. And Sunshine could not use her own magic because Lord had turned into steel, and her magic could work or react with the steel.

Then the fear appeared on Sunshine's face as she had noticed that Lord was already near to her. And suddenly Lord started screaming like there was a light that was getting out from Sunshine's eyes and shining on him. Then Lord fainted on the ground like a dead body, and Sunshine walked until near Lord and looked at him and said, "This is Luna's magic." Then Sunshine turned and walked until her car and she got in the car, then she drove away.

The children and Abraham were still in the living room, and they were all talking together. The children were asking questions to Abraham about the ancestors of the kingdom. And suddenly, the conversation was interrupted by Aaron who said that it was strange that Sunshine was still outside.

And Aaron added that it was already midnight, and that he was worried about Sunshine. And Mia said that Aaron was right that they must go out to look for Sunshine, mostly that the kingdom was not safe because the monsters could appear in the kingdom at any time.

Asher looked at Luna and told her that she must take them where Sunshine was. Luna looked at Abraham and she asked Abraham if he could give her the sheet of paper that he had drawn the third bridge on it. And Abraham asked Luna where she was going with this sheet of paper? Luna answered Abraham that she was going to look for Sunshine.

Abraham told Luna that it was not safe for her to go outside alone. Luna told Abraham that she was not going alone, that she was going with her companions. And Abraham told Luna that he was coming with them because he would not let them go outside alone.

Luna told Abraham that it was too late for him to go outside, and that he should be in bed now. Abraham told Luna that he could not let the children go outside without him. Luna told Abraham not to worry because everything would be fine.

Abraham told Luna that he could not let the children go outside without him because he would die if something happened to the children outside and that he was not with the children to protect them. Luna told Abraham not to worry because she could protect her fellows by using her magic in case of danger.

Suddenly, Luna and Aaron turned their heads towards the door, as they had heard a noise coming from the door, and the smiles appeared on their faces as they saw Sunshine who was walking in the room. Aaron told Sunshine that they were worried about her. Sunshine replied to Aaron that she was sorry if she took a longer time than expected, and that the reason why she had taken so long was because she had had an accident on the road.

And immediately, everyone's expression changed, and they were all staring at Sunshine with fear on their faces as they had heard Sunshine say that she had had an accident on the road. And Aaron asked Sunshine if she was all right? And Sunshine answered Aaron that yes, that she was fine. Then Sunshine added that she needed their help outside.

Then all of them got up from the floor and they rushed through the door by asking Sunshine what was going on. Sunshine answered them to follow her outside. Then they all got out and they walked until they were near the car. And except Luna, the rest of them were surprised to see John's wife and John in the car when Sunshine opened the car's door.

And Asher asked Sunshine where she found John's wife and John? Sunshine answered Asher that she would explain everything to them later, but that they must take John and his wife into the house. Then some of them carried John's wife into the house, and others succeeded in waking up John and they helped John to walk to the house.

Then the children laid John's wife in a room, and they went and woke up the doctors and nurses. And everyone who was asleep woke up to the noises of children, and they were all surprised to see John's wife who was lying in the bed unconscious.

And at the same time, they were very afraid that maybe John's wife was dead or maybe that the child who was in the womb of John's wife was not doing well. Then Doctor Thomas demanded to leave the room and wait in the living room because he and the nurses were going to take care of John's wife.

Except the doctors and nurses, the rest of the people were in the living room and they were asking questions to Sunshine about how she found John and his wife. And Sunshine was trying to answer their questions as she could, but Sunshine was not telling them the truth.

And only Luna knew that Sunshine was not telling them the truth, and Luna knew that Sunshine was lying because Sunshine did not want people to know that she(Sunshine) was born with the powers and magic. And people had tried to talk or even ask questions to John without success because John was not talking. And John was just sitting in the chair and he was looking tired and sad.

Then Doctor Thomas got out of the room, and almost everyone rushed towards Doctor Thomas by asking him how John's wife was. And there was silence, and all the eyes were focused on Doctor Thomas, but Doctor Thomas had his mouth closed.

And people were very worried about the silence of Doctor Thomas, and they were wondering why Doctor Thomas was silent. And some had even the fear on their faces, while the hearts of others were beating faster than the normal. Then Sunshine asked Doctor Thomas why he was silent? Doctor Thomas took a deep breath and answered that John's wife was in a critical condition.

And suddenly, the expression on everyone's face changed, and their faces were full of sadness, and some of them had their mouths opened but no word was coming out. Then some of them turned their heads and looked at each other without uttering a word, and there were some of them who wanted to talk but their mouths were shaking that they could not pronounce a word.

Then Sunshine asked Doctor Thomas how they could save John's wife? Doctor Thomas answered Sunshine that they must provoke the delivery of John's wife, or else she would die with the baby in her womb. And Sunshine asked Doctor Thomas what he needed to provoke the delivery of John's wife.

Doctor Thomas answered Sunshine that he needed a lot of equipment but that this equipment was in the hospitals. Sunshine told Doctor Thomas that she and her fellows could go to the hospital to carry all the equipment he needed. Doctor Thomas replied to Sunshine that it would be not possible to get in the hospital because he had called his colleagues to know if he could get the equipment to the hospital or even take John's wife to the hospital, but his colleagues told him that there were monsters in front of all the hospitals of the kingdom.

Sunshine told Doctor Thomas not to worry, and that she and her comrades had already fought against the monsters. Luna said that Kalus had made the monsters appear to prevent them from getting in the hospitals with the pregnant women. And Luna added that she and her companions were going to get the equipment that Doctor Thomas needed.

Abraham told Luna that the monsters could come into this house to kill the pregnant women if she and her comrades went to the hospital. Luna told Abraham not to worry because even if the monsters come into this house to kill the pregnant women, the monsters would not succeed in getting into the house because she would use her magic to lock the door from outside.

Luna also added that she would use her magic to watch the house when she would leave, and that if she noticed that the monsters were around the house, she would come with her fellows to fight the monsters.

Abraham asked Luna if her magic could protect the house by preventing the monsters from breaking down the door to enter the house. Luna told Abraham not to worry because she knew the powers and strength of the monsters, and that the monsters could not break the door that was locked through her magic.

Then Abraham told Luna that she and her comrades must go now to take the equipment that Doctor Thomas needed. Luna looked at Doctor Thomas and asked him which kind of equipment he needed? And Doctor Thomas answered Luna that a nurse would come with her, and this nurse would show her the equipment he needed. Then Sunshine, Luna, the nurse and others left.

It was 12:15 a.m., the moon and stars were shining in the sky, and there was the wind that was blowing outside. Sunshine was driving the bus towards the parking of the hospital, and there were Sunshine's comrades and the nurse in the bus.

Then Sunshine parked the bus in the parking lot and they all got off the bus. And they started to walk towards the entry door of the hospital. And suddenly the expression on the faces of some of them changed, and they were looking at the monsters with the terror on their faces as they were seeing the monsters in front of the hospital. And they had noticed that these monsters had swords and that some of these monsters had wings.

Then Luna's eyes started turning, and she lifted her head through the sky, and she handed her hand through the space, and the swords started flying into the space. And Luna's fellows had all lifted their heads through the sky and they were seeing the swords flying towards them. And some of them also noticed that there were two horses that were running towards them.

Then Luna looked at her fellows and said that only she and Sunshine were going to fight the monsters. Asher told Luna that he was going to fight the monsters too. Luna told Asher that he could not fight these monsters because some of these monsters had wings, and he could be easily killed by these monsters. Because the monsters that had the wings were very dangerous. Asher told Luna that he was ready to die, and that nothing was going to prevent him from fighting the monsters.

Luna told Asher that he could not fight these monsters because he did not have the abilities to fight these kinds of monsters because to fight these monsters he needed to fly into space. Asher told Luna that if Sunshine could fight these monsters, it meant that he could fight them too because even Sunshine could not fly into space.

Luna looked into Asher's eyes and told him that he did not know well who Sunshine was. Then Luna turned and walked towards a horse, before Asher opened his mouth to say a word. Asher was looking at Luna and Sunshine who were getting on the horses with the mouth opened wondering what Luna meant by he did not know well who Sunshine was.

Sunshine and Luna were on the horses and they had grabbed the swords in their hands, and the horses were running towards the monsters, and there was rage on the faces of Sunshine and Luna. Sunshine and Luna knew that they must get rid of the monsters as soon as possible because they knew that they did not have enough time because John's wife was in danger, and they must get the equipment that the doctors needed to save John's wife.

Then Luna and Sunshine saw the monsters who were running towards them, and Sunshine and Luna turned their heads and looked at each other. Luna said, "I would fight into the space, and you would fight on the ground." Sunshine replied, "It's a great idea." And she added, "We would make sure that the monsters would not cross us because if the monsters cross us, our fellows who are behind us would be killed by the monsters." Luna asked, "Are you ready?" Sunshine answered, "I am willing."

Then Luna lifted her head through the sky and she saw some monsters who were flying in the space, and her eyes started spinning then she flew into the space with her sword in her hand. Luna started fighting the monsters who were in space, while Sunshine was fighting the monsters who were on the ground.

Asher and others were watching the fight with fear on their faces, and they were afraid that Sunshine and Luna could get killed by the monsters, even if Sunshine and Luna were winning the fight by killing the monsters. But they knew that the worst could happen at any time and Sunshine and Luna could be killed by the monsters. Asher, Khloe, Aaron, Mia and Isac were thinking about how to join the fight, but it was impossible because there were no swords and horses. And Luna had just made two horses and two swords appear.

After a few minutes, Sunshine and Luna were still fighting the monsters, and they were fighting by preventing the monsters from crossing them because the monsters were trying to cross them to go kill those who were behind watching the fight. Luna was flying into space by killing the monsters, while Sunshine was moving on the horse by killing the monsters.

Then Luna flew and landed on the ground as she had killed all the monsters who were in space. Then, Luna got on the horse and she joined Sunshine and together they killed all the monsters who were on the ground.

Then Sunshine, Luna and others walked until inside the hospital, and the nurse showed them the equipment that the doctors needed. Then they carried the equipment that the doctors needed and left the hospital without security men who were in the hospital saying a word.

After fifteen minutes, the bus parked in front of the house of Khloe and they got out of the bus. And they carried the equipment that was in the car and they entered the house with it. Then the doctors, nurses and children installed these equipment in the bedroom where John's wife was.

Then the children left the bedroom, then the doctors and nurses stayed in the bedroom and they were taking care of John's wife. The children were in the living room waiting for the doctors to get out of the room and to tell them how John's wife was doing.

And there was silence in the living room. And some children were sitting in the chairs with their hearts beating faster than normal, while others were walking in the living room with fear on their faces. And all the children were afraid and worried about John's wife.

After a few minutes, people who were sitting in the chairs got up from the chairs and they rushed towards Doctor Thomas who had just got out of the room. And all the children had their eyes focused on Doctor Thomas, and they were waiting for him to talk.

Then Doctor Thomas told the children that John's wife was still in a critical condition and that they were still waiting. And Doctor Thomas added that the good news was that John's wife was not in a coma, and that John's wife was no longer unconscious and that she had the eyes opened, but just that she was so tired and weak to utter a word.

Luna asked Doctor Thomas what was the solution? Doctor Thomas answered Luna that they must wait because John's wife was too weak and tired to give birth by pushing the baby. Luna asked Doctor Thomas if he was thinking of performing surgery on John's wife?

Doctor Thomas answered Luna that the surgery was a risk, and that the operation was not being considered at the moment, but that in a few hours if the situation did not change they would be forced to take a risk and to perform the operation on John's wife.

Luna told Doctor Thomas that he would not perform the operation to John's wife because she had the solution. Doctor Thomas asked Luna what was the solution? Luna answered Doctor Thomas that she would crush the leaves of the tree called Baoba that she and Sunshine had come from the sacred forest with.

And John's wife would drink the juice of these tree's leaves, and it would help her, the juice of this tree's leaves would not only give the strength and energy to John's wife, but the juice of these tree's leaves would also help John's wife to give birth safely. Then Luna turned and walked towards the kitchen and she was followed by her companions.

Luna was standing up in front of the sink and she was washing the tree's leaves. And Luna was talking with her comrades, and her comrades were asking her the questions to Luna about these tree's leaves. Luna was answering the questions of her friends.

Then Luna asked the blender to Khloe, and Khloe gave the blender to Luna, and Luna started to crush these tree's leaves. Then the children were joined in the kitchen by Abraham. Abraham stood up near Luna and he was looking at Luna who was crushing the tree's leaves in the blender with the tears that were flowing down his cheeks.

The children were staring at Abraham with the sadness on their faces as they were seeing the tears that were flowing down her cheeks. And Luna asked Abraham why he was crying? Abraham told Luna that he looked at her as she was crushing the tree's leaves and he remembered his childhood life. And he remembered how he and his friends used to go to the sacred forest with their parents to look for the tree's leaves, the herbs, the tree's bark and the tree's roots.

And Abraham added that he remembered how he grew up by seeing the people around him taking the traditional remedy, and that he himself had grown by taking the traditional remedy when he was sick. Abraham went on and said that despite the fact that there were already the hospitals and the pharmacies when he was born, his parents had never taken him to the hospital when he was sick.

Because there were the traditional remedies at home for any kind of illness, and that even most of the inhabitants of the kingdom did not go to the hospitals and pharmacies because there were the traditional remedies at home. And that people used to go to the hospitals only for emergency cases.

Abraham continued and said that everything had changed since Kalus became the king of this kingdom because Kalus banned the inhabitants of the kingdom from going to the sacred forest and he also banned people from using traditional remedies.

George looked at Abraham and he told Abraham not to worry that everything would change in the kingdom because the reign of Kalus was over. And that people would continue to go to the sacred forest, and people would use the traditional remedies as in the past. And Abraham thanked George for his words and Abraham also told George that he could not wait to see all the changes that would be made in the kingdom.

Sunshine looked at Abraham and she told him that the changes in the kingdom would start today because George would sit on the throne of the kingdom today. Abraham smiled at Sunshine and he told her that the changes had already started since the day she and fellows had organized their first protest to demand the return of education to the kingdom.

Then Luna said that they must continue the conversation in the living room because John's wife was ready. Abraham looked at Luna and the smile appeared on his face as he noticed that Luna had grabbed a small red cup and this red cup contained the juice of the tree's leaves that Luna had crushed.

And Abraham told Luna that she was not only a princess, but she was also the mother of the kingdom, then Luna smiled at Abraham and she thanked him for his words. Then Abraham told the children that they have to go to the living room. Then Abraham and the children left the kitchen.

They reached the living room and they saw Doctor Thomas who was waiting for the remedy, and Luna gave the red cup that contained the remedy to Doctor Thomas. And Doctor Thomas thanked Luna for the remedy and he went to the room to give this remedy to John's wife.

Then the parents and children were waiting in the living room, and most of them were worried about John's wife, and they were hoping that everything would be fine. But there were a few of them like Sunshine, Asher, Luna and others who were confident that everything would be fine.

Suddenly, the expression on everyone's face changed, and they were looking at each other with astonished faces as they had seemed to hear the cries of a baby. And suddenly, there were the screams and they all jumped for joy as they had heard the cries of a baby coming from the room where John's wife and the doctors were. And the children were jumping and screaming, while the pregnant women were clapping their hands with smiles on their faces, and the parents were dancing.

Then Sunshine calmed everyone as she had heard something strange, and all the eyes were focused on Sunshine and they were all wondering why Sunshine had interrupted their celebration. Then Sunshine broke the silence and said that it seemed that the kingdom of Manitoba had just welcomed the twins.

And immediately the expression on everyone's face changed and they were all looking at Sunshine with amazed faces wondering what was going on with Sunshine. And Sunshine noticed that everyone was looking at her with astonished faces as if she was crazy, and she asked them what was going on? Asher replied to Sunshine that they were waiting for her to tell them what was going on because she was the one who had interrupted their celebration.

Sunshine asked Asher if they did not hear what she had said? Asher answered Sunshine that no one in the room had heard what she had said, and that they were still waiting for her to tell them why she had interrupted their celebration.

Sunshine looked into Asher's eyes and said that John's wife had just given birth to the twins. Asher looked at Sunshine with an amazed face and he asked Sunshine if she was all right? Sunshine answered

Asher that she was fine. Asher told Sunshine that he thought that she needed to rest and get some sleep because John's wife had given birth to one baby and not to two babies.

Suddenly, there was a silence and they were all hearing the cries of the babies with astonished faces, and only Sunshine who was not surprised to hear these cries coming from the babies. Aaron said that Sunshine was right that John's wife had really given birth to the twins. And Asher said the one who needed to get rest and sleep was him and not Sunshine because the only crazy person in the room was him.

And they all started laughing, then the children started yelling by jumping and they were clapping their hands as they were hearing the newborns who were crying loudly. The parents were watching at the children how the children were celebrating the arrival of the twins with smiles on their faces, and some parents even had tears that were flowing down their cheeks.

And looking at the parents, we could see that the parents were very proud of the children, and the parents were feeling that the children had not only saved the kingdom, but the children had also saved the lives of all inhabitants of the kingdom. And the children had specially saved the future of the kingdom and the future children of the kingdom.

Then the parents and children turned their heads and looked at the door as they heard a noise coming from the door. And they all rushed towards the door as they had seen Doctor Thomas who was staring at them with a smile on his face. And they all stopped near Doctor Thomas and they were looking at him with faces full of smiles while waiting for him to talk.

Then Doctor Thomas opened his mouth and announced that John's wife had given birth to the twins who were two little girls. And Doctor Thomas added that the two girls and John's wife were doing well. But that the two girls were in the incubators because they were born premature.

And Sunshine thanked Doctor Thomas for his amazing work. And Doctor Thomas told Sunshine that she did not need to thank him because he was just doing his work. And Doctor Thomas added that he was the one who would thank all the children for saving the kingdom and the lives of the future generations of this kingdom.

And that he especially thanked Luna for everything that she had done so far for this kingdom, and he thanked Luna for the remedy that had been made for John's wife because this remedy had helped a lot. Also, he thanked Luna for the fact that he had been tortured by her a few days ago because if he had not been tortured by Luna, he should not be in this house practicing his work by making history by fighting against the laws of Kalus.

Doctor Thomas went on and said that he also specially thanked Sunshine who was the one who had started this fight against the laws of Kalus more than a year ago. Because without Sunshine, the whole kingdom should still be subject to the laws of Kalus, and the inhabitants should be still living according to the laws of Kalus.

Suddenly, Doctor Thomas was interrupted by Luna who was clapping her hands, and the rest of the people followed Luna by clapping their hands. Then Luna walked face to Doctor Thomas and she hugged him, and the rest of the children hugged Doctor Thomas too. Then everyone got in the room to see the newborns.

The children were standing up around the incubators and they were all staring at the babies who were in the incubators with their faces full of smiles. And looking at the expression on the faces of the children, we could see that they were very happy to see these twins in the incubators. Sunshine's face was full of joy, and she was very happy that she had succeeded in saving John's wife. And the parents were looking at the children, how the children were looking at the babies in the incubators with the joy on their faces, and some parents even had tears flowing down their cheeks.

Then Sunshine turned her head from behind as she had heard a voice called her name, and Sunshine was staring at John's wife as she had noticed that she was called by John's wife. And John's wife asked Sunshine to approach the bed with her comrades.

Then Sunshine told her fellows that they were all called by John's wife. Then they all walked until near to the bed and they had their eyes focused on John's wife who was lying in the bed. And there was a silence in the room, and they were staring at John's wife who had opened her mouth to talk but no word was coming out from her mouth.

Suddenly, the tears started running down the cheeks of John's wife, and she broke the silence by introducing herself like Sarah. Then Sarah thanked the children not only because the children had saved her life, the lives of her babies, and the life of her husband, but because the children had taken their courage to fight against Kalus and against the laws of Kalus.

Sarah went on and said that the children had succeeded where the parents had failed, and that she had no word to thank these children for what they had done for this kingdom. Because no word was enough to thank these children who were risking their lives to save this kingdom and the future generations of this kingdom.

Sarah added that it's been more than a year that she was watching on television the fight of these children. And that she had been astonished by the courage and the determination of the children to save the kingdom. And that she was more amazed when she opened her eyes in this house in this bed, and she was completely lost when the doctors told her that she had been found by Sunshine.

Because she had never imagined that this time should find her alive. Because she had made the decision to die with her babies in her womb when the king Kalus had announced the new laws of Kalus which banned the births in the kingdom and which forced all pregnant women to have the abortions.

Sarah continued and said that she was fifty years old and that these twins in the incubators were her first pregnancy because since she was twenty years old when she got married, she had never got pregnant. And she had spent thirty years looking for a pregnancy without success.

And the worst day of her life was when she was diagnosed infertile by the doctors, and she had spent the years crying the days and nights, and she had even lost the desire to live. And she was no longer eating, sleeping and working, and that she was spending her time by wondering why she could not get pregnant, and what she had done to deserve not to give birth.

And the only thing that she wanted was to die, and she had tried to kill herself three times, but she had been saved on time by her husband named John. And that the third time that she had been taken to the hospital because she tried to kill herself, the doctor announced the best news of her life, and the best news was that she was pregnant.

And at the beginning she did not believe that she was really pregnant because she thought that the doctor had announced that she was pregnant. Because the doctor wanted her to stop trying to kill herself. And she had never believed that she was pregnant because she was already fifty years old because she was wondering how a woman of fifty years could be pregnant, until the night she felt a miracle in her womb.

And this miracle was when she had felt that she was really pregnant, and it was incredible and it was like a dream, and from this moment she had recovered her joy of living. And she was very happy to go to bed every night and to wake up every morning till the cursed day where the king Kalus had announced the new laws of Kalus that banned the births in the kingdom and that forced the pregnant women to have the abortions.

And she had decided at that moment that Kalus had banned the births in the kingdom that she was going to die with her babies in her womb because it was not even possible for her to have an abortion. And to die with her babies in her womb was only the solution because she had lost the envy for life when Kalus banned the births in the kingdom, and her husband decided to die with her and their babies.

Then she and her husband spent a day and night walking without drinking water and without eating, and mostly without knowing where they were going. But the only thing that they knew was that they wanted to die and they were walking with the hope that nobody would find them, and with the hope to die as soon as possible.

Because it was very hard for her to walk with two babies in her womb, and she was feeling hungry and thirsty, and every step she was making was very hard, and she was hoping that this step was going to be the last and that she would faint and die with her babies in her womb.

Everyone in the room was listening to Sarah with the tears that were flowing down their cheeks, and with their faces full of sadness. And looking at them, we could see that it was very hard for them to listen to Sarah who was telling her story.

And Sunshine had the anger inside her by listening to Sarah, and Sunshine was realizing how Lord and Kalus had tortured Sarah and also all the inhabitants of the kingdom. And for Sunshine the only responsible were Lord and Kalus, and it was time to kill Lord and Kalus. And even if Sunshine did not know how to kill Lord, she was determined to kill Lord and Kalus this morning.

Sarah continued and said that the last thing that she remembered was that she was walking between the trees and she felt a strange thing in her body and she fainted, then she opened her eyes in this house in this bed. And that she did not even know how Sunshine had found her because she could not have imagined that she could be found, and she even did not know how she had appeared in this tunnel where she had been found by Sunshine.

Because she was wondering how she ended up in this tunnel especially since the road leading to this tunnel was locked by the king Kalus. And Sarah added that she had been very surprised when the doctors and nurses told her that she had been found in the tunnel by Sunshine.

Suddenly, Sarah was interrupted by Luna who told Sarah that she was so sorry about what Sarah went through, and that she was so sorry if she was not able to protect the kingdom as she was destined to do. Because even if people said that she was very brave, it was not true because if she was really brave, she should prevent Kalus from destroying this kingdom.

Because she was the only responsible for everything that had happened in this kingdom, and she was also responsible for the suffering that the inhabitants of this kingdom were living now. But now, it was time to put an end to the suffering of the inhabitants of this kingdom, and it was above all time to bring peace in the kingdom.

Then Luna turned and she started to walk towards the door, but she was stopped by Abraham who asked her where she was going. Luna answered Abraham that she was going to kill the devil Kalus. Abraham told Luna that it was dangerous to fight against Kalus. Luna replied to Abraham not to worry about her because she knew who Kalus was.

Isac told Luna that he was coming with her, but Luna refused and she told Isac that it was dangerous, that he could not come. And Isac told Luna that if it was dangerous it meant that she could not go alone. Sunshine told Isac not to worry because she was going with Luna. Asher said that he was going with Sunshine and Luna. Then the rest of the children in the room said that they were going too.

Luna said that it was very dangerous and that she was going only with Sunshine because Kalus would use his magic to fight and Kalus would not hesitate to kill people who would be with her. Asher told Luna that he was not afraid of Kalus, and that he was ready to die.

Luna looked into Asher's eyes and she told him that he could not come with her because if he came, she would be forced to protect him from Kalus. And it would be harder for her to fight Kalus by protecting her fellows at the same time, mostly that Kalus was very dangerous with the satanic powers he possessed.

Asher said that he did not care if Kalus had the satanic powers, and he even did not care to die because it would be a dream come true to die by fighting the devil named Kalus. Luna looked at Asher and she told him that she knew that he was very brave and that he was very courageous and she also knew well that he was not afraid to die.

But she also knew that it was not only she and her comrades who needed him alive because the whole kingdom needed him alive, and the kingdom needed him. And Luna also told Asher that it was useless to risk his life now because the whole kingdom needed him alive. Because he needed to live to protect the kingdom in the future in case the kingdom was invaded by the enemies.

Suddenly, there was silence in the room, and everyone had been touched by the words of Luna. And all those who wanted to go fight Kalus had changed their mind because they had realized through Luna's words that Luna was right.

Then Abraham broke the silence and said that only Sunshine and Luna were going to fight Kalus, and they would all wait for Sunshine and Luna at home. Then people started talking to Sunshine and Luna to be careful. But there were some parents in the room who were very afraid, and they did not want Sunshine and Luna to go fight Kalus.

Then Sarah got out of bed, and she walked till near to the incubators, then Sarah opened the incubators and carried one of the twins who were in the incubators and she handed this baby to Sunshine by looking into Sunshine's eyes and said, "This baby is your namesake, and I named her Sunshine like you, and I want you to come back to look after your namesake because you are the one who would raise your namesake." Then Sunshine took the baby in the hands of Sarah with the smile on her face, and she thanked Sarah.

Then Sarah carried the other twin who was in the incubator and she walked till face to Luna with this twin in her hands, and she handed this baby to Luna by looking into Luna's eyes and said, "This baby is your namesake and I named her Luna like you, and I want you to come back to take care of her because you are the one who would educate your namesake." Then Luna took the baby in the hands of Sarah with her face full of smiles and she thanked Sarah.

Then everyone in the room started to applaud with smiles on their faces, and all the eyes were focused on Sunshine and Luna who had carried the babies in their hands. And Remy was still filming what was happening with his camera. And Sarah told the rest of the children that she was sorry because it was not possible to give the name of everyone to the twins, and that the fact that only the names ofSunshine and Luna were given to the twins did not mean that Sunshine and Luna were more important than others. Because all the children were important, no child was more important than the others.

Then all the pregnant women who were in the room promised to the children who had not yet had the namesakes, that each of them would have a namesake because the babies who were in their wombs would be their namesake. Then everyone was surprised when John thanked all the children for their fight to save the kingdom.

Sunshine told John that she was very happy to see that he was doing well because she was worried about him because he had not opened his mouth since they got home. John replied to Sunshine not to worry that he was doing well, just that he was traumatized by what was happening. Then they continued to talk.

After a few minutes, Sunshine and Luna put the babies in the incubators. And everyone gave a hug to Sunshine and Luna by wishing good luck to Sunshine and Luna. And some had the eyes wet of tears, while others had the tears that were running down their cheeks.

And there were also some with faces full of fear, while others had faces full of sadness as they were wishing good luck to Sunshine and Luna. And despite the fact that Sunshine and Luna promised them that everything would be fine, they were very worried.

Then Sunshine and Luna left the house, and they had locked the door from outside through their magic. Then Sunshine and Luna decided to mix their magic to be more powerful and stronger when they would fight Lord and Kalus. Sunshine transferred a part of the energy of her magic in Luna's body, and Luna also transferred a part of the energy of her magic in Sunshine's body. Then both Sunshine and Luna flew into space.

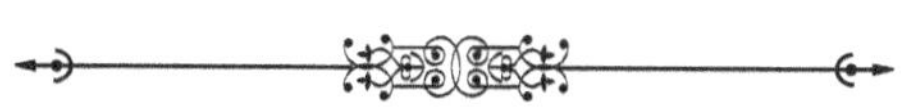

CHAPTER X

THE DEATH OF LORD AND KALUS

It was three in the morning, there was darkness outside, and there was no moon and stars in the sky. Lord and Kalus were sitting on the tree's trunk in an empty forest, and they were talking about the kingdom and about Sunshine and Luna.

And the Lord was telling Kalus that this empty forest was his house, and that this house had been destroyed by Sunshine. Then there was silence, and Lord took a deep breath and said that everything was over, and that Sunshine and Luna had won the fight.

"Everything is over?" Kalus asked.

"Yes, everything is over," Lord answered.

"What do you mean?" Kalus asked.

"Sarah gave birth to the twins," Lord said.

"We must kill these twins," Kalus said.

"It's too late," Lord said.

"Too late?" Kalus cried out.

"Yes, because we can no longer kill these twins," Lord answered.

"Why can we no longer kill these twins?" Kalus asked.

Suddenly, the expression of the faces of Lord and Kalus changed and they were looking with worried faces as they were feeling a strong wind that was blowing. Then they lifted their heads through the sky as they had noticed the light that was shining and they saw the moon and stars in the sky.

And they understood that the light was shining because the moon and stars had appeared and this light was coming from the moon and stars. Lord told Kalus that Sunshine and Luna were coming. Kalus asked Lord how he knew that Sunshine and Luna were coming? Lord answered Kalus that the moon and stars that had appeared were a message.

Suddenly, the expression on the faces of Lord and Kalus changed and they were looking with surprised faces as they were seeing Sunshine and Luna who were flying into space. And Kalus had the mouth opened but no word was coming out from his mouth.

And looking at the expression on Kalus's face, we could see that he was surprised to see Sunshine and Luna, even if he was told by Lord that Sunshine and Luna were coming. And Kalus was more surprised by the abilities of Sunshine and Luna to fly in space. Then Lord and Kalus got up and they were still looking at Sunshine and Luna who were flying towards them.

Then Sunshine and Luna landed face to Lord and Kalus. Sunshine and Lord were staring at each other in the eyes, while Luna and Kalus were staring at each other in the eyes. And the faces of Luna and Sunshine were full of anger, while the faces of Lord and Kalus were full of smiles, and there was silence between them.

"Welcome to your grave," Kalus said.

"I am glad to see that you are still alive," Luna said.

"You missed your chance to kill me a few days ago, when you opened my magic room," Kalus said.

"I am here because I want to keep my promise, the promise I have made to the whole kingdom to kill you," Luna said.

"I am the one who is going to kill you," Kalus said.

Luna looked into Kalus's eyes with rage on her face and she said, "I promise you that no one would cry for you in this kingdom, your name would never be used or even be pronounced in this kingdom.

The children who are growing up and who would born would not even know about your existence." And Luna added, "I would erase your name in the history of the kings of this kingdom, I would make sure that no one would remember about you."

Kalus smiled at Luna and said, "Stop dreaming."

Luna looked into Kalus's eyes and said, "George would sit on the throne and would wear the crown of this kingdom today."

"You must kill me first before you crown George as the king of this kingdom," Kalus said.

Suddenly, the expression on the face of Kalus changed and his face was full of anger. And Luna was looking at Kalus, and she was not really surprised to see the anger on Kalus's face, then Luna noticed that Kalus's eyes were turning. Then Luna's eyes started turning as she had understood that Kalus was using his magic to fight.

Then there were four swords that were flying into space, and these swords were flying towards Sunshine, Luna, Kalus and Lord. And two of these swords were coming from Luna's magic, while the other two swords were coming from Kalus's magic. And the two swords coming from Luna's magic were flying towards Luna and Sunshine, while the other two swords coming from Kalus's magic were flying towards Kalus and Lord.

Then each of them grabbed a sword, then Luna and Kalus started walking towards each other by holding their swords in their hands, and by looking at each other in the eyes. While Sunshine and Lord were walking towards each other by holding their swords in their hands by looking at each other in the eyes. Suddenly, they stopped near each other and they started to fight by using their swords, and their faces were full of anger as they were fighting.

After a few minutes, they were still fighting with the anger on their faces and with a lot of determination, and the fight was very hard. Sunshine and Luna were fighting by using the space, they were flying into the space, and the fact that Sunshine and Luna were flying in space was making the fight harder for Kalus and Lord.

Because Lord and Kalus were forced to fly in space to fight because the fight was led in space by Sunshine and Luna. Lord and Kalus had difficulty flying in space by fighting, and they had difficulty fighting in space by flying not only because they were not used to fighting in space by using the swords, but mostly because they had trouble breathing in space. And they had difficulty breathing in space for two reasons.

And the first reason was the fact that Kalus and Lord had trouble breathing with the strong wind that was blowing. And the wind that was blowing was preventing Lord and Kalus from breathing well because this wind was natural. And the fact that Kalus's body and Lord's body contained the satanic powers was making things difficult for Lord and Kalus because the natural wind could not match with the satanic powers that were in their bodies.

The satanic powers that were in the bodies of Kalus and Lord could not handle the air that was entering in the bodies of Kalus and Lord through the nostrils of Kalus and Lord. Because the air that was entering the bodies of Lord and Kalus through their nostrils was coming from the wind that was blowing, and it was impossible for Lord and Kalus to prevent this air from getting in their bodies because they were flying in space.

Kalus and Lord had tried to prevent this air coming from the wind that was blowing to get into their bodies without success. And the fact that Lord and Kalus were flying in space by fighting was preventing them from controlling the air that was getting in their bodies through their nostrils because it was impossible for them to focus because they were moving in space by flying and fighting.

And the only chance for them to prevent this air from entering their bodies was to concentrate on rejecting this air which was entering their bodies, but they did not have time to focus because they must fight to kill their opponents and to defend themselves. And the air that was entering their bodies was preventing them from using their satanic powers to breathe well because Lord and Kalus used to breathe well through their satanic powers.

And the second reason was the fact that Lord and Kalus had mixed their powers to be more powerful and stronger during the fight, and it meant that Kalus's body contained his magic and a part of Lord's magic, and Lord's body contained his magic and a part of Kalus's magic.

And Kalus had difficulty to manage Lord's magic that was in his body because Lord's magic that was in Kalus's body was very strong. And the fact that Kalus had difficulty managing Lord's magic that was in his body was making things more difficult for Kalus to breathe and to fly faster in space. And Lord had difficulty to manage the Kalus's magic that was in his body because Kalus's magic contained the natural powers and satanic powers.

And the fact that Kalus's magic contained the natural powers and satanic powers, it meant that Lord's body contained the natural powers coming from a part of Kalus's magic that was transferred in his body. And Lord had difficulty managing the natural powers of Kalus that were in his body because Lord was a monster, and Lord's body was made only with the satanic powers. So, the natural powers that were in Lord's body were preventing Lord from flying faster and breathing well.

Lord and Kalus were trying to lead the fight towards the ground, but Sunshine Luna had understood that Lord and Kalus had difficulty fighting in space, and that it was the reason why Lord and Kalus wanted to lead the fight on the ground. But Sunshine and Luna were still leading the fight into space, and even worse they were flying more and more into space to fight.

And the fact that Sunshine and Luna were flying more and more into space to fight was putting Lord and Kalus more in difficulty. Because Lord and Kalus were forced to fly more and more into space to be on the same level as Sunshine and Luna, and to have the balance to fight Sunshine and Luna.

But the problem was that Lord and Kalus had more difficulty breathing as they were flying more and more into space. And the fact that Lord and Kalus had difficulty breathing was having an effect on the fight because they were fighting with great difficulty. Lord and Kalus wanted to land on the ground but they knew well that they could not fight on the ground, while Sunshine and Luna were in space.

Because if Lord and Kalus were on the ground, while Sunshine and Luna were in space, it would be impossible for Lord and Kalus to fight Sunshine and Luna. Lord and Kalus knew that on the ground, they would not be able to lift their swords to fight Sunshine and Luna who would be in space.

Because Sunshine and Luna in space would have a huge advantage on them. Lord and Kalus knew that even if they had difficulty breathing in the space, they were forced to fight in the space because they needed to have the balance and they needed to be at the same level as their opponents to fight their opponents who were Sunshine and Luna.

After fifteen minutes, the fight was still going on, but Sunshine and Luna were having the advantage. The fact that Lord and Kalus were having trouble breathing was making them lose their concentration on the fight and they had started to get tired.

Sunshine and Luna had found the weaknesses of Kalus and Lord, and they were using the weaknesses of Kalus and Lord to dominate the fight. Lord and Kalus were not fighting to win because they were not going towards Sunshine and Luna to kill Sunshine and Luna. Lord and Kalus were fighting for the purpose of defence and they were only fighting to defend themselves to prevent Sunshine and Luna from killing them.

Suddenly, Kalus pushed a loud cry as he had been injured in his shoulder by Luna's sword. And the fight was still going on, but Kalus was fighting with a lot of difficulty and he had difficulty wielding his sword because he was feeling pain in his shoulder as he had been injured by Luna.

And Kalus had been injured on his right shoulder by Luna, and the worst was that Kalus was holding the sword with his right hand to fight. Then Kalus changed the hand with which he was holding the sword, and he passed the sword on his left hand because it was impossible to keep holding the sword with his right hand to fight.

Because the pain that Kalus was feeling in his shoulder was getting more and more strong. The fight between Lord and Sunshine had not changed, and they were still fighting with the same energy and determination, even though Sunshine was dominating the fight.

But Lord was defending well against Sunshine. Kalus had completely lost control of the fight and he was no longer able to defend himself against Luna. And Kalus was bleeding on his forehead and in his left hand because had been injured by Luna.

And Kalus was not able to defend himself against Luna not only because he was injured, but mostly because he was having trouble wielding his sword by using his left hand. Because Kalus was normally right-handed. And Kalus could not use his right hand to fight because the injury that was on his right shoulder was preventing him from using his right hand to fight.

Lord had started to become tired, and the fact that he was tired was making him weak. And Lord had difficulty defending himself. Then Lord turned his head to the left as he had heard a loudly scream coming this side, and suddenly the eyes of Lord opened widely and he was looking with a face full of terror as he was seeing Kalus's hand and Kalus's sword that were falling to the ground.

And Lord was understanding that one of Kalus's hands had been cut off by Luna, then Lord understood that he needed to save Kalus because Kalus could no longer fight Luna. Then Lord tried to fly towards Kalus, but Lord was stopped by a strong pain that he had felt in his stomach and he push a yell as he had felt this pain.

Then Lord turned his head and he saw Sunshine's sword in his stomach, and he understood that he had been stabbed by Sunshine. And Sunshine had succeeded to stab Lord because Lord was distracted by what was going on between Kalus and Luna. Sunshine and Lord were staring at each other in the eyes without saying a word, and Sunshine's face was full of anger, while Lord's face was full of surprise, and Lord was surprised because he was still not realizing that he had been stabbed by Sunshine.

Then Sunshine removed her sword from Lord's stomach. Then Lord pushed a loud cry as he had been again stabbed in his stomach by Sunshine. And Lord was feeling pain that was preventing him from defending himself from Sunshine. Then the fear appeared on Lord's face when he saw Sunshine who had lifted the sword to cut off his head.

And suddenly there was a loud noise coming from the sky, and there was a yellow light that was shining in the sky. And Sunshine tried to cut off Lord's head, but unfortunately her hand which she had grabbed the sword was not making any movement. And Sunshine looked at her hand and she noticed that nothing had caught her hand, and she tried to make a movement with her hand but she was not succeeding.

Sunshine was really surprised by what was going on, she did not understand why she could not make a movement with her hand, and it was as if her hand was mystically blocked by someone. Lord was staring at Sunshine with a surprised face and looking at the expression on the face of Lord, it was obvious that he was not understanding what was going on.

And Lord was completely lost, he did not understand why Sunshine was not able to make a movement with her hand with which she had grasped the sword. And Sunshine was still trying to make a movement with her hand with which she had held the sword without succeeding.

Luna and Kalus were looking at each other with silence, and the face of Kalus was full of surprise, and Kalus was surprised to see that Luna could not make a movement with her hand that she had held the sword with. And Luna was trying to stab Kalus with her sword.

But unfortunately, she was unable to make a movement with her hand. And it was as if Luna's hand that had grabbed the sword was mystically blocked, as if there was a mysterious person who was preventing Luna from stabbing Kalus. And Luna was completely lost and she did not understand what was going on.

And Luna was looking at her hand that she had grabbed the sword with, and she was noticing that there was nothing that had grabbed her hand, but she still could not make any movement with her hand. And Luna was completely lost because she did not understand what was going on.

Suddenly, the expression of the faces of Lord, Luna, Kalus and Sunshine changed, and they were all looking with the astonished faces as they were seeing yellow light that was shining. And they all very surprised and they were wondering where this yellow light was coming from. Then they all lifted their heads through the sky as they had noticed that the yellow light that was shining was coming from the sky.

And suddenly the smiles appeared on the faces of Lord and Kalus while the fear appeared on the faces of Sunshine and Luna. And they were all staring at the cloud that was opened and they were seeing a yellow light in the cloud. And looking at the expression on their faces, it was obvious that they had not heard the strong noise that had happened in the sky a few minutes ago.

Sunshine and Luna were understanding that they could not use their swords to kill Lord and Kalus. Because their hands with which they had grasped the swords had been mystically blocked by this yellow light that was shining in the cloud. Sunshine and Luna understood that they could not kill Lord and Kalus because this yellow light was mystically preventing them from killing Lord and Kalus.

Sunshine and Luna also understood that they could not anymore fight Lord and Kalus because they could not anymore . use their swords to fight as the yellow light that was shining was mystically preventing them from using their swords. Sunshine and Luna knew well that they were in danger as they could not anymore fight Lord and Kalus.

Suddenly, the expression of the faces of Sunshine and Luna changed and they were looking with astonished faces as they were seeing this yellow light coming from the cloud shining on Lord and Kalus. Sunshine and Luna understood that this yellow light was shining on Lord and Kalus to give strength to Lord and Kalus.

And they also understood that Lord and Kalus were receiving the powers from this yellow light. Sunshine and Luna understood that this light yellow was coming from the master, also called god of Kalus and Lord, that the god of Kalus and Lord was giving the powers to Lord and Kalus through this yellow light.

Then Sunshine understood that she must do something, and she started to fly towards Luna. After a few seconds, Sunshine was near Luna and she told Luna that they must land on the ground. Then Sunshine and Luna flew and they landed on the ground, and they lifted their heads through the sky, and they saw Lord who had carried Kalus on his back and Lord was flying towards the ground.

And Lord had carried Kalus on his back because Kalus could not fly as Kalus's hand had been cut off by Luna. Then Lord landed on the ground with Kalus. Lord and Sunshine were looking at each other in the eyes, while Kalus and Luna were looking at each other in the eyes. The faces of Lord and Kalus were full of smiles, while the faces of Sunshine and Luna were full of anger. And there was silence between them.

Then, Lord broke the silence and said, "I am the winner."

"The war is not yet over," Sunshine replied.

"It's over because I am going to kill you now, and Kalus is going to kill Luna now," Lord said.

"I am here to keep my promise that I had made to you," Sunshine said.

Lord laughed and asked, "The promise to kill me?"

"Yes," Sunshine answered.

Lord started laughing, then he looked into the eyes of Sunshine and said, "I am immortal."

"You are bleeding now," Sunshine said.

"Even if I am bleeding, I can not die," Lord said.

"I promise to kill you today before sunrise," Sunshine said.

"I promise you to have the control of this kingdom, and to turn this kingdom into a vampire kingdom before sunrise. And I also promise you that the future generations of this kingdom would be the vampires," Lord said.

"Have a good trip to hell," Sunshine said.

"Have a good journey to paradise," Lord said.

Then Lord turned his head and looked at Kalus without saying a word, and Kalus understood the message of Lord like Lord was staring at him, then Kalus's eyes started spinning. Sunshine turned her head and looked at Luna and both were looking at each other with silence, then Luna's eyes started spinning, like Luna had understood why Sunshine was looking at her. Then Lord, Luna, Kalus and Sunshine lifted their heads through the sky, and they saw four swords that were flying towards them.

And two of these four swords were coming from Luna's magic, while the other two swords were coming from Kalus's magic. And the two swords coming from Luna's magic were flying towards Luna and Sunshine, while the other two swords coming from Kalus's magic were flying towards Kalus and Lord. Then each of them grabbed a sword. Then Luna and Kalus started to walk towards each other, while Sunshine and Lord started to walk towards each other.

Suddenly, they turned their heads to the left as they had heard a noise coming from this side. And immediately the expression of their faces changed. Then Sunshine, Luna and Kalus were looking with astonished faces, while Lord was looking with a face empty of expression as they were all staring at a human that had appeared in the form of a robot.

And they were all staring at this robot. Sunshine, Luna and Kalus were wondering what was going on? And where did this robot come from? But unfortunately, they could not answer these questions. But looking at the expression on the face of Lord, we could see that

Lord knew what was going on, and we could also notice that Lord was not surprised to see this robot.

Then the robot opened its mouth and said he was not a robot even if he looked like a robot. Sunshine asked, "Are you a human?" The robot answered that he was not a human but that he was instead a magic. Sunshine cried out, "A magic?" The robot answered that he was the reason why Lord and Kalus had banned the births in the kingdom. Sunshine said, "I do not understand."

The robot said that he was a magic coming from the bodies of the twins that Sarah had given birth to. And that the twins that Sarah had in her womb had the magic and that he was this magic, and that he was sent by the gods of the kingdom to help Sunshine and Luna to save the kingdom.

Luna told the robot that he did not tell them the reason why Lord and Kalus had banned the births? The robot told Luna that Lord and Kalus knew that there was a pregnant woman who carried in her womb the twins, and these twins had the magic that was dangerous for Lord and Kalus.

But that Lord and Kalus did not know exactly which woman carried these twins, and it was the reason why Lord and Kalus chose to ban all women to give births and to force all pregnant women to have the abortions. The robot added that Lord and Kalus wanted all pregnant women to have the abortions because they did not want to take a risk that the woman who carried these twins give birth, as they did not know exactly the woman who carried the twins.

Luna looked at the robot and asked if it meant that he was the reason why the births were banned in the kingdom? The robot answered Luna that yes. Luna asked the robot if it meant that the twins who were born an hour ago named Sunshine and Luna had the magic?

The robot answered that no, that the twins named Sunshine and Luna did not have the magic. And the robot added that these twins named Sunshine and Luna had just carried the magic that he was in their bodies, that the magic that he was had left the bodies of these twins to come and help to save the kingdom. Luna told the robot that she did not understand.

The robot told Luna that he was a magic that was sent by the gods of the kingdom to come and help to save the kingdom. That the gods of the kingdom had mystically sent him through the twins that were in the womb of Sarah. And that Sarah had carried him(magic) in her womb during her pregnancy without even knowing that she was not only carrying her twins, but she was also carrying the magic that would help to save the kingdom.

Sunshine looked at the robot and asked the robot why the gods of the kingdom had chosen Sarah to carry him and not another woman? The robot answered Sunshine because Sarah was pregnant with the twins, and that he was a magic who could be carried only by the same sex twins. And that Sarah was only the pregnant woman who had the twins of same sex in her womb.

Sunshine asked the robot why only the twins could carry him? The robot answered that all the twins had a special gift to do things that others could not do. And the robot added that it would be dangerous and risky if he was carried by a child or even children who were not twins. And that it would be even impossible to be carried by a child or even children who were not twins.

Sunshine asked the robot how it was possible that she had found Sarah in the tunnel of the bridge while the road that led to this bridge was locked? The robot answered Sunshine that Lord had found out that Sarah could be the pregnant woman who carried the twins, and Lord was determined to kill Sarah.

And the Robot added that it was the reason why he had mystically helped Sarah to escape from Lord, and that he was the one who had mystically helped Sarah and John to appear in the tunnel of the bridge. Sunshine asked the robot what would happen now? The robot answered Sunshine that she and Luna would continue to fight Lord and Kalus, while he was going in the sky to fight the evil spirit that was helping Lord and Kalus to stay immortal.

Sunshine asked the robot what would happen after the fight? The robot replied to Sunshine that the only way to save the kingdom of Manitoba was to kill Lord and Kalus, and that it was important that she and Luna kill Lord and Kalus during the fight.

Because if Sunshine and Luna failed to kill Lord and Kalus, and that they were killed by Lord and Kalus, it meant that the kingdom of Manitoba would be turned into the kingdom of the vampires. And the future generations of this kingdom would be the vampires and the laws of the world of the vampires would be established in the kingdom of Manitoba.

Sunshine told the robot not to worry because the kingdom of Manitoba would never be turned into the kingdom of the vampires. Sunshine added that the future generations of the kingdom of Manitoba would never be the vampires and the laws of the world of vampires would never be established in the kingdom of Manitoba.

The robot replied to Sunshine that the fear of the gods of the kingdom was to see that one day that the kingdom of Manitoba had been turned into the kingdom of the vampires by Lord and Kalus. And that the gods of the kingdom were very afraid that the future generations of the kingdom could be the vampires and that the laws of the world of the vampires could be established in the kingdom.

And the robot added that it was the dream of the gods of the kingdom to save the kingdom by preventing Lord and Kalus from turning the kingdom of Manitoba into the kingdom of the vampires. Luna looked at the robot and she told the robot not to worry because Luna and Sunshine would not disappoint the gods of the kingdom.

Because the kingdom of Manitoba would stay the kingdom of Manitoba forever, and the kingdom of Manitoba would keep its traditions, cultures and values forever. Luna added that the future generations of the kingdom of Manitoba would be raised and educated according to the traditions, the cultures and values of the kingdom of Manitoba.

The robot said that the gods of the kingdom would be very happy to hear that and mostly to see that the kingdom of Manitoba has remained the kingdom of Manitoba with its traditions, cultures and values forever.

Sunshine asked the robot if the robot would come back to the kingdom after the fight? The robot answered Sunshine that he was sent by the gods of the kingdom especially for this mission, and that after the fight he would return near to the gods of the kingdom. But if one day the kingdom was attacked again by the enemies, the gods of the kingdom could decide to send him again to help and save the kingdom.

Sunshine asked if the twins who were born and who had carried him(robot) would grow up with the magic? The robot answered Sunshine that no, that these twins did not have the powers and magic, and that these twins had just carried him, and he had gotten out from the bodies of these twins.

Suddenly, the conversation was interrupted by a strange voice in the sky, and they all lifted their heads through the sky to see who was talking. But unfortunately, they were not seeing the one who was talking, and they were all hearing a voice who was saying that he was ready to fight, and this voice was asking Lord and Kalus to kill Sunshine and Luna.

And this voice was also saying that the kingdom of Manitoba would be turned into the kingdom of the vampires. And that the future generations of the kingdom of Manitoba would be the vampires who would be raised and educated according to laws, the traditions, the cultures and the values of the world of vampires.

The faces of Sunshine and Luna were full of surprise, while the faces of Lord and Kalus were full of smiles. And looking at the expression on the faces of Sunshine and Luna, it was obvious that they were wondering who was talking. But looking at the expression on the faces of Lord and Kalus, it was obvious that they knew who was talking in the sky. Suddenly, the facial expressions of Luna and Sunshine changed, and the fear appeared on their faces as they had noticed that this voice had stopped talking, and that the cloud was shaking.

And Sunshine asked, "What is going on?" 'The robot answered Sunshine that it was the evil spirit that was in the sky who was making these noises to express the anger of the god of the world of the vampires. And the robot added that it was also the god of the world of the vampires who was talking through this evil spirit. Then the robot wished good luck to Sunshine and Luna. Sunshine and Luna thanked the robot for coming to help them to save the kingdom of Manitoba. Then the robot flew through the sky.

Sunshine, Kalus, Luna and Lord were watching the robot that was flying through the cloud with the faces empty of expression, then they saw the robot get into the cloud and disappeared. Then they started to hear the noises coming from the cloud and they noticed that the cloud was shaking, and they understood that the robot was fighting against the evil spirit. Then all four turned their heads and looked at each other.

Then Luna and Kalus started walking towards each other by holding their swords in their hands and by looking each other in the eyes with faces full of anger. Sunshine and Lord started walking towards each other by holding their swords in their hands and by looking at each other in the eyes with their faces full of terror. Suddenly, they all started fighting with anger and determination. Luna was fighting against Kalus, while Sunshine was fighting against Lord.

After a few minutes, they were all still fighting with the same determination and anger. And the fight between Sunshine and Kalus was very balanced, while the fight between Luna and Kalus was dominated by Luna.

And Luna was dominating the fight against Kalus, not only because Kalus did not have balance like the right hand of Kalus had been cut off by Luna a few minutes ago, but mostly because Kalus had difficulty using his left hand to wield the sword. And the cloud was still shaking, and the cloud was shaking because the robot and the evil spirit were still fighting.

After fifteen minutes, the fight was still going on, but Kalus had already almost given up the fight and he was tired and weak, and he was no longer able to defend himself against Luna. And the whole body of Kalus was full of blood because he had been stabbed all over his body by Luna.

And if Kalus was still alive despite the fact that he had been stabbed everywhere on his body by Luna, it was because Kalus was mystically linked to the evil spirit that was fighting in the cloud. So Kalus could die only if this evil spirit died first because the satanic powers that were in Kalus's body were linked to this evil spirit in the cloud.

The cloud was still shaking, but it was shaking with less violence and strength, and the cloud was shaking with less strength and violence because the evil spirit had started to become tired and weak. The fight was still going on between Sunshine and Lord, but the fight was dominated by Sunshine because Lord had started to become tired and weak. And the Lord had become tired and weak because the evil spirit that was in the cloud was tired and weak. So, Lord was mystically linked to this evil spirit, and Lord was getting his powers, energy and strength from this evil spirit.

Suddenly, Kalus pushed a scream as he had been stabbed in his stomach by Luna, then the blood started to get out from Kalus's mouth. Kalus and Luna were looking each other in the eyes, without saying a word, and the face of Kalus was full of sadness, despair and regret, while the face of Luna was full of anger. Luna was seeing the blood that was getting out from Kalus's mouth without saying a word, and she understood that Kalus was dying.

Then Luna lifted her head and looked at the sky and she noticed that the cloud had stopped shaking and that there was no more noise in the cloud, and she understood that the evil spirit had been killed by the robot. Then Luna also understood that Kalus was dying because the devil spirit who was protecting Kalus and who was making Kalus immortal was dead. So, the satanic powers that were in Kalus's body and that were linked to this evil spirit were dead.

Then Luna pulled her sword out of Kalus's belly and Kalus fell to the ground. Then Luna walked a step towards Kalus and she looked into Kalus's eyes and she noticed that Kalus's eyes were closing.

Then Luna said, "I had promised you that you were going to pay for all the evil things you did in this kingdom. I had also promised you that you would pay for all the deaths of the children that you had mystically killed and drunk the blood. I had promised you that you would pay for all the tortures that the inhabitants of the kingdom had suffered because of you. I had promised you that this kingdom would never be the kingdom of the vampires and that the future generations of this kingdom would never be the vampires, also that the laws of the world of the vampires would never be established in this kingdom. I had promised you the end of the laws of Kalus of this kingdom. I had promised you that George would be the king of this kingdom and that the kingdom would recover its traditions, cultures and values. And I had promised you that you were not immortal and that I was going to kill you. And I did everything that I had promised to do, and I kept all my promises." Then Kalus closed his eyes, and he was dead.

Then Luna turned her head and looked with a face empty of expression at Sunshine and Lord who were still fighting. Sunshine and Lord were still fighting, and Sunshine was bleeding on her forehead because she had been injured by Lord. But despite the fact that Sunshine had been injured by Lord's sword, Sunshine was dominating the fight, and there was blood on Lord's body because he had been injured by Sunshine. And suddenly, Lord opened his mouth and he yelled out and there was blood that was coming out of his mouth as he had been stabbed in his heart by Sunshine.

Sunshine and Lord were looking each other in the eyes, and the face of the Lord was full of despair and sadness, while the face of Sunshine was full of rage. Then Sunshine lifted her head and looked at the cloud and she noticed that the cloud was no more shaking, and she understood that the evil spirit who was protecting Lord had been killed by the robot. Sunshine mostly understood that Lord was dying because the evil spirit who was linked to Lord and who was making Lord immortal was dead.

Then Sunshine looked into the Lord's eyes and said, "I had promised you that you would never have this kingdom. I had promised you that this kingdom would never be ruled by a monster like you. I had promised you that you would pay for all the evil things that you had done in the kingdom and to the inhabitants of the kingdom. I had promised you that this kingdom would never be the kingdom of the vampires, and the future generations of this would never be the vampires, also that the laws of the world of the vampires would never be established in this kingdom. I had promised you that you would regret having appeared in this kingdom. I had promised you to kill you. And now I kept all my promises." Then Sunshine removed her sword from Lord's heart and she cut off his head. Then, Lord's head went and fell away and the rest of his body fell to the ground.

Then Sunshine walked near Luna and they looked each other in the eyes without saying a word. After a few seconds, Sunshine broke the silence and said, "Thank you to you, we did, our kingdom is saved forever."

Luna replied, "Thank you to you, we succeeded to save our kingdom and the future generations of our kingdom, also the future of our kingdom." Then the tears started flowing down their cheeks and hugged each other.

After a few seconds, they heard a noise, and they turned and looked around and they noticed that the forest was burning, and they stared at the fire and the corpses of Lord and Kalus who were on the ground. After less than a minute, the fire was almost everywhere, and Sunshine said that it was time to leave. Then Sunshine's eyes and Luna's eyes started spinning and they flew in space and there was the wind blowing on them in space and their hairs were lifted by this wind as they were flying.

CHAPTER XI

GEORGE CROWNED THE KING OF THE KINGDOM OF MANITOBA

It was six in the morning, the sun had not risen yet, and it was a bit cold outside. And the streets of the kingdom were full of people who were celebrating the death of Kalus. The death of Kalus had been announced early this morning on the microphone of Remy by George.

Since the news of Kalus's death, people have been celebrating. And the inhabitants of the kingdom had declared this day a holiday to celebrate the death of the devil Kalus. And there were noises coming from the horns of the cars and motorcycles in the streets. And some people were even drinking and singing to express their joy. And there were people in the streets who were burning the photos of Kalus.

And it was the first time in the history of the kingdom that the death of the king was not mourned, but instead celebrated. And the tradition of Manitoba usually required seven days of mourning upon the death of the king or the death of the queen, but for the first time the tradition would not be respected by the inhabitants of Manitoba.

And no one in the kingdom was sad, no one had shed the tears of sadness or the tears of regret. But people had instead shed the tears of freedom, the tears of the end of suffering and tears to have a new and better kingdom and the tears of happiness. And people had spent the whole day celebrating the death of King Kalus.

The next day, George and Mia got married, and George had been crowned the king of the kingdom of Manitoba. And the whole kingdom was very happy to see that George had become their king. And the whole kingdom shed tears seeing George sitting on the throne of the kingdom and with the crown on his head.

Then George put an end to the laws of Kalus and he also pardoned all the prisoners of the kingdom. And George created an independent government for the first time in the history of the kingdom. Abraham had been appointed Minister of the Culture and the advisor of George. Remy had been appointed minister of Youth and Communication, and other people had also been named in the government.

Abraham had decided as minister to pay tribute to all the children who had fought for freedom of the kingdom. And Abraham had decided to build the status of all the children who had fought to save the kingdom and he had also built a museum in the name of these brave children who had saved the kingdom. And there were the pictures and the stories of these children inside the museum. Then the kingdom had recovered its traditions, cultures and values.

Remy had decided as minister that the story of the children who had fought to free the kingdom would be taught in school. And George had decided as the king to honor all his companions of the fight with a medal of honor, and George had also decided to name some streets of the kingdom after the names of his fighting friends.

Then George had decided to name the two largest cities of the kingdom to the names of Sunshine and Luna. And the whole kingdom had paid tribute to all these brave children who had fought the days and nights and who had risked their lives to save the kingdom.

And all the children of the kingdom had retaken the way of the school. Even George and Mia had retaken the way of the school with their fellows. But Sunshine and Luna were no longer the teachers because all the teachers had been very happy to retake their jobs and to teach the students again. Sunshine and Luna were now the students and they were going to school each morning with their comrades and they were also spending time together after school.